SPIRELLI PARANORMAL INVESTIGATIONS: SEASON ONE

EPISODES 1-6

KATE BARAY

EPISODE 1: THE DISAPPEARING CLIENT

ABOUT THE DISAPPEARING CLIENT

A human investigator in a magical world...what could possibly go wrong?

Jack Spirelli, paranormal investigator, public debunker of supernatural frauds, and private fixer for the magic-using community has opened his doors.

Between exposing paranormal hoaxes and handling cases of a more magical nature, Jack's juggling more business than he can handle. It's past time to hire an assistant, another investigator, and some additional muscle – but maybe the dragon who just walked in and applied will do for now.

1

Jack fiddled with the inner workings of his ancient cash register. He needed a newer machine to better track sales, because—surprisingly—The Junk Shop actually had a few sales to track. Who knew boxes of garage sale rejects would be so popular? The store hours were erratic, and the stock ranged from recycled trash to bizarre trinkets, yet the store still received stellar online consumer reviews. It didn't have a website. So how did the yuppies, hipsters—whoever the hell was writing the reviews—find it?

"You know, that car outside looks like it needs a little work. I might know a guy, if you're interested."

Five foot and a lot, the woman attached to the voice would be hard to miss, with her fiery red hair and overly bright green eyes. Jack left his barstool perch behind the counter and had a long look at her.

He'd missed her entering the store, and her voice had startled him. Quite a task, considering he had a tight ward on the store. And he was hardly an unobservant guy.

"How can I help you?" Jack worked to produce a convincingly relaxed tone.

Face expressionless, the redhead said, "I'm here to apply for the position."

"We're not hiring at the moment." When she didn't reply and she also didn't leave, he added, "Look around. We're a small shop, but maybe something will catch your eye."

Sure, The Junk Shop was a retail location, but it had begun primarily as a front for Jack's work with the magic-using community. A discreet physical location was a bonus when meeting with clients who wanted to stay under the radar. He looked around the small store. For a front, it was becoming increasingly and uncomfortably popular.

She looked around. "Uh-huh. I'm not here for . . . bric-a-brac. I'm sure you've got a position open. My sources are excellent."

Jack hadn't posted the position. Where would he? He could just imagine how that ad would read. *Wanted: Paranormal investigator's assistant. Complete discretion and some ass-kicking required. Part-time help in The Junk Shop mandatory. A high tolerance for the unexplainable preferred.* No.

And Jack had only mentioned to a select few that

he was looking to hire: his highest-ranking Inter-Pack Policing Cooperative contact, Harrington; the Texas Pack leader, John Braxton; and IPPC's temporary chief of security for the Prague library, Ewan Campbell.

"Who's your reference?"

"My stealth entry into the store wasn't reference enough?" She gave him a toothy smile.

That smile made him incredibly uncomfortable. Green eyes, creepy feeling—alarm bells were ringing. Damn. His stealthy, green-eyed Amazon was a dragon. He'd bet cash on it. He stared back without answering.

She shrugged. "Lachlan McClellan, but that might not be entirely to my benefit when you check my references."

"Head of the McClellan clan?"

The guy led a powerful clan of dragons, but he was also a dick with a crap sense of humor. And Jack didn't see him being particularly enlightened about female employees. Although he was surprised Ewan had mentioned Jack's staffing needs to his clan leader.

She hesitated before responding. "We're from the same clan."

Oh, hell—dragon. He knew it. "You want the job?"

She raised an eyebrow. "I'm here, having this conversation with you."

Her non-answers were annoying as hell. More importantly, he didn't see them becoming less annoying with time and proximity.

"Pass." Jack turned back to the register.

"Wait. Yes, I would like the job." She continued to speak to his back. "Please. I would very much like this job."

Slowly Jack turned around. "Then tell me why I should hire you? Besides your stealth entry into a warded store. That only tells me you're a thief."

A brief flicker of fiery green flashed in her eyes, but quickly dimmed. "I'm unemployed and unable to return to my previous employer, which makes me highly motivated to be successful here. Also, I understand you're looking for muscle. My combat skills are excellent." She blinked. "I can demonstrate."

She gave him another smile with just a shade too many teeth.

"No thanks. A dragon kicking my very human ass isn't much of a demonstration. Besides, I'd hate for us to break my bric-a-brac." Jack sat down behind the counter and picked up a pen. Having a dragon would be a huge tactical advantage in most fights, regardless of technical competence.

"Talk to Lachlan. Whatever else he might say, he'll tell you I'm honest and hardworking." She placed a slight emphasis on "honest." She swallowed, the first sign of nervousness she'd displayed since walking into his store. "Please."

Apparently he'd hit a nerve when he'd compared her to a thief. A highly motivated, well-connected dragon employee—he'd be an idiot to walk away just because she wasn't exactly right. Especially since he didn't know what "exactly right" was. What type of person wouldn't drive him nuts with continuous contact? The shelf life of most of his relationships, regardless of the type, was pretty short.

"What's your name?"

"Marin." She didn't offer her hand.

Jack knew the right answer, yet still he hesitated. Damn. He had a job coming up day after tomorrow that could use some dragon muscle.

"All right, Marin. Come back tomorrow at ten. If your reference comes through, we'll discuss employment terms." He narrowed his eyes. "I don't pay well."

She ducked her chin once in acknowledgment and headed out the door. This time, Jack saw her pass through the ward, and a shower of green sparks, visible only to him, fell in her wake. He felt a corresponding pinch from the ring he wore on his right hand. No way he'd missed the ward triggering when she'd first entered the store. If this whole thing worked out and she joined Spirelli Paranormal Investigations, that was one of his first questions.

Jack picked up his cell and scrolled through his

contacts, looking for Ewan's number. Jack was pretty sure Ewan would put him in touch with Lachlan. After a quick mental calculation, adding seven hours to account for Prague time, Jack decided it wasn't too late and dialed Ewan's number.

Ewan answered on the first ring. "Jack. What's up?"

"Hey, Ewan. Any chance you could put me in touch with Lachlan? I had someone come by the shop asking about that assistant's job. Remember, I told you I was looking for someone? Lachlan came up as a reference."

"Sure." Background noise filtered in. "Heads up —you're on speaker."

"Thanks, man. You might actually know her; she's from your clan. A tall redhead named Marin?"

The background noise abruptly disappeared. Ewan must have turned the speaker function off and picked up his phone. "Yeah." The word came out so short, it almost sounded like a grunt.

Something about Marin had drastically changed the tone of their conversation. Jack contemplated for a split second whether to ask. He closed his eyes. Had he lost his mind?

After a few seconds of silence, Ewan said, "Marin is my daughter."

Jack sat on his favorite barstool, the one positioned in front of the shop's register. Careful to make his tone as neutral as possible, he said, "I didn't know that."

"Clearly."

Jack didn't get it. Ewan seemed pissed, but the guy hadn't said a word about not hiring his kid. Since Jack wasn't eager to get singed or mutilated due to an unfortunate miscommunication, clarification was the wisest course. "So, are you telling me you don't want me to hire her?"

"Not at all."

Jesus. Really? Jack rolled his shoulders. "Are you telling me you want me to hire her?"

"What did you want to know?" Ewan's voice had lost some of its edge.

"Uh, okay." Jack figured Ewan had enough patience for about two questions, so he erred on the side of caution and limited himself to one. "Would you recommend Marin for the job?"

"Yes. We done?"

Good enough.

"Yeah. Thanks again." As he pocketed his phone, he caught a flash of movement out of the corner of his eye.

Staring at the now empty shop floor, he said, "I know you're there, little guy. You better be glad I know what rat poison does." He couldn't commit to chemical warfare—even in the pursuit of pest control. It was a weird quirk. Whatever. People who used rat poison must not know what that shit did to the insides of an animal. He snorted. Or they just didn't like living with rats. "Fuzzball, you're damn lucky I don't actually live in this pit."

Jack shook his head. He really needed to stop talking to the rats. It probably made them feel welcome. But he couldn't resist one last warning. "You better not touch the coffee, Fuzzface."

2

———

Jack's ring tightened on his finger, interrupting his morning coffee ritual. He ignored the jingle of the front door bells and the flash of green light in his peripheral vision.

"You're early." Jack didn't raise his voice. He figured dragons had good hearing.

A few seconds later, Marin joined him in his office at the back of the store. "Nice bells."

Overkill maybe, but after Marin had surprised him yesterday they'd seemed like a good addition. "They were sitting around the store. That happens a lot, actually. I need something, have a look around, and there it is."

"Really?" She raised an eyebrow and tilted her head.

"What? It's a junk shop. It's not like I keep great

records on my stock. I buy most of this crap by the box." He opened the small fridge under the coffee station and pulled out milk.

"Hmm." She sat down in one of his client chairs. "And, by the way, I'm only five minutes early."

"The front door was locked." Jack tried to be pissed that she'd picked his front door lock, but he couldn't quite work up to it.

Marin stared back at him without comment.

"And I haven't had my coffee."

She glanced at the half-empty pot of coffee.

"I've only had one cup of coffee. And quit being such a smartass." When she didn't apologize—as if he thought she would—he asked, "Would you like a cup?"

"Yes, thank you."

He handed her a cup of black coffee. If she wanted milk or sugar, she was on her own. Once he'd sat down behind his desk, he said, "Minimum wage. Forty hours a week, no overtime, no benefits. You work in the shop or on cases, as I decide."

"Minimum wage?" She looked amused, rather than worried.

If she wasn't working for the cash, then why? He mentally thumped himself. Didn't matter and he didn't care. If it became relevant, then he'd worry about it.

"You came to me," Jack reminded her.

"Yes." She wrapped her hands around her coffee

mug. Closely trimmed nails, no polish—practical.

He waited. He could use her. Needed her, really. But he wasn't about to start this relationship from a position of weakness.

Marin gave him an odd look he couldn't interpret, then said, "If that was an employment offer, I accept."

Jack opened a drawer and pulled out a few forms. He pushed them across the desk and handed her a pen. "You're hired." He turned his attention to his computer, trying to figure out the best travel options for the two of them and whether his travel budget would cover it. When he saw that she hadn't yet picked up the pen, he said, "You've got five minutes to finish that. One of my gigs just got moved up."

Marin perked up, clearly waiting for details.

Jack pointed to the paperwork. "Five minutes."

Marin grabbed the pen and started writing.

Five minutes later, Jack figured driving was the only option. No problem—he'd just hired a driver. Sort of. And with Marin behind the wheel, he could get in some work.

Marin handed her paperwork to Jack.

"Any chance you have a go bag?" Jack asked.

She nodded.

"With you?"

"Yes." Her eyes widened slightly, the only sign that she was dying of curiosity. She had to be. She was the type: one part puzzle geek, one part adventurer, and two parts control freak.

Great, his inner grumpy voice moaned. That meant four parts pain in his ass.

Stuffing her paperwork in his to-be-filed drawer, Jack said, "We're headed to Louisiana."

"Now?" She didn't look ruffled as she asked.

"Now." Jack left her sitting in his office while he went to the back to fiddle with the air conditioning. He wasn't leaving the A/C running on high while he was gone.

On his way to the door, he called over his shoulder, "You coming?"

Before he'd flipped the sign to closed, she was standing behind him. Okay. Mental note: dragons are strong and fast.

As he locked the shop door, he told her, "We're driving."

Marin looked skeptical. "Uh, maybe I'm driving?"

"Oh, yeah. I have to work on the way." He stopped when Marin fell behind. "What?"

She looked at his car parked in the street about ten feet away, blinked, and said, "I meant that we can take my car."

Why was everyone so distrustful of his Jeep? The thing ran and ran. It was a great car.

"Which one's yours?" He grinned when she pointed to a Range Rover Sport. "Done. Why am I paying you? Are you sure you don't want to work as an unpaid intern?"

"Too late. You already hired me." She raised her eyebrows slightly. "And I am not intern material."

"Whatever you say." Jack retrieved his laptop, go bag, and cell charger from the Jeep, then slammed the door shut. "SPI doesn't pay mileage."

"Spy? Ah, S.P.I. Spirelli Paranormal Investigations. Cute." Her voice indicated it was anything but. Marin climbed into the driver's seat. "As for mileage —I figured. But you're definitely paying for gas. You have an address for me?" Her hand hovered over the GPS.

"Miersburg, Louisiana. I'm not sure where we're staying yet." Jack plugged in his cell charger and started charging his phone. Then he set up a hot spot and pulled out his laptop. "We'll be gone overnight, possibly a few days. No dog at the house, right?"

"No dog, no significant other, no roommate, and no plants." Marin glanced at Jack. "I don't suppose you're planning to murder me, cut me into little pieces, and bury the parts in five states?"

"Only if you really piss me off." Jack rubbed his neck. "Okay. Only if you really piss me off, I suddenly become fire resistant, and there's zero chance of being hunted down by a pack of dragons and tortured in retaliation."

"Uh-huh. It's a clan of dragons, by the way. Or a

flight or a weyr, not a pack. Bad idea to compare dragons to Lycan. It's a sensitive topic." As she spoke, Marin was slowly making her way out of East Austin and heading to the highway.

She didn't look offended.

"Seriously?" Jack couldn't resist asking. The dragons he'd met didn't seem all that sensitive.

"Yup."

Jack turned his attention back to the case file notes on his laptop. "So—SPI was hired to escort Charlotte Sneed, a Louisiana earth witch, on a shopping expedition in Austin."

"Shopping. In Austin. She needed a bodyguard for that?" Marin tapped her fingers on the steering wheel. "Never mind. Why are we driving to Miersburg for an Austin babysitting job?"

"Because the job has changed. Calvin Sneed, the client's husband, contacted me this morning. His wife disappeared yesterday, and he's refusing to contact local police. He's asked us to find her. I told him he really needed to call the police, but that just made him more agitated."

Marin snorted. Quietly, but it was unmistakable.

"I get it—her disappearance is likely related to the magic community or he wouldn't have SPI looking into it." Jack tipped his head back onto the headrest and closed his eyes. He hated complicated jobs. Bodyguard on a shopping trip in a town where he knew many, if not all, of the players in the magic-using community—that wasn't complicated. He turned to look at Marin. "Don't suppose you know anything about the magic-using community in Miersburg?"

Marin glanced at him then pulled her gaze back to the road. He took that to mean: Hell no, you idiot.

Eyes back on his computer, he said, "You have a lot of attitude for someone on probation."

"Or an acceptable amount, considering we're in my car and left Austin city limits at least ten minutes ago."

Jack shrugged and went back to his computer, looking at the few notes he'd made over his first cup of coffee—before Marin had arrived. "No pack in Miersburg, but I'm waiting to hear from the Texas Pack leader—John Braxton—about any strays that may be in the area."

"Any other witches? Is Charlotte part of a coven, for example? Or does she have any local competition?" Marin asked.

"Not according to the husband. The closest witch lives about two hours away and is a friend of Charlotte's. What exactly would be competition for a local earth witch? There's no active Coven of Light branch in the area." Jack had checked on Coven connections before he'd taken the job. They were, basically, a large institution of whackadoo witch zealots, and he wasn't getting anywhere near them if he could help it.

"You know, earth witches are tied to their communities. Special teas for the sick, gardening advice for the neighbors, PTA president. That kind of thing can generate jealousy and a sense of competition, especially in such a small town." Marin glanced at the GPS screen, tapped the screen to bring up the route map, then said, "This place has to be under twenty or thirty thousand, based on what I'm seeing on the GPS."

Jack stopped typing and watched her closely as he asked, "You're from a small town, then?"

Marin's gaze didn't waver from the road. "Or maybe I just know witches really well."

"Whatever. No local Coven of Light, no local witch rivalries. And the husband had no idea about other magic-users." Jack googled Miersburg. "Around ten thousand. A town that small, I'm betting they'd know if there was a spell caster running around."

"Maybe." Marin tapped her fingers on the steering wheel. "Don't suppose there's any chance you'd pay a speeding ticket?"

"No."

Apparently, she was willing to pick up the ticket herself. That, or riding with him was driving her nuts, because she didn't reply and sped up to around eighty-five. Fine by him.

Before he got wrapped up in research and forgot,

he asked, "How did you get through my ward at the shop?"

Marin pressed her lips together. "What do you know about dragons?"

Jack squinted and adjusted his visor. "Let's assume not much."

Marin sighed. "We're not like Lycan, because we don't shape-shift. I'm a dragon, and I'm a woman."

"Right—I got that part."

Marin huffed in annoyance. "I'm not sure you do. I'm dragon and human—at the same time."

She glanced at Jack, possibly to gauge his reaction. But he wasn't even sure what his reaction was. What she described didn't make sense. "Then why do I see either a dragon or a human whenever I'm around you guys? It seems like you're picking one."

She didn't quite roll her eyes—but it sure felt like she had. "I choose which part of myself you see. Which part interacts on a physical plane with this world, but that doesn't mean I'm not both dragon and woman at the same time. You're thinking in terms of humans with magical talents—a human who can use his magic to shift to a wolf, or crocodile, or jaguar. But I'm not a human with some magical ability. It's not a question of having magic—I am magic."

What the hell? Jack asked the first question that came to mind. "Are you supposed to tell people this shit?"

She gave him one of those toothy smiles. "Most are smart enough not to ask."

She definitely used that creepy smile to intimidate.

"Cut it out with the dragon grin. How does all of this apply to walking through my ward?"

Marin shrugged. "I choose which part of myself exists at any given time in this world, but I can choose, for a very brief moment, to allow neither of my forms to exist in this world."

"So you're saying that you didn't walk through the ward? That you unexisted yourself through it?" Jack shook his head. "That sounds like teleportation to me."

"Not teleportation. A nonphysical part of myself remains, an anchor in this reality. It's that anchor that moves and to which my physical body returns. Neat, right?" She gave him a brilliant smile. A genuine one, not her creepy alligator smile.

Jack laughed, her excitement catching. "Yes. That's a handy skill."

They both fell silent, but it wasn't an uncomfortable quiet. Jack was pleasantly surprised she'd shared so much. He'd keep his mouth shut, and clearly Marin knew that. One small step forward in his first employer-employee relationship. He tried not to cringe. Relationships with people—even professional ones—were always so damned complicated.

3

Calvin Sneed ushered Jack and Marin into his study. "Can I offer you a drink?" When they declined, Calvin motioned for them to sit down. Concern was etched across his face and his eyes looked tired, like he hadn't slept well.

Jack pulled out a notebook. "What can you tell me?"

Calvin dropped into the chair behind his desk. "I didn't want to say over the phone, but the reason Charlotte hired a bodyguard . . . I mean, she's been shopping in Austin by herself for years. She buys—I don't even know what—things she can't get locally. But you don't care about that." He cleared his throat. "We hired you as a precaution, because I was worried her Aunt Sylvia might try to meet with her in Austin, maybe even recruit her. Sylvia's with the Coven of Light."

"And that worried you? That Charlotte might run into her aunt?" Jack asked.

Calvin looked confused. "The Coven of Light? I thought you'd know about them, since you're an insider."

"I'm familiar with the Coven, but I don't know of any Coven activity in Austin. Why now and why Austin?"

"Charlotte's Aunt Sylvia called a few weeks ago. She was recruited by the Coven at least ten years ago, and Charlotte hadn't had any contact with her in that time, except an occasional letter. Then she calls out of the blue. Charlotte was polite, but she didn't encourage further contact. When her trip came up, I was a little nervous about her being so far from home." Calvin sighed. "We don't know where Sylvia lives now, but Charlotte's family is originally from the Austin area. So traveling back to Austin so soon after they'd spoken . . . it just made Charlotte uncomfortable. Well, me, actually. Charlotte wasn't afraid of her aunt."

Calvin stalled—overcome or lost in thought, possibly. Jack prompted him quietly. "So you called SPI."

"Right. We figured that if you met her and kept an eye on her while she was in town and she headed straight back, there shouldn't be any problems." Calvin blinked dazedly. "But then she didn't come home yesterday, and we already knew about you, so I called."

"Did Aunt Sylvia make any threats?"

"No, nothing like that. They parted on good terms. But she's with the Coven." Calvin looked at Jack like he'd lost a few marbles.

"I understand. I'm just trying to get a full picture." Jack tried for a reassuring, sympathetic smile. Not his strong suit. "Is there any other reason that you suspect the Coven of Light is involved? Other than the proximity of Aunt Sylvia's call?"

Calvin rubbed his face hard with both hands. "No. But I don't know what else could have happened. Everyone loves Charlotte. She's a genuinely caring person. She's generous—with her time, her enthusiasm for projects . . . You don't understand. She heads up the annual Plants & Fans for Seniors fundraiser, mentors the Junior Geologists at the high school." He paused, hesitating, and then continued, "She also does important work for the town. Not a job; Charlotte is a stay-at-home mom. But she's working on a project for Miersburg."

Marin nudged his foot. More discreet than an I-told-you-so, but equally annoying.

Jack ignored his sidekick and focused his attention on Calvin Sneed. "I understand—she has a lot of friends in town and people who look up to her." When Calvin seemed satisfied that they appreciated his wife's popularity and lack of enemies, Jack asked,

"What can you tell me about your wife's schedule yesterday?"

Calvin looked at him blankly. He closed his eyes briefly, and when he opened them, he looked more purposeful. "Like I told you this morning: I realized she was missing a little before dinner. Yesterday was her night to cook, and we eat around 6:30—my son and Charlotte and I. I called at six, but she didn't answer."

Jack jotted down the beginning of a timeline.

"Where was Charlotte planning to be before dinner?" Marin asked the question in a voice Jack hadn't yet heard from her. She sounded . . . compassionate.

"Looking for plants, herbs, flowers—that kind of thing." Calvin smiled. "Hunting—that's what we call it. Our little joke since—unlike most of Miersburg—we don't hunt."

Jack paused, letting Calvin drift back into the here and now at his own speed. Once Calvin made eye contact, he said, "And what about the rest of her day?"

Jack jotted down everything Calvin could remember about Charlotte's schedule earlier in the day as he recounted it. When Calvin seemed tapped out on details, Jack asked him, "Do you mind if we have a look around?"

"Of course not. Do you want to start with Charlotte's office? Her calendar will be there." Calvin stopped and took a breath. The man looked exhausted.

Jack nodded, and Calvin immediately stood up, ushering both his guests out of the study to the back of the house.

Jack shouldn't have been surprised to find that Charlotte's "office" was actually a tidy little shed attached to a greenhouse. As he and Marin stood inside, he couldn't help but notice the sharp contrasts. A rough tin shed on the exterior, her office was pleasantly clean and comfortably furnished on the inside. In fact, the interior was larger than it appeared from outside. He and Marin both fit comfortably with room to spare— enough for a large modern desk, an ergonomic chair, and a love seat. Charlotte spent some time in her office.

Calvin stood awkwardly in the doorway of the well-lit shed.

Jack scanned the room, spotting a large desk calendar blotter, as well as several deep desk drawers with no apparent locking mechanisms. "I think this will keep us busy, Calvin, if you don't mind giving us a few minutes." Calvin nodded, looking relieved. As he turned to go, Jack said, "One last thing: your wife's phone number—the one you provided on the form—that was her cell number?"

"That's right." Calvin rattled off the number Jack had scrawled in his notes. With a pained smile, he backed out of the doorway and closed the door carefully.

Immediately, Jack turned to Marin and pulled out his phone. "Have a look at her calendar." He dialed his tech contact's number, and turned his back to Marin when Christina answered. "Hey. I have a cell number for you. Can you get a location for it?"

Christina, or Chris as her Pack buddies called her, replied in a distracted tone, "Now?" The sound of an insistent toddler echoed in the background but was quickly drowned out by a little girl's screech.

Jack felt a hint of the discomfort he always experienced in Chris's hectic household. Three kids were a lot of kids—especially when they were all moving at once. Her kids were mini-hoodlums—lovable little squirts, but always into something and constantly in motion. He muffled a groan. Apparently, Chris's brood was overwhelming long-distance, too. Save him from a herd of small children. "Ah, soon? I've got a missing woman and the husband's continuing to refuse our recommendation to report it."

"Text the number, and I'll be back to you in ten with an answer or update." Then Chris hung up on him.

Jack pocketed his phone after texting her Charlotte's name and number. Turning back to Marin, he asked, "Whatcha got?"

Marin wrinkled her nose. "A pretty boring life. Basically what the husband said: worked in the shed in the morning, picked up her son, Charlie, and dropped him at home, went 'hunting.' Then mysteriously failed to appear for dinner. We need to find out where she went hunting."

"Yeah. And where her cell is." Jack flipped through the contents of the top desk drawer. "Don't suppose you found a map marking all her favorite collection spots?"

"No. But I did find what might be her collection list." Marin pointed to a list of plants scrawled in the margins of the desk blotter calendar that covered a good portion of the desk's surface.

Jack pulled out his notepad and wrote down the seven plant names: pine-barren deathcamas (crow poison), redbay, le sureau, swamp willow, black nightshade, cattails, and mayapple. Several of them had lines running through them, as if they'd been ticked off a grocery list. Three remained, and he put an asterisk next to those. And crow poison—or pine-barren deathcamas, what the heck?—was underlined three times.

"Uh . . . you know you can use your phone for that. For documenting evidence." Marin waved the phone in her right hand at him. "I already snapped a picture of the list. And the calendar."

He stuffed the pad back in his jeans pocket and squatted down to sift through a mostly empty wastepaper basket. "What are the chances hubby knows where she collects her ingredients?"

Marin flipped through the previous few months on the calendar. "No idea."

Done with the trash, Jack stood up and moved back to finish the desk drawers. "I didn't say a word about your driving, right?"

"Yeah. What's wrong with my driving?"

Jack lifted his eyebrows, but refused to answer. "You can extend me the same courtesy. I like how I record case notes. I have a method. And yes, I do know my phone takes pictures and that I can take notes on it. Thanks, but no." Geez, she was annoying. Why was he bothering to explain himself? Especially to someone who was barely an adult. Jack stopped rifling through the middle drawer and closed his eyes. He'd forgotten that weird dragon quirk. He opened his eyes to examine Marin. She looked mid-twenties. "How old are you?"

Marin leaned down to start working on the bottom drawers on the opposite side of the desk. Red hair swept down and covered her face. "In human years?"

Whatever the hell that meant. Instead of asking, he said, "Calendar years."

"A hundred and three." She attacked the papers in the drawer with renewed vigor, still avoiding his gaze. "That's kind of like twenty-one for you guys, but my license says twenty-five."

"Whatever. If you're 103, I'm not taking tech advice from you."

Marin snorted and—finally—looked up at him. "Dragons are very . . . current. It's a function of exceeding the life span of the culture we've chosen to join. Every day a dragon has to choose to live in the now."

And if a dragon didn't live in the now? She called it a choice, but it sounded more like a rule. Maybe a law. "If some ancestor decided to join humanity, that means you can choose to leave, right?"

"Not particularly," Marin muttered, and ducked her head back to the contents of her drawer. "Ha!" She lifted a bundle of letters. "Check it out—letters from Auntie. These might be useful, right?"

"Maybe." A buzz emanating from his back pocket interrupted him. He snatched the letters out of Marin's hand, stuffed them in a back pocket, and then yanked his phone out from the other back pocket. He flipped immediately to the text. "Sweet. We've got GPS coordinates on Charlotte's phone." Jack opened up the door to the greenhouse and quickly catalogued the general layout and contents, and then he swept the shed room, looking for any last pieces of relevant info. "Can you do that blood-hound trick? Where you scent magic?"

A look of distaste crossed Marin's face. "I can discriminate the individual scent of a person's magic. Could you not compare me to a dog, though?"

Unapologetically, Jack said, "Right. So—you've got Charlotte's scent?"

"It's all over the plants in the greenhouse and the one on her desk." When Jack continued to stand unmoving in front of the shed door, she said, "Yes. I have the signature for Charlotte's magic."

Opening the shed front door, he waved Marin through. "All right. Let's see if Calvin knows where his wife collects her plants." He carefully untucked his button-down shirt and smoothed the wrinkles as best he could. Sloppy and maybe a little unprofessional, but the thin bundle of letters in his back pocket wouldn't be visible.

4

Calvin looked much more composed, and more present in the moment, as he greeted Jack and Marin at the back door to the house.

"Charlotte has a few favorite spots, but I only know three locations. I marked them on a map, just in case. And you mentioned this morning that an extra key might be helpful." He handed Jack the map and a car key. "But like I said, I'm sure Charlotte wouldn't lock her car."

Jack pocketed the key and glanced at the Google map. Red felt lines clearly marked three areas outside of Miersburg city limits. "Thank you. This is helpful, Calvin." Jack made eye contact and repeated himself. "Really. We're going to check on a few things, but before we leave—are you sure you don't want to report Charlotte's disappearance?"

"Tomorrow morning. If you don't have any information for me by then, I'll visit the chief of police after I drop my son at summer school. The chief doesn't exactly know about Charlotte. And he won't know what to do, how to handle something like this, if the Coven is involved."

Jack nodded. "I'll call with an update as soon as I have any information for you."

Calvin escorted them to the front door wordlessly. After the door closed behind them, Marin turned to Jack and started to speak.

"Shut up," Jack said under his breath. "In the car."

Marin clamped her mouth shut and headed to the car. After she shut the driver's door with unnecessary force, she said, "Seriously? You're not going to tell that clearly terrified man that we have a lead?"

Jack ignored her, intent on retrieving his laptop and pulling up Google Maps. If he could plot the phone location, he'd know if it fell in one of the three areas provided by Calvin. Finally, the map he needed downloaded.

"Can you at least tell me where we're going?"

Jack stared at the screen on his laptop. "No. Shut up—I'm working."

Marin smacked the steering wheel. "You're a f—"

"Tscht." Jack located the cell GPS coordinates on the map. He did some rapid topography comparisons. Bingo. On the far southern edge of one the areas. "North. Drive north." If he bothered to listen, Jack was sure he'd hear the grinding of Marin's teeth. "You didn't seem this moody in your interview."

"You weren't quite this much of an ass." Her nose twitched. "And I wanted the job."

"Huh." Jack turned back to the computer screen. "The cell is located in one of Charlotte's favorite collection spots. We'll hit that one first. Then we'll move clockwise to catch the remaining two."

"So if you know exactly where we're going now, can you at least plug in the location on my GPS? I'd hate for Charlotte to have to sleep out in the woods a second night because we got lost."

"I think we both know Charlotte didn't wander off a trail and get lost in the woods." Jack lifted up his hands defensively when Marin glowered in his direction. "Okay, I'm entering it already."

Two minutes, three at most, and Marin said, "What's the plan?"

"Already told you: we look for Charlotte, her car, her phone, or any other sign of her at the coordinates Chris gave me. No luck there, then we check the collection area. No luck there, then we check the next collection area." Jack pulled Aunt Sylvia's letters out of his back pocket. He angled his shoulders away from Marin, hoping she'd get the hint. He couldn't work with her chattering in his ear. Maybe having a driver wasn't actually worth it.

Fifteen minutes later, they rolled up on a blue

Volvo station wagon parked under a tree on the side of the road—just about where the GPS coordinates were pointing. As Marin pulled up behind the Volvo, Jack said, "That's close enough."

Jack retrieved the fact sheet Calvin had emailed him as Marin and he had driven to Miersburg. It was a simple form with some standard questions: name, age, basic physical description, description of her car.

Marin grumbled unintelligibly to herself.

"What? Speak up." Jack compared the license plate of the Volvo they'd found to the number provided by Calvin. "That's it. That's Charlotte's car." He turned to Marin. Her lips were thin. "What?"

"I can't believe you've had a cheat sheet all day and didn't mention it."

"I emailed it to Calvin when he called this morning. You think I was just hanging out and drinking coffee all morning?" Jack moved to open his door, then paused. "You ready to try to catch Charlotte's scent?"

Marin sighed. "Magical signature—not a bloodhound. But yeah, definitely."

They exited Marin's car, and Jack watched as Marin circled the car.

"Don't you think it's weird that Charlotte left her cell in her car?" Marin opened the car door. She gave Jack a concerned look. "Her unlocked car."

Jack circled the car, looking in the windows.

"We're three side roads off the main highway. It's a small town, and she knows everyone. She's a trusting person. She likes to work uninterrupted by the outside world. She forgot—"

"Okay. I get it." Marin leaned in, had a quick look around, and then backed out of the car with a dissatisfied look. "I suppose it makes sense an earth witch wouldn't do a lot of magic in her car."

"Not getting anything?" Jack opened the passenger-side door and sat down. He popped open the glove box. "Cell was in the glove box." He lifted it up to show Marin, but she'd disappeared.

Scanning the roadside, he found her two hundred feet off the road, down what looked like a path. If she didn't want the dog analogies, she shouldn't run off like a freaking hound on a trail. He shrugged. He'd catch up if she didn't check back in within a few minutes. He checked the battery on Charlotte's phone—no password required—and found it low. He quickly flipped through the recent texts, but nothing jumped out and grabbed him. Phone calls were the same; all came from saved contacts and most were from her son and husband.

He climbed out of the Volvo to find a pissed-off dragon waiting.

"What kind of earth witch doesn't do some kind of magic out in the middle of all this vegetation?" Marin swatted at a mosquito, then turned to Jack. "Do you have any bug spray?"

Jack tried to hide a smile, then decided he didn't care and grinned. "City dragon, huh?"

"Sure, if that gets me some mosquito dope." She scratched at her neck. "I've got nothing in this area."

"That sucks, since it's still light for at least a few hours. Don't suppose you can do a flyover of the area in full light?"

"Hm. I can, actually. Seriously, where's the bug spray?"

Jack rifled through his go bag and pulled out the Ziploc that contained his outdoor stash.

As she picked through the rub-on repellent, sunblock, and high-Deet-content bug spray, Marin looked like she'd hit gold. "Thank God." She slathered her neck with the ointment. "Bugs love me."

Jack shook his head. "Don't you heal fast?"

"Sure. But bites itch. And the buzzing—ugh." She generously doused herself and only after she was thoroughly covered did she answer his earlier question, "I have some ability to camouflage. If you're looking for me, it doesn't work—but out here? I don't see why not."

Jack searched through what little he knew about dragons, and he definitely couldn't remember anything about camo.

Marin sighed. "We're just like you guys; we don't all have the same talents. My nose for magical signatures isn't great, so I have to be pretty close. But it's easier for me to get closer since I have some chameleon talent."

Jack blinked at the bright blue summer sky and puffy white clouds. "Chameleon? As in sky-blue dragon?"

"Jesus, Jack. This is why we don't talk about this shit. For all you know, my dragon form is baby blue."

Jack turned to Marin's car and plugged in Charlotte's cell. "Okay, whatever." He hated to be caught in what might be perceived as juvenile curiosity. But seriously—baby-blue dragons? He turned back just in time to catch his bag.

"So, I can carry a cell but can't use it without landing. You'll have to keep an eye on me for a general direction of travel, and I'll call in what I find after I land. And you'll have to attach the phone to my dragon self. If I carry it in my jeans pocket, it won't work until I land. My phone and clothes stay with my human form."

Jack blinked. Weird. But that was his superpower. He seemed to have an infinite capacity to accept the weird, the wondrous, and the unbelievable. "Okay. Where's the best place? I've only ever seen one of you guys, and that wasn't exactly up close and personal."

"Forearm, probably." Marin gave him a probing look. "You're not going to freak?"

Jack didn't bother to answer, just dug around in his bag. He had some paracord packed that should work. As he worked on a cradle for the phone, he reviewed the plan. "You change. I attach the phone. You follow a search grid to cover the wooded areas north and east of here."

Marin nodded. "Got it. The entire area has to be less than a hundred acres. It won't take me long."

Holding up Marin's phone, now cradled in paracord, Jack said, "Land and send me your search info, including your landing point, if you see anything. Then call in and I'll meet you."

"All right, already. Let's get going."

"You know, something out there might have harmed Charlotte." Jack paused, waiting for some kind of reaction from Marin. Nothing. He tried his damnedest not to roll his eyes. "I'm saying be careful."

"I get it. I'll be fine." Marin stepped away from the car, and then she was gone.

She was every color and none. Or, rather, the dragon resting on its haunches about ten feet away was. Every hue of the rainbow seemed to glint off a silvery backdrop then fade into a shimmer of . . . nothing. Giant wings flexed, and Jack could see her outline. Not clearly, but the shape and the impression of movement were there.

I'M MORE CLEARLY VISIBLE IN MOTION.

Jack clutched his head. The voice—Marin's voice —screamed. Stabbing pain pulsed through his brain. Several seconds later, he blew out a harsh breath. It took him another few seconds before he could speak. "Ow."

The iridescent dragon shimmered into view, again fully visible. Her long, sinuous neck flexed, displaying a rainbow of colors. It took Jack a moment to realize she was ducking her head.

"Don't tell me: that was an accident."

Reptilian eyes blinked and a bony head dipped in a nod.

Jack closed his eyes and pinched the bridge of his nose. When he looked up again, Marin was smiling—probably. "Any chance you can try for a whisper?"

Another nod.

"And maybe not smile? All those teeth are distracting."

Dragon teeth immediately disappeared.

Better? The voice in his head was thin, reedy.

"Yeah. Feel free to knock it up a half notch. Not one of your better talents, is it? The dragon mind-meld. Or whatever you call it."

Giant reptilian eyes narrowed to slits. *Mind speech. And I don't suck; you're my first human.*

"And that's finally just right, Goldilocks." Jack lifted up the cell phone. "Am I okay to attach this?"

Dragon Marin lifted her left foreleg and tapped the ground.

"My, Grandma. What big claws you have." Okay, maybe the dragon was making him a little nervous.

That or he'd reached a new level of cheesiness for some other, unknown reason.

As he leaned down to attach the phone, Marin flexed her claws. His breath caught. "Seriously? Charlotte could be injured in the woods and you're messing with me?"

She leaned down and huffed hot air in his face. Nice.

He smacked her leg. "Done. Let me grab my glasses before you take off."

Returning with his field glasses and a small handheld GPS unit, he said, "All right. Whenever you're ready." He still wasn't completely comfortable with Marin venturing off alone, given her lack of concern for the inherent risk. But he certainly felt better after he saw her flex her wings and take flight. Witnessing a dragon shove its massive body into the air using muscular haunches, straining wings, and will power was terrifying. He was pretty sure he could admit that without being a wimp.

While her takeoff had been a demonstration of brute force, watching Marin in flight was something else entirely. Graceful. Beautiful, even. Jack took his field glasses out. As soon as she'd taken off, she'd shimmered into what looked like nothingness, but her movement let him pick out her camouflaged form from the blue of the sky. He could even make her out when she was gliding, but just barely.

As Jack watched her circle the search area in a

spiral pattern, he had to wonder: how exactly could dragons fly? Yes, her wingspan in mid-flight was truly an amazing sight. But her body must be roughly the size of an elephant. Even as long and strong as her wings clearly were, her flight was a physical impossibility. And yet he watched her skim the treetops. She'd claimed to be a thing of magic, and here was the evidence.

Marin's abrupt descent interrupted his thoughts. Her head lifted and her rear fell, almost as if she was standing in the air, and then she dropped from his sight. Magic. He noted a landmark near where she'd landed, and used that to determine his heading. He saved his current location on his GPS, made a rough estimate of the distance, and entered a destination waypoint.

Jack grabbed a small daypack out of his bag and scrounged around for the essentials. He wasn't going far and shouldn't be long, but he should have received a text and a call from Marin by now. Dammit. He shoved every magical gadget and doodad he'd brought with him into his pack. Except his warded glasses. He replaced his sunglasses with a pair of warded horn-rimmed glasses. With these on, he should be able to see any wards—any magic, actually—that was in the woods. Not nearly as functional in this environment as Marin's magic signature detector, because the glasses were limited to line of sight. And, unlike the spell caster who'd warded the glasses, he couldn't interpret what kind of magic he was seeing. Not yet. He was hoping that with some practice, he might figure that out.

Still nothing from Marin. He called and her phone rolled immediately to voicemail. Dammit. He stopped and drafted a quick email with a brief sketch of the situation. He paused before he hit send, but he didn't have much choice. Someone needed to know what the hell was going on in Miersburg, Louisiana, if he didn't manage to make his way out of the woods.

5

Fifteen minutes of light hiking in the woods, and Jack remembered with painful clarity how much he hated snakes. Every downed tree he climbed over, every sweep of knee-high grass he waded through, gave him the creeps. It wasn't like he had an actual phobia, but he wasn't ashamed to admit that snake gaiters and decent hiking boots took the edge off and made outings in the snake-infested outdoors less nerve-racking. Only, he'd left his freaking gaiters at home.

"What the hell?" Jack scrambled backward, almost tripping.

The brown snake he'd startled disappeared into the grass.

Jack closed his eyes and counted to ten. He hated snakes. Hated them. His eyes popped open. What the hell was a brown snake doing out in the middle of the day in the middle of the summer? Just what he needed: suspicious snake behavior in the middle of the woods, where his dragon and his client had disappeared. Jack checked his GPS and then entered a small clearing, trying to push the thought of a freak snake attack out of his mind. His scalp was still crawling when he spotted the crushed grass impression of what must have been Marin's landing spot.

Jack scanned the clearing for her exit point. He found it, but the crushed grass trail out of the clearing had definitely been made by a very human, two-legged Marin. Why hadn't she called in when she landed? No signal in the clearing? He checked his phone and found four of five bars visible. He dialed Marin's number, and again got her voicemail. At least his cell was working.

"You're getting this message because I'm pissed and can't yell at you in person. If you get this message before I get to you, call me. Immediately." Jack pocketed his phone.

Maybe the phone had dislodged mid-flight. Given the spiraling flight path Marin had taken, no way would he be able to rule out that possibility by finding her phone. But she should have had the sense to stay in place at the clearing once she'd landed and found her phone gone.

If he found her in one piece, he might take her up on that offer of hand-to-hand that she'd made yesterday. As pissed as he was, he might just beat her.

Jack grunted in annoyance and pushed up the warded glasses that had slid down his sweaty nose. And there it was. Not plainly visible, just a faint outline of a shadow that wasn't quite a shadow. He let the glasses slide down his nose and peered over the top of them: no shadow.

Jack fixed the glasses firmly in place and followed the dark outline. Now that he knew what he was looking for, he could see where it transected Marin's path exiting the clearing. She'd passed directly through what might possibly be a ward. Certainly, the shadowy edge was magic. Had she walked through it, unaware? Or had she used her particular dragon skill of avoiding wards and "unexisted" herself to the other side?

As Jack contemplated his options, a scraggly rabbit darted through the clearing and disappeared behind that shadowy line. Jack dipped his head to catch sight of the rabbit with unaltered vision over the top of his warded glasses. But it was gone. Not hidden in tall grass or brush, just gone.

Well, that ruled out one possibility. He couldn't follow Marin's path through that smudge of magic, because who knew where he'd end up. Or what happened to whatever—whoever—crossed that line. How the hell had his ward-hopping dragon not seen it?

Keeping a minimum of ten feet away from the shadow line, Jack followed the edge. It didn't take long for him to notice the curve of the shadow's edge. He checked his GPS tracks and saw he'd managed to traverse an almost perfect half-circle. It looked like about a half-acre, assuming the circle continued. He tried not to jump to conclusions, but it was looking like this little bubble had trapped Marin, whether she'd stumbled into it or ward-hopped through the barrier.

Jack was less than fifty feet away from where, he suspected, the dark shadow of magic he'd been following completed a circle. The oddly dark shading of the magic, the disappearing rabbit, the circular barrier, and two disappearances: the whole situation reeked of a trap. He had no clue how he was getting inside, and he'd almost completed his sweep of the perimeter. Jack started to run through a list of backup resources—he wouldn't need them, but just in case—when an object hit him hard on the ass. He quickly scanned the area, looking for a threat. He found sunlight, a few birds, and a bold squirrel who appeared to be scolding him.

Looking at the squirrel, Jack muttered, "Don't suppose you just nailed me with a nut?"

The squirrel chittered in response and ran up the tree he'd been clinging to. Jack turned his attention to the ground, looking for whatever it was that had hit him. And there it was. He picked up a phone wrapped in a bright yellow OtterBox case about four feet behind him. Marin's phone. No way he'd missed that as he'd walked the shadow's edge. He shoved his glasses up his nose and gave the phone a solid inspection. Determining it magic-free, he squatted down and flipped the thing over so the screen was face up.

A smile slowly spread over Jack's face. "Brilliant." He picked up the phone and stood up before he read the message on the screen.

Charlotte found alive & well. Trapped in warded bubble powered by death magic. Do NOT cross ward. Can see & hear you. Need water. Have shelter. No clue how to leave. C & I maybe not alone in bubble. Marin

Water was simple enough. He had a bladder in his pack and a bottle of water. He removed the bladder and chucked it with some force through the shadow barrier. The small bottle he kept for himself for now.

He looked at the barrier. If he could talk to squirrels, he shouldn't be so uncomfortable talking to someone he couldn't see. He hesitated then slowly raised his hand and waved. "Ladies." Yeah, awkward. "I've got a stash of water in the car if you need more." Jack grabbed a protein bar from his pack. Lifting it up, he said, "Coming your way."

As for them not being alone . . . Marin seemed to have some common sense. He wouldn't have hired her otherwise. And she hadn't mentioned immediate danger. He pulled her phone out and drafted a quick reply. Who's with you? Can they hear/see me?

Jack lifted the phone up and pointed in the direction he planned to throw it. He waited a few seconds then chucked it. Hopefully ghosts didn't have a way to interfere with electronics.

It didn't take long for Marin to reply, and this time the phone arrived with startling accuracy, thrown almost directly into his hands.

Not certain – possibly a spirit. Dead spell caster? Trapped victim? Suspect spirit can see & hear what's directly outside bubble. Giving me a bad feeling. Ideas on getting us out?

Great—the dragon was worried. Time for reinforcements. He pocketed Marin's phone. There was only one person Jack knew who had solid spell-caster knowledge and probably knew about ghosts: his English buddy Harrington at the Inter-Pack Policing Cooperative. According to Jack's sources, the guy had a spirit living in his library.

It wasn't like they were tight, but Jack had done a little job for him and still had his number. And it had been Harrington's idea to bring Spirelli Paranormal Investigations into the light, to make the business official. Hell, Jack had a website now that he could almost completely blame on Harrington.

"Grabbing some more water from the car. Be

back in thirty minutes, this spot." Jack hesitated, then went ahead and added, "Be safe."

He dropped a waypoint on his GPS, verified the direction of the car, and booked it. He needed to get out of earshot—whatever the hell that was for a ghost—and call Harrington.

He arrived at the Range Rover slightly out of breath. Maybe he'd been drinking a few too many beers lately. He retrieved his cell and dialed Harrington. Jack only had a landline for him, so he crossed his fingers and waited.

"Harrington." Crisp, clear British tones came across the line.

"Jack Spirelli here. I need some information on dispelling wards and some background on ghosts."

Jack could hear the creak of old leather in the background. He could just see Harrington leaning back in an old-fashioned chair, twirling a moustache, contemplating what he could extort in exchange. Yeah, maybe his imagination was in overdrive after the whole silver dragon thing earlier.

"You'll owe me a favor."

And the negotiating had started. Jack sighed quietly. "Local only; that includes Texas and not the surrounding states. And no more than two days' work." He kept a steady watch as he spoke, scanning the surrounding woods, the small road, and the two parked cars.

"Three, and you work for anyone, not just me."

Hell. He closed his eyes an considered his options, then a thought occurred. "Spirelli Paranormal Investigations for three days, local work only, transferable. Deal."

Harrington made a sound that might have been a laugh. Apparently, his substitution of the business name hadn't gotten by Harrington. He must not have an aversion to working with dragons, because he said, "Agreed. I assume this relates to the cryptic email you sent earlier. What do you want to know?"

"Yeah. But it's under control for now. There's a ward around an area about the size of a suburban lot that looks like a shadow, even in direct light. It allows entry but prevents exit, and acts like a one-way mirror. I can't see inside, but I have contact with people on the inside who can see out."

"You're using those warded glasses I gave you for that last job?" When Jack confirmed that he was, Harrington continued, "First, the physical description sounds like death magic. You're likely not seeing a shadow, but rather a complete absence of light. If the ward mimics a shadow, it might be fading, which means it's quite old. That's in your favor, because wards powered by death magic are strong." Harrington paused. "Very strong."

"All right. How do I break the ward? I've got an earth witch and dragon on the inside. And outside I've got the warded spectacles, a magically powered light source, and a strengthening potion from an earth witch. Jack cringed at using up his entire store of magical objects. He'd been trading whenever possible, trying to gather a stash of goods that might even the playing field on his magical jobs. So far this paltry stash, plus a few items he'd left at the house, were all he'd come up with.

"If you don't have a spell caster who can deconstruct the ward, the easiest way to defuse one is to exhaust the power source," Harrington said.

"Are you saying trigger the trap until there's no more juice?" Jack managed to not throw the phone —just barely.

"Yes. But there's no way to know if the next cricket who crosses the ward will expend the remaining energy or if the body mass of five hundred dragons would even make a dent. If it were a regular ward, set and abandoned, it likely wouldn't function for long. But a ward powered by death magic has exponentially more magical reserves."

Jack tried to give Harrington's words some thought. "So you're telling me my people are screwed."

"Without a spell caster? Yes, that's likely." Harrington's tone divulged no overt concern for the players in Jack's little drama. "But a talented spell caster, someone like Lizzie Smith—"

"Or you." Jack cringed to think what kind of trade he'd have to negotiate to get Harrington to Louisiana.

"True. I could likely deconstruct it with a little time." Harrington paused, the absence of an offer temporarily stalling the conversation. "Your dragon —Marin?—she's already tried to evade the ward?"

"I'm assuming the ward-hopping thing didn't work or she'd have done it. And even if she could, that would leave our earth witch still stuck in the trap, possibly with a ghost."

"Possibly?"

Jack started stuffing water bottles into his pack. He was running low on time if he was going to return within thirty minutes, and he had another call to make. "Yeah. Marin's not sure, but she thinks there's a ghost in there with them. Is it possible a ghost could be trapped inside the ward?"

"It depends on how the ward is structured. But if your dragon thinks there's a ghost, then there's a ghost. Marin's young, but dragons generally have impeccable magic-detection ability."

Unless there was a death magic ward in play, apparently. Jack pulled his phone away to check the time. He needed to leave in the next five minutes.

"No other thoughts on breaking this ward down?"

"Get a spell caster." Again, Harrington refrained from offering his own services.

Jack scowled. He definitely planned to pawn off his favor-in-trade on Marin. He swung his pack on his back. "What can you tell me about ghosts?"

"They have limited interaction with the physical world. There exists an assumption that ghosts are tied to their physical remains, or the geographic location where the physical body died if there are no remains, which limits their movement through space. I'm unaware of a reliable method of dispersing a ghost's energy." Harrington paused. "Theoretically, if a method was created to disperse the energy of a ghost, there would be ethical questions. Is dispersal of ghost energy akin to the death of physical body? Or perhaps not, since the physical body has already died? Perhaps it's a death of the soul?"

Who was he talking to? Harrington, waxing philosophical, was simply bizarre.

Jack interrupted him before he went too far afield. "So, what about magic? Can a ghost utilize magic? There's a decent chance that the ghost inside the ward is the spell caster who laid the trap."

"Or the victim the spell caster used to power the ward. A more likely scenario for the creation of a ghost."

Jack started heading back to the meeting point, but he kept to a leisurely pace. "Sure. It could also be a hiker who was trapped and died. Regardless, do we need to be worried about a magic-wielding ghost?"

"No guarantees, but I'd say no. Manipulation of items in the physical world? Yes. Using the ghost's own magic? I don't think so." Background noise filtered through the phone, then Harrington added, "Call a spell caster. Get the ward defused." And he hung up.

Jack would love to flip the guy the bird. Wasn't this exactly what IPPC was for? Sure, they were primarily a European and British organization, but IPPC had extended some tentacles into the States. And they were the only policing organization that existed with jurisdiction over the magic-using community. Shit, who even knew about the magic-using community. But no. Evidently Jack should just go ahead and take care of this mess, since he happened to be here. Freaking annoying guy.

Jack shrugged off his annoyance and called Chris.

Chris picked up, but this time she was cheery, and no kid noises percolated in the background. "What's up, Jack?"

"Hey. Just need a little info on the area I'm in. I need you to look into any known deaths around a specific set of coordinates. Murder, suicide, accident —doesn't matter. I'll text coordinates when I hang up. Oh, missing persons also. No specific time frame." Jack paused to verify his route. He grimaced slightly, then said, "And I need it as soon as possible. I'm in a bit of a bind."

"I have time now. Hubby has the kids out at the playground for the afternoon. You're intruding on my 'me' time, but I forgive you."

"Thanks. Gotta run." Jack hung up and texted the coordinates.

Jack picked up the pace and made it back to the meeting point in just under thirty minutes. He pulled out Marin's phone and typed a quick update.

My source says ghosts can move things but not do magic. Working on the ward issue. Any new info re: ghost or ward?

"Hey, guys. I'm back with more water and protein bars. You there?" And still, Jack felt like a complete ass, talking to the air.

A small branch whizzed by Jack. "Guessing that's a yes. Incoming," he called before he chucked Marin's phone and then three water bottles over the shadow. As he reached for the fourth bottle, he noticed a group of spikey white flowers directly in front of the shadow ward. Quickly, he scanned the surrounding area for markers he'd made note of earlier. He'd be damned if the ward wasn't shrinking. This particularly large bunch of the distinctive flowers hadn't been visible before, so that meant at least six or eight inches in a half-hour.

Jack lobbed the fourth bottle past the ward and said, "Send your phone back so I know you guys are okay."

Nothing.

He called again. "Send the phone back, Marin."

He waited impatiently for at least three minutes, and then a bright flash caught his eye.

"Shit." Keeping a close eye on the ward, he circled around to the area where he'd spotted with his peripheral vision what must have been dragon flames. The top few branches of a tree smoked, but the branches hadn't sustained a flame. He ran the rest of the distance.

When he found the tree, he searched the area systematically for any signs of spreading fire. All it took was a stray ember or two and the right type of fuel, and he'd have a fire on his hands. One that could easily bypass the ward. Marin and Charlotte would be trapped inside with an approaching fire they couldn't escape.

As Jack completed a last sweep of the area, he heard an alarm sound. Scanning the area, he spotted Marin's bright yellow phone. She must have missed him this time. But at least she'd had a backup plan. He picked it up and read the message.

Def'ly have a ghost. Peeved, thinks we're target practice. Phone throwing makes it angry. Marin-dragon is protecting me. We're moving around a lot. Out soon? Thx! Charlotte.

Jack could imagine them running around in circles, trying to stay away from some demon-like spirit as it threw miscellaneous pieces of forest debris at them. If Marin hadn't felt the need to turn dragon to protect Charlotte, it might almost be entertaining. But he had no real idea what kind of danger they were in, so—not entertaining.

Jack's phone rang. The sound was unexpected and jarring in the silence of the woods. He pulled it out of his pocket. "Hey, Chris. That was fast."

"It's been like twenty minutes. I thought you were in a rush?" Chris huffed out a put-upon sigh. "Listen. There's not much. A few missing persons, all eventually found. Not a lot of serious crime out in Miersburg over the last half-century, and no notable deaths. But—and this is good—there's a local legend about a witch living in the woods. It dates back to the turn of the century. I found it in a search of the parish history. What do you think?"

"I think spell caster or witch; it's the same difference to the non-magical townspeople of turn of the century Miersburg." Jack saw another flash or orangey-yellow flame. This time angled much higher and clearing any trees. What the hell was going on in there? "So—what's the story? My timeline's getting a little tight over here."

"It looks like an affluent local woman married a philandering ne'er-do-well. They moved into the family home; once the money was gone, he left. She lived in her family's cottage waiting for him to return, even after everyone saw he wasn't coming back and her family had died. I'm paraphrasing, but that's the gist. I sent you the article. The locals thought she was odd. Eventually the townspeople started calling her a witch."

"Huh. Where's the magic? Why do they call her a

witch?" Jack scanned the treetops, trying to catch any other flashes of flame in the sky. If Marin set the woods on fire while he was getting a history lesson from Chris . . .

"She was alone and lived outside the town proper. And her story was a huge scandal, enough to make it into a little old lady's recollections of the town. That was enough back then to get you labeled a witch. I don't have a specific location for her house, but—in the woods, north of town, isolated. Could be your gal."

"Got it. Keep looking. See if you can find her name. And the name of her husband and whatever happened to him."

"Seriously?" Chris's voice had turned peeved. "That kind of stuff isn't easy to find on short notice. Whatever. I'll see what I can do." And she ended the call.

Jack had to remember to throw in a word of thanks every once in a while. Chris got prickly when she felt underappreciated. Right. Next time.

No more flames had popped up while Chris had briefed him. Avoiding a massive fire seemed like a good plan, regardless of whatever else he did. So, bonus.

Jack tried yelling a few times to attract Marin's or Charlotte's attention, but he got no response. He'd lost contact with both of them. Unfortunately, neither of them knew that the ward was shrinking—

probably being drained by containment of two large, mobile bodies. What would happen if the ward collapsed in on them? Or what if they simply stayed near the edge and the ward moved past them, leaving them on the outside of the trap, like the flowers? That could be the solution—an escape for them both. Or maybe not.

Regardless, there were now a few options available and no way to convey them reliably to the women. Jack pulled out his phone and drafted two very short emails: one to Charlotte's husband and one to Harrington. Then he stepped across the barrier.

A silver dragon crouched, hissing steam at a —Jack did a double take—floating iron skillet. Marin swatted massive claws at the skillet, and knocked it to the ground. After the odd weapon fell with a solid thud, Jack saw that small wounds sprinkled her body. Each wound oozed blood. And that was when he realized: Marin's scales had flexed and turned with her body as she'd taken off in flight. They hadn't been the rigid, overlapping scales he remembered from the only other encounter he'd had with a dragon.

Jack mentally thumped himself and then jogged toward Marin, keeping half his attention on the prone frying pan. As he approached, something slammed into his side. He stumbled, choking, coughing. He shoved his knuckles into the grass, pushed hard, and lurched upright. And fell again. His shoulders burned. He rolled to the side and a flying branch pounded the grass next to his head.

Get behind me.

Marin's voice brushed through his mind as he scrambled to dodge another blow.

Now.

Before he could stand, Jack was enveloped in a dragon wing. The silvery hide of her wing shielded him, giving him just enough time to stand.

"I'm good," he yelled.

As Marin folded her wings close to her body, Jack ran behind her.

"Charlotte huddled behind Marin, one hand resting on Marin's silver scales. "The ghost should run out of juice soon. Ghosts can't—"

A dragon grunt interrupted her.

Jack scanned the area for an improvised weapon. Then realized— "Shit. We can't hurt it."

"No." Charlotte's brow furrowed and she gave Jack a dark look. "If the dragon—Marin—weren't still immature, her scales wouldn't be so soft."

Hey. I can hear you guys.

"I didn't send her here to be a pincushion. And she sure as hell wasn't supposed to end up trapped." Jack was interrupted as Marin shifted, maneuvering quickly to the right. Following her as she moved, Jack asked, "Why exactly are we using a soft-scaled dragon as a shield?"

He'd just spotted a tumbledown cabin not far away.

Better than having your tender human skin pummeled. And I heal faster. But this shit is getting old. How much longer can it hold out?

Charlotte said, "Not much longer. I hope." Turning to Jack, she said, "We were heading to the cabin when you showed up."

A hiss of steam spewed from Marin's snout.

Since scales rippled under his hand at the same time, Jack figured those hisses were pain responses. So the few flashes of fire he'd spotted might have been accidents. He edged closer to Marin's tail until he had a clear view over her back. But all he saw were the objects the ghost was using as projectiles. No ghost, cloud, figure—nothing. Stones flew at high speed and pinged off Marin's body. And branches darted through the air like arrows. After watching for a moment, Jack realized the missiles came one at a time.

"I think our ghost can only manipulate one object at a time." As Jack spoke the words, he searched the surrounding area for incoming missiles, but couldn't spot the next attack.

She's gone. For now. Dragon Marin blinked out of existence, replaced by her human self. "Mind-speaking with you both is exhausting. Easier this way." She gave Jack a peeved look. "You have some water in your pack?"

Jack pulled out a bottle and handed it to her. "I lost contact and I needed to pass along important information. And I'm not a complete idiot. We have backup coming if we're not out of here by the morning."

"The morning?" Charlotte's eyes got wide. "Seriously? And my husband must be losing his mind with worry. Please tell me you at least told him where I am."

"Just that we'd found you and were extracting you." Jack handed Charlotte a bottle of water. "Do you want him trying to get you out? Getting stuck in here?"

"Of course not." Charlotte's shoulders slumped. "I'm just so tired. And I want to go home, see my family." She groaned. "Sleep in my own bed."

"We're almost there." Marin wrapped a comforting arm around Charlotte. Turning to Jack, she narrowed her eyes and said, "Right?"

Jack sidestepped the question for now. "How much time do we have? Before the psycho ghost comes back?"

"With our luck, she can hear you, Jack." Marin let go of Charlotte and started toward the cabin.

Charlotte followed right behind her. "I'm not sure, but several minutes. Manipulating objects, interacting in any way with the physical world—I know that takes effort, and there's a limit to how much a ghost can do in a short period of time."

Jack hustled to catch up, since it looked like
Marin was about to walk through the doorless entry
to the small cabin. "Okay. First things first: the ward
surrounding us is powered by death magic."

"We know. We told you that in the text—remember?" Marin answered just a hair before she ducked
into the doorway. A few seconds later, she said,
"Whoa. And I might have found the sacrifice. Or
maybe a victim of the trap? Used the cabin for
shelter and didn't ever leave . . . " She popped back
out. "Don't suppose you saw bones when you
checked out the cabin yesterday?"

Charlotte shook her head frantically. "Truly. I'd
have said. I wouldn't forget to tell you guys something like that. I mean . . . " Her lips twisted. "I didn't
actually go in. It's creepy, you know? And there's a
nasty vibe. I just ducked my head through the door
to make sure no one was in there."

"So, how do you feel about skeletal remains?"

Charlotte sighed. "At least I'm not going in
alone." She was about to walk through the door, but
she paused to ask, "Uh, just bones, right? No squishy
parts?"

Jack bit his lip. It was just too bizarre not to be
comical, but he was damn sure Charlotte wouldn't
appreciate him laughing.

"Bones, clothing scraps. That's all," Marin
replied, disappearing back into the cabin.

Jack stopped Charlotte with a hand on her

shoulder and walked in before her. "Any chance either of you noticed that the ward is shrinking?"

The smell of must and decay filled Jack's nose. No door, and whatever had originally covered the windows was long gone, but much of the roof remained intact. Damp had gotten in, but no direct sunlight meant the interior had moldered.

A gentle push on his back reminded him Charlotte was directly behind him. He took several steps into the room then approached Marin and crouched down next to her as she examined the pile of bones. "The ghost is definitely female, and the remains are female—but I have no idea if these are the ghost's bones."

Jack raised an eyebrow. "You can ID sex from bones?"

"I'm assuming she's female because of her size, the shoes—" Marin pointed to a sturdy pair of women's boots that had outlived much of the wearer's clothing. "And see the small buttons scattered on the ground? Women's clothing. And from the quality and number of buttons, the style of the shoes, I'm guessing early nineteen hundreds. Not a poor woman."

Charlotte joined them, but remained standing. "If the ward is collapsing, that may be why our ghost wanted us away from the perimeter." She shrugged. "Maybe? Because she wasn't bothering me until Marin arrived and we both started tracking your progress around the perimeter of the ward."

"I don't suppose either one of you know what would happen if the ward passed us by, rather than us trying to walk through the ward?" Marin looked at Jack and Charlotte hopefully. "And Jack, before you ask, when you approach the ward, it's like a strong shove. The closer you get, the more it pushes back. And the more force you use, the greater the rebound. I tried a running start with less than stellar results."

"No clue. But if it would just shove us away—basically if it still works—why was the ghost so pissy about us lingering near the perimeter?" Charlotte looked thoughtful. "Why does the ghost even care about the ward?"

"I've got some local history for you that might help with that." Jack repeated what Chris had told him: local affluent woman, abandoned by her scumbag husband, isolating herself after her parents passed, labeled a witch by the locals.

"We do have local lore about a witch in the area. But I can tell you with complete certainty, there are no local witches in this area, and haven't been for a very long time." Charlotte smiled. "I checked before we moved here. But—you're thinking the story is about a spell caster?"

"If it is, I'm betting this is her." Jack motioned to the small pile of bones and shoes on the ground.

Marin shook her head. "But being labeled a witch has nothing to do with magic. She acted oddly, was a woman, and lived alone. That could easily equal witch in nineteen hundreds rural Louisiana."

"Okay, the fact that they call her a witch is a coincidence," Jack said. "Crazy woman in the woods, left by her husband. If she's a spell caster, she kills herself, and as her last dying act sets this ward. Crazier things have happened."

Marin shook her head. "We're making a lot of assumptions, the greatest being that the bones belong to the ghost, and the ghost is our spell caster. We have no real proof of that. And if we did? What good does that do us?"

Jack smiled. "I do know that the place of death or the physical remains tie a ghost to a location. That means that our ghost is tied to this place because she died here or because her bones are here, regardless of who she actually is. We want to get rid of the ghost. I say we get rid of—"

A thundering crack sounded and debris dropped on Jack's head.

"JACK. COME ON. WAKE UP, JACK."

A sharp pain pulsed behind his right ear. He tried to speak, but his mouth was full of dirt. The realization of which immediately resulted in a fit of coughing. Searing pain flashed in his eye, his head. Coughing turned to retching.

"Don't move." A woman's voice. Charlotte.

He tried to speak and finally managed a croak on the third try. "Marin?"

"Over here," Marin replied.

Jack cracked an eye open, and blinding, gut-wrenching pain forced his lid closed. But he didn't puke. A cold sweat covered him, probably from all the churning his stomach had been doing. Oh, yeah, maybe from the pain. "What happened?" His voice was steadier now, his thoughts less jumbled.

"That bitch cracked the roof's supporting beams and dumped a bunch of roof on top of us." That acerbic comment originated, surprisingly, from Charlotte.

"That bitch is gone for now, by the way," Marin added in a milder tone. "It must have taken a good bit of juice to break the beams. They're pretty stout." She cleared her throat. "About that . . . any chance you might be able to move anytime soon?"

"Head injury. Give me a break," Jack grumbled with his eyes still closed.

"It's just that Charlotte is pretty sure you're not about to croak. And I can't move until you clear out of the cabin." Marin's voice was matter of fact, but there was a tenseness underlying it that was curious.

Jack steeled himself and opened his eyes. The light was getting dimmer as the sun set, which might have helped with the pain. He could see about half of the cabin from where he'd been knocked out. And there was Marin, near the corner, trapped under one of the split beams. "Shit. Sorry."

"It's all good. I can get out. But when I shift the beam, the rest of the rubble will move. Not particularly safe for you and Charlotte. So, uh, you got a time frame on getting up?"

"The wound is already starting to clot, but there's a good chance you'll vomit when we move you. And maybe pass out again." Charlotte sounded apologetic.

"It's fine. Do you think a strengthening potion might help?" Jack asked Charlotte as she started moving some small pieces of wood and plant matter off him. "I got it from an earth witch. Something to do with increasing endurance and strength."

"It won't fix your head, but it'll make you feel better." Charlotte pursed her lips. "A lot better if it's a good recipe and the witch had any skill." She muttered something about potions under her breath, and then asked Jack, "In your backpack?"

"Yeah. It's in the blue Platypus—the reusable plastic water bottle thing. I only brought a liter—is that enough?" Jack asked quietly. He'd closed his eyes again. It was just easier. And puking sucked.

"More than enough if it's done right." Charlotte dug through his pack and then crowed with delight.

"Oh, yes! This is Marceline's work. You couldn't ask for better quality."

Jack managed to prop himself up on an elbow without ralphing.

Charlotte handed him the potion and told him to drink about a third of it. "No need to waste it, and more won't make a difference for at least a day."

"Got it." The first sip made Jack's stomach turn, but the second settled it. By the time he finished a third of the bladder, standing up seemed like a reasonable option. "Any chance this works on dragons? Maybe you guys can split the rest?"

Charlotte removed the cap and downed her portion. Once she was done, she handed it off to the still prone Marin. "I think it's worth a try, unless you think it might be harmful."

Marin took the container, gave it a sniff, then said, "Bottoms up," before finishing the potion. "Now get your ass out of here before our friendly neighborhood ghost returns and decides to do something worse."

Jack was already struggling to his feet. "If there's any chance, can you try to grab—"

"Yeah. But the walls have ears, and all that."

With a little support from Charlotte, Jack made it out of the cabin in good time. By the time they'd exited, his headache had dulled to a tolerable throb. The sun had fallen below the treetops, making it less startlingly bright, which also helped. He and Charlotte shared a look then turned to stand back to back, on the lookout for the return of the angry spirit.

A loud crash made both of them jump, but Charlotte stopped Jack when he would have returned to the cabin. "Her dragon could shift the debris more easily, so she was going to push her way out in dragon form."

"Ah. That conversation happened when I was passed out, I'm guessing."

Marin emerged through the doorway just as human as they'd left her, and in her hand she clutched a pelvic girdle, two long bones, and a skull.

"I'll scout for the edge of the ward." Jack took off at a jog in the opposite direction of the cars.

The last thing they needed was that crazy thing blocking their escape route. When he reached the area he estimated to be near the ward's edge, he pulled out his glasses, surprisingly only slightly bent but otherwise intact. He searched for the edge and found nothing. Maybe the darkening sky made the edge more difficult to see? He thought about using his special flashlight, but opted against it, since both it and the ward were magic and he had no clue how they'd both appear together through his warded specs.

He lifted his gaze and looked further into the distance. And he saw it: a retreating shadow. It was moving at a good clip. He turned back to Marin and

Charlotte, who'd been following behind him. He raised his hand, hoping they'd get the idea. Marin stopped, shooting him an odd look. He turned back, and this time he found the ward's perimeter more quickly. The now *stationary* ward. When they'd stopped moving, the ward had also stopped.

He sprinted back to Marin and Charlotte and relayed his conclusion as fast as he could get the words out: "The ward's not tied to a physical perimeter. It's the bones. It's tied to the bones. That's why the ward was shrinking as its magic drained, as we threw objects through it and pushed against the edge of it. If it was tied to a boundary, it would have just faded away in place. But since it radiates outward from the bones—"

Jack stopped and caught his breath. His sprint through the woods had aggravated his head injury, even with his super potion, and he was close to puking. "Throw the damn bones. As far as you can. All of them at once." He yanked his pack off and dumped the contents.

"Shit. The ghost is coming. I can feel her," Marin said. But she hesitated. "When the ward passes by us?"

"No idea. Do it." Jack didn't want to spend the next twelve hours beating back a psycho ghost with an irrational grudge. He handed her the pack. "Do it."

Charlotte swallowed. "Do it."

Marin stuffed the bones in the pack. And the wind began to gust madly. She hefted the pack and threw it like her life depended on it.

A horrible rush of energy gathered. Loomed.

Jack yelled, "Ward hop!"

In an instant, Marin was a dragon and had wrapped her wings around Charlotte and Jack.

Jack felt cold. No—nothing. A cold nothingness. His limbs were gone; only his core existed, and only in a floating space, as if gravity had faded slowly away. Then his body collapsed in on itself and every particle of his being screamed. He screamed. But there was no sound. There was silence. And again there was a nothingness, a weightlessness to his body. For seconds, minutes. Forever.

"Wake up, Jack." Marin's voice, thin and reedy, reached his ears.

"Holy hell." For the second time in one day, he was laid out flat with his face in the dirt. "What the holy mother of hell was that?"

Charlotte said, "A dimensional shift." Her teeth chattered. "I think I might be in shock."

Marin caught her and lowered her gently to the ground.

"Brilliant idea. Let's take the humans through a dimensional portal." Marin fell to the ground next to Charlotte. "I might complain about being called young, but you know—I actually am kinda young. I'm not supposed to do that kinda shit." She sounded more confused than angry. Tired, certainly. "Didn't really know I could."

Jack pushed himself up into a sitting position and looked around. "Oh, shit."

Marin closed her eyes. "What now?"

"Thank you," Jack said with feeling. He really liked living. He was sometimes reckless and took risks he shouldn't—but that didn't mean he had a death wish. And one look at the ground around them told him that nothing—except maybe the plants—had survived that massive magical energy rush. The bodies of insects, birds, a squirrel, were scattered around them. He said it again. "Thank you."

Marin had wrapped her arm around Charlotte, and the two of them were sitting quietly. She opened her eyes, and Jack tipped his head toward the carcass of a small bird a few feet away.

Marin closed her eyes again. "Oh."

Jack hated to ask—but if they weren't out of trouble, they needed to get moving. "Do you feel the ghost? Is she still here?"

The color had returned to Charlotte's face, and Marin looked more herself. Marin replied, "I don't know if she's gone—but she's not here now."

Jack checked his face, and amazingly found his specs still propped up on his nose. He stood up, ready to scout for the new location of the ward—so they could avoid it. Before he'd scanned further than the immediate area, his phone rang.

"That's a good sign," Charlotte murmured.

Jack checked the number, then quickly answered. "Harrington. You got my email."

"I'm calling about the massive magical explosion that just reverberated through a tiny little town called Miersburg." Harrington's voice was ice cold. "Don't suppose you can tell me anything about that?"

"Any damage done?" Jack asked.

"Yet to be determined."

Jack knew that meant no. At least for now. Time to fess up. "There was damage to the local wildlife near the coordinates I gave you. I'm not sure how extensive. I haven't verified if the ward is still standing, and, if so, the current location of the ward. Also, I'm not sure where the ghost has planted itself."

"You relocated a ward powered by death magic." It wasn't a question. And Harrington spoke so quietly, Jack wasn't sure if the man was in shock or about to completely lose his shit because he was so mad.

"I've got to get everyone home as soon as possible, so . . . " Jack hoped he could at least get off the phone and do some assessment before the shit completely hit the fan.

"There's an IPPC subcontractor on the way from New Orleans, estimated arrival in an hour. Get your client home and my guy will call if he has any questions." Harrington paused, and when he spoke again, his voice was frigid. "You will answer your phone."

"Will do." Jack ended the call before any talk of payment, favors, or other unpleasant consequences were mentioned. Once he hung up, he did the math. "That bastard. He called his guy as soon he got off the phone with me earlier today."

"Sorry?" Charlotte was on her feet and looked ready to go.

"Not important. There's a cleanup crew on the way to defuse the ward—if there's still a ward. So we're good to leave and get you home."

The walk back to the cars was uneventful, thank God, because all three of them were exhausted. Jack was so tired, even the thought of snakes didn't faze him as he waded through knee-high grass.

Charlotte asked if Marin could drive her car, and she called her husband on the way home. So when the two vehicles pulled into the Sneeds' drive, Calvin and his son were both waiting. Effusive hugs and some tears were shared by all three family members.

Jack waited just long enough for Calvin to remember he owed them a check. He handed Jack an envelope and pumped his hand enthusiastically.

Just as he and Marin were about to slip away, Charlotte pulled them both aside. "If you'll head south out of town, you'll be driving in the right direction to hit a healer I know. When I get into the house, I'll text you his address."

Jack drew a breath, intent on protesting.

"No. She's right, Jack." Marin peered at him. "It's either that or we have to stop off at the hospital. You may not be feeling it, but there's a head injury hiding under the effects of all that witch juice you drank."

"It's late—"

Charlotte pulled him into a hug. "It's fine. He owes me a favor."

Stepping away, Jack looked a little to the side of Charlotte's right ear and said, "Thanks. I appreciate it."

Jack didn't argue when Marin took the keys from him and pulled him toward their car.

Marin waved a farewell to Charlotte, and opened the door for Jack. "In."

It only took them about forty minutes to reach the healer's house, but it seemed like forever to Jack. He was exhausted but couldn't sleep—possibly a result of the potion. And he hurt, but in a muted way that he knew wasn't natural. Hopefully his brain hadn't been bleeding this entire time. And on that happy thought, Marin pulled into to the healer's circular drive.

"Hey. How you doing?" Marin poked him in the arm.

"Jesus. Stop already. I'm awake." Jack opened the door to get out and found that a young man, maybe mid-twenties, with tats and chin-length hair, was waiting on his porch for them. He had a beer in one hand.

The kid put his beer on the ground and said, "Hey, I'm Kai. Have a seat on the porch, and I'll take a look at you."

It didn't take long for Kai to establish that: no, Jack's brain wasn't bleeding; yes, he had a concussion; and, sure, he'd be fine to skip the doctor's office after Kai was done with him.

"But you really need to get some rest, man." Kai lifted his beer in a toast.

Jack reached out a hand. "Thanks. I'll do that. And we really appreciate your help."

Giving Jack's hand a firm shake, Kai said, "No worries." Shaking Marin's hand, he added, "I've never actually met a dragon. So—cheers. And you guys drive safe."

Jack wasn't sure which one of them would crash first from their endurance potion high, but he wanted them both home when it happened. So when Marin drove like there was a psycho, projectile-hurling ghost on their tail, he didn't bitch. He might have actually dozed off for a bit because when his phone rang it startled the crap out of him.

Jack almost didn't pick up, but then he remembered Harrington's borderline threatening command to answer his phone. Not a number he recognized. He leaned his back against the headrest and answered. "Yeah."

"Harrington here. Put me on speaker; I have information you'll both want to hear."

Jack flipped his speaker on. "We're both here."

"The cleanup crew found a journal in the debris. It was relatively intact inside an oilskin in the back of a dresser." Harrington cleared his throat. "The woman who lived in the cabin was insane long before she died. The bones you found belonged to Mary Elizabeth Potter. She was the owner of the home, and a spell caster."

Marin said, "Any ideas as to why she set the ward?"

Jack made an annoyed sound. "Or why she hung around to haunt the place?"

Harrington let out a long breath. "We can tell from the journal that her husband left, and it wasn't long after that she discovered she had syphilis. Certainly a possible cause of her insanity. The last few coherent entries demonstrate an obsession with her husband returning and with keeping him near."

Jack pinched the bridge of his nose. "And from

there it's not a leap to assume she used her own death to power one last ward."

Marin groaned. "You're saying her dying act was a twisted attempt to keep her cheating husband with her forever? That's sick."

"We can't know for sure, but yes," Harrington said, "that's what we're thinking. The ward was gone when the crew arrived. But they secured the bones."

"Which secures the ghost, right?" Jack asked.

"Yes." Harrington didn't sound nearly certain enough for Jack. But it wasn't his problem any longer. "Any other good news for us?" Jack asked.

"Be glad IPPC isn't seeking reimbursement for the cleanup crew." Harrington ended the call.

Jack struggled to keep his eyes open. Even tales of crazy wives and their creepy eternal love couldn't keep him awake.

Marin glanced at him. "We're almost home. You passed out after we left the healer's house."

"Ah."

She sighed. "I'm fine. Whatever Kai did must have offset the side effects of the endurance tea you drank, but that stuff still has me wide awake. Go back to sleep."

He thought he agreed, but maybe he just fell back asleep.

JACK'S HEAD rolled forward as the car came to a stop. He cracked his eyes open slowly and saw that they'd pulled up in front of The Junk Shop.

After she put the car in park, Marin sat quietly, unmoving. After several seconds, she said, "Well, that could have gone better."

Jack gathered his gear and opened the car door. "Yeah." He paused. "Coulda gone worse, though." He stepped out into the street and let out a jaw-cracking yawn. "See you tomorrow at ten?"

Marin nodded.

Jack raised his eyebrows in pseudo-excitement. "Tomorrow's the crash course on using the cash register."

Marin laughed. "Awesome."

She sounded like she meant it. Cool. He slammed the door and headed into the shop.

EPILOGUE

One week later

Jack crouched down and dumped the contents of the tin he held into a tiny porcelain dish.

"Oh my God. Are you feeding your rats?"

Jack jumped to his feet, surprised. Turning, he saw his sister Hannah. "No. I mean, I'm feeding my — How did you even get in the store? I didn't hear the bells." Jack cleared his throat.

Hannah peered at the can in his hand. "You're feeding your cat?"

"Sure."

"Jack. You cannot feed the rats. And seriously—crabmeat? Do you know what this dump will look like in a month, once you start feeding them? You're completely insane."

Jack scowled at his sister. "I'm not nuts. And whatever it is, it isn't a rat. It's house trained."

Hannah waved a dismissive hand. "Like you'd know. You can't see the rat poop for all the dust, funk, and rubbish piled up."

"I sweep." Jack tried not to sound offended, but really . . . "And I'm telling you: whatever Fuzzball is, he sheds and doesn't leave any crap on the floors. That's not a rat."

"Ugh. You're impossible, and this place is disgusting, but that's not why I'm here." Hannah straightened the cuff of her shirt. "You need to get a real job."

"I have a real job."

"Oh, I see that you have a new job. It's not bad enough that you run a store filled with rubbish, but now this." Hannah pointed to the shiny new sign that ran along the bottom of the display window. Passersby could now see that The Junk Shop was also home to Spirelli Paranormal Investigations.

That's right. He was legit. Completely out in the open, listed in the yellow pages, searchable online, with a sign on his store. And now the final step had been achieved: he'd been officially outed to his family. If his sister knew, then so did everyone else in his family. They'd be so proud.

"You're basically advertising yourself as a fraud —or a fruitcake. And you're doing it using the family name. What in the world are you thinking, Jack?" Hannah's brow crinkled with worry.

Let the paranormal investigating begin.

Keep reading for Jack and Marin's next case, Episode 2: The Forgotten Memories*!*

EPISODE 2: THE FORGOTTEN MEMORIES

ABOUT THE FORGOTTEN MEMORIES

A true medium or just another fake? Jack's on the case.

Conrad Blevins speaks with the dead. Or does he?

Is Conrad a psychic for hire or a fraud preying on the recently bereaved? Jack Spirelli and his dragon side-kick Marin hunt for the truth, even as the pursuit endangers their lives.

1

The Junk Shop's front door swung open, the attached jingling bells announcing a new client. Jack ducked his head and stared at his computer screen, hoping his assistant Marin would field this one. Ever since he'd put the sign in the window advertising Spirelli Paranormal Investigations, he'd dealt with more crackpots, posers, and nosey neighbors than his limited patience could tolerate. And it had only been a week.

Marin poked her head into his office. "There's a Mrs. Wallace here to see you."

Jack glared.

"She'd like to discuss a potential fraud. Of the paranormal variety." Marin smiled brightly.

She was enjoying his discomfort with the suddenly very public face his business had assumed. His own fault, but that didn't make it any easier.

"Show her in. Please." Jack stood up and mustered a halfway enthusiastic smile.

Marin disappeared briefly and reappeared with a petite brunette.

Jack's prospective client extended her hand. "Dottie Wallace. Nice to meet you."

"Jack Spirelli." After releasing her hand, Jack pointed to the chairs in front of his desk. "Have a seat, Mrs. Wallace."

"Dottie, please. And thank you so much for seeing me without an appointment." Jack made a dismissive gesture with his hand but didn't manage a response before Dottie chattered on. "I saw your sign in the window. I was getting my hair done—just two doors down—and you know there's only street parking here. So I was walking to my car and I saw your sign." She practically bubbled over with excitement that the fates had smiled on her and put Jack's sign in her path. "I wasn't sure exactly what that meant, paranormal investigation. So I came right inside and asked. And I can't tell you how excited I was to find out that it's exactly what I need."

Jack held back an impatient sigh. His tiny shop had been a steal, such a steal that he'd bought it outright. And then the neighborhood had exploded. Trendy hair salons were just the beginning. Two art galleries, a boutique law firm, a coffee shop—and clients like Dottie Wallace. Generally good for The

Junk Shop's balance sheet, but not exactly what he'd expected or wanted when he opened the biz. Jack spied the rock on Dottie's left hand. Really, though, the woman was nice enough.

"How exactly can SPI help you?"

"I was telling your assistant..." Dottie looked around.

"She's keeping an eye on the shop."

"So I was telling your assistant that my mother has recently started using the services of an untrust-worthy person. I'd like you to prove that this person is...unreliable before she spends any more money." Dottie's face flushed a light pink. "He's taking advantage of an elderly woman. It's disgraceful. And my mother is especially vulnerable right now. My father passed just a few months ago."

Jack pulled a legal pad out of the top right-hand drawer. "I assume we're talking about suspected fraud? And do you have a name?"

"Conrad Blevins. And I can tell you, he is *not* a local man." Dottie gave Jack a significant look.

Clearly she expected some response, so Jack nodded solemnly. "Of course not. What service is he claiming to provide?"

"He says he can speak to the dead and that he's in contact with my father. He encourages my mother to speak to Dad through him. She brings him some-thing of Dad's, pays him, and she gets messages in return." Dottie sat a little straighter. "It's bull. Can you help me?"

Jack wanted to say yes. Not only did she look like she could afford their services, there was also the possibility her father actually was a ghost. That he'd found a way to communicate with Blevins. If Dottie's father had possessed some magic in life, and on his death had actually become a ghost... The chances were slim, but it was possible.

"Where did you say your mother lives?"

Dottie frowned. "I'm not sure I did. A little town just the other side of the Louisiana border, DeRotan is the name. That's not a problem, is it?"

"Louisiana?" Jack tried for a bland look. He'd had more than enough of Louisiana recently.

Dottie bobbed her head. "Yes, that's right. Of course, I'll pay all your travel expenses. I'm sure we can agree on a per diem rate that suits you." She smiled faintly. "A local investigator simply isn't an option, you understand. And there's a lovely B&B I can recommend. I know the owner."

Dottie might look like a bit of fluff, but Jack would bet cash this woman had a spine of steel.

"That's great, Dottie. I'm sure we can work out the details."

"WE'RE TAKING TWO CARS, RIGHT?" Marin lounged in Jack's office, her feet propped on the corner of his desk.

She'd clearly overheard some of his conversation with Dottie. At least the part about the job being in Louisiana.

Whatever her reasoning, two cars meant two gas bills, and that cut into Dottie's generous but finite per diem. Straight-faced, he leaned back in his chair and said, "I don't think that makes a lot of sense."

"Hmm." Marin considered the toes of her shoes. "If we're driving separate cars, technically I'm meeting you at the job location. And if we're meeting there..."

"I don't have to pay for your hours in transit. And if I offer you transportation—"

"Which I'll decline," Marin quickly added.

"Then I don't have to pay mileage on your car, although I'm sure you would like some gas money." Jack squeezed his eyes shut. "Do I want to know why you want to take two cars so badly?"

Marin moved her head indecisively from side to side. "Maybe not." When he gave her a blank look, she sighed. "Okay. I'm not keen on sharing a car for five hours on the way home...if you almost get me killed again."

Before Jack could deny the possibility—what were the chances of a repeat of the Miersburg case?

—Marin was saying, "And I might take a quick trip to New Orleans when we're done."

"For the record, I have no intention of getting us blown up, or even almost blown up."

Their last Louisiana job had been unexpectedly hazardous. Technically, his actions had resulted in a near-miss explosion of a small town. But how was he to know moving a ward powered by death magic would cause a cataclysmic reaction? And yes, the car ride afterward might have been awkward—but it was all hazy. He'd been sleeping off the lingering effects of a head injury.

"Uh huh. Because you planned on it last time?" Marin shrugged. "It's cool. Just trying to minimize coworker stress, maintain a good work environment,

Jack laughed. "You are so full of shit. But if I drive you that crazy and it keeps you from charring me on the drive home, two cars is fine. And I'll chip in for gas."

"And I get my own room at the B&B."

Pushy, for someone whose job description included dusting recycled garbage and taking out the shop trash.

Jack paused a moment, as if considering her counteroffer. "Only if you drive once we're in town."

Dottie had booked two rooms at Jack's request, but he hated letting go of leverage. And Marin had a sweet ride.

"Done." Marin cocked her head. "You're a complete pain in the ass. You know that, right?"

"And yet all the women love me. You good to leave this afternoon?"

"*Jack.*" Marin shook her head. "All the *twenty-year-old* women love you. They think your ratty car and your chaotic life make you cool."

The look on her face made her thoughts on the subject clear. Whatever.

2

Around seven that evening, Jack pulled into the B&B directly behind Marin's Range Rover. He pulled into a parking space and sat in the driver's seat, staring unseeing through the windshield.

Marin tapped on his window.

Jack opened his door. "Just taking a second to make sure all my parts are intact."

"I didn't top eighty-five—I set my cruise control." Marin stepped back from his door. "You'd prefer to arrive in the middle of the night?"

Stepping out of the car, Jack said, "I'm not complaining, just recovering." He slammed the door shut and stretched. Close to five hours in a car made his knees stiff these days. "All right. Let's check in."

When Marin and he walked in the front door to

the small reception area, no one was in sight. Marin picked up a small bell on the counter and rang it.

After a few minutes passed, Jack started to consider the feasibility of walking up the staircase to the second floor and knocking on doors.

Marin was getting bolder with her explorations. She walked behind the reception desk, checked the small office there, and found no one. "You have a number for these guys? Otherwise, I'm picking an empty room and letting myself in."

Jack was already reaching for his phone. "Just a second; I've got the confirmation email."

An older man, wheezing with exertion, came in the front door. Sweat dripped down his nose, and he pulled a huge, old-fashioned handkerchief from his back pocket and dabbed at his face. "Hi. How can I help you folks?"

Not exactly what Jack expected, after hearing Dottie Wallace's glowing recommendation.

"We have a reservation. Under the name Spirelli." Jack debated pulling up the confirmation email, because Marin and he were clearly unexpected.

"Spirelli, two rooms, booked for three days." A deep furrow appeared between the man's eyes. "You canceled."

Jack almost didn't want to argue, the guy seemed that put out. But he needed a place to sleep. "I did not."

The man heaved a frustrated sigh, then immediately his demeanor changed. "My apologies. Please come in and have a seat." He motioned to a grouping of chairs placed next to the winding staircase. "It will be just a moment for your rooms. My name is Milton. I'm one of the owners."

Marin caught Jack's eye, and said quietly, "Bags."

Jack nodded and threw her his keys. Then, ignoring Milton's offer to sit, he approached the counter. "Does that happen a lot?"

Milton stopped typing on his computer. "Hmm?" Again, his brow furrowed.

"Do reservations get canceled in error frequently?"

"We've had a few odd occurrences recently. Maybe our new reservation system..."

Milton seemed unconvinced his reservation system was to blame, which opened up too many questions. Jack hated complicated jobs. And this check-in mess was beginning to reek of complications.

"We may need to stay longer than three days." The words reluctantly left Jack's lips.

Milton nodded in an agreeable fashion. "We'd be happy to have you. Our snowbirds are long gone, and there's not been a summer rush yet. Plenty of room."

Jack nodded, still uneasy, and accepted the two keys Milton handed him.

"Dottie Wallace called. I talked to her myself—before the cancellation—so don't you worry about the bill. That's to go directly to her."

Marin came in with two bags, so Jack didn't answer. He smiled in thanks then turned to grab his bag from Marin. He headed up the stairs, hoping nothing bizarre was hiding in the closet or buried in the garden. Because something definitely felt off.

Maybe Marin felt it too, because she followed him to his room.

After he unlocked the room, she said, "I'll just have a quick look. Maybe check for any signs of a recent magical signature."

Jack held the door open for her. "Please." His warded, magic-spotting glasses were still in his bag. After she slowly walked around the room, he said, "Anything?"

Marin didn't answer immediately.

Jack walked into his room, letting the door close behind him. "You found something?"

Again, she hesitated. Finally—"No. But something's weird."

"If nothing's crawling out of the woodwork to melt my flesh, let's call it good. I've got some work to do."

Marin's lips pinched. "I don't perceive an immediate physical threat." She gave a small shake of her head then turned and walked out of the room without another word.

JACK'S EYES SHOT OPEN. He glanced at his rumpled clothes then at the clock. Two thirteen. He pushed his laptop, perched precariously half on and half off his stomach, onto the bed next to him. He rolled out of bed, stretched, and unbuttoned his jeans. Before he'd shucked them, he heard a woman bellow. *Shit.*

He tried to shake off the last remnants of sleep before he walked into the hall. Blinking at the image he stumbled into, he figured he'd failed. He was hallucinating, dreaming, something. A huge-headed creature—a cat?—was plastered on the front of a T-shirt that swallowed Marin. And her feet were covered in fluorescent-pink fuzzy socks.

"What the hell are you wearing?"

Marin scowled. "Button your pants. And hurry up." She was already headed down the stairs.

Jack tucked in the half of his shirt that had escaped while he'd slept, and buttoned his pants, all while following closely behind Marin. "Do you have any idea what that woman was yelling?"

Marin paused on the stairs, cocked her head, and said, "Something about being late for school?"

"What the... School? Aren't we the only guests?" But he was talking to the back of Marin's head.

About halfway down the stairs, Jack could hear faint kitchen sounds. He and Marin followed the sounds around to the back of the house, where a spacious kitchen was situated. Sounds of clattering dishes and humming emanated from within.

Jack shared a glance with Marin and he motioned her ahead.

"Thanks," Marin mouthed quietly. But she walked in.

Jack followed directly behind her.

"Sleepyheads, you're going to be late for school. Sit down at the table and eat your breakfast." An older woman with neatly styled hair, a practical but tidily pressed dress, and a slightly damp apron motioned to the table located in a small eating area adjacent to the kitchen.

Marin started to move in the direction of the table. Jack grabbed her arm and shook his head.

"What if she's sleepwalking?" Marin whispered. "If we wake her up and she realizes two strangers are in the kitchen with her in the middle of the night, she might freak out."

"Do you really think it's that simple? We both know something freaky is going on." Jack turned to the older woman. He tried to catch her eye but she wouldn't look directly at him. "Ma'am? I'm Jack."

"Yes, dear. Eat your breakfast. You'll miss the school bus." The woman washed dishes as she spoke, her attention completely absorbed by the task.

"Where's Milton?" Jack had directed the question

quietly to Marin, but it caught the woman's attention.

"Milton?" The woman Jack was beginning to think might be Mrs. Milton wiped her hands on her apron and turned in Jack's direction. "Milton shouldn't miss breakfast."

"I'll just fetch him quickly." Marin headed back the way they'd come.

Jack cleared his throat. "Ah, Mrs...." Shit. What was Milton's last name? "Um. We're not your children. Do you understand that? I'm Jack and—" Marin paused in the doorway when Jack pointed to her. "This is my colleague Marin."

The woman paused, her hands bunched in her apron, with a blank look on her face. And then her face changed. Like she'd just woken. "Of course you're not my children. You're guests. Mr. Spirelli plus one." And she made eye contact for the first time. Looking at Marin, she smiled. "Would you like some breakfast?"

Marin came back into the kitchen. "I'm sorry. I don't know your name. Are you Milton's wife?"

Extending a hand, she smiled again—a relaxed, comfortable smile. "Rose Perrin. Yes, I'm Milt's wife."

Marin shook her hand gently, as if she might break. Rose didn't look frail; she looked like a fit, active woman. But her physical appearance aside, she conveyed a sense of fragility.

Marin backed a step away, giving Rose room to

move about the kitchen. Already, Rose was hand-drying the dishes she'd washed earlier. "Rose." Marin waited for her to turn. "You know it's the middle of the night?"

Rose slowly, carefully stacked the dish she'd dried on top of several others on the counter. Her shoulders stiffened. "No. I didn't know that." She smoothed her hair and turned around. "I'm so sorry to have disturbed your sleep. If you'll excuse me, I'll let you get back to bed."

After Rose left the kitchen, Marin tipped her head to the kitchen table. "Late night snack? That early dinner we had was a while ago."

"I'll keep you company."

Jack let a few minutes pass, long enough for Marin to finish her eggs. "So?"

Marin swallowed. "These are really good. You're sure...?" She pointed to his plate.

Wordlessly, he handed her the plate.

"I think she understood the situation enough to be embarrassed." Marin stuffed half a slice of thick-cut bacon in her mouth.

Jack watched in fascination as the rest of the bacon disappeared off her plate. "How can you eat that much and not be fat?"

Marin wiped her mouth and placed her napkin on the table. "I don't think she was sleepwalking."

"Agreed. Not that I have any evidence."

"A gut feeling? Me too." Marin stood up and pushed her chair in.

Jack looked at the pristine countertops, the neatly stacked dishes on the counter, and the dishwater in the sink. "I guess we should do the dishes."

Marin grabbed both plates. "Yeah."

Standing side by side, him washing, her drying, Jack figured this was probably as close as they'd ever come to being friendly.

Marin took the last plate from him. "Only jack-asses ask women about their weight."

Okay—not so friendly.

"Sorry." Jack pulled the plug on the dishwater.

"Just a friendly piece of advice. In case your dating pool broadens beyond coeds." Marin yawned. "What time are we meeting in the morning?"

"Breakfast is from seven thirty to nine, and we have an appointment with Dottie's mom, Betty Lasserre, at ten. But maybe you'll want to skip—"

"I'm always hungry. I'll catch breakfast at eight, in case you want to meet before we leave."

Jack headed upstairs. "Good."

3

Jack had eaten breakfast around eight thirty and had an awkward encounter with Milton. He'd apologized profusely for the late night disturbance, which was fine—but there was an underlying desperate tone to the conversation. Jack suspected Rose of previous bouts of similarly disturbing behavior.

If there was a magical excuse for her behavior, Jack would be thrilled to find it. And this time it wouldn't be about a paycheck.

"You have a plan?" Marin asked from the driver's seat of her Range Rover.

"Sure. Dottie's been vocal about her suspicions. So when she told her mom she'd hired us to vet her psychic, it didn't exactly shock her." Jack turned his phone to silent. They were almost there.

"But was she upset?"

"You tell me. When Mrs. Lasserre found out we were arriving yesterday, she immediately invited us for coffee."

"Strange," Marin said, but her attention had already turned to the modest house on the right. "This is it?"

"Yeah—not exactly what I expected either."

Dottie Wallace had possessed a sleekness, an elegance, and a huge diamond that had indicated to Jack a certain level of wealth. But her mother's home didn't fit that image.

Marin pulled slowly into the drive, clearly double-checking the house number. She must have gotten the same impression of Dottie as Jack. "Huh. This is the right address."

Marin parked the car, and they both approached the house with more caution than either the tidy house or its elderly inhabitant warranted.

When Betty Lasserre opened the front door, Jack held back a grin. Elderly his ass. The woman who opened the door vibrated—with energy, with vitality, with cheerfulness. She didn't look elderly, though she was surely well into her seventies, and she didn't look like a recent widow.

"Mrs. Lasserre?"

Betty smiled warmly. "Yes. And you must be Jack Spirelli and Marin Campbell. It's nice to meet you. Please call me Betty." She motioned for them to come inside. "I hope you've been enjoying your visit to DeRotan."

"Yes, thank you." Marin led the way into the living room.

The house was even smaller inside than it had appeared from the driveway, and the front door opened directly into the living room. Though small, the room was beautiful. The furnishings were sparse but elegant—antiques, probably quite valuable.

Betty invited them to sit. She'd laid out a coffee setting, complete with a silver urn and fine china.

Marin sat down on the sofa Betty had indicated. "Thank you for inviting us into your home."

After Betty had seated herself in a matching brocade chair, Jack sat down next to Marin. The setting, the whole situation, was a mix of casual and formal that Jack found confusing.

"When my daughter told me she'd hired an investigator, I thought it best to speak with you directly. I see no reason for anything but a forthright conversation." Betty leaned forward and poured a cup of coffee for Marin. "Cream or sugar?"

Marin shook her head and accepted the black coffee.

"My daughter's talent for managing financial transactions doesn't extend to managing her personal relationships."

Jack wasn't sure how to respond to that bomb, so when Betty turned and asked about his coffee, he had to bite back a thankful sigh. "Cream, please. Thank you."

Jack shared a quick glance with Marin, just long enough to see she was equally at a loss.

After pouring herself a cup and adding two lumps of sugar, Betty said, "You know my daughter's an attorney? She has an amazing head for numbers and did fabulously in law school."

Apparently Jack needed to make an effort to check some of his rampaging stereotyping tendencies. He most certainly did not know Dottie Wallace was an attorney. Mergers and acquisitions? Tax law? Why hadn't he run his usual check on her? Not that it mattered—he just hated looking and feeling like an under-prepared, ill-informed twit.

Jack declined the small piece of cake Betty offered. "She's concerned that Conrad is taking advantage of you at a time when you might be vulnerable."

"Do I look like I'm in a fragile, susceptible state?" Betty sipped at her coffee, giving Jack a bright, inquiring look.

Marin must have thought Jack enough of an ass to actually answer that question, because she quickly intervened. "I'm sorry for the loss of your husband. Were you married long?"

An inane question. The kind that popped out of a person's mouth when confronted with an uncomfortable topic like death.

A blank look passed over Betty's face. It was as if the animation and liveliness of her features were stilled for a brief moment—then she recovered. "Years. We were married for years."

Marin nudged his foot. As if he was an idiot. No recently bereaved widow forgot how long she was married.

"I'm sorry, Betty. When did your husband pass?" Jack quickly pulled together a few questions that he could *almost* reasonably ask a recently bereaved spouse.

"It's almost six months now." Betty didn't hesitate in answering.

"You're both from the Lake Charles area originally?" Marin asked.

"My family has lived in DeRotan for almost a hundred years." Betty took another sip of coffee, blithely ignoring the question regarding her husband's origins.

Jack asked, "Where did you meet your husband...? I'm sorry—what was his name?"

Panic flashed across Betty's face, and her lips opened without releasing a sound. "Robert," she finally said. "My husband's name was Robert." She spoke firmly. Trying to reassure herself she hadn't forgotten?

"Did you attend the same school as your husband? Maybe you met there?" Marin tipped her head to the side, looking politely inquisitive.

That same blank look crossed Betty's face and then it was gone. She smiled, but it was thin. A different thing entirely from the broad, welcoming smile earlier. "That's enough about me. You're here to discuss Conrad." She folded her hands in her lap. "Conrad is a good man. He's helped me to deal with the grief of losing a loved one."

The consistent shift from her husband to herself was noteworthy. And her reactions to questions about Robert were at the least strange, if not disturbing. Jack stared into his coffee. What was he saying? The woman had lost her husband. Grief expressed itself in a variety of ways. Damn. Not enough information.

Jack took a drink of his coffee, savored the strong, smooth flavor, and swallowed. "Can you tell us something of how Conrad works?"

"His process, you mean? Certainly." Betty immediately became more comfortable. "I bring him small objects, little trinkets that remind me of my husband or that had special meaning to us as a couple."

"Can you give us an example?" Marin's voice was low and undemanding.

Betty smiled. "Yes. I'm to bring his car keys. The fob was a gift on his sixtieth birthday."

"I see. And what other items have you brought?"

Again that blank look. After a moment, Betty

said, "When I give him the object, we talk about why it's special."

Marin shot Jack a worried look. "And Conrad uses these special items to reach your husband, to reach Robert?"

"It's not like Conrad can speak directly with him. He gets feelings and impressions. And Conrad shares those with me."

Jack placed his coffee cup and saucer carefully on the coffee table. "Mrs. Lasserre, Betty, what happens to the items you give Conrad?"

Betty's gaze drifted away from Jack, alighting on a clock placed on her mantel. "I'm so very sorry. I have an appointment in town. If you don't have any more questions, we'll just finish up. And you can let my daughter know everything is all right. She's such a worrier."

Jack and Marin both stood up.

"The coffee was excellent. And I appreciate you making the time to see us." Jack paused, taking a moment to scan the walls. "I don't suppose you have a picture of your husband I might see? It's just that we've been speaking of him, and I'd love to see a picture of the two of you."

Betty gave Jack a small, polite smile. "I'm afraid they're all packed up." And before Jack could squeeze in another question, Betty had ushered them both out of the house.

Marin slid into her seat and slammed the door.

Staring at the car key in her hand, she said, "That sweet woman's brain is Swiss cheese." She shoved the key into the ignition and started the car.

"But only on the subject of her husband," Jack responded grimly.

"You mean the one whose name she can't say? Whose name she can't even remember?" Marin thumped the steering wheel with the heel of her hand. "This is just wrong. And actually—we don't know she's only hazy on her husband. There could be any number of topics we didn't cover that have faded away." Marin blew hard at a piece of bright red hair that hung in her eyes. "Ugh. For all we know, she has some form of dementia, and this has nothing to do with Conrad. Or with magic."

"What about her inability to reconcile her complete confidence in Conrad with her bizarre memory loss and the apparent theft of several personal items? And her rapid mood swings? She was happy to have us, but she didn't want to discuss her husband at all." Jack grunted. "What am I saying —that sounds like grief."

Marin snorted. "But the car keys? That con artist is making off with her husband's car, I guarantee it."

"I don't know." Jack rubbed his neck. "I don't know. I was planning to visit Conrad, but now—I'm thinking we head back to the B&B and have a serious talk with Milton. There are too many similarities between Rose's and Betty's behavior. Yeah. Back to the B&B."

Marin shoved her hair behind her ears then took a breath. "Right. You got it, boss."

Jack did a double take. He hadn't detected even a hint of sarcasm.

4

Milton had been hesitant to talk in the house, but he'd agreed to have lunch with them in town—Lake Charles, not DeRotan—though not until one o'clock, when his sister was available to come stay with Rose. Apparently there was only one diner in DeRotan, and that was too public.

After killing a few minutes on his computer with some fact-checking he should have already done on his client, Jack knocked on Marin's door and told her he'd meet her at the car in five.

Once they were both seated in Marin's car, she asked, "Any reason we're leaving a half-hour early?"

Jack programmed Conrad's address in the GPS. "I want to run by the psychic's house and have a quick look, sniff, whatever it is you do to pick up magic signatures." He pulled out his glasses from his breast pocket. "And I'll take a look with these."

"Then we're headed to Lake Charles? No lingering around the bad guy's place, right?"

"That's the idea." Jack kicked back in his seat. "And don't jump to conclusions; we don't know he's a bad guy."

"Sure we don't."

Jack closed his eyes and leaned back against the headrest. Apparently Marin got the hint, because she didn't say a word to him until they arrived several minutes later.

"Wake up. We're here."

Jack opened his eyes and cleared his throat. "Not sleeping—reviewing the players. By the way, Dottie Wallace is a partner in a tax law firm."

"Am I supposed to be surprised?"

Jack shrugged. "Mom owns her house outright and has lived there for fifty years. No signs of severe financial distress. Also, I found at least a dozen addresses for Conrad just within the last five years, and no convictions."

"He likes to move, or he has to move?"

"Excellent question." Jack pulled out his warded glasses again and put them on. "How close can we get to this guy's house without him catching our scent or tripping a ward of some kind?"

"He's not Lycan. I'm almost certain. Moving frequently, conning people. Sorry—*probably* conning people. Probably charming, comfortable with new people and new environments. That's a far cry from the typical Lycan." Marin's gaze panned across the street as she spoke.

"I'd agree." Jack completed his scan of the area surrounding Conrad's rental house. "I'm not seeing anything that looks like a ward."

"Maybe he's your garden variety, regular human psychic with an electronic security system."

"You really think that?" Jack asked.

"Of course not. I'm playing devil's advocate." Marin squinted at Conrad's house, half a block away. "You asked how close we could get without tripping a ward, or being scented—I don't know. Without knowing what this guy might be, other than human, I just don't know."

"How close to the house do you have to be to sense any kind of magical signature?" Jack worried they'd have a replay of Miersburg.

"You're so transparent. The only reason I tripped that crazy woman's death magic ward was because I was texting my location to you—and it was a faint ward." Marin tipped her head first one direction then the other. "So really, it was your fault I tripped it. Your plan, your fault."

"Your failure in execution does not make the plan flawed. That's deeply flawed reasoning and you know it."

Marin waited.

"Okay." Jack lifted both hands in surrender. "Have at it. If you think it's safe..." He hesitated a moment. "If you think it's safe, I trust you."

"Be still my heart. If only I'd caught that on tape." Marin had hopped out of the car and was a few feet away before Jack could even begin to consider a response.

He kept forgetting how fast she could be.

He couldn't help but roll his eyes when she walked right down the sidewalk on Conrad's side of the street and passed his house. She was moving at a good clip, for a human, but it still seemed needlessly reckless. She came back down the street on the opposite side of the road. The whole thing probably took less than three minutes, but he wanted to strangle her.

"Don't get your boxers in such a twist," she said as she slid into the driver's seat.

"First you blame me then you take risks. Just drive." Jack punched the diner's address into the GPS.

"If I didn't know better, Jack, I'd say you were worried." Marin pulled out onto the quiet street. "But the reason I got so close? There wasn't a hint of any magic. As you should know by now, a magic-user has to actually *do* magic to leave a trace signature. Either Conrad's not using magic, or he's doing it strictly indoors. No traps or wards that I could detect." Marin shifted in her seat then finally added, "And I didn't smell Lycan."

"I knew it. You huff about the difference between Lycan and dragons, but I knew you guys had a nose."

Marin snorted. "It's better than yours, anyway."

It took less than twenty minutes to reach the restaurant. Jack spent the drive sorting through the people involved in the case, considering possible motivations, and estimating the likelihood of magical influences. He checked his notes, but mostly he just gave it some thought. Marin hummed.

"Closer than I thought it'd be," Jack commented as they pulled into the parking lot.

"This place is on the edge of town." Marin waved and smiled. "There's Milton. He's a little early, too."

Jack and Marin hopped out of the car, Jack pulling his laptop bag with him as he came. Slinging his bag over his shoulder, he motioned Marin ahead of him. He kept a close eye on Milton as he followed Marin inside, but all he saw was a tired old man.

They were seated immediately in a booth, and the waitress greeted Milton by name.

After she'd taken their drink orders, Jack leaned forward and asked, "When did you start noticing problems with the reservation system?"

"I think you know the problem isn't our computer." Milton clasped his hands together on the table. "My wife gets confused sometimes. She forgets who's booked. Or mixes up the names of our guests. Sometimes she forgets where she is." He looked down at his hands. "What year it is." He glanced back up, an earnest look on his face. "But that doesn't happen very often. She usually knows the day. What happened last night—that doesn't happen very often at all. It's usually the little details that she confuses."

"Has she been to the doctor?" Marin asked.

Milton puffed out an angry breath. "Doctors. They run a bunch of expensive tests and don't tell you anything. I keep at 'em and they say Rose is just getting old."

The waitress came back with a cup of coffee for Milton and two glasses of water.

Milton ordered a hamburger when Marin deferred to him. "Good hamburgers here." He gave Jack and Marin an encouraging look.

"Okay, then. Hamburgers. I'll take mine with cheese, mustard, onions, and pickle." Jack handed the waitress the single-page, plastic-coated menu.

"I'll have the double with cheese, lettuce, tomato, and mayo. Can I get extra fries? And some onion rings?" Marin must have caught Milton's surreptitious head shake. "Sorry—no onion rings. I'll have the..."

"Fried pickles." Milton smiled. "They're good." Once the waitress had left, he said, "So many young ladies now don't like to eat a good meal."

Jack hid his grin, but Marin still kicked him under the table.

"I've always had a healthy appetite. It runs in the family."

Jack raised his eyebrows. "She wasn't that nice when I brought it up."

"That's because Milton is a gentleman." Marin smiled sweetly at Milton. "Thanks for the pickle recommendation."

Milton looked between Jack and Marin. "Have you been working together long?" When Jack replied in the negative, Milton closed his mouth and made a noncommittal sound.

Glancing at Marin, Jack saw she looked as clueless as him. "When did you start to notice Rose's behavior change?"

Milton's wrinkled hands twisted together. "Well, everyone forgets the small things sometimes: a dentist appointment, where you put the keys, that kind of thing."

"Maybe you noticed when she started forgetting the little things more often?" Marin prompted him. It was clear the topic was difficult.

A red flush rose in Milton's face. "No, I didn't. Well, not till after. She had an incident with one of the guests. It wasn't breakfast in the middle of the night, but the same idea. And then, when I started to look back, I could see there'd been a problem for several weeks."

"If possible, we'd like to establish a timeline."

Jack pulled a small notepad and pen from his pocket. "Can you narrow down the date?"

His brow furrowed. "I thought you were here to investigate Conrad Blevins? I'm not sure what Rose's illness has to do with that."

Jack set his pen down. "Marin and I interviewed Mrs. Lasserre this morning, and we noticed some similarities in their behavior."

Milton nodded and leaned toward them. Before he could speak, the waitress returned with their orders. It took several seconds of shifting and settling before everyone had their meal and the waitress had left again.

Marin shoved her plate a few inches away. "You were saying—about Betty and Rose and how they were having similar difficulties?"

"I think it's in the water." Milton looked grim. "Something's in the water in DeRotan, and it's making people lose their memory."

Jack and Marin exchanged a glance. Marin nudged his foot, and when he didn't immediately speak, she nudged harder, so Jack asked the million-dollar question. "Why do you think the water's contaminated?"

"First it was Eric Miller. Then Betty, and Rose was next. All in the last six months. All three having mental difficulties. And we all live within a mile and a half from each other." Milton looked down at his plate. He didn't look nearly as hungry as before.

"You know what—we can talk about this after we eat. The burgers look great, and we should try to enjoy them." Marin pulled her plate close again and picked up her burger.

Milton started to say something but changed his mind and picked up his burger.

They ate in silence for several minutes until Marin spoke. "The pickles are fabulous, Milton. Thank you for the recommendation."

Milton looked around then said quietly, "The onion rings aren't crunchy. They come out slimy on the inside and soggy on the outside."

"Soggy is no good for onion rings. My burger tastes fabulous, almost as good as the pickles." Marin packed away another mouthful of burger.

Milton wiped at the burger juice dribbling down his chin. "They make a good burger."

They finished the rest of the meal quickly. Jack hadn't realized how hungry he was until he started eating. And when he wiped his fingers after the last bite, he wanted to sit back and enjoy the afterglow of a well-cooked meal with just the right proportions of protein and grease.

Milton flagged the waitress and asked for a warmup, a good sign he was ready to talk again.

"I'll take a cup," Jack said.

Marin added herself to the list, and a few moments later they all had a hot cup of coffee and some privacy.

"If it was the water, don't you think more people would have symptoms?" Jack flipped his small note-book open.

"Well, the water makes a lot more sense than Conrad Blevins." Milton gave Jack a funny look.

"We're not saying Blevins is responsible," Marin said. "They are simply some commonalities we're trying to explain."

"Well, other than the geography, Eric Miller's little girl died recently. Cancer. And Betty lost her husband. But Rose still has me, and the kids have been doing really well." Milton shook his head. "Since you're so keen on Blevins, my Rose has seen him a few times—but not like Betty. She just wanted to see what all the fuss was about. Betty went on about him, so she set up an appointment or two."

Jack underlined "Eric Miller" in his notebook and made a note about Rose seeing Blevins a few times professionally. "Can you tell us what happened to Eric?"

Milton heaved a sigh. "Eric didn't make it." His eyes locked on to Marin's. "You can see why I'm so worried about Rose, can't you?"

Very carefully, Marin asked, "Are you saying that Eric Miller died recently?"

"Shot, in his own home. Terrible mess for his wife to find. He never would have done that if he hadn't been sick. If you knew Eric... His wife can't even go in the house. She moved back in with her mother." Milton shook his head. "He wasn't himself. And he changed all of a sudden. Not directly after his daughter's death, but maybe two months later. He started to act oddly and then he was gone."

"Is there a reason you think his death is tied to the water and to Betty's and Rose's condition?" Jack asked.

"Sure. Like I said, he lived close. And he started to act strange: confused, forgetting things, angry all the time." Milton gave Jack another strange look. "And I definitely didn't think Conrad Blevins had anything to do with it. Eric wasn't the kind to pay a psychic. I don't know if they even knew each other. Blevins had only lived in town six months when little Corinne Miller passed." Milton shook his head. "That was a terrible, terrible thing for such a little girl. May God rest her soul."

Jack waited what he thought was an appropriately respectful moment then asked, "Do you think Eric's wife might speak with us?"

"I don't know. First her daughter then her husband—she's had a hard time. I'm sure she's trying to move on with her life."

Marin gave the old guy a hopeful look. "Can you ask her if she'd be willing to meet with us? The request might be easier for her to hear coming from you."

Milton's lips pursed. "I'll try."

Apparently those green eyes could be persuasive

when they weren't all lit up and glowing, dragon-style.

"You want me to call now?" Milton pulled a slick new smartphone out of his pocket. After a few murmured words of thanks from Marin, he headed outside to make the call.

Jack slipped a few bills on top of the check. "What do you think?"

"I think three people with Swiss cheese brains—all developed in a short period and after Conrad's arrival—in a town with fewer than three thousand people is nuts." Marin tipped her head. "No. It's batshit crazy nuts."

Jack looked at his notes and went through the cast of important players. "There's no tie between Blevins and Miller."

"That we know of. Milton wouldn't necessarily know if Eric was seeing a psychic, even though he's convinced Eric wasn't the type. I mean, what's the type? Lots of people consult with psychics." Marin waved through the window. "I think Milton is done. You ready?"

Jack slid out of the booth and offered Marin a hand.

Taking his hand, she asked quietly, "You up for a grieving widow?"

Jack tugged a little harder than he should, and Marin gave him a look.

As they emerged from the diner, Milton

approached. "She'll see you, but she says to come right away, quick as you can."

JACK WALKED into Karen Miller's living room, trying to pick out something of her personality in the fussy, cluttered room. "Thank you for seeing us."

"Come on in. My mom's out shopping for at least another half-hour. I don't think she'd be comfortable with this. And she wouldn't understand why I'd want to talk about Eric." Karen ushered them further into the room as she spoke and gestured for them to sit.

The immediacy of the appointment made sense. And at the mention of her mother, Jack recalled this wasn't Karen's home. He looked at the figurines crammed haphazardly on the mantel, then at Karen, perched on the edge of an old-fashioned recliner. Tidy hair, a crisp sleeveless shirt, and no makeup that he could see—not really the fussy figurine type of woman.

After settling on the sofa, Jack said, "It's a difficult topic. We appreciate you speaking with us."

Karen made a small sound that could have been the beginning of laugh or a sob—Jack couldn't tell. "It's a relief. Truly. My husband's death is like some terribly kept secret. Everyone in town knows—or thinks they know—what happened, but no one will discuss it, especially not with me. The entire town walks around pretending it never happened." Her voice was bitter, and anger bubbled just below the surface. She rubbed her forehead with her fingertips then said, "I'm moving next month. I've found a job in Houston, and I'm getting out of here. It's the best thing for me."

"What can you tell us about your husband's death?" Marin's question, although direct, was voiced in a calm, compassionate tone. It seemed to do the trick, because Karen answered without hesitation.

"It was always about our daughter." Karen smiled, as if a happy memory played out in her mind. But her smile quickly faded. "Corinne was sick a long time. By the time she—" Karen drew a sharp, hiccupping breath. It took her a moment before she started to speak again. "By the time Corinne left us, Eric and I thought we'd be prepared. We'd known for so long that she wasn't going to make it. But all the preparation, the counseling, it doesn't mean much when your child dies. The first few months were a terrible time for both of us. But then he seemed to be doing better. He joined a support group—I wasn't ready, but he said it was helping."

Karen paused. Not overcome by grief that Jack could tell. She simply sat on the edge of the recliner showing no strong emotion at all. It was then Jack first noticed that her clothes were just a little too big. And her eyes had purplish shadows that had defied her attempts to mask them with makeup.

When she spoke again, Karen's voice was measured and even. "I found him holding her picture one night, crying. And he said he couldn't remember. It didn't make much sense to me at the time. He would ask me to talk about her, to tell him stories—and I couldn't. It was just too soon." She stopped suddenly. "It was a week or two before I could see that he couldn't remember significant events. Not small things, though that would have been bad enough. Important events, things I'd never imagined he could forget, he could no longer recall: Corinne's first dance recital, her ballerina Halloween costume, how excited she was when we went to the petting zoo and she met the baby goats."

Jack and Marin both waited, neither eager to interrupt. Karen was taking this opportunity, one that had been denied to her by her friends and family, to sort through events. And to say out loud what must have been in her mind for some time now. And Jack wasn't about to stem the flow.

Karen fiddled with the fussy lace coverings on the arms of her chair. Eventually, she continued. "I thought that was his way of dealing with the grief, and I was so angry." Karen's eyes got wide and she looked straight at Jack. "But that can't be right, because he didn't want to forget. Really didn't want to forget. When he realized some of his memories were slipping away, it made him even more upset. He desperately wanted to remember." She sighed quietly—the barest hint of audible exhalation. "He left a note. I burned it, didn't want anyone to see it."

"Do you remember what the note said?"

Karen turned toward Jack, but it was a moment before her eyes focused on him. "He said he was sorry. And that he couldn't stand to lose any more of Corinne. That's all."

"There was no question about the cause of death?" The question had left his lips before Jack realized how inappropriate it was. He could have kicked himself.

It was like something clicked in her brain, and Karen asked them, "Why did you want to know about Eric? Milton didn't say. Just that it would be helpful if I didn't mind discussing what happened to Eric with you."

"Rose Perrin and Betty Lasserre are both suffering from memory loss," Jack said. "Betty's condition, much like your husband's, may be limited to memories of one person."

"Her husband passed—from heart problems, I believe—less than a year ago," Karen said. "Is that who...?" Jack murmured a quiet agreement, which triggered a perplexed look from Karen. "But I don't really see why Eric's death would have anything to do with either of them. Rose and Betty are both

older than my grandmother. Aren't memory problems normal for really old people?"

Really old? Betty and Rose weren't that much
older than Jack—younger than his parents. He didn't
think forty was particularly old, but right now he felt
the weight of each year. "Losing cognitive function
can happen as we age. But the symptoms in Betty's
case are very similar to what happened to your
husband."

"Very similar," Marin said. "So similar that we're
trying to determine if there might have been a
related cause for both of them."

Karen's brow furrowed. "I don't think I understand. Psychological problems aren't contagious, are
they?"

"No. It's nothing like that." Jack tried not to
wince. Just what they needed: the whole town to
pick up on Milton's contaminated water theory. And
he still hadn't asked about Conrad. Shit. "We're
simply reviewing some trends and trying to find
some common factors."

"Yes. For example, do you know if your husband
used a psychic's services?" Marin, the clever girl, had
picked up what he was after. "Or had his palm read
or a tarot reading?"

Shaking her head firmly, Karen said, "No. Definitely not. He thought all of that was silly. Although
—you know, I do wonder if he changed his mind a

little. Not that he believed, but after he met that new man—"

"Conrad Blevins?" Jack asked.

"That's right. He met Conrad in grief counseling. I can't imagine Eric ever believing in psychics, but he wasn't bothered that Conrad believed in spirits and all that."

Jack heard the mechanical sound of the garage opening. Quickly, he asked, "They were friends?"

Karen tipped her head at the sound of the garage door opening.

Jack asked again, "Eric and Conrad were friends?"

"Yes, I suppose they were. They shared their grief in a way that Eric and I couldn't. That much sadness brings some people together, but it tears others apart." Karen glanced toward the back of the house again and rose from her seat. "I'm sorry, but it's probably best you leave now. And I don't know how else I can help you."

"Of course." Marin stood and pulled on Jack's arm until he was following her.

They managed to miss Karen's mom on the way out.

Marin dragged Jack along the drive. "Hurry up."

"What has you in such a snit?"

"If we can get in the car and down the drive before Karen's mom sees us, then she can tell her mother whatever she likes. For whatever reason, that poor woman doesn't want to explain our visit to her mother." Before she hopped in the driver's seat, Marin gave Jack a significant look, and added, "It's the least we can do."

"Right." But he was talking to air. Marin was giving him a hurry-up look from the driver's seat. Damn, he really was feeling old today.

5

"You're sure this is a good idea?" Marin asked for the second time since Jack had told her Conrad's house was the next stop.

"No."

"We have no idea how he does...whatever it is he does." Marin continued driving to Conrad's, even as she pointed out what an incredibly poor choice that might be.

Sometimes, Marin was a halfway decent employee.

"Whatever it is he does? How about stealing people's souls?"

Marin shot him a sidelong glance. "That's a little melodramatic."

Jack stared out the passenger window, considering her accusation. Bullshit. "Not at all. He rips away those things that make us who we are: our experiences, our memories, and all the emotions that go along with them. If that's not stealing someone's soul, then—well, it's stealing something just as vital. Someone has to stop him."

"I agree. But maybe we do a little research first."

Jack snorted. "Right. You have an expert on soul-sucking psychics." He shot her an annoyed look—and that was when he caught it. Uncertainty. "You do. You actually have an expert. Who do you know and why aren't we reaching out?"

Silence.

"Pull over, Marin."

Marin sighed and pulled the car over to the shoulder.

"I know IPPC has nothing. I sent Harrington an update after our midnight meeting with Rose. Harrington's the cog that keeps everything turning in that organization. If IPPC had any information, he would know about it and have at least passed on a warning by now."

Reluctantly, Marin turned to Jack, hands still on the wheel. "IPPC may not—but my dad might know something."

"Your father works for IPPC—so isn't that the same difference?"

Marin laughed. "Sure. Like Dad's sitting down with some tech and cataloguing hundreds of years of experiences. I don't see that happening anytime soon. He's security, not a walking database." She shook her head slightly. "But I'm sure he's helpful enough when he can be."

"So?"

Marin pinched the bridge of her nose. "So—give me a second. Dad and I aren't exactly tight right now." She scrunched her eyes shut. "And it's not like he's a walking encyclopedia of rare magical talents."

Jack knew something was up between her and her father—but he hadn't asked. Didn't want to be involved, because his own family drama was more than enough for him. Well, shit. "Do we need to talk about it?"

Marin opened her eyes. Distracted, she looked at her phone but didn't pick it up. "What?"

"Do you want to talk about whatever it is that's going on with you and your dad?"

Marin gave him a perplexed look. "Not really. Not now." She took a deep breath and blew it out. Then she picked up her phone and dialed.

"Hi. Yeah. Quick question. What do you know about magic that steals memory?" Marin tilted her head so she could hold the phone against her shoulder then reached across Jack for a pad and pen in her glove box. "No, not total amnesia. And still walking and talking." She jotted a few notes down. "Yeah—selective memory loss." She turned to Jack and asked, "Happy or childlike demeanor? Or more confused? Confused, right? Jack's with me, Dad."

Marin tipped the phone slightly so Jack's answer would get picked up.

Jack reviewed his interactions with Betty and Rose and what Karen had told them about Eric. "One confused victim. One angry victim. But we've got one who's more...distant. None of them have what I'd consider a happy or a childlike demeanor."

"Two are missing memories of recently deceased family members." Marin made a few more notes then her lips thinned. "Well, yes, of course. But do you know any way to counteract—" Her nostrils flared. "I get it. But if you've not got anything useful —" She scribbled on her pad again.

Jack caught her attention before she could end the call. "He might be using and keeping personal items from his victims."

"Did you hear that? Yes." Marin's eyes got all squinty. "I'll make sure not to hand him any tokens, Dad. I get it. Gotta run." Marin blew at a stray wisp of bright red hair. "Ah—hi to Heike." And she quickly ended the call.

She closed her eyes, leaned back against the headrest, and let out a long, low groan. "Family."

From Jack's perspective of the conversation, Ewan had been helpful and hadn't asked a lot of unrelated questions. But Jack wasn't going anywhere near that landmine. He glanced at her notepad but couldn't make anything out. "Didn't you learn to write, like, eighty years ago?"

Marin turned to look at him. "What are you talking about?"

"Shouldn't you have good handwriting? I thought that was a thing back then." When she just stared at him like he'd lost his mind, he looked away from the scraggly, indecipherable scratches on the pad she was holding and asked, "What do we know?"

"Definite exclusion of a few possibilities. And through elimination, he's got a best guess." Marin shrugged. "I told you: it's not like he has an encyclopedia of weird and wonderful creatures. Also, Dad's memory is decent, but you have to remember that dragons are very much creatures of the now."

"Yeah, I remember you told me about that whole concept of living in the moment. Something to do with how long you guys live, right?"

Marin nodded. "So that leaves us with a disturbing prospect. Dad called it a created man. Think Frankenstein or a golem." She pulled back onto the road.

"Are you telling me that Conrad has a partner? A creator?" Jack grabbed her discarded notepad.

"Technically. Assuming he's this created man Dad was talking about. But these created men, they don't wander the countryside stealing memories if their creators are still hanging around. The creator's life, memories, magic, or something keeps the thing alive. But if the creator dies—"

"Good Lord. Some egomaniac creates his own personal human Gumby servant and then forgets to flip the off switch before he dies." Jack chucked the useless notes into the glove box.

"Yeah. Basically. Although Conrad is focusing on specific memories, which is apparently not the norm. Well, assuming there is a norm. So we've probably got a vessel, previously powered by his master's magic, with a dying battery that he somehow recharges by stealing memories from grieving humans."

"Don't forget Rose."

"Actually, Rose's symptoms are what Dad described—the confusion about time and place. Something like nonspecific senility. So the bereaved victims are unique to Conrad. Oh, and tokens are important to some created men." Marin gripped the steering wheel. "I think it's a terrible idea to go to Conrad's without some kind of plan."

"Since you're driving ten miles under the speed limit, we should have plenty of time. And there's some urgency here. The active attacks on Betty and Rose, combined with the fact that we don't know how exactly he's causing the damage or if it's reversible—all of that means now is better than later. And we don't really want him prepared for us, do we?" Jack scrubbed his hands over his face. "So how do we kill this thing? And we're not calling him the created man. That sounds goofy as hell. He's basically a golem, so—golem."

"A golem is a subtype, and that's probably not what Conrad is." Marin must have caught Jack's eye roll, because she quickly added, "But sure—golem works."

"And...?"

"And—no idea. Chop his head off, burn him. Maybe he dies just like any other person. Dad didn't know, which is why he insisted I be careful."

"He's your *dad*. What do you expect? Hey, I'm just saying." Jack lifted his hands. "Okay, our next stop is the hardware store."

Marin's lips curved into a hint of a smile. "Yippee. Axes, duct tape, lamp oil, and a shovel, here we come."

"It's disturbing how quickly you came up with that shopping list."

And that made her grin outright.

"ONE MURDER KIT—CHECK. One body disposal kit—check. Escape car gassed up—check. I feel like a well-prepared criminal." Marin dropped the last bag into the rear of her Rover and slammed the rear hatch.

"Why don't you announce that a little louder?" Jack

waited until they were both seated inside the car before he said, "I'd love to spend the rest of my life in jail for killing a mass murderer who's not even human."

"Potential mass murderer. We don't have a body count. But the sudden disappearance or death of Mr. Blevins is an issue. We're clearly the prime suspects if something happens to him: new to town, digging around his clients, asking questions about him, and purchasing a variety of suspicious materials immediately before his death." Marin tapped her fingers on the steering wheel. "I think a house fire."

Jack tamped down all-too-vivid images of buildings—homes—aflame. "Are you kidding? We could light up the whole town. Or at least the neighborhood."

"Really, Jack. Magical fire, dragon—remember?" Marin turned and blew a small puff of smoke in front of Jack's face. "And we've had an unusual amount of rain lately."

Damp, warm air touched his face. Steam, not smoke. "That's creepy as hell—but I get it: you have excellent control." He waited a few seconds then said, "A little heavy-handed."

Marin smirked. "What's the plan, boss?"

"Arrive, subdue, remove the head, burn the body, burn the house." Jack couldn't help but cringe at the house-burning, magically controlled or not. "What do you think?"

"Are you actually asking my opinion? Give me a second to recover from the shock."

"My mistake. It won't happen again." But the words slipped out with no conviction. Just something to say as he thought about Marin, himself, their professional relationship. Yeah, something needed to change, and he didn't want a repeat of Miersburg. Jack cleared his throat. "Uh, yeah. So?"

Marin peeked at him out of the corner of her eye. "Don't let him have anything that belongs to us. Tokens are important to created...uh, golems—whatever that means."

"I'm betting they help him steal memories."

"Or give him power over the token's owner. Or are just trophies he keeps to remind him of past successes. Whatever. Best to avoid dealing with it, so hang on to your stuff."

Jack grunted in agreement. "And we can't forget how much everyone likes this guy. He must be charming."

"It's possible he's *literally* charming his victims, that he has a magic talent that influences how people feel about him."

Jack groaned.

"Right." Marin's lips twitched. "In theory, I should be immune—or at least less affected."

"Well, that's good anyway. Because if he has super strength or some kind of physical advantage—"

"Like not being alive and therefore impossible to kill?"

"Smartass. Yes, like that. You're the obvious one to get close and try to immobilize him, since you've got the super strength and lightning speed." Jack had a gut-churning thought. "So if Conrad is a vessel for his master's magic, how exactly did his creator make him? Not the golem—the vessel?"

"We're almost there, so I'm circling the neighborhood before we head in." Marin made an immediate right turn a few streets before Conrad's. "The simple answer: his creator took some poor soul's body and repurposed it."

"If that's true, then we forget taking his head. We immobilize him and incinerate his body. No body, no vessel for whatever the hell it is that makes Conrad alive." Jack nodded. "All right. We walk in, overpower him, gag and tie him, and then burn him."

"Without giving him a chance to talk or touch us —those are the most common vehicles for persuasive talent," Marin added.

"Or letting him take a personal object from either of us." Jack dug around in his pockets and dumped out the change, a small pocketknife, and his wallet. He stashed the wallet and knife in the glove box.

"We're parking and knocking on his door?"

"No. That gets him too close. In through the back

and we try to surprise him." Jack reached down to check his ankle holster and gun. "Preferably before he calls the cops. If we could *not* get stopped by the police at any point today, that would be great. Especially since I'm carrying concealed."

"You're worried about a concealed weapon?" Marin snorted. "If he calls the cops and then ends up dead, no accidental house fire. That's a much bigger problem."

"Yeah. That too."

Marin pulled into a small neighborhood park. From there they could easily walk to the house that abutted Conrad's. "No way in without being seen now. We wait till dark, I assume?"

"Yep. Should only be an hour or so. I'd say wait until he's asleep, but for all we know he doesn't sleep."

Marin's brow furrowed. "And Rose's nighttime adventure in the kitchen makes me wonder if he has a way to reach them at night."

Jack nodded. "As soon as it's dark, then."

Jack gave Marin's ass a firm push. He'd given her a leg up over the fence, but she'd looked about ready to drop back down. Once she'd cleared the fence, he clambered over behind her and saw why she'd hesitated. A stout rose bush, thorns included, was just on the other side. He shimmied several feet down the fence then hopped off.

Thankfully, Louisiana in the summer meant all the houses in this little neighborhood were locked up tight with the curtains pulled and air-conditioning units running full blast. So with only a little luck, no nosy neighbors to stumble on them. And Conrad's house only had lights on upstairs. Jack could just make out the faint outline of yellow in one room where the light leaked through the corners of the curtains.

"Thanks," Marin whispered in Jack's ear when he reached her.

Jack shrugged and motioned to the back door. As he watched, Marin approached the door and disappeared. He squinted in the dark. He thought the weird steam-breath was creepy. Marin disappearing into nothing made the hairs on the back of his neck rise. Before he could go completely mental, Marin quietly opened the back door and motioned him inside. He'd have to figure out why walking through a door was freakier than walking through a ward—but his brain had decided that it absolutely was.

Once inside, he could hear the low hum of a television in the background. Just enough noise to mask any small noises he and Marin might make.

Or not.

Because Conrad was headed down the stairs. Jack could hear him. Conrad wasn't making any attempt to move quietly; the guy was whistling.

Had they tripped a ward unknowingly? Or an armed security system that neither he nor Marin had spotted?

They both moved to the back of the room and to the side, the spot least visible to a person descending the stairs. Jack reluctantly drew his gun. They needed to avoid the sound of gunfire if their original accidental house fire plan was going to work. But he also liked breathing.

Jack pointed at Marin. She was their only silent

option at this point. Jack just had to make sure he didn't hit her if that plan failed, because he'd be poorly placed for a clean shot.

And then there he was: their very own ninja memory assassin. A slightly receding hairline, soft in the middle, average height. Conrad looked like he worked behind a desk all day. He looked like that guy, Bob, the one who grills burgers for the block party and waves at passersby when he's working in the yard. He looked like everyman and no one in particular.

While he'd been cataloguing Conrad's appearance, Jack's gun had slowly lowered and the muzzle now pointed at the ground. He didn't remember deciding to lower it.

Marin approached Conrad, but slowly. That wasn't the plan. Jack knew it, but he wasn't really concerned about it.

As Marin slowly closed the distance between her and Conrad, she said, "Jack. Why do I not want to smash this walking piece of excrement's face in?"

Marin sounded curious. Not frantic. So there must not be any urgency.

"I don't know—but I'm feeling like he might be kind of a good guy." Jack paused. *That* wasn't right.

"I'm a really nice guy. You should get to know me before you make any hasty decisions." Conrad smiled pleasantly, his bland expression matching his bland tone. "Jack, why don't you give me your gun?"

"Sure." Jack started to walk toward Conrad. Wait. Bad idea. Really bad idea. "No. I think that might be a bad idea." Was that his voice? It sounded wrong to his own ears.

"I'm sure you're right," Conrad said. "Go ahead and shoot the redhead instead. I think that's a good idea."

"Okay." The word slipped past Jack's lips, but he didn't move. Shooting the redhead seemed like an even worse idea than giving Conrad his gun. No. He really shouldn't shoot Marin. He kind of liked Marin. Then his arm was wrenched and the pain brought a moment of clarity. "Shit."

"Yes." Marin held tight to his forearm and yanked him along behind her. "You going to shoot me?"

"Hell no." Jack looked over his shoulder. "Conrad's headed to the garage."

Marin pulled him through the back door.

"Let go." Jack pulled at his arm. "I'm fine."

As they hoofed it across the yard and Marin made a run at the fence, pulling herself over in a smooth move, Jack had a fleeting thought: were they retreating or being chased?

After holstering his gun, Jack joined her, huffing slightly, on the other side of the fence. No curious neighbors yet.

Right before she took off again, Marin said,

"We're agreed that you shoot him if you get the opportunity?"

"Yeah." Jack jogged at a good clip, just keeping pace with Marin. "Wouldn't have shot you."

Reaching the car, Marin tugged open the driver's door and hopped in. Jack was a hair behind her.

After he closed the door, Jack repeated, "Whatever I said, I wouldn't have shot you."

"I know that. But it's pretty damn disturbing that Conrad's persuasion is that effective from such a distance." Marin pulled out into the street. "Those poor women didn't have a chance. And Eric—ugh. I want to beat this creature to a pulp."

"It would be pretty cool if you could manage that. Maybe earplugs?" Because Jack knew they had to finish this tonight. That, or Marin and he could easily become Conrad's next victims. Or he'd skip town and continue harming innocent people who caught his eye. "Do you think he's running?"

Marin checked her rearview mirror. "Nope. Definitely chasing. And I can tell you, his persuasion is tied to proximity, and it's definitely not his voice. Visual? A smell? Hormones of some kind? The magic is dense near him and dissipates further away, but there's no fluctuation when he speaks. Hell, it may not even be a natural talent. He could be using borrowed magic—a potion, maybe. I can't tell—the magic just looks...off."

As Marin shared what she'd discovered, Jack

watched a green Subaru gain on them. The same green Subaru that had been parked in Conrad's drive earlier.

"Do I want to know how fast you're going?" Jack slipped his seatbelt on.

"Nope. At least there's no traffic." Marin continued to check her rearview mirror with startling frequency.

"I'd love to avoid a car accident. I'm squishy and breakable, remember? No magical bells and whistles. No extra healing ability."

"Then it's a good thing our buddy Kai lives around the corner." Marin gave him one of her toothy, mildly terrifying grins. "You remember Kai? The healer who magicked your head back into reasonable shape. After your concussion—"

"After I almost blew us up. Right, I remember. It was like, what? Two weeks ago? Of course I remember." Jack had forgotten the kid's name, not that he'd patched Jack up. "He's close?"

"Yeah. Closer to us than to Miersburg." Marin gripped the steering wheel. "I think Conrad is going to run us off the road and either kill us or have us kill each other."

Since he'd reached the same conclusion, Jack couldn't argue. "Bad news, because that means he's not worried about any injuries he might sustain."

"Yep."

The car jerked as the Subaru tapped their

bumper, but Marin had already accelerated.

"Shit—sharp turn coming up ahead." Jack struggled for a half-ass decent out. "A good chance you survive a collision with this asshole?"

"Very good."

Quickly now, Jack said, "Slow down for the turn as much as you can, and I'll jump out."

"He'll rear-end me...ah. And you'll shoot him after the crash."

"That's the plan."

Marin squeezed the steering wheel. "Wait till I say go."

"You're sure—"

"I am."

"Dammit, I love this car," Jack muttered.

Marin smiled broadly. "I know. I'll get another one. Get ready." She braked hard.

Jack did his best to think only: exhale; relax. He cracked the door open. Exhale. Relax. They slowed down significantly, probably to twenty or fifteen miles an hour. He could survive that. Right?

"Go!"

Jack let himself fall from the car, exhaling as he went.

Burning, wrenching, rolling. Panicky gasps of breath. *Relax and roll. Relax and roll.* And he rolled and burned and rolled.

It took him a moment to realize he was stationary and just his head was spinning. Immediately, he tried to even out his breath. Slowly reaching for his ankle holster, he scanned the area as best he could from the ground. Minimal movement should make him less visible. He hoped.

The Range Rover was off the road but upright. Jack couldn't see if Marin was in the front seat. The country road they'd ended up on had no streetlights, and the headlamps from the Subaru shone at an angle to the Rover. No movement near Conrad's car. Jack searched the wreckage of the car for any sign of Conrad—but from his position on the ground he couldn't see much.

Jack had been at least fifteen feet from Conrad when the guy had half convinced him to pull a gun on Marin. Massive adrenaline dump, road rash, a jacked shoulder, fear—he couldn't count on accuracy at a hundred feet. Fifty? Could he risk getting that close?

Jack did a few calculations then rolled to his feet and ran to the Rover, a good hundred feet from the Subaru. Conrad must have clipped the left edge of the Rover's bumper in the turn, spinning the cars away from each other. The thought slipped through his head, crammed together with the ache in his shoulder, the sharp pain in his hip, and the slow burn down his back.

Marin was in the car, slumped slightly to the side.

"Shit." Jack kept half an eye on Conrad's car,

while he tried to get to Marin. "Marin, can you hear me?"

Marin cleared her throat. "I'm okay, but you've got a hitch in your step." She coughed. "Freaking air bag fumes. Hey, relax. Conrad hasn't left the car."

"You sure?" When she nodded, Jack said, "You didn't black out?"

"Screw you, too. I'm sure. Now get me out of this cloud of chemicals."

Jack opened the door and gave her a hand out. It took her a few seconds before she was steady on her feet.

"I haven't seen any movement around the car, but I can't see him."

Marin sneezed. Eyes watering, she said, "The bastard's still in the front seat. Maybe his legs are broken."

"Are you sure you're okay?" Jack couldn't help but notice the wheezing, sneezing, and tearing up.

"You take care of you. I'm fine."

Jack rubbed his bruised hip absently. "I can't shoot him if I can't see him. And no way am I getting close." A pleasant thought perked him up. "Can you just incinerate the car? We're in the middle of nowhere."

Before Marin could respond, Conrad's clear and even voice resonated through the air. "Burn me and their memories are gone forever."

Jack checked that Marin still looked like herself

—still was in control of herself. "Are you feeling compelled?"

Marin shook her head and quietly murmured, "But I'm not quite up to flying and fire at the moment."

She did look paler than she had a few moments ago. And she was sweating. Marin didn't sweat. Something was wrong. *Shit.*

Raising his voice, Jack said, "Okay. What do you want?" He tried to sound reasonable, but even to his own ears he sounded pissed off.

Conrad's car door swung open, followed by the appearance of his legs—clearly not broken. "I want what every man wants. To live free, unmolested by my fellow man."

"Are you fucking kidding me?" But Jack spoke quietly. He counted to three and then raised his voice. "And what about the people you molest? Your victims."

"The old. The weak. Unmissed by society when they fade away. Where's the harm?" Calm, dispassionate, Conrad's reply made Jack queasy.

"Jack." Marin was leaning against the Rover. "His master."

Immediately, Jack turned around and yelled, "What about your creator? Is that what he believed? That people were there for you take? That the weakest were there for you to abuse? To injure? To kill?"

Conrad stood smoothly from the car, fluidly turning to present a minimized target. "But Jack, I don't kill."

He'd left no center mass target, the asshole.

Jack grabbed frantically at the last thread of the conversation. "Eric—what about Eric?"

Soothingly, Conrad said, "Eric killed himself. He was weak, unhappy. Ready to die."

"Not weak, Conrad. He was in pain. Pain that you caused." Jack raised his gun and fired.

"Tsk, tsk. If you shoot, you shouldn't miss." Conrad took a casual step toward Jack and Marin, appearing completely unruffled by the near-miss. "Don't you want to save Rose's sanity? Betty's memories of the love of her life? Shame on you." He took another step.

Doubt crept in. Could they get Betty's memories back? Rose's, too? Jack glanced at Marin.

Lips trembling, forehead beaded with sweat, Marin said, "He lies. He's using persuasion, Jack."

By the time he'd turned back to Conrad, the creature was several feet closer. Jack fired, clipping his shoulder—but Conrad kept walking.

"His creator, Jack," Marin wheezed.

"The man who made you..." Jack searched frantically for some argument. Something to distract. "He's ashamed, Conrad."

Conrad hesitated for a split second.

Bingo.

Conrad continued to walk forward. He was maybe seventy feet away. "You're wrong. They nourish me, and he would want me to live. If you knew my father, you would know this."

"He wasn't your father. He was your creator. He was human—like I am. Like Betty, and Rose, and Eric. You're not human, Conrad." Jack spat out the last sentence like an accusation, and fired.

A miss. His freaking shoulder was killing him, making it impossible to get a steady aim.

Conrad cocked his head, seeming to consider Jack's statement. "I'm better than human. I don't age. I don't tire or become sick. I'm not weak."

Jack made a quick guess—everyone without a soul wanted one, right? And surely this thing, whatever it was, didn't have a soul. "But you can never be better than humans, because you have no soul." No reaction, so Jack switched tracks. "Your creator had a soul."

"Yes, and he shared his soul with me." Conrad was about fifty feet away.

An easy enough shot on any other day.

Jack dropped his gun hand. His shoulder couldn't take it, and this wasn't working. "So when your creator, your father, died, he took away your soul."

Conrad turned to face Jack, and the hate in his eyes burned. "He shouldn't have—"

One shot, center mass, silenced him. Jack stared

down the sight of the gun he'd raised and fired
without conscious thought. Already his feet were
moving, bringing him closer. He fired again—heart.
And again—head. The last remaining shot he fired
through the shredded remains of what passed for
this creature's heart.

Seven shots. Looked like Conrad was just human
enough to die. Jack leaned down, about to check its
pulse, when he realized—did the thing have a pulse
to begin with?

On the way back to the car, he picked up his
shell casings, but his gaze never strayed far from the
crumpled figure of Conrad. Where was all the
blood? Whatever Conrad had been, it didn't seem to
bleed much.

He picked up the last casing and turned to find
Marin crumpled in a heap next to the car. Pale,
damp, unconscious.

"Shit. Shit." Jack rushed to her side and reached
down to feel for a pulse.

Marin's eyelids flickered. "Please. Get a grip,
Jack." She wheezed and coughed. "I'm not dying."
She stopped to catch her breath. "I pierced a lung.
Hurts like crazy."

"Holy shit. That is *not* good."

Marin's eyes were now firmly open and she
looked pissed off. She narrowed her eyes. "My
phone. Call Kai. You idiot."

"Right. Got it." Jack retrieved her phone from the

Rover and scrolled through the contacts. There was only one Kai, and he had a Louisiana number. He dialed the number and flipped it immediately to speaker.

"Hey, it's Jack. The guy—"

"Yeah—I remember. The guy with the head injury. Any reason you're calling from Marin's phone?" Kai asked.

Well, that was interesting... Before Jack could map out the various reasons for Kai to have Marin's number programmed in his phone, Marin started wheezing.

"Hey." Marin started coughing immediately, which made tears stream down her face.

"Jesus—can you shut up for five minutes?" Jack barked.

Immediately a sharp pang of remorse hit. It wasn't her fault he had nasty, inadequate, and help-less feelings piled on top of guilt. His idea to inten-tionally crash the car. But he still wanted to throw the phone at her.

Jack grunted in frustration. "Sorry, Kai. Marin's punctured a lung and needs help right now. The faster you can get here the better, because she won't stop talking." He took a breath, briefly meeting her eyes. "And she looks like shit. And definitely is in a lot of pain."

"Already in the car and heading down the drive. Where am I going?" Kai's words were confirmed by the soft dinging of the seatbelt warning bell in the background.

After Jack gave him directions, Kai said, "Just keep her still and quiet. I'll be there in fifteen."

Jack ended the call and pocketed Marin's phone. "Not a word."

She glared at him but didn't utter a sound. She did, however, bite the hell out of her lower lip.

It seemed like a never-ending fifteen minutes to Jack, as he waited for someone, somewhere to have heard the shots and come to investigate. Or for another traveler to venture down this back road and report the accident before they could clean up the scene. He could only imagine how rough it was for Marin, in pain, worried about discovery, and just dying to tell him how to deal with the cleanup.

Thirteen minutes later, Kai pulled up in his old Wrangler.

Kai jumped out and jogged to Marin. "At least I know why you guys weren't coming to me. That's a serious shame about the Range Rover."

"Right?" Jack said. "I'm going to miss that truck."

Marin glared at both of them.

It didn't take Kai long to heal Marin sufficiently so that she could talk without excessive pain.

She stretched, grimaced, and then said, "Don't worry. I'll incinerate the whole mess." Jack must have looked confused, because she immediately explained, "That is what you've been sitting here stressing out about for the last twenty minutes, right?"

Jack winced. "No comment."

Marin snorted. "I get it." Turning to Kai, she asked, "You can get the tear repaired, right? The rest is fine, I just need the lung intact before I set fire to that corpse over there."

Kai sighed. "I was trying really hard not to notice the three-hundred-year-old corpse. Thanks for the reminder."

"What the hell—are you serious?" Jack looked back at the heap of clothing and twisted limbs that used to be Conrad.

"Sure. I mean, it looks fresh—and I don't want to know how that happened—but he's definitely at least three hundred years past his sell-by date." Kai turned back to work on Marin. Without looking up, he said, "Really. I don't want to know."

"Got it." Jack glanced discreetly at his watch.

"I'm almost done." Kai's lips twitched. "Maybe five more minutes. This lady has enough juice to heal worse injuries to a critter five times her size."

"Cute," Marin said.

"Are you saying you're using Marin's magic to heal her wound?" Jack watched the two of them with curiosity.

"Yeah. That's why you guys—non-magical people—are harder. No juice but my own involved." Kai gave Marin a serious look. "Deep breath."

When she'd complied, he asked, "How does that feel?"

Marin gave Kai a glowing smile. "Much better than just patching the tear. Thank you."

Jack pulled his gaze away from three-hundred-year-old Conrad and said, "Yes. Thank you. I hope we didn't wreck your entire evening."

Kai grinned. "Are you kidding? You guys are the only excitement I get. I was thinking about moving closer to New Orleans, but if you keep this up, I'll start to feel almost useful."

Marin stood up and offered Kai her hand. "Glad to provide entertainment. And thanks again."

Kai pulled her close for what looked like a friendly, but not over-friendly, hug. "Stay safe." He lifted a hand in Jack's direction and headed back to his Jeep.

"Wait till he's gone then blow the whole thing up into unrecognizable bits?" Jack asked hopefully.

Marin huffed out a small laugh. "Don't you wish. We call the locals and report the accident, but I think incinerating the body is a good idea. Who knows what an autopsy would reveal."

"He hit us, we were confused, by the time we got out of the car, he was gone." Jack shrugged. "Maybe."

"I need the body away from the scene. Somewhere that a char mark won't be noticed. The woods."

Jack started to head in Conrad's direction, but

stopped when his hip protested. "Shit. Why didn't I hit him up for a little healing boost?"

"Because you were so worried about me." Marin towed him along behind her as she headed to collect Conrad's body. "Or you forgot how much you hurt because you'd been still in one place for so long."

"Yeah. Not to burst your bubble, but once I realized you weren't dying... So, uh, definitely the second one." Jack braced himself to pick up the body. "I get a warm bath after this. Promise me, please. And no teasing if I break down into tears."

"I'm laughing my ass off if you cry."

They bantered back and forth the entire trip to the woods, each of them desperately clinging to any topic but the lifeless creature they carried.

Once the body was safely burned, the cops called, and the accident reported, two hours had passed. The police had been suspicious. Conrad was, not surprisingly, well liked. But when it came right down to it, he wasn't a local. And Marin and Jack hadn't done anything wrong from what the officer could see. It was clear the Range Rover had been rear-ended. After Marin passed a Breathalyzer, and both she and Jack had emphatically refused medical treatment, they both piled into the cab of the tow truck and hitched a ride to the B&B with the driver.

It wasn't until the tow truck was pulling away that Jack realized he and Marin hadn't discussed what they'd tell Milton. And Rose. And Betty. And Dottie. Or if they'd tell Karen anything at all. He scrubbed his hands over his face. "I desperately want that soak in a bath."

"Yeah. But there's no better time to check out Conrad's house than now. No way is that officer gaining access this evening."

"Dammit, you're right." Jack closed his eyes and let his head roll back. "Ow."

"Your neck hurts too?"

Jack sighed. "Apparently. All right. Let's head in. And if Milton's up, we spill the beans tonight—otherwise we do it tomorrow after a decent night's sleep. What the hell are we going to tell him?"

"The truth, I think. It's not much crazier than someone contaminating the water supply." Marin shrugged. "It's just a question of whether we say magic, hypnosis, drugs...or something else."

"Karma is a complete bitch." Jack smiled weakly.

Marin tipped her head quizzically.

"That call to your dad that I pushed you to make? I'm making my own uncomfortable little call. Harrington is going to make the call on magic, drugs, hypnosis, or something else."

"Oh." Marin shot Jack a sympathetic look. "That sucks."

Drugs, hypnosis, memory loss, and cover-ups. Not the conversation Milton had likely expected when he'd come down to check on the late arrivals. The tow truck lights had woken him when they'd flashed through his bedroom window.

Milton sat very still, wrapped in his bathrobe, his hand clenched around a mug of herbal tea. "So you're saying that he drugged Rose and used hypnosis to make her forget certain things. Why would he do that?"

"Because he's sick, Milton. Really sick. But he's gone now. Jack and I made sure he couldn't keep hurting people." Marin looked so earnest that even Jack was starting to buy the story. And, really, most of it was true.

"I don't understand why the police aren't

involved. What am I supposed to do to help her get better? What do I tell the doctors?" Milton's worried gaze dug at Jack.

Here was the tricky part.

"Like I said, Jack and I aren't with the police, but we work with a law enforcement agency out of Europe, where Blevins has committed similar crimes. That agency has contacts with the FBI and Interpol, and we've been authorized to provide you with the name of a representative from each of those organizations." Marin pulled out her phone and carefully copied the names of two people and their phone numbers. "If you have any questions, you can ask either of these two people—but it's quite important that you only speak with these people." She gave him a soft, compassionate look. "Do you understand?"

"I understand what you're saying, but I'm not sure I understand why." Milton took a sip of the now cold tea. When Marin was about to explain further, he shook his head. "No. I don't care. I just need to know what I can do for Rose."

Jack leaned back in his chair and clasped his hands together. "The good news is that Rose isn't sick. The memories are gone, but you can tell her stories, share your memories, and fill in the gaps. We also think that her confusion will diminish over the next few weeks now that Conrad isn't actively interfering with her perception of time."

An educated guess that he and Marin had made —something had made Rose's symptoms different from Eric's and Betty's.

Milton's bushy grey eyebrows pulled close together. "And if it doesn't?"

"Then you can call one of the contacts we've given you and they'll help you," Jack said. He suspected that the FBI or Interpol contact would have Kai or another healer come by to check on Rose.

Milton shook his head. "So she won't remember, but she doesn't have Alzheimer's. That's good news." His whole body relaxed into the kitchen chair. "Really good news."

SITTING in the passenger seat of Milton's car, Marin said, "Do I want to know how many favors you owe Harrington for getting the Inter-Pack Policing Cooperative involved in this mess?"

"After that frantic middle-of-the-night call—or early morning, in his case—I expected Harrington to wring me dry." Jack started the car and began the familiar drive to Conrad's house. "But as soon as I gave him the details, he immediately offered up two contacts. Either Harrington was pissed off about the types of victims Conrad was choosing, or he was appalled by the sheer number of victims out there.

In three hundred years, there's no telling how many people's lives and families he destroyed." Jack shifted in the seat, trying to find a comfortable position for his throbbing hip. "There's no way to know—Harrington didn't share. But those are my two best guesses."

"Hm. I think it more likely Harrington's worried about the exposure risk." Marin frowned. "Really, you can pull over and let me drive. How finicky can this hunk of junk be?"

"With an attitude like that, very. Besides, I'm fine." Jack groaned. "But I'm not looking forward to hopping fences. Surely it's late enough to park on his street. No one's going to be up at three in the morning, right?"

"Let's hope."

Fifteen minutes later, Jack was back to being creeped out by Marin's walking-through-walls act, though he had to admit it was less bizarre the second time. The door opened and Marin poked her head out. "Come on already."

Jack slipped in and quietly closed the door. "I'll check the bottom floor and you do the top—assuming you're pretty sure nothing's warded in here."

"Should be good," Marin whispered over her shoulder as she headed to the stairs. "I'll pick up the pieces if I'm wrong."

Jack was way too tired to even think about being

annoyed. He just wanted to get this search over and get some sleep before he had to face Betty and Dottie in the morning. It had been a difficult decision, but Marin and he had agreed to leave Karen out of the follow-up. Nothing they could say would change the fact that her husband was dead, and she was trying to move on. Jack had no idea if that was the right decision, but it was the one they'd made.

He was standing in front of the fridge, getting up the nerve to open it—all he could think about was finding a bunch of hacked-up body parts—when his phone rang. He pulled it from his pocket and answered after he saw that it was Marin. "Hey, can you hang on just a sec?"

He opened the door. Whew. Gatorade, lemonade, iced tea, orange juice. Not a speck of food. Mr. Blevins liked his fluids. "Weird. He's got no food in the fridge or cupboards, but about ten different kinds of drinks. What's up?"

"You need to come upstairs." Marin hung up.

Jack considered jogging for about two seconds then decided cryptic didn't equate with urgent. And his freaking hip was killing him.

By the time he arrived, Marin had her hands on her hips, her foot tapping, and a look that lacked all sympathy for his battered state. "This is not good."

"Hey—I hurt. You didn't say I needed to hurry."

"Not that." Marin swung open the door to what looked like a study. "This."

The walls were covered with shelves, but there weren't any books. Just things. Trinkets. Doodads. Scraps of paper. Rows and rows, covering all four walls.

"What is this?" Jack had an uneasy feeling, but he wasn't sure why exactly.

"A trophy room, I'd guess." Marin clutched her arms, hugging herself. "All these pieces have a tiny bit of magic—some kind I've never seen—attached to them. I think maybe there's something of the item's owner still clinging to the objects."

Very slowly, Jack said, "But—that's not bad. If the objects hold an imprint of the previous owners, then why does this room make me want to hide in a closet somewhere?"

A moue of distaste crossed Marin's face. She shook her head. "I don't know. All I know is that there's something bad here."

Jack nodded to the door and followed Marin out as she left. He took a deep breath out in the hallway. "So—not trying to return these to their former owners, right?"

Marin frantically shook her head. "No. No-no."

Jack put a hand on her arm. "Hey. It's okay." When she nodded, he asked, "Is there a computer?"

"A laptop in the bedroom." Marin wrinkled her nose. "You can go get it if you want it."

"That's fine." He gave it a little more thought then said, "Okay. I retrieve the laptop, and you burn the trophy room with everything in it. If it's that bad, we shouldn't leave that stuff lying around. Any way to make it look like an electrical fire?"

Marin huffed. "Piece of cake."

"That's terrifying," Jack said, shaking his head. "Arson aside, we good with the plan?"

Marin nodded.

"Where's the bedroom?"

Marin pointed to the last door on the hallway.

Jack made a detour to the bedroom, grabbed the laptop from Conrad's nightstand, and hoofed it out of there. Meeting Marin in the hallway again, he asked, "We sure we have everything?"

"I'm good. Let me just take care of the tokens or trophies..." Marin's nostrils flared. "Whatever they are."

"Um, do I need to leave? Or do we do it from outside?" Again, Jack had a vivid image of a neighborhood engulfed in fire.

Marin sighed. "Seriously? Just wait behind me. I promise not to set you on fire. But don't chatter. Fire in human form is more difficult."

Jack pressed his lips together and took a step back.

It was bright. White then brilliant blue then white—like it couldn't decide. Jack's eyes burned from the light. He closed and rubbed his eyes. By the time he opened them, there was nothing. "What the hell. Where's the smoke? The heat? And how did you do that?"

"I flash-burned it at high heat. I told you I wouldn't set the neighborhood on fire." Marin shoved on his good shoulder. "Get a move on. We should leave just in case that light freaked anyone out. Remember, you can see a bit through the corner of the curtains."

Jack stood staring at the blackened room. "And this is going to look like an electrical fire?"

"I made sure the origin is clear. They're going to wonder what the heck Conrad had on his shelves that burned like liquid lightning—but that's not our problem." Marin blew a bright red wisp of hair out of her face. "Makes him look more suspicious, right?"

Jack laughed. "You think?"

By the time they'd driven back to the B&B—with Marin behind the wheel—they'd outlined a slightly different tack to take with Dottie. Tightened up the story, practiced what they'd say. They'd provide the report by phone, have their FBI contact immediately follow up, and make sure there was an in-person meeting scheduled for tomorrow afternoon. Dottie was a tougher nut than Milton, but when Jack finally sank into his tub in the wee hours of the morning, he was pretty damn sure they could pull it off.

EPILOGUE

"**S**PI, how can I help you?"

Jack pointed a finger at Marin in warning. She'd started answering The Junk Shop's second line, the one he very occasionally used for Spirelli Paranormal Investigations, with the SPI abbreviation. It seemed a little over the top.

She just rolled her eyes and ignored him for the most part.

"Yes, sir." Marin tapped a button and replaced the handset. "Jack, we're on speaker with Harrington." Marin walked to the office door and shut it.

No customers in the shop, but the room warded to be soundproof when the door was shut.

"I have some news for you regarding that laptop you shipped to us." Harrington sounded tired.

Jack took a seat behind his desk. "Okay. Go ahead."

He and Marin exchanged a glance. Harrington didn't usually openly share information, and Jack hadn't asked for anything in exchange for the laptop. He'd wanted someone who could use the information to have it, so he'd shipped it to Harrington.

"First, your guy had no psychic skills. From what we can tell, he used a combination of research, psychology, cold-reading, and persuasion to achieve the psychic effect."

"Marin and I had guessed as much."

"Yes, but I should add that his persuasion talent was incredibly strong," Marin said.

"What I called to tell you, well—" Harrington cleared his throat. "IPPC would like to thank you for your efforts in this case. We'll also be forwarding a reward that was posted a number of years ago by a Spanish magic-using family who ran into Conrad using a different alias. I'll spare you the details, but they were eager to have him caught."

"Thank you." Jack knew his tone was flat and he should be more thankful, but something about this case had hit him wrong from the start. It was hard to work up a healthy level of excitement. "There's more, I assume?"

"Yes." When he spoke next, Harrington's tone was brisk. "We've calculated his feeding requirements based on information he used to track and plan his...his meals. It appears Blevins required from four to seven victims annually."

"No." Jack moved to the edge of his seat. "No, that can't be right."

"I'm telling you it is," Harrington replied grimly.

"I don't think I mentioned it when we spoke last, but we had a healer in the vicinity of the corpse—purely by chance. He was convinced Blevins had died over three hundred years previous." Jack clenched his teeth. "I'm not doing that math."

"We suspect Blevins has been actively stealing memories for the last two hundred, maybe two hundred fifty years. If his creator used a different method to sustain him, that would account for the discrepancy." The sound of shuffling papers traveled over the line then Harrington said, "Again, we'd like to thank you for your efforts. If you could send a report to IPPC detailing the specific method of execution and what brought Blevins to your attention, that would be most helpful." A dial tone sounded.

"Of course he ends the call before I can decline the request for a report. That seems about right for Harrington." A stupid thing to bitch about—but Jack's head was spinning with the possible numbers.

Marin settled back into her chair. "Maybe, but that was the only thing remotely normal about that call. I get the impression Harrington feels like he owes you. I've definitely not heard him that uncomfortable before."

"And the giant white elephant?" Jack asked.

"Yeah—how the hell did he get away with it for so long? I don't know, Jack. Staying mobile? Victim choice? Let's just be glad Dottie Wallace loves her mom so much, that she likes trendy hair salons, and that she decided to walk into your store." Marin nodded. "Yeah, I'm calling this a good case."

"Sure. Okay." Jack rubbed his temples. "We did catch the bastard."

"No, seriously." Marin smiled—a genuine smile, not one of her terrifying, toothy dragon grins or snarky half-smiles. "We did something good."

"Yeah, I guess we did." Jack turned back to his computer. "And it's our store, not mine."

Keep reading for Episode 3: The Fleeing Witch!

EPISODE 3: THE FLEEING WITCH

ABOUT THE FLEEING WITCH

Jack Spirelli describes the Coven of Light as a cult-like organization, with dangerously powerful members and no love for mundane humanity. He was also on record as categorically refusing to involve himself in a case that took him anywhere near the Coven.

Why then had Jack agreed to take the case of a defecting Coven member? His dragon side-kick Marin may not speak to him again–ever. But sometimes the right thing to do wasn't convenient, comfortable, or safe. It's also possible the stash of magical potions the fleeing witch had used as partial payment might have played some part in his decision.

1
———

Sparkling red lights flashed in front of Jack's eyes, and his ring tightened on his finger. Red lights...witch? Blue was spell caster. White, healer. Yellow, Lycan. Green, miscellaneous other magic. Yeah, red was witch. In his shop, right now. And the day had started out with so much promise, so beautifully uneventful.

He kicked his feet off the edge of his desk and headed into the retail area of The Junk Shop.

A woman wandered in between the tables of junk, her gaze never lingering for long on any one object. Late forties or early fifties, casually dressed, and nervous, if her darting gaze was any indication.

Jack checked the register area but didn't see Marin. "Anything I can help you with?"

She turned to face him and immediately started twisting a chunky ring on her right hand. "Charlotte sent me. She said you might be able to help me. You do protection work, correct?"

"Sometimes. I'm Jack Spirelli."

Clearly she knew that, but his other option—who the hell are you?—seemed to lack tact.

Worry lines deepened on her forehead and around her mouth, making her look pinched. Older. "Sylvia." She started to extend her hand then changed her mind and clasped her hands together. "Sylvia Baker."

Why did that name ring warning bells? It took a few seconds, but all of the tiny connections finally came together. He'd walked out of a former client's office with a stack of letters from her aunt. The client had been missing, the letters might have been relevant, and he'd been short on time—so he'd grabbed them. And read them. More than once. Jack felt a fleeting twinge of guilt when he remembered he'd stashed them in his bottom left desk drawer. Well, hell. He'd *meant* to return them.

Sylvia peered at him. "So how does this work? How do I hire you for protection work?"

"Just to be clear, you're Charlotte Sneed's Aunt Sylvia?"

Sylvia's eyebrows lifted. "She mentioned me?"

"You came up in the context of the Coven."

Jack would normally invite a prospective client into his office at this point, but the Coven of Light connection changed everything. The Coven was a batshit crazy, cult-like organization, with a lot of powerful members and no love for mundane humanity—no thanks.

Sylvia pulled a sheet of paper out of her purse and fanned her face. "Sorry—do you have someplace we can speak more privately? Perhaps..." She looked over her shoulder in the direction of Jack's office.

As he hesitated—she was a Coven witch, even if she was Charlotte's aunt—Sylvia fiddled with her ring. Before Jack could respond, she lifted her hand, pursed her lips, and blew.

"What the—" Jack stared at his computer screen in confusion. He'd been in the shop. Not his office. How'd he get here, sitting at his desk, when his last memory was standing in the store? And who was the lady sitting across the desk from him? "What the hell? Who...you're Charlotte's aunt." Slowly, in fits and starts, it came back to him: Charlotte's Aunt Sylvia, the Coven of Light. "What did you do to me?"

Sylvia's nose wrinkled up in some combination of dismay and vexation. "You really shouldn't remember. I need to work on that one." Her eyes widened as Jack rose from his seat. "No, no. It's completely harmless, really. Just makes you a little more compliant for a few minutes. It doesn't last, or do any damage."

"Your idea of 'completely harmless' and mine are clearly not the same. If you do anything like that again, I'll pick you up and throw your ass out of my shop. I don't care whose aunt you are." Jack glared. "Or what witchy shit you have up your sleeve."

Sylvia bit her lip. "I thought you were going to send me away."

"You thought correctly. That was me exercising free will. I'm a big fan of it. You've got thirty seconds: why do I not kick you out now?"

"I want out, but I need help getting out of the country." Sylvia sat up very straight and quickly ticked off the following points on her fingers. "I have excellent magical potions to trade. I can pay well. And we're stronger together than apart." She cleared her throat. "It's possible the Coven has drawn a few conclusions and already knows I'm here."

Jack could feel his right eye twitch. "Why would I believe someone—a Coven member, no less—who's already poisoned me?"

"I need you." Hands clenched tightly in her lap, she added, "I don't have any other options."

"Why now?" At her confused look, Jack said, "Why are you leaving now? Why not ten years ago, or five?"

"At first, it was all about learning. I liked learning new things. And I'm good. Very good, actually." Sylvia pushed greying bangs out of her face. "But you only go so far before the Coven asks for more. I woke up one day and realized I was mid-level management. The only way up is death magic, and there's no treading water in the Coven." She sat up straighter and lifted her chin. "I won't do death magic."

Well shit.

Jack hated a moral quandary. That combined with being drugged put Sylvia right at the top his five most annoying people list.

But death magic. Jack only hesitated a moment before he picked up his phone and called Marin. "Get your ass back to the shop and bring your go bag."

He hung up before she could ask any questions. Because, really, what the hell was he going to say?

Sylvia sat wide-eyed, silently watching him.

"Okay, why SPI?—wait." Jack held out his hand. "Before we get into that, give me the ring."

Sylvia's lips quirked. "It's empty. Really." When Jack's hand remained outstretched, she sighed and removed the ring.

Before Jack took it, he asked, "How does the substance work? Through contact? Inhalation?"

"Contact."

Jack withdrew his hand and retrieved an envelope from his desk drawer. Once Sylvia had dropped the ring into the envelope, he said, "I assume there's some way to neutralize the powder."

"Dunk it in water. Or rinse it under the tap." Sylvia shrugged. "I told you, it's...um, not very potent."

"Harmless? Right." Jack shook his head. He retrieved a bottle of water from the small fridge in the office and poured it into a disposable cup then dropped the ring in. "Why did you come here? In what universe is that a good choice?" Jack eyed the cup of water with the ring suspiciously.

"You have connections with the Inter-Pack Policing Cooperative, right?"

Jack shook his head. "Not formally. And IPPC has a strict hands-off policy when it comes to the Coven. You should know that. They won't help." Seeing Sylvia deflate, Jack said, "You must have had some idea of that."

Sylvia made a sound that was suspiciously like a growl. "But I'm, you know, defecting." She waved her hands.

Jack stopped rummaging in the office closet for his second-string travel bag. "Watch the hands, lady."

"Sorry," Sylvia mumbled.

He hadn't repacked his go bag after the last trip, so he'd be relying on his back up. He yanked it out from under a box of crap he'd meant to have Marin sort through for the shop. He unzipped it and checked the contents. A crisp, clean scent puffed out. He ruffled through pressed, folded clothes. Pressed? He didn't press his clothes.

"Does this mean you're taking the case?" Sylvia clasped her hands in her lap.

Clean smells, pressed clothes—who cared? What the hell was he going to do about the Coven? The freaking Coven. "Tell me about this magic stash you're willing to trade."

Sylvia brightened. "I have some exceptional specimens. I've been experimenting with the concept of portable plant-based weapons. I'm particularly fond of the exploding pomegranates. But I can't pass anything along until...well, until we..."

Jack quirked an eyebrow at her. "Defeat the Coven?"

Sylvia turned red and fanned herself. "Escape."

Marin triggered the ward and appeared in the office door a few seconds later. Her face was slightly flushed. "What's going on?" She scowled at Jack. "Why are you covered in witch magic?"

"The Coven's after our new client, and we're leaving town." Jack picked up his bag.

Marin face was tight with some emotion. "Why does the Coven want you?" Her face went blank. "You're a Coven witch."

"I'm defecting." Sylvia's face scrunched. "I thought I was defecting. But it turns out IPPC probably isn't interested, so...I'm a refugee?"

"Jack," Marin drew out his name like an accusation, and her eyes turned a startlingly bright green. "Do you have any survival instincts? Seriously? The Coven is into torture, death magic, crazy shit. They do not like non-magical people. Hell, they don't like anyone who's not a witch."

Sylvia stared at the wall, overtly avoiding eye-contact, while she was discussed.

"Oh, I tried to say no. Then I got witch-dusted." Jack turned to Sylvia. "Something that won't ever happen again." She nodded so vigorously that stray wisps of her hair bounced. Jack acknowledged her agreement with a curt nod. "And that's when our new friend told me we'd fare better against the Coven together."

Marin snorted. "And you think they'll give us as much grief if we walk away now? We pass on this job, and she's is no longer our problem. The Coven's not our problem. How do we even know she's really defecting?"

"Fleeing, not defecting. And we know because I've read her letters." Jack reached down into his desk drawer and pulled them out. He tossed them at Sylvia, who snatched at the bundle before it fell to the ground. "It's all there. You have to read between the lines a little, but the discontent, the fear, it's there."

Sylvia clutched the letters tight. "These were private."

"Your niece was missing, and they were a poten-tial clue at the time." Jack shifted the bag on his shoulder. "But we don't really have time for this. Sylvia's from Austin, and I'm the only paranormal investigator in town—or at least the only one with ties to the magic-using community. And Charlotte was a SPI client just a few weeks ago. So Sylvia's right—they could well be on their way."

As they passed through the shop, Marin gave Sylvia a hard look. "If this blows up, I know exactly who to blame."

Jack stepped between the two women. "Is your car out of the shop, Marin?"

"No, I'm still in a rental," Marin said.

"Right. We'll take my car." Jack shot Marin a warning look and murmured, "Not one word."

Marin rolled her eyes, but didn't utter one negative word about his Jeep. "Sylvia, how did you get here? And where are your bags?"

Bags, in other words, magical stash. Jack turned a sharp gaze on Sylvia. "Where *are* your bags?"

But Sylvia didn't reply. She was standing in front of Jack's Jeep with her mouth parted slightly. "Is it safe?"

Marin let out a rolling laugh.

Jack ignored her. "Definitely safe, and it runs great." Jack yanked hard on the back door to open it for Sylvia. "Bags?"

"Oh. At my motel." Sylvia settled into her seat then flinched when Jack slammed the door shut. She waited until Jack was in the car before she replied. "I couldn't exactly tote them all around with me, could I?"

Marin slammed her door harder than necessary. That door didn't stick—much.

"You left your..." Jack struggled to remember how exactly Sylvia had labeled her experiments. He groaned. "Portable plant-based weapons. You left them in your motel room."

"I didn't have much choice, did I?" Sylvia made a small, annoyed sound. "I took precautions."

Jack just hoped those precautions didn't include some kind of booby trap. Pulling out into the street, Jack said, "Fine. Which motel?"

After Sylvia provided the name, the three continued the ride in silence. Probably the best possible option at this point, because the tension was wearing on Jack.

2

When Jack pulled up in front of Sylvia's room, he was surprised to see it slightly ajar. "You did put the privacy sign out, didn't you?"

Sylvia leaned over Jack's shoulder, squinting at the cracked door. "I could have sworn that I did."

Jack shared a look with Marin. He took the keys out of the ignition then handed them to Sylvia. "If we're not back in three minutes, leave."

Jack took a breath and hopped out of the car.

"Do we have a plan?" Marin, close on his heels, asked.

"Not run into a water witch who can drown me in my own body fluids."

"First, disgusting. Second, only the really powerful ones can do that. And third, that is not helpful." Marin bumped into him as he paused on the stairs. When he turned around to give her a look, she said, "What?"

"Do *you* have a plan?"

"Clock's ticking. Get a move on." Marin shoved his shoulder for emphasis.

That's what he thought. But Jack refrained from comment and jogged the rest of the way up the stairs. When he got to Sylvia's door, he paused just long enough to see Marin was on his heels and walked into the room. No gun, no plan. He needed to do some life choice evaluating soon.

A young woman with earbuds and a cleaning cart wiped down the mirror above the sink. She caught sight of Jack and Marin in the mirror and screeched. She clutched the Windex drenched paper towel to her chest.

Relief rushed through him. Then he realized their late teen cleaner still look terrified. Apparently he looked scary even without a gun. Jack held both hands out. "No cleaning today."

No luck. He glanced at Marin and did double-take. Unnaturally green eyes flashed. He put an arm around her shoulders, whispered in her ear, "Eyes."

"Okay, honey bear. I'll just head down to the car."

Honey bear. And for that he felt completely justified in smacking her ass on the way out, the snarky shit.

"I'll come back tomorrow. But you need to put the 'Do Not Disturb' sign up if you don't want your room cleaned." The cleaner's accusatory tone left no doubt as to her feelings about the situation.

Jack didn't have long to wait before Sylvia appeared in the door with Marin.

"You are terrible at this." Jack shut the door behind them.

"What?" Sylvia's gaze darted around the room. "You found it?"

Jack shook his head. "You're terrible at being on the run. You forgot the door sign. And coming to Austin when you're from here...Not ideal."

"Too late to fix that." Sylvia's gaze darted around the room as she spoke. "Where did I put that chest?" She pulled something—a handful of dust, perhaps —out of her pocket and scattered it. No moer than an eye blink later, a blue plastic ice chest with a thick white lid appeared. "Besides, that's not my expertise. All of that running around and fighting and chasing. Much more appropriate for a fire witch or a water witch." Her lips pinched. "No, no. Not my area of expertise."

Jack had a bad feeling about "her area of expertise." He eyed the chest like it was a ticking bomb.

Marin pressed her lips together. But clearly she couldn't restrain herself. "An ice chest? You have your magical stash in an ice chest on wheels?"

Sylvia snapped the retractable handle up. "You have a better idea? I thought this was clever. A more stable temperature, easy to transport. It is very heavy, so it's difficult to get in and out of the car and up and down the steps. I took the elevator when I checked in. Otherwise, it works great."

"That's great, Sylvia," Jack said. "But is it safe?"

Sylvia patted the lid affectionately. "Of course." She blinked. "I mean, mostly."

Jack closed his eyes. "Okay. Is it safe enough for me to carry to the car?"

"Oh, definitely. Yes." Sylvia stepped away from her precious stash.

Jack decided that was an invitation, so he took charge of the chest. As he carried it down the steps, he decided that Marin could carry the damn thing next time. It was heavy as hell.

As he loaded it in the back of the Jeep, a thought occurred. "How exactly did you plan to get this on your flight?"

Sylvia wrenched the back passenger door open then gave him an innocent smile. "I was hoping you'd help sort out those little details, but I will be leaving a good portion of the content with you."

"Exactly how much do you have budgeted for expenses?" As he pulled carefully out into traffic, Jack tried not to think about what a rear end collision would do to his precious cargo.

"Enough. I think. Why?" Sylvia clutched at the big purse she had tucked under her arm.

Jack tried not to roll his eyes. "Do you have a large quantity of cash in your purse, Sylvia?"

Sylvia's lips twitched and she clutched her purse tighter, but she didn't answer.

"Jesus. Okay, never mind. We're getting a private plane out of Dallas. I hope." Jack chucked his phone at Marin. "Call Max and ask him to hook us up with a flight out of Dallas. Quiet, as little security as he can manage, as close as possible to an airport with a connecting flight to the UK." Jack shifted uneasily in his seat. He had an itching sensation at the back of his neck that didn't bode well. "And keep an eye out for other magic-users. Ii can't shake the feeling the Coven already has eyes on us."

"I'm not picking up anyone close, but I'm on it." Marin shot Jack a worried look then started hunting through his contacts for Max.

As Marin relayed their request to Max, Jack got on the northbound access road to the I-35 that itchy, uneasy feeling only getting worse.

Max would come through for him. The guy was a pilot and had connections all over the place. And if he didn't, Jack would just keep on driving. Maybe Canada. Then a freighter to England. Shit. He hoped it didn't come to that.

Marin hung up. "He thinks he can find us a flight on a small private plane out of the DFW area."

With no definite escape route confirmed, Jack wasn't surprised at his persisting twitchiness. But it made for an uncomfortable trip to Dallas.

. . .

THE "DFW AREA" turned out to be a tiny town thirty miles north of Dallas. Which left Jack grinding his teeth he weaved through miles of metroplex traffic and dodged the homicidal Dallas drivers en route to the airport. And the flight was only so far as a private strip near Boston. But Sylvia's ice chest made it on the plane, the owner-pilot of the plane didn't even blink when handed a wad of crumpled bills in payment, and the trio were that much closer to England. All in all, a win. Jack couldn't believe they'd managed to avoid the Coven. Perhaps he'd underestimated Sylvia's stealth skills. Jack had just about convinced himself of this cheerful analysis when they landed in Boston. He was even feeling charitably disposed toward Sylvia in the taxi on the way to Logan airport. Yeah, he should have known better.

3

"You're freaking kidding me." Marin smacked Jack on the shoulder. "Our friends beat us here."

The cab had just pulled into the terminal's drop-off area, so whoever Marin sensed must have been waiting for the three of them. Jack scanned the slow stream of late night drop-off traffic. A useless endeavor without his specially warded specs, since he couldn't see or feel magic any better than the next non-magical guy. "Where?"

"Not sure yet." Marin leaned forward from the back seat of the taxi van. "But I can feel it. My scalp itches with—" She stopped and shot the taxi driver a quick look.

He didn't seem to be paying any attention.

How did the bastards know about Boston? Jack gave Sylvia a look. "No cell phone, right?"

"I already told you: no. I didn't have one before I left. And I wasn't about to get one for this."

"Who doesn't have a cell phone these days?" Marin asked, still scanning the travelers.

"Are you kidding me? You of all people—I mean, someone your age—should get that." Jack, sitting in the front seat of the taxi, waved the driver on as he began to slow. "Keep going."

Marin pointed. "There."

Jack pushed her hand down. "Never mind. Let us out here. Right here." When the taxi driver started to protest—there wasn't room at the curb because he'd passed up the previously open spot—Jack interrupted him. "It's fine."

Jack shoved a hundred in the guy's hand and hopped out. He fetched their bags from the back of the van while Sylvia searched the crowd for the offending Coven member.

"Just because there's a witch here, that doesn't mean they're Coven. Witches do travel a little."

Marin pulled the chest out of the back. She scanned the immediate area then said, "Like we'd be that lucky." She slammed the hatch down, snapped out the handle on the chest, and glared at the rolling stash of magic goodies like it carried the plague—or something less curable. "We can't get this on the plane; why are we even messing with it? And how the hell are we going to outrun them now? They know we're here."

"We're in a massive public airport. What are they going to do?" Jack picked up both his and Marin's bags.

Sylvia and Marin shared that look he sometimes got from magic-users—the one that said, Jack's an idiot.

Jack shifted the bags to one shoulder and grabbed Sylvia's. "Come on."

As he moved to the airport entrance, Marin crowded in from behind him. She spoke in low, even tones. "A woman is approaching from the left. Mid-thirties, dark brown hair, glasses, no luggage."

"Got her." Jack couldn't miss her. Everyone in the vicinity had some kind of bag or purse—except the witch. "She doing anything?"

"Gaining on us. Walk faster," Marin said as she almost clipped Jack's heels.

"Wait." Slightly out of breath, Sylvia tugged on Marin's shirt. "Air witch." She heaved a breath. "Need to—I" She gasped. "Line of sight." And then she stopped speaking. It took everything she had to keep pace with Jack and Marin.

"Shit." Marin's head swiveled from left to right and back again. "That bitch witch is suffocating her, Jack. We need to get her out of sight. All of us out of sight."

Jack pointed to the food court up ahead. If they could make it that far. Sylvia was starting to stumble and gasp for breath. Jack threw an arm around her shoulders and propped her up while he pulled her with him. Three bags, a stumbling middle aged woman, and an aggressive air witch on his ass—he might be getting a little too old for this.

They finally made it to the food court and not a moment too soon. Sylvia swayed under his supporting arm and her lips had a faint tinge of blue. Jack tried to get her to sit on the cooler, but she shoved away his assistance.

"No—" As soon as she spoke, Sylvia erupted into a fit of coughing.

Jack looked around at the handful of curious passers-by. Even as thin as the crowds were, much more of this and security would definitely show up. He smiled blandly. "She's fine. Asthma." Turning to Marin, he lowered his voice and said, "And the security cameras? Don't suppose you can do anything about that?" Marin was kneeling in front of the chest. She'd flipped it open so the contents were hidden by the wall on one side a Jack and Sylvia on the other. "Maybe. What do you need, Sylvia?"

"Red...blood." Sylvia waved a hand and pointed, but she hadn't recovered enough to speak.

Jack popped his head around the corner. "Shit. Pick one. She's almost here."

Marin fumbled around and pulled out a red plastic container.

"No!" Sylvia's hastily barked response brought forth a fit of coughing. "Flow...flower." She pursed her lips, mimicked blowing, and with her fingers illustrated movement away from her mouth.

"Got it." Marin pulled out an upside-down glass jar. Inside was a brilliantly red, spiky flower.

Jack motioned for the plant, but Marin ignored him and approached the corner, unscrewing the cap as she went. She carefully pulled the glass up and away from the flower and held the cap—to which the plant was firmly affixed—then she stepped out from their temporary hiding spot.

She didn't go far, maybe three steps, and then held the flower up and—nothing. The lights flickered for the space of a heartbeat.

The next thing Jack saw, Marin held a plant with a nude flower. The spiky petals lay withered at the feet of their pursuer.

Jack turned to Sylvia. "What exactly does this thing do?" He started to gather the bags he'd dropped.

Before Sylvia could answer, Marin was already beside him. She hadn't lingered to witness the result, just retreated. The color had washed away from her face. "I suspect the coven has some way of shielding this type of mess from mundane law enforcement, but if..." She swallowed, her face twisting in a grimace. "Hopefully the cameras didn't catch anything important."

"Are you ok?" Jack asked.

Marin gave him a curt nod and then avoided his gaze.

Message received. But he made a note to ask at some point in the future when they weren't in mortal danger.

Jack darted a quick look over his shoulder. Their tail was on the ground, heaving her guts up. Not quite projectile vomiting, but she was still making a wide-spreading, foul-smelling mess. She clutched at her stomach and heaved again and again. "What does that flower do, exactly?"

Sylvia's color had returned, but she spoke slowly, first taking a measured breath. "It's similar to food poisoning. Basically harmless." She erupted into a fit of coughing.

Jack hesitated, and then put a steadying hand under her elbow. "Uh-huh. We don't share the same understanding of *harmless*."

After a few clear breaths, Sylvia picked up the pace, leaving the moans and putrid stench of her victim behind. "Very bad, mostly non-lethal, food poisoning." She shrugged. "Harmless."

Jack thought back to Sylvia's reaction when Marin had pulled out the red plastic container. If instantaneous food poisoning was "harmless" then whatever was in *that* container must be terrifying. Jack tried to look inconspicuous as they moved through the terminal. Easier now that Sylvia no longer appeared to be in distress. The ice chest didn't help, but they weren't drawing many curious looks.

"I'm not really sure how a blown dart reached an air witch target, but one must have," Marin said. Her color looked normal but she still didn't look quite right.

"All of them." Sylvia's tart response interrupted Jack's speculation of what Marin had done to dim the lights, and why it had made her so ill.

An image of the withered petals at the air witch's feet came back to Jack. That was one nasty plant.

"They're hungry little flowers." Sylvia spoke with a fondness that reminded Jack of an aunt speaking of a favored niece or nephew.

"Clever." Marin shot Sylvia a respectful look.

Sylvia tipped her head, acknowledging the compliment. Finally, something they could bond over: cool weapons.

Jack shook his head. Giving Marin a pointed look, he said, "Hey. You need to be scanning the area for the second wave."

Sylvia confirmed, "She won't be alone. And that was my only blood lily." Her lips twisted, and then she added slowly, "Some of my other inventions aren't so crowd-friendly."

Again Jack thought of the red plastic container. "Well, there are hardly crowds of people this late at night. So think about what might work if we can get them alone but in an open space."

Sylvia nodded, her eyes getting a faraway look.

So Jack kept an eye on Sylvia, and Marin kept an eye on everyone else as they headed to the ticketing area. Unfortunately, it didn't take long for Marin to spot the next wave.

"We've got a pair this time. Maybe fire witches?" Marin hovered for a second indecisively.

"Not very powerful, probably muscle." Sylvia blinked when both Marin and Jack stopped and looked at her. "What? That's why you can't tell for sure, Marin. Not much juice."

"Well, it doesn't take much magic to start a fire— just to control its movement and the damage," Marin said. "Much more dangerous in a public arena than more powerful witches."

And the witch duo was, of course, in between them and the ticket counter.

"All right. What can they do?" Jack pulled his two companions to the side, near a wall. Hopefully making them less conspicuous.

"Set things on fire, control heat—"

Jack interrupted Sylvia's list. "Specifically to us, not the environment."

"Ah. Well, setting people on fire magically is harder than you'd think. Probably not that." Sylvia's tone was matter of fact.

Jack rubbed the bridge if his nose.

"Yay," Marin said in a flat tone. "Not burned alive —probably. Tortured—definitely."

Sylvia tilted her head. "But probably no permanent harm."

Jack looked at the petite salt and pepper-haired woman. When was he going to stop being surprised by the words coming out of this woman's mouth?

"Hey, guys? They're headed this way," Marin said.

Turning to the ice chest, Sylvia said, "I have two things..." She leaned in and dug around.

"Shit. Security is headed this way, too." Not that Jack was surprised. They'd lurked, lugged around a suspicious ice chest, and were now weirdly huddled.

"Oh, yes. I have the perfect thing." Sylvia shoved a cookie in Jack and Marin's hands. She took a bite of her own. "Eat. Hurry up. All of it." Immediately she returned to dig in the chest.

Marin didn't pause, just shoved the cookie in her mouth. The entire thing. Since Marin could perceive magic—its type and sometimes its function—Jack steeled himself and then followed her lead, hoping she hadn't suddenly discovered blind faith in Sylvia's concoctions.

He'd barely formed the thought that the chewy center had a pleasant lemon-ginger flavor, when the air filled with a fine powder. Jack covered his mouth and nose, but it was too late. He choked down the half-chewed cookie in his mouth and struggled not to gag. His nose had already filled with powder. Tears streamed from his eyes and he punched at his thigh. He was keeping that damn cookie down. No time to think what the powder would do if he didn't.

As his vision cleared, he saw the two fire witches bent over, gasping and coughing, only feet away. They'd clearly received the bulk of the...whatever the hell it was. Dry-eyed and breathing easily, Sylvia calmly walked away from the group. In one hand, she clenched the extended handle of the ice chest. and in the other she firmly clasped Marin's hand. Marin followed blindly, her eyes swollen and her face tear-drenched. Sylvia motioned with her head for Jack to follow.

Where were the security guards? Jack scanned the surrounding area as he slowly stood upright. The guards were walking away slowly, their hands outstretched, reaching into the air. Blind? Both men moved erratically but without panic. Confused?

Sylvia hadn't paused in her retreat and she was almost to the exit doors, when she called over her shoulder. "Jack? We *are* leaving?"

Jack trotted in her direction, their bags banging against his side. He nodded as he chuffed out a hoarse breath. He couldn't cough. Once he started, he wouldn't stop. His throat burned with his efforts to hold it in. When he reached Sylvia and Marin, he turned to see their fire witch friends recovered enough to see them walk through the exit door.

"Shit. They saw us leave. What the hell was that?"

"Devil's weed." Sylvia tipped her head. "Tweaked slightly."

Marin dabbed at her eyes with her sleeve. "More than slightly. That's some powerful shit."

Sylvia raised her hand to flag a cab. "But not lethal." She frowned as a cab pulled up. She turned to look at Marin. "You must be very young for your eyes to be so sensitive."

A low growl emanated from Marin's vicinity. But she didn't say anything as she packed the ice chest into the taxi's trunk.

Jack dropped their bags in next to the ice chest.

"Well, at least you have lungs of steel." Jack hopped into the cab after Marin. Lowering his voice, Jack asked, "What exactly does devil's weed, *your* devil's weed, do?"

Keeping her voice low, Sylvia said, "Confusion, temporary memory loss, hallucinations. My potion's not lethal—I made sure." The last was added in an earnest tone.

Since everyone had been alive when they left, Jack figured she *had* made sure—but that the question even came up was telling. About devil's weed or about Sylvia's potions, he wasn't sure.

"Where to?" The cab driver interrupted them and shot the trio an uninterested look over his shoulder.

Jack rolled his shoulders, trying to think of a good escape route. He didn't know Boston.

"Someplace central, public, lots of space," Marin told the driver. "And not far."

The first glimmer of interest sparked in their cabbie's eyes. "Boston Common? It closes at 11:30, but that gives you an hour or so."

"That works." Marin dropped back against the cushion of the seat. "You don't have a phone. Do you have any kind of electronic device, Sylvia?"

"Something with a GPS signal, specifically?" Jack added.

He and Marin both turned to look at Sylvia.

A perturbed look crossed her face. "I've already told you: no. But how we managed to fly into Boston of all cities." She gave both Jack and Marin an annoyed look. "Boston? It's a hotbed of Coven activity."

Jack closed his eyes. Very slowly, he said, "Now you tell us."

"How am I supposed to know what information you do or don't have?" Sylvia's aggravation leaked into her voice, raising it somewhat.

"All right," Marin said sharply. "Boston's not the best choice, but it was the one option we had at the time. We need to figure out if the Coven has some way to track you, or if they've just been incredibly lucky. What did you bring with you?"

Sylvia took a deep breath. "What I'm wearing, my bag, some toiletries, three changes of clothes, and the ice chest filled with my projects."

"Your purse?" Jack reached a hand out.

Sylvia passed him the large bag she'd held clutched against her chest.

"If there's nothing, it might be geo-locater." Marin wrinkled her nose and scrunched up her eyes. "That would suck."

Jack looked up from rummaging in Sylvia's purse. "That would suck."

"Here." Marin took the purse and dumped its contents in between her and Jack. She examined the empty bag and then plopped it down in Sylvia's lap.

Marin rummaged through the items, replacing them in the purse when she was done with them. A small toiletry bag, a nightgown, a sandwich, a veggie-juice drink, a wallet with no personal photos inside, an envelope with a wad of cash, and a small notebook with a fancy pen tucked into a holder on the side.

When all the items were once again in Sylvia's bag, Marin said, "Nothing looks suspicious."

Sylvia hugged her arms close. "Of course not. I checked. My bag and the ice chest, too. There's nothing that has the taint of another witch's magic."

"Hey. We're almost there. Any place in particular you want to be dropped?" The cab driver didn't even bother to look back when he spoke.

Apparently the little trio had lost their driver's interest during the uneventful trip. That was one piece of good news: their driver must not have gotten an earful.

"No," Marin said. "Anywhere's fine."

He didn't acknowledge Marin's response but he did pull over about two minutes later. Jack was curbside, so he hopped out and went to the front passenger window to pay while Marin grabbed their bags.

Jack handed the cabbie a fifty.

The driver hesitated, and then said, "One piece of advice. You wanna avoid the Coven, you ditch the witch and leave Boston as soon as you can."

Jack looked at the driver closely for the first time. Deep wrinkles etched grooves in his tanned face, dark brown eyes peered out from beneath shaggy white eyebrows—then the cab was gone.

Jack turned around to see Marin and Sylvia looking equally perplexed.

Marin shook her head. "Don't ask. He felt human to me."

Jack finally turned his attention to the park and got his first look at Boston Common. "Holy shit. How big is this place?"

"Big. Let's get rolling; I don't want to stand around on the street with a huge sign that says: Coven of Light, come take me now." Marin turned toward the Common, but she turned back when they didn't immediately follow her. "We just need a spot to sit down and figure out next steps. Preferably where we can see them coming."

"Sorry," Jack mumbled. He couldn't move past the taxi driver knowing about the Coven, and Marin was already tackling the next problem. He wasn't exactly on his game.

They entered the Common on a well-lit path, the ever-present ice chest rolling along behind.

4

J ack, Marin, and Sylvia traveled down the Common path at a moderate speed. Much more and Jack couldn't miss the strained breathing sounds Sylvia made. Since he didn't particularly want to carry her, they kept to a speed that Jack found teeth-gratingly slow. He couldn't help but imagine the hot breath of Coven pursuit on his neck.

"Um, hello." Sylvia caught up the few feet she'd lagged behind. "I think—"

"Yeah, they're here. I can feel them." Marin's terse statement jerked Jack up short.

"How the hell did they find us?" But if Marin or Sylvia knew the answer to Jack's question, they'd obviously have said something long before now. A plan—he needed to move forward. "How far?"

Marin turned to look behind them, walking

backward down the path for several steps. She scanned the surrounding area. "Nothing I can see."

"You really want to avoid line of sight with most witches." Sylvia supplied this information in a helpful tone.

"Yeah—I'm getting that." Jack stopped. A plan. He laughed and shook his head as the cab driver's words came back to him.

Marin gave him a nasty look. Her frustration was palpable. "On a timetable here, Jack."

"Our cabbie was brilliant. 'Ditch the witch and leave Boston.'" Jack surveyed Sylvia and her gear: no jewelry, the clothes on her back, the purse he'd already gone through, her bag—which they hadn't yet made time to search. "Ditch the bag and strip off your clothes."

Marin hesitated just a hair and then lifted the bag she'd been carrying for Sylvia ever since they'd left the cab.

"Wait!" Sylvia grabbed the bag. "My letters," she explained as she rummaged through the bag. She pulled them out and shoved the bundled stack into her purse.

Marin yanked some jersey shorts and a t-shirt out of her bag. "My PJs will have to do." She scanned the area for passers-by then said, "Quick, before someone comes along."

Jack turned his back and alternated between studying the map he'd pulled up on his phone and keeping an eye out for anyone walking up the path. There were just enough trees that you couldn't see into the distance—so no line of sight. But it was hardly heavily wooded. He could just imagine explaining to Boston PD why they'd been hanging out with a naked woman on a public path.

"All right," Marin said.

When Jack turned around, Sylvia was dressed in navy knit shorts that reached to just above the knee and a bright green shirt. Oversized flip-flops covered her feet. She leaned down and picked through the contents of her purse, now dumped on the ground. She huffed out a harsh breath and then shoved the cash and the letters into a reusable cloth shopping bag that Marin must have provided and left the rest.

"Whatever you're going to do with this stuff, do it now." Marin caught Jack's gaze. "They're close."

Sylvia rummaged in her ice chest.

"I'm developing a love-hate relationship with that thing." Marin eyed the chest suspiciously.

Sylvia pulled out a glass flask that had been bubble wrapped. "Oh, maybe we should move them to the path. I don't want to kill the grass."

Marin rolled her eyes. "I could have set them on fire." But she quickly moved the items onto the main path in a tidy path.

Jack bit back the natural response: why didn't

you? Because, really, he should have thought of that himself.

Sylvia shooed them away, then tossed the flask on the pile from about three feet away. As soon as the glass broke, the entire pile blazed with bright flames. She briskly walked away, grabbing the ice chest handle as she passed it.

As the threesome walked away, Jack looked around at the green grass, the trees—the fuel that surrounded them. "Are we going to be reading tomorrow about the Common going up in flames? You can't tell me that stuff was harmless."

"Mostly harmless. A little creosote bush and torchwood powder won't set the park on fire." Sylvia winced and limped along for a few feet. Ill-fitting flip-flops weren't exactly the greatest footwear for a woman on the run.

Jack grabbed the chest handle from her. "Yeah, but we're talking magically enhanced torchwood. I'm guessing the regular stuff doesn't burn when exposed to air."

"Seriously, Jack, I hope you had more in mind than getting rid of Sylvia's gear," Marin said. "For all we know, her ice chest is bugged. Or she is."

"No. I don't think that's possible. The ice chest is a last minute purchase and wasn't out of my sight before I left—and you can't bug a person without them knowing." Sylvia huffed a little, trying to catch her breath. "I don't think."

Jack could only think of a few possibilities. He grabbed the handle of the retracting handle of the chest from Sylvia. "The entire city is warded, or—"

"No way," Marin said. "Las Vegas was a bizarre anomaly from everything I've heard. And impossible to miss when you passed through the ward. And don't forget, that's big spell caster magic. I don't see any Coven members playing well with local spell casters."

That was an understatement considering what happened to two Coven members who'd recently tried. Jack wouldn't soon forget the sight of a man drowning in his own body fluids. "Yeah. What about a geo-locater?"

Sylvia stopped to catch her breath. "Where are we headed?"

"Park Street Station," Jack said, glancing again at his phone. "Shouldn't be much farther."

Marin handed Jack her bag. "Come on. I'll give you a ride."

"I'm sorry?" Sylvia blinked at her in confusion.

"Piggyback. You must have done it as a kid. Come on." Marin couldn't hide the grin spreading across her face as Sylvia wrapped grabbed hold of a bunch of t-shirt to stabilize herself. Sylvia's discomfort was clearly cracking her up.

Jack gave Marin a narrow-eyed look

"Whatever. They're still back there checking out the pile of ash we left."

Once Sylvia and Marin had figured out the dynamics of piggyback transport and they were headed to the station again, Jack said, "So—geo-locater? Do we think that's a reasonable possibility?"

"Oh, my. That would be bad." Sylvia seemed to have gotten over her embarrassment. Now her attention was focused primarily on not losing her flip flops as Marin trotted along at a good clip.

Jack tried not to shake his head. Surely Boston Common had seen weirder things?

"Any chance you know how to block a geo-locater?" Sylvia sounded a little huffy.

"We don't know how to keep you from being tracked—by a geo-locator or anyone else. But at least if we can figure out how they're doing it, we can try. So I'd say that's a good next step." Marin managed to reply and shift Sylvia around to a more comfortable position without slowing.

Thank God for dragons. And maybe he should up his running schedule to four times a week.

"I'll call Harrington and see what he knows. We need to 'ditch' you metaphorically. Make you look like you've disappeared. Preferably like you've died. Then we quietly slip away home while you travel on to England. Because, at this point, they'll be looking for you wherever Marin and I go."

Sylvia's eyes got big. "You're going to kill me off." Before Jack could assure her that they weren't actually going to off her, Sylvia said, "Why didn't I think of that?"

The subway station finally appeared. Not much further. *Thank God.* Jack unclenched teeth that felt cemented together.

Marin gently lowered Sylvia to the ground at the entrance of the subway station. And Sylvia had even managed to hang onto her flip-flops.

Jack checked the schedule on his phone. "Five minutes, if it's running on time. How close are they?" He started to dial Harrington's number but paused before connecting, waiting for Marin's answer. When she didn't reply, he looked up.

Marin stood completely still, facing the direction they'd just come from. Her stillness was so complete, Jack could feel the hairs rise on the back of his neck. He rolled his shoulders. He shouldn't let her creepy dragon shit get to him. He couldn't believe that it still did.

Finally, Marin turned around. "I think we lost them. They're not getting any closer. Maybe we ditched the tracker?"

"There were at least three or four turn offs between here and there," Sylvia said. "And witches can't track like Lycan. Or dragons."

Marin frowned in response, but didn't correct Sylvia's misperception that dragons could track by scent. Jack didn't get why the Lycan-Dragon scenting comparison bothered her so much.

Addressing Jack, Marin said, "Do you have an end destination in mind?"

"If we've lost them, I'd love a crash pad." As he spoke, an unengaged cab rolled by. Jack flagged him down. "If they're not on our heels, we're getting a room. You're sure?"

Cautiously, Marin said, "I can't sense any magic-users in close proximity."

Sylvia's mouth twisted. "I could really use some sleep—if we think it's safe."

"Enough with the sleep talk already." Marin stifled a huge yawn then threw open the door of the cab that had rolled to a stop in front of them.

Sylvia got in first and as she pushed through to the far seat, she said, "Know of a motel outside of town that takes cash?"

The driver's answering grunt must have meant yes, because she pulled out into the road as soon as Jack closed the door.

As the cab pulled away from the curb, an uneasy feeling crawled up Jack's spine. Their escape had been too simple and the loss of their Coven tail much too easy. Much as he hated to keep falling back on Harrington, he was Jack's best source. And Jack had to figure out how the Coven had been tracking Sylvia. Otherwise, how was he going to kill her off?

5

Jack closed the bathroom door of the cheap room he, Marin and Sylvia had just checked into. He'd gone with something outside of town in the hopes of escaping the Boston hotbed of witches. He flipped the cover of the toilet down and planted himself on the seat. Before he could talk himself out of it, he dialed Harrington.

Harrington picked up on the second ring. "How can I help you, Jack?"

Jack cringed. He already owed the guy one favor. "I might be able to help *you* out. I've got access to some recently developing intel that might interest you."

"In exchange for...?"

And here was the tricky part. Trying for a casual tone, Jack said, "Information for information. I could use a little background on magically tracking a person."

Harrington's response was immediate and sharp. "I'm not putting you in touch with Cliff."

Jack shifted, trying to find a more comfortable position on the hard seat. "I get it. I'm not asking for your precious geo-tracker. Just some information from you."

"Done. What have you got?"

"A Coven witch on the run, headed your way. Well, headed IPPC's way, to London. Not sure where she'll end up, but she'll be passing through London."

"Jack," Harrington chided. "You know we can't help. We have a strict non-interference agreement."

"Right. I'm not asking you to interfere. I'm letting you know she'll be in the area and, more than likely, open to answering some questions. If you have any." Jack shifted the phone to his other ear. "Or not. If you don't think she'd be useful."

"When?"

Just as Jack expected, Harrington couldn't pass up commitment-free intel on a rival organization, regardless of whatever non-interference agreements the two groups had in place.

"Not sure yet when she's landing, but I can update you."

There was silence on the other end of the line for several seconds. Finally, Harrington said, "Agreed. What do you want to know about tracking?"

"What methods are there? And is there a way to block them? Hypothetically, I'd like to make someone untrackable."

"You know about geo-locaters. As you're already aware, there's a way to tag a person or object so that a geo-locater can still actively track them from a distance. Then there's scent tracking."

"There's been no evidence of Lycan," Jack said.

"Lycan aren't the only magic-users capable of scent-tracking. But they do all utilize basically the same principles. Could you have been tracked by scent?" The tapping of keys in the background punctuated Harrington's response.

"Doubtful. Maybe in conjunction with some detective work and some other magical means—but not alone. Any hints for finding a geo-locater's tag? There are no electronics: no phone, no computer." Jack couldn't help but hope they'd destroyed whatever tag might have existed when they destroyed Sylvia's gear.

"Well, tracking through technology requires a gifted geo-tracker. You know they're rare. Fire is good if the tracking device is an object. But if the subject has ingested the marker and it's been absorbed into the subject's system, then only time will dissipate the signal."

Jack closed his eyes and let his head fall forward. "How long?"

"Two days? Three? No more than five at the most."

Shit. "Wait," Jack said. "Wouldn't Marin have picked up on the magic?"

"Possibly with an item. But if it had a relatively weak signal and she didn't know exactly what to look for, maybe not." Harrington tapped away on his computer. After a few seconds, he added, "And even less likely with an ingested tag."

"So it's likely there's a geo-locater involved. How the hell are we supposed to hide from someone whose gift is finding people?" Jack rubbed at his temple where a nagging throb had begun.

Harrington muffled some noise that sounded suspiciously like a laugh then the typing in the background started again. "My source doesn't think there's much talent locally. If a geo-locater is involved, they're close."

"Wait a second: are you IMing with Clifford?" Jack couldn't keep the incredulity from his voice.

Harrington made a noncommittal noise.

"That bastard. When I went looking for him, he didn't have a phone let alone a computer." Jack couldn't help a huff of laughter. "Good for him."

"He sends his greetings."

Jack smiled. Cliff was a funny little guy, and it was good news he was crawling out of his hole—well, his Welsh fortress-castle-prison—even if it was only virtually. "So, exactly how far does Cliff think the local talent could stretch?"

"Ten or twenty kilometers, but it's possible he's underestimating. He seems to think the local talent barely qualify as geo-locaters."

Jack considered the logistics of a short range tracker. Best guess, the Coven had used some old fashion detective work to track them to Boston. And once there, the fleeing trio had stepped into a web of Coven contacts—so their tracker could easily be in Boston. An escape plan was slowly forming.

"What about blocking? Scent, geo-trackers, whoever might be looking." Jack stood up and stretched out his back.

"You need a spell caster. A decent spell caster."

Of course he did. In retrospect, Jack couldn't believe his luck when Marin walked in The Junk Shop just weeks ago and asked him for a job. But, damn, a spell caster would be handy.

"Anyone reliable in the area who would considering subcontracting?" Jack asked.

"You're in Boston, Jack. A heavily Coven-inhabited area. Any remotely trustworthy spell caster will be well outside the city. I think we've got a few contacts in the vicinity." Harrington typed away on his computer, but it didn't take him long. "I can give you three names, but—"

"I know. IPPC didn't refer me, isn't asking them

to help me, and generally has nothing to do with any of this."

Harrington sighed. Audibly. "Correct."

Jack opened the bathroom door and as he walked out made a writing motion at Marin. "I get it. Go ahead."

Marin handed him a piece of paper and pen, and Jack jotted the three names down. "Where are they?"

"Salem," Harrington said. "Outside the city limits, but not far by rail or ferry."

"You're kidding. Salem?" Jack underlined the word Salem on the scrap of paper several times.

"It's not a witch-friendly town, in part due to its history. And that has made it somewhat welcoming to spell casters. It's not exactly a thriving community; it's too close to Boston. But it's close."

"I thought you weren't particularly well-informed when it came to the Coven and witches in general."

"Improving intel has been a recently added objective. The information and the contacts are good." Harrington's tone was terse. "You'll update me with arrival information?"

"Yeah."

Jack pocketed his phone. Typical Harrington— no goodbye.

Jack retrieved the scrap of paper off the dresser, headed to the sofa, and collapsed in a heap. He was exhausted. "I've got the names of three local spell casters. With any luck, one of them will bite on a paying job involving a witch."

"A *Coven* witch," Marin said.

They both turned to Sylvia. Curled into a ball on her side, she dozed on top of the covers still clothed in Marin's T-shirt and shorts, the flip-flops abandoned next to the bed.

"You look like crap. Take a quick a nap, and I'll try to sort out a meeting with one of these guys. What exactly is it that we want?" Marin rummaged first in the dresser and then the closet where she pulled out a blanket. She threw it at Jack.

"A shield from tracking. Most likely a low- or mid-level geo-locator is involved." Jack shook the blanket out and tipped his head back against the cushions. "Or some other tracking method that's completely unknown to you, me, and IPPC."

"Right. I'll leave that part out, why don't I?" Marin picked up one of the key cards they'd been issued. "I'm going to grab a few snacks from the vending machine before I call. Be right back."

Jack grunted and pulled the blanket higher.

He must have slept soundly because the next thing he knew, Marin was shaking him awake. She shoved a small paper cup of coffee in his hand as soon as he sat up. God love her.

"Thanks." Jack downed half the cup in a few swallows. The coffee was still hot, so he hadn't been out long. He glanced at the bed and found Sylvia still asleep. "What have you got?"

"An appointment." Marin pushed aside a packet of cheese crackers, a bag of chips, and some jerky to retrieve the scrap of paper he'd given her earlier. There was an address scribbled next to one of the names. "Uh, Jack, I recognized one of the names. A guy who used to do some work for my dad every once in a while. I called him."

Jack took a sip of coffee, hoping it would settle the churning in his stomach. Where would he be without Marin? It was getting ridiculous, how much he relied on her. He chugged the rest of the coffee "Right. How long do we have?"

"We need to leave in five minutes. We're meeting in Salem."

Jack scrubbed his hands across his face. "All right. Give me a few minutes in the bathroom and wake up Sylvia."

JACK, Marin, and Sylvia huddled around a table at a small Salem coffee shop, warm drinks clutched close as they waited for their spell caster to show. Jack eyed the door, waiting for the mysterious spell caster Arthur to show up.

When a small, unassuming older man walked through the door, Marin tapped the ring on her middle finger against the table. Jack nodded at her then stood up and motioned to him.

Extending his hand, Jack said, "Arthur. We appreciate you meeting us this early."

Arthur shook his hand with surprising firmness. "'It's alright. I don't sleep much these days. You're Jack?" When Jack nodded, Arthur turned to Sylvia with a questioning look.

"Sylvia. Thank you for your help." She pumped Arthur's extended hand with an excess of enthusiasm.

Arthur smiled politely at Sylvia—without judgment as far as Jack could tell. When Sylvia eventually released his hand, he turned to Marin and a broad smile spread across his face. "Very nice to finally meet you. Greetings to your Dad."

After they'd all settled into their seats again, Arthur clasped his hands on the table. "You need to make someone untrackable?"

Sylvia raised her hand, a sheepish expression on her face. "That would be me."

"No idea how they're tracking you?" Arthur's eyes narrowed and he raised his hand. "Don't answer that."

Arthur studied Sylvia for several minutes. So long that Sylvia started to shift uncomfortably in her seat. Eventually, she clasped her hands and stared fixedly at them.

Arthur reached over and placed a hand on top of

Sylvia's. "Nothing too complicated. You must have eaten a warded item. Seeds work nicely. And beans, especially raw. It would have been within the last few days. Can you think of what...?" Arthur removed his hand and leaned back in his chair.

Sylvia's lips had thinned, and her face tensed.

"You know what it was?" Arthur asked. When she hesitated, he said, "Or you suspect."

"Sunflower seeds. A friend—" Sylvia cleared her throat. "Another Coven witch brought some by a few days ago. I had no idea." She gave her head a small, firm shake and attempted a smile. "I know what they're like. I'm not sure why I'm so..." She shook her head again.

"Well, the seed is long gone at this point, but with a tracking ward a person only has to ingest it for the ward to tag them," Arthur said. "After consumption, it's simply a matter of how much juice the geo-locater invested in the tag. I'm guessing not much. The duration of the tag is affected by the magical energy attached to the tag. The distance the subject can be tracked is a function of both the magical energy attached to the tag as well as the talent of the tracker."

As Arthur detailed the exact nature of geo-tagging, it occurred to Jack that the man had a great deal of information. Jack didn't want to alienate their newfound and very informative source, but once his suspicions were raised... "You know a lot about geo-tagging."

"Arthur's partner was a geo-locater." Marin mouthed "sorry" to Jack.

Jack made a mental note never again to nap and leave Marin in charge. Ever. And a reminder to smack himself when he wasn't so damn tired.

Before Jack could feel like crap for not apologizing—because he wasn't about to—Arthur had picked up the narrative again.

"As I was saying, this tag has neither great distance nor great duration. Not surprising, really. Not much local talent." Arthur's gaze drifted away, unfocused for a moment then he seemed to collect himself. "By locally, I mean in the States. We don't have much geo-locating talent. Wales, the East Indies, a sprinkling in Australia and New Zealand—that's where the tracking talent is. And a few outlier pockets scattered here and there, of course."

"We appreciate you coming out of retirement for this, Arthur." Marin shot Jack a warning look. "Any chance you can give us some specifics? A timeline? A range?"

Sylvia, looking confused, said, "How do you retire from spell casting?"

Arthur smiled and a lightness overtook his features for the first time since they'd sat down. "I suspect in much the same manner you're leaving the Coven." He tilted his head to the side. "Without the life-threatening flight. I moved and didn't connect with the local community—what little of it there is. But back to the matter at hand, before the young man has a coronary. Two days, at a guess, before your tracking tag fades. But that's immaterial. I can create an invisibility ward that extends well beyond your tagger's talents."

Sylvia's eyes went wide. "But I won't be actually invisible? I've never heard of such a thing."

"No, not invisible. If you want to be untrackable, that's an invisibility ward. You'll be hidden from the nosy folk: geo-locaters and on a more limited basis from Lycan and other scent trackers." Arthur waggled grey eyebrows at them. "I'm very good at invisibility wards. Not many spell casters are."

Jack found himself smiling even though he was pretty sure they were sitting ducks in the café, and he was pretty sure he'd be on a Coven hit list after this. Arthur was likable. Speaking of being sitting ducks... "It's been about 2 and a half hours since we last ran into the Coven. We thought we'd destroyed whatever was tracking Sylvia. But now that we know we didn't—how exactly did we manage to evade them for that long?"

"An unreliable local tracker, maybe. Perhaps you ventured outside the tracker's range." Arthur gave Jack a sad smile. "You'd never have shaken Francis. My partner. Francis was a gifted tracker, one of the best. He was Welsh, of course. Not American."

A heavy silence followed. Clearly, Arthur had lost his partner. And just as clearly, he'd been devoted to the man.

Arthur cleared his throat. "So, I'd guess that either luck or an incompetent tracker might have helped you along."

Sylvia rubbed her eyes. "Thank the heavens for the Coven reluctance to associate with other magic-users. They probably have no idea their tracker is sub-par." She tipped her head. "Though I suspect they're learning and he won't outlive this particular assignment."

Jack shook his head at her callousness. "Yeah..."

"On the off chance that your pursuers have managed to track you through other means to the area, I've set up some security for our meeting this morning. I scrambled the geo tag. It will read like Sylvia's popping in and out of range. I didn't want to mask the tag entirely." Arthur lifted both hands in casual gesture. "Without knowing your plans, it seemed the safest course of action."

"Arthur, you are a gentleman and a scholar." Jack leaned forward. "Here's what I'm thinking. Sylvia, you have to disappear before you leave the country. And the best way to make sure you disappear is to kill you."

Sylvia clapped her hands together. "I love it. If I'm dead, no one's following me. It's perfect."

Arthur nodded. "I can ward a piece of jewelry or

clothing. It's easy enough to make a ward that activates when it's worn. Then once you've been killed off officially, you can trigger the invisibility ward."

Marin removed a ring from her left thumb, a simple silver band she wore most days, and handed it to Arthur. "Will this work?"

Arthur took the ring, examined it briefly, and nodded.

"But how do we kill me?" Sylvia asked.

That was the question.

J ack scanned the small outdoor area. He hoped sticking around in Salem had been the right plan. That this was a good place to implement their plan. He rubbed his temple, hoping the looming headache would fade. At least Salem had to be better than Boston.

"Jack! This is important." Sylvia held up a glass container. "These aren't labeled."

Jack pulled his attention back to the small table where Sylvia had placed a few of her potions. He couldn't help it; the crawling sensation on the back of his neck was telling him something wasn't right.

"I got it. The round, chemistry-set-looking flask is fire. The peanut butter container has glitter that sticks and burns. The test tubes with the corks fluoresce after they've been shaken."

Sylvia closed her eyes and inhaled slowly. "Vigorously shaken."

When she opened her eyes again, Jack said, "Vigorously shaken—got it. So I'm a little distracted. Can you blame me?"

She sighed. "No—but you need to know what each of these containers holds. And the peanut butter jar isn't glitter. Those are small seeds. Don't let them touch your skin. They won't actually burn you, but any contact and you'll feel like you're on fire." Sylvia fiddled with the material of her new skirt, bought a half hour earlier from a small boutique they'd stumbled across as they'd put their plan in place. "I can't believe they didn't catch up with us while we were shopping."

Jack glanced at his phone. Almost noon. "Exactly how incompetent is this tracker?"

Sylvia raised her eyebrows. "Maybe Arthur's scramble was better than he intended. Or they had to dig deep for some better evil-henchmen talent? Whatever the reason, my feet are grateful. Those flip-flops were terrible."

Marin appeared, a large takeout bag in one hand and a felt marker in the other. She handed the marker to Jack. "Great. Like the regular bad guys weren't bad enough. My vote's for Arthur. He probably tied their geo-locator's antennae in a knot."

Jack passed the marker to Sylvia. She shook her head but took it. "It's important you understand how each of these works." She started to carefully print instructions on the glass and plastic containers.

Jack took a bite of his burger, while Marin pulled out the rest of the food. He had a handle on the contents...then he remembered the insta-fire. A little caution was warranted. He turned to keep an eye on Sylvia's scribblings.

Marin stuffed a fry in her mouth. "Let's hope the supervillain angle is crap."

"I might be a traitor, but I'm still a witch. The run-of-the-mill Coven member may have no qualms about performing death magic on humans." A deep furrow appeared between Sylvia's eyebrows. "And others. But not witches. If you're drinking the Coven Kool-Aid, you believe witches are a higher form of being."

"Long story short, they may have more limited resources than appears at first glance." Marin said, and shoved another fry in her mouth.

Sylvia nodded. "But I'm pretty sure we haven't worked our way through Boston's squad of enforcers or upper management—all of whom would happily see me dead."

Jack had picked their outdoor location for visibility and ease of escape. He just wasn't planning for them to escape very far. "All we need is one of them to make a move. If they're much longer, we'll have to move to another spot. We don't want to broadcast the plan by making ourselves too available."

Sylvia replaced the cap on the marker with a firm snap. "Done. And I'm very uncomfortable with this part of the plan. This sitting around and waiting to get jumped part."

Marin and Jack exchanged a glance. They couldn't predict exactly how the Coven would strike next. Unanswered questions meant gaps—weaknesses—in their plan. But the plan was in place and rolling forward. Some fire and a little sleight of hand and, hopefully, Sylvia would be in the clear.

Jack didn't understand how Sylvia was protected from the flames, but Marin said it could be done. And having witnessed the complete control his dragon side-kick had displayed on a previous case—lighting up an entire room in seconds, destroying the contents but nothing else, then extinguishing the flames and leaving the charred remains cool to the touch in an equally short amount of time—yeah, Jack believed she could keep Sylvia safe.

"Jack."

From her irritated tone, Jack guessed wasn't the first time Marin had called his name. Not good; he had to stay sharp.

"Yeah. You got something?" Jack started to gather their trash.

"Not close, but approaching," Marin said. "Definitely witch."

"I guess it's time. There are three of them, by the

way." Sylvia stood up and grabbed the extended handle of the ice chest.

"You've got the ring?" Jack asked.

Without the warded ring that Arthur had created for them that morning, the plan would fail. Invisibility, his ass. Well, there'd been no way to verify it worked because she couldn't put it on until she'd "died." They were all placing a great deal of trust in Arthur.

Sylvia pulled at the ribbon hanging around her neck and showed him the attached ring. When he nodded, she stuffed it back under her shirt.

Marin stood up, scanning the surrounding area. "Let's go." Briskly, her hand on Sylvia's elbow, Marin ushered her in the direction of the small wooded area about fifty yards from the table.

That had been the point of choosing this particular area: food, a picnic bench, and a handy wooded area in which to disappear. Jack resisted the urge to actually cross his fingers as he jogged the few feet separating him from Marin and Sylvia. The short stretch to the woods seemed like a mile given their slow pace. And Jack still hadn't spotted their three pursuers.

And there they were. Jack caught sight of two men and a woman over his right shoulder. All three were weaving with determination through the light crowd of midday foot traffic.

Jack placed a hand on the middle of Sylvia's back. "Just a little faster."

She panted and almost tripped. "I am not—" She took a quick breath. "I'm in terrible shape."

"Panic doesn't help." Jack glanced over his shoulder again. They weren't going to make the pre-arranged spot. "You see that thick tree, the one with the low hanging branch?"

"Yes."

"That's where we're headed," Jack said.

"Jack?" Marin shot him a worried look.

"It'll work. It has to." Jack tipped his head, indicating their pursuers.

By the time they'd made it to the tree, one of the men and the woman were within thirty feet. Just as Jack slid behind the large tree, hugging close to Marin and Sylvia, the first salvo arrived. A glass shattered against the tree and a fog began to coalesce and rise from the ground.

"Water and earth. The fog is just fog—probably to obscure sight." Sylvia had caught her breath and spoke clearly. "But—ah—don't touch where that potion landed. I'm pretty sure it's a contact poison. Definitely not harmless."

"Wait—poison?" Jack said. Shit. "Not harmless" in Sylvia-speak meant *lethal*. "I don't remember any antidotes in your ice chest."

"I said, don't touch it," Sylvia snapped at him. "What happened to the third man? I think he's a low-level water witch. No boiling your insides or drowning you in your own blood." Sylvia spoke so matter-of-factly, without any sign of strain; it was disturbing. Jack wondered if that was key to keeping her calm: give her a task and keep her occupied. Or discuss torture. She seemed really comfortable with torture. And poison. And fire.

"Hey," Marin muttered. "The fog. The third man."

"Yeah, see if you can sense him in the woods." Jack turned to Sylvia and whispered in her ear, "We need to make sure he's not blocking your exit."

A loud, booming noise echoed through the small wood. And kept echoing. Jack sank slowly to the ground, the bark of the tree at his back digging into his flesh. That should hurt.

"...tree...poison." A woman's voice in the background.

Right. He shouldn't be touching the tree. God knew what that poison would do to him. Oh, yeah—kill him. He tried to get up. Couldn't.

Marin grabbed him and pulled him a few feet away. That was good. Poison was bad.

She was saying something—but the echo wouldn't stop.

Sylvia shoved a handful of weeds at him. She was digging into his shoulder. Burning him. He tried to scramble away. Couldn't move. Burning, everywhere. His shoulder. And the smell, the noxious smell of burnt flesh. His nose filled with it. He gagged. The world wavered.

Then Marin was holding his head between her hands. Hard. He blinked away the sweat in his eyes.

"Can you hear me?" Marin asked.

"Yes." Jack's voice sounded strange in his ears.

Still holding his head, Marin said, "You've been shot. Sylvia's stopped the bleeding."

"Weeds..." Jack wasn't sure what part weeds played. His muddled mind finally landed on the answer: earth witch, bleeding wound. Why was his brain so slow? And then he felt it: the fierce burning in his shoulder. He'd been shot. Marin had said.

"The yarrow will keep the bleeding in check. And Marin's fried the shooter. But I need to..." Sylvia pulled out the ring from under her shirt.

"Right." Jack reached his right hand over to hold the plants in place on his shoulder. Only halfway there and his vision swam.

Marin, still holding his head, squeezed hard. "Don't pass out, you jackass. Not until we're done."

"Awww, honey." Jack gasped as he inhaled. "I didn't know you cared."

Marin snarled something obscene, grabbed his right hand, and shoved it over the bunch of weeds on top of his wound.

Jack couldn't manage pressure, but he could hold them in place. For now. "The other two?"

"Inspecting the crispy remains of the shooter—

but likely not much longer." Marin's attention was riveted to some distant spot in the woods. "And local law enforcement is a problem."

The fog had dissipated, so the water witch had either lost his concentration or couldn't hold the fog for long.

"So—it's time to burn some shit already. How do we get them closer?" Jack asked.

Marin raised an eyebrow, "*You* sit there and try not to bleed. Besides, looks like they're headed this way already."

Jack couldn't see shit from his vantage point. But even if Marin couldn't see them approach, she'd feel it. What he wouldn't give for that ability.

They'd get closer, Sylvia would misfire a fire potion and appear to be consumed by flames, Marin would cover her in a protective layer of flame—Jack still didn't actually get how that would work—and Sylvia would put on the ring and slip quietly away behind a wall of flames. Simple.

But Sylvia's escape route had changed. And the angle of pursuit was different, changing the visual effect. And the cops might be on the way. And he was bleeding—barely, but still— and immobilized on the ground. *Shit*

Marin and Sylvia must have been talking while Jack had zoned out.

Sylvia rolled her stash closer to Jack. "We need

you to throw the fire flask." She pulled out a tiny perfume bottle and knelt next to him.

Jack knew he looked like shit—he felt like death. "Are you nuts?" But he swallowed as Sylvia the tipped the liquid down his throat.

As she held his head and Jack swallowed the last drop, Sylvia said, "Not nuts and mostly harmless." She leaned in whispered fiercely in his ear, "Thank you." Then stepped away.

It was heartfelt; Jack knew it. It wasn't the words; it was the look in her eyes—sad, hopeful, exhausted, grateful, all mixed together.

"Angles have changed, and I need to make a little more fire. That stuff should perk you up." Marin grabbed the chemistry set-looking flask, the one that basically exploded on contact with air and would set a good five by five area on fire. Handing it to Jack, she said very quietly, "Fire on three."

Jack pulled his right hand away from his shoulder, waiting for the pain, the burn, the fading vision. Nothing. He wrapped his good hand carefully around the neck of the flask.

Marin held up one finger, two fingers—

Jack could see movement out of the corner of his eye. Three fingers and an explosion of fire.

Tears ran down Jack's face as smoke stung his eyes. He cringed away from the flames only a few feet away. He couldn't see Marin. He couldn't see Sylvia. Had she remembered the ring?

Jack started to stand. He should have a few minutes left on that potion he'd swallowed. The world wobbled, his vision narrowed, but he focused on breathing, beating back the nausea. Finally, the world assumed a more stable aspect. Minor planning fail: how the hell was he supposed to stop the two pissed-off witches just on the other side of the wall of flames?

Jack reviewed his mental notes for some potion that would help him. But those notes were crap. Labels. Shit, he hoped that would work. He leaned down, expecting to feel faint, but found he was surprisingly clear-headed. Digging through the chest, Jack grinned as he realized that the two witches were still after him. Closing the gap, in fact. *Not* chasing Marin or the now invisible Sylvia.

Maybe their little gambit had worked. He pulled out the red plastic container that had freaked out Sylvia in the airport. Marked in clear capital letters, the container read, "NOT HARMLESS."

Jack choked in pain as a laugh escaped.

In smaller letters, there were instructions to throw, very far.

No mention of what it did or how fire would

affect it; it was a gamble. Jack checked the progress of his witch buddies, and that was the tipping point. They'd just about found their way around the edge of the flames and were closing in.

Plastic wouldn't break, so he averted his head and opened the container. Inside were four tiny bundles. Net sachets filled with God only knew what and tied with little pink ribbons.

He picked one up, careful to only touch the netting at the top, and closed the container again. He ducked out from behind the tree that hid him from the witches and hurled the pink ribbon sachet.

Light flashed, the ground rumbled. Jack fell back against a tree, clutching the red plastic container. As debris fell from the sky, Jack hunted some sound past the ringing in his ears. But the world was silent.

He looked down at the container in his hand. Hell. The cops were definitely coming now.

Jack took a breath, steeled himself for a possible witch zap and stuck his head out for a look. One still coming.

He opened the container and grabbed a second sachet-grenade. As he tossed the second grenade, he realized the guy was probably too close...blackness engulfed him.

Jack gained consciousness suddenly. Rhythmic punches of pain shot through his body. Acrid smoke filled his nose and burned his throat. His head felt like it was going to explode.

"Jesus, put me down." He tried to yell, but a weak croak emerged and his breath huffed out on a gasp with every other word.

Slung across Marin's shoulders in a fireman's carry, he bounced with each step jogging step.

No answer and the feeling of his skin, muscle, bones shredding with each step wouldn't stop.

Still. Quiet—no more thudding of his own pulse pounding in his ears. He opened his eyes, took a clean breath of air. He must have passed out again, because he could see the road where only trees were before.

They moved to the road, but in a gliding, smooth motion. A silver Mercedes. Nice. He really shouldn't get blood on—

"Jack. Come on; wake up." Marin's voiced drifted further, closer, and further.

A vice closed around Jack's finger. "Ahhh!" His eyes flew open.

Marin let go of his hand. "The healer needs you awake."

"Wha—" Jack was wedged into the backseat corner of a large car with Marin to his right.

The car door was open and a man was leaning in.

Jack tried to shift in his seat. "Shit." Pain. A gunshot. Bleeding.

Now he remembered. He held himself as still as possible. Too late. The wound throbbed to the beat of his heart. He shivered as a gentle breeze brushed against his wet skin. It was dark outside.

The man at the door leaned in further. "I have to touch you to evaluate and start the healing."

Jack winced, but he forced a response from his lips. "Yep. Permission given." Freaking healers and their bizarre code of ethics. Maybe if he got a little pissed about that, he could distract himself as the man poked.

"Fuck!" Jack yelled as the guy pulled material away from the wound. Jack panted and tried to catch his breath, make his ribs move less, be still, anything to lessen the pain.

A cool wash of numbness started in his shoulder and flowed to his weakened arm, his throbbing head, his aching and exhausted body. Jack closed his eyes and almost cried in relief. He took a pain-free breath and then another. He opened his eyes. "Thank you."

The man, dark-headed but with a bright red beard, nodded without letting his attention waver from Jack's wound.

Jack didn't want to say—but it had to be said. "Marin, I—"

"It's fine." Marin's lips were thin, her face tight. "It could easily have been me. I lost the shooter. That's why he got the shot off."

Jack coughed out a laugh. "Only one though."

"Yeah."

The healer stepped away. "I can't do much more. Mundanes are harder to heal—no magic to borrow."

The guy looked embarrassed, like he'd failed.

Jack was confused. "I feel a lot better. I mean, seriously better."

The healer shook his head.

Another man approached the open door of the car. Arthur. Where did Arthur come from? "Oh—this is your car?"

"It is," Arthur said. "What Ryan is trying to tell you is that your improved state won't last long. You need to see another healer when you get back to Austin."

"He needs blood." Ryan—apparently that was his healer's name—gave him a hard look. "Magic can't replace what's not there, and you've lost a decent amount of blood. Even with your witch's poultice, all the movement opened up your wound again."

"I can't go to the hospital. Any chance you have some saline? Wouldn't that get me by?" Jack looked between Ryan and Arthur, trying to gauge how big of a problem his injury was going to be.

"It might, but I don't have any. And, honestly, your witch didn't do you any favors when she juiced you with, what? Uppers? A strength potion? Not a great idea for a guy who's leaking blood." Ryan scanned the horizon.

Jack looked around. They were parked in the middle of nowhere. "Where are we?"

"New Hampshire," Arthur replied. And when Jack gave him a curious look, he shrugged. "I'm retired. I have a car. It wasn't a problem. Besides, I'm not particularly worried about pissing off the locals. I've decided Salem isn't really a good fit for me."

Great. Jack's guilt ratcheted up about five notches. They'd put their friendly, retired spell caster in the shit with the local Coven reps. Not that the guy seemed remotely concerned.

Ryan reached out and touched Jack's shoulder again. "If I can't convince you to go to the hospital, then get to another healer as soon as you can. I've done everything I can."

Jack could almost feel the magic flowing from the man as he gave Jack one last healing push. Certainly, he could feel the effects. He reached out and firmly shook the man's hand. "Thank you."

Ryan nodded and walked a short distance to a parked truck.

As the threesome loaded into the car, Arthur driving and Marin in the back with him, Jack tried to fit all the pieces together in his head. The entire afternoon was a tangle of partial memories and flashes of intense pain. "Sylvia's safe?"

"I think so. Either our sleight of hand worked, or I completely fried her." Marin lifted her hands. "I'm kidding, Jack. I didn't fry the client. She's fine. Safely uncooked and on her way. Whether she makes it to the cargo ship, that's another question."

Jack winced. "We didn't have a choice, but cargo sure as hell wouldn't have made my top ten."

Arthur caught Jack's gaze in the rearview mirror. "I doubt the Coven would consider it in their top ten, either. You're lucky you found a ship headed the right direction."

Jack tipped his head back against the seat cushion. "Two weeks to Germany, then from Germany to —" Jack stopped himself. Arthur was trustworthy, but there was no reason to burden him with the information. Eventually, after a few stops and possibly an IPPC debrief, Sylvia would make her way to England.

"With some luck, we'll hear from her in a month." Marin frowned.

"Says the dragon who didn't get shot. The client's tail was shaken and means provided for a relatively safe getaway. Mission accomplished." Despite his words, Jack couldn't suppress a desire for more closure. Not knowing sucked.

It hadn't taken them long to get to the Manchester airport. After a pit stop at a gas station where Jack changed his shirt and washed up, he and Marin boarded a perfectly normal, economy class flight to

Dallas where Jack's buddy Max would meet them. One brief text and Max had agreed to fly into Dallas, pick up Jack's car from the tiny airport outside of town, stock up on some basic medical supplies, and meet them at the DFW airport. With any luck, a little saline and some pain killers would keep Jack going long enough to make it home to Austin.

And it almost happened.

Marin and Jack's connection in Chicago was uneventful. And the first half of the flight was pretty good. That's how Jack remembered it. Marin said he looked airsick and the flight attendant checked on him three times. But Jack knew with certainty that the second half hadn't gone to plan because he remembered drifting in and out of awareness several times. And Marin being pissed at him and poking him a lot, and finally Max carting him around in a wheelchair at the airport. Yeah—not so great.

When Jack woke up the next morning in the hospital, Marin was slumped in a chair near his bed. He didn't think that was allowed, but it was good to see a familiar face so he wasn't complaining.

He desperately needed a pee. That had to be a good sign for a guy that had major blood loss recently. As he got up to hunt down a toilet, Marin's head jerked up.

She rubbed her eyes. "You look better. Marginally, but at least you can stand on your own."

"Yeah. Hey, what happened to my stash?"

Marin covered a massive yawn. "Your welcome, Jack. It was no problem carrying your ass through the woods. Or finding a healer in the middle of backwoods New Hampshire. Or faking my way through a flight with a recently gunshot nitwit. Or convincing the hospital staff to treat your serious anemia without running twenty diagnostic tests. No problem at all. But, yes, I did take care of your stash. Arthur's mailing it. I did let him pick something out as a thanks for packing it up and getting it here."

Jack couldn't restrain a massive grin. He even leaned down and hugged her like madman. Until he remembered he was wearing a hospital gown and had to pee like a racehorse.

"Hey, before you run off—Sylvia made it on board. One of Max's buddy's works at a travel agency, and she has a friend, who knows this guy... You know Max. He worked his connections."

Jack grinned. "That's all right."

By the time he got back, Marin had thrown his clothes on the bed and made arrangements for him to check. "Against your doctor's recommendation, by the way. They still want to run a bunch of tests. They don't understand why you were so dehydrated, had low blood pressure and anemia but couldn't find signs of recent trauma or other signs of blood loss."

"I'm a medical mystery."

"No, you're an accident-prone toddler who needs a high-level healer on staff."

Jack could hardly argue, given the number of times he'd needed a healer recently. "Yeah, but a spell caster sure as hell wouldn't hurt, either. Um, you're driving, right?"

Marin rolled her eyes and jingled the keys in her hand at him. "You drive like an old lady."

But Jack could see the worry behind her teasing. She must not be too pissed off at him. But that didn't lift the weight that had firmly settled over his chest.

EPILOGUE

Several days had passed since he and Marin had returned from Boston. They'd received a wire from a numbered account. Sylvia of course. Jack had worried. He couldn't agree that she was mostly harmless, but at least she knew where to draw the line. And the woman had mad skills in the garden.

But one question kept nagging at Jack. There'd been an unsettled, uncomfortable feeling between him and Marin since they'd returned. He wasn't sure if asking would push the atmosphere at The Junk Shop into an even murkier place or maybe clear the air. Either way, the question buzzed in his mind like an annoying gnat, and he wanted the answer.

He stepped into the doorway of his office, and he asked, "Why do you work for me?"

Marin dropped the file folder in her hand back

into the filing cabinet, and then she turned to look at Jack. But she didn't reply.

Jack walked into the office. "You don't need the money."

Although not a question, Marin shook her head slowly in response.

Her reluctance fueled his curiosity. Or maybe it was his anger. He didn't want to need her—but after several brushes with death it was clear he did. "You have better contacts. You're stronger, faster. You have magic." Jack shoved his hand through his hair. "It's your world, not mine. So, why do you work for me when you can do my job better than I can?"

Marin sank into Jack's chair. "You're wrong."

But she didn't explain.

"That's not good enough. Maybe we've only been together a few months, but the shit we've been through, the number of times you've dragged both our asses out of—" *His messes. His bad choices.* It made him even angrier to acknowledge it, but he wasn't about to lie to himself. He wouldn't be that guy. "I haven't worked out kinks, and I don't know the best ways to navigate in this world, but you still stay. Why?"

"Jack..." Her eyes shone bright, but she rubbed at the corners before anything resembling a tear could fall. She snorted. "Even my dad doesn't make me cry. Thanks for that." Her head fell back against the chair and she stared at the ceiling. She groaned then lifted her head. "Dragons don't really do their own thing. The entire clan is tied to McClellan's security company. In one way or another. And young dragons don't leave home."

Jack settled into one of the client chairs and kicked his legs out in front of him. "But you're young, and you don't work for McClellan. So apparently you *can* do your own thing."

"The jury's out. We live in a precarious place. The world moves by very fast, and we have to stay in touch with time as it passes."

Jack nodded. "You've said before. Some dragons go mad when they stop living in the present. But what better way to stay in touch than to live amongst the little people."

Marin curled her lip. "It's not funny. You're an impetuous shit, but I still like you enough not to want to see your life flash by in a series of short moments. I guess that's how the older dragons experience time...toward the end. Or if they lose touch with time."

"I'm still not seeing the problem. You bucked a cultural trend and left the nest."

"Supposedly, we don't do well alone, outside of the clan." Marin shrugged.

Jack narrowed his eyes, peering at her.

She sighed. "I can't work in an office. It's not the work—but the sameness, the routine, the small rooms. And I couldn't start a business by myself.

Show up to an empty building, go weeks without seeing the same person twice. It's just not for me." She looked up at the ceiling briefly—praying to the dragon gods for patience?—and then said, "So this —The Junk Shop, SPI, this job—it's a real option for me. And that's down to you."

"Are you seriously telling me that I'm your link to good mental health, dragon-style?"

She wrinkled her nose. "Let's just say you're *one* option."

It sounded like she needed him, too. He could breathe, really breathe, for the first time in a while.

Jack nodded. "Got it. Let me know if another option pops up." After a moment, he added, "I like having you here." He stood up. Past time to end this particular conversation. "I'll see you tomorrow."

"Yeah. Tomorrow."

For more of Jack and Marin's adventures, grab your copy of Spirelli Paranormal Investigations: Episodes 4-6! Keep reading for an excerpt from Episode 4: Something Nasty in the Attic.

EPISODE 4

SOMETHING NASTY IN THE ATTIC

ABOUT SOMETHING NASTY IN THE ATTIC

A new case with a surprising client...

Jack knew the critter living in his shop, affectionately referred to as Fuzzface, wasn't a rat. But what exactly was he? It wasn't surprising Jack was in the dark, since the creature had never let himself be seen. Small, clean, and with a preference for canned crab, Fuzzface had become an invisible but comforting presence in the shop.

Imagine Jack's surprise when he learns Fuzzface isn't an unobtrusive shop pet, but his newest client.

Jack pushed off from the counter and spun his new swivel stool. "I don't think you mentioned—why did you move out of your dad's house?"

Marin didn't bother to look up. "None of your business. Where did you get this crap? We'll never be able to sell this stuff." She pulled out a tangle of colorful plastic beads.

"Not true." Jack spun around again on his stool. "Mardi Gras."

"That's months away, but you're probably right. These will make great decorations. Or they will after someone untangles them all. And yes, I know that's me." She picked at the knotted mess, glancing periodically at Jack. Finally, she said, "Jeez, Jack. Stop it. You're going to puke."

Jack spun the stool one more time, just because

—why not? When the world around him stilled, it occurred to him that maybe, just maybe, Marin had been right. He didn't feel lightheaded, but he was pretty damn sure he was hallucinating. "Marin." His gaze remained fixed on the small creature that had appeared in front of him.

"What?" she snapped.

Without looking away from it, he asked, "Do you see a small, white, furry, uh, something near the office door?"

"Hey, that's exciting. Your hedgehog is coming out to say 'hello.' They're usually so shy." The sound of beads clattering on the table muffled her words. "Although you have been feeding him crabmeat."

Its nose twitched, and its big brown eyes moved from him to Marin and back again. If Jack didn't know better, he'd swear the thing smiled when Marin mentioned crab.

Jack sat as still as he could manage. "That is *not* a hedgehog." It looked more like a lab puppy than a hedgehog. But definitely not a puppy. He had no tail, a round body with short, stubby legs, and large brown eyes. It was the big, brown, mournful eyes that reminded him of a puppy.

"He won't disappear if you blink, Jack. Obviously he wants something."

In response, the furry creature dropped back on its haunches into a position that resembled a dog sitting.

"See. He's even getting comfortable." Marin's voice was getting closer.

It lay down.

"Uh, I think—this sounds nuts—but I think he understands you." Jack would swear the creature sighed.

"He definitely understands. Jack, meet your Arkan Sonney." Marin said, "Sir, may I present Jack Spirelli, as you know, the proprietor of the shop. I'm Marin Campbell. It's a privilege to meet you."

The little furry creature stood back up on his four legs and executed what looked to Jack like a very credible bow.

Jack wasn't sure what he was supposed to say. "Hi?"

Marin poked him in the ribs with an elbow. "A 'thank you' wouldn't hurt. This gentleman is the reason your shop is doing so well."

Rubbing his side, Jack said, "Thank you." He shot Marin a hard look. He moved out of poking range then said, "I'm not exactly sure what I'm thanking you for—but I have enjoyed having you here. You're good company."

Jack couldn't look the little creature in the face as he added that last sentiment. It was a little embarrassing.

"He says you're good company, too, and the food's good."

Jack shifted his gaze to Marin. "He's communicating with you? I don't hear anything."

"He can communicate telepathically." Marin tilted her head, studying their new friend. "I didn't know that. Can I ask why you didn't speak before now?"

A slow smile spread across Marin's face, and she nodded.

Jack sighed. This was going to get old fast. "Maybe you could share? Since I can't hear him?"

"Fuzzface—" Marin's grin reappeared. "—*Bob* didn't have anything to say before."

"Bob?"

Marin crossed her arms. "Bob."

Awkward. Jack had given the dude a pet name because—he thought he was a rodent of some kind. But Bob?

"Bob, uh, apologies for the nicknames. I didn't really know what to call you." When Fuzzface dipped his head, Jack said, "Any chance of you speaking to me?"

Fuzzface's—Bob's—furry head turned to Marin.

"He is." Marin opened her eyes wide, giving Jack an innocent look. "Bob's a guy of few words. I think he can communicate with me because we both have the ability. You're probably out of luck. And I don't think Bob sees any problem with me acting as translator."

Bob blinked his big eyes at Jack. He seemed to be waiting.

"So, uh, I'm glad to meet you." Jack rubbed his neck. This one-way conversation thing was gonna kill him. What did the little guy want?

"Thanks for the crab. I like shrimp, too." Marin's lips pulled into a smile as she translated. "Arkan Sonney are really good luck. Those mysterious items that always seem to show up when a customer asks, those great finds you've stumbled across at garage sales when you're just picking up random boxes of leftovers…" Marin pointed to Bob.

"Seriously?" Jack whispered to Marin. When she just raised her eyebrows and nodded, he turned back to Bob—and the fuzzy little body that housed some serious raw magical talent. "I had no idea. And, um, sure, shrimp's no problem. I mean, if you have a list—" Jack looked to see what Marin was getting in response.

She gave a subtle shake of her head.

"Or, you know, crab and shrimp are great." Jack had experienced some weirdness in the last few months, but this was beyond bizarre. *Roll with it, Jack.* "I can buy crab and shrimp. Is there anything else?"

"My friend—sorry, Bob's friend—needs help." Marin frowned. "Let me close the shop, and we can talk about this in the office without being interrupted."

Bob must have thought that was a grand idea, because he trotted off in the direction of the shop. Jack watched a tiny corkscrew tail disappear into his office then he turned to Marin. "How have you not mentioned this to me before?"

Marin flipped the sign to closed and shot the bolt. "Yeah. That's tricky. They're really shy, and they usually work in secret. Honestly, I thought he might leave if I told you. Or if you made a big fuss about him. I don't know; maybe I was wrong. So, you do realize that he's hiring us, right?"

John exhaled a loud breath. "Sure. Right. Okay. I think Bob's probably a pretty good guy. I have a good feeling about this one."

When they walked into the office, they found Bob curled comfortably in one of the client chairs.

"So what can we do for you?" Jack asked.

2

———

Jack's radar was clearly off. Any good feelings about Bob's case he might have imagined had vanished as soon as he'd learned more. Come to find out, Arkan Sonney were communication minimalists. Not much for chitchat generally, and danger didn't seem to make them any more talkative. At least not their buddy Bob.

"Something nasty in the attic." That was the message Jack and Marin had gotten out of Bob. He'd provided a few additional details—a location down the street from the shop, that the shop was his Arkan Sonney buddy's crash pad—and repeated his thanks for the crab. Then he'd disappeared. Sneaky fast? Temporarily invisible? Teleportation? Jack wasn't placing bets. An hour ago, he hadn't even known there was such a thing as an Arkan Sonney.

As he and Marin approached their destination—

a charity thrift shop—Jack couldn't help but be thankful. At least the "something nasty" wasn't in *his* attic.

"Turn here." Jack pointed to the right.

Marin slowed down but didn't put her blinker on.

"Turn right—that parking lot, right there."

Marin ignored him then sped up and passed the small charity shop parking lot.

"Shit." The color had washed from Marin's face. "Shit, shit, shit."

"Okay. You're freaking me out a little. What's the problem?"

Marin looked at Jack, her eyes huge. "I am in so much trouble." Her fingers flexed around the steering wheel, and Jack could see her pulse leaping in her throat. "We are in so much trouble."

Jack decided it was time for him to assume a role that was somewhat foreign in their relationship: levelheaded sidekick. "Explain to me exactly what the problem is, and we'll deal with it."

Marin shook her head. "Just—let me get us out of here. Before he realizes I'm here. Not the shop... too close. Your place?"

"Okay. Turn right at the next light."

Jack had a sick feeling that *he*, whoever *he* was, was a scary sonofabitch. Because Marin was terrified.

It took fifteen minutes to reach Jack's house, and

in that time he could see Marin ease out of her terror. By the time she turned into his driveway, she looked almost calm.

As she drove up the winding drive, her eyebrows climbed. "Seriously?"

"What?" Jack tried to keep a scowl off his face. He hated explaining his personal life. That shit was nobody's business.

"First—not what I imagined. Second—I clearly need a raise."

"This place predates SPI and The Junk Shop. Since I'm hustling to make my property tax payments, no, you cannot have a raise." Jack pointed to a spot where she could park.

"Why don't you sell? A small acreage like this, right in Austin..."

"It hasn't always been *in* Austin." Jack said. "And I bought the place with some money my grand-mother left me. I can't just sell it."

Marin pulled the key out of the ignition and then slowly turned to face him. "Are you telling me you're keeping the property for sentimental reasons?"

Jack didn't reply. Didn't even look at her.

"Oh my God," Marin said. "This is why you're such an asshole about money."

He wanted to thump her, but why bother when he had a legitimate reason to pry into *her* personal shit.

"Why were you so worried at the charity shop?

And who is the 'he' you're so concerned about running into?"

"Oh, Jack." Marin collapsed back into her seat. "I seriously screwed up. I'm talking big, huge, massive screw-up."

"Glad it's not me for a change. But what exactly did you do?"

"I think, maybe, I let an ancient, exiled dragon back into the world." Marin winced. She shut her eyes and sighed. "Pretty sure I did, actually, unless there's another dragon in Austin. Or someone with dimension-hopping abilities."

"And it's living in the attic of a charity shop?" Jack shook his head. "Never mind. How did you do that exactly?"

"You remember how I hop through wards? Nonphysical anchor here in this reality and the physical part of me in another place?"

Jack couldn't forget if he tried. When Marin had pulled both him and their client through that doorway on a previous case, the sensation hadn't been one he'd ever wanted to repeat. He still didn't understand exactly where they'd gone. It had been cold and empty. He'd felt transparent. No, he'd felt hollow. Actually, he wasn't sure how he'd felt. His body hadn't worked like it should in that space, but he'd have peed himself if it had. "Yeah."

"I opened that door when we were at the airport trying to get Sylvia out of town. But I opened it really wide. I thought that might fry the lights for just a moment."

"Oh, yeah. I remember that. I meant to ask you how you did that. You're telling me that you shorted out the airport lights by opening up a huge inter-dimensional doorway?" Jack tamped down his incredulity. He did stupid shit, but that was epic. "That's—"

"Asinine. I know that *now*." Marin scrunched up her face. "In the moment, it seemed like a good idea."

"I was going to say creative—but if you let something nasty through the door, then maybe asinine is a more accurate. Why didn't you say something?"

Marin choked. "You think I knew the essence of some ancient and probably batshit-crazy dragon snuck through? I didn't know other dragons could even do that. I thought my door worked for me. You know, that only I knew it was there." She frowned at the look on Jack's face. "There's no handbook, Jack. And it hasn't come up before."

"Well, okay. Let's think about this. If it's just his essence, he can't really do anything, can he?"

"Who knows what he can do? I don't think some-thing like this has ever happened. He's from the time before."

"Before what?" Jack asked.

"I told you, remember? Dragons made a choice

to live in the now. In this culture. He's from before. He made the choice to leave."

Jack had a nasty feeling in his gut. "Please tell me that our dragon visitor hasn't been living in that dimensional pit stop of nothingness for centuries."

Marin shrugged and gave him an uncertain look. "Maybe? Or maybe my hidey-hole has doorways to other places. I don't know. Oh my God." The color fled her face. "I have to tell my dad." She covered her face, her words muffled. "And I have to tell Lachlan."

"I don't suppose we can fix this on our own."

"No." Marin groaned. "This is the kind of mistake staying close to the clan is supposed to prevent."

Jack didn't know what arrangement she'd made with her dad and Lachlan, only that they weren't thrilled about her leaving the nest so young—especially her dad. "Will you have to go back to the clan?"

She shrugged. "I won't go. Anyway, we have bigger concerns."

After debating with himself for several seconds, the only certain conclusion he drew was that being the reasonable one on the team wasn't all that much better than being the guy blundering along with not much of a clue. Attempting a confidence he didn't he feel, he said, "Here's what we're going to do. You're going to call your dad. Better now than after something worse has happened. And you never know—

he might have an easy fix or tell you it's less of a problem than you think."

"You didn't feel him in your head. It's a big deal. He's really old." But Marin grabbed her phone.

"Hang on." Jack opened the car door. "I'm not staying for this conversation. I'm going inside to call Harrington. He needs to know there's a potential threat in Austin." Jack held up his hand when Marin started to protest. "Dragon business or not, IPPC and Harrington are the only thing remotely resembling law enforcement or a magical infrastructure that we have in the U.S. He needs to know. And when we're done, we're heading back to the shop. We can't avoid the place. And it can't be a coincidence that this evil essence is squatting so close to the shop."

"It's me. It has to be; I'm the only dragon for miles. And I've been practically living at The Junk Shop lately, dealing with all the new stock you've been digging up and reorganizing SPI's client files."

"If he's drawn to you, then we can't avoid him. And better he stay in one predictable place, right?"

"Sure." Marin stared out the front windshield then nodded once. "All right. Let me do this before I have a coronary."

As Jack let himself in through the side door, he couldn't help wonder how bad the situation was. He'd never seen Marin so rattled. Or act so much like the twenty-one-year-old human girl she was supposedly equivalent in age to.

He headed for the kitchen. After his meeting that morning with Bob, he wasn't about to run out of crab at The Junk Shop. He was already here, and anything that dropped a few more bucks into his bank account was a priority. And, he had to admit, having Bob in the shop, even before he knew his unseen companion was Bob, had been...nice. He liked leaving food for him.

He dialed Harrington as he started poking around in his pantry for canned crab. He'd just found three cans hidden behind a bag of basmati rice when the call rolled to voicemail.

Jack couldn't remember ever having gotten Harrington's voicemail before. The guy must sleep with his phone attached to his body, because he always answered. Except for now.

Shit.

"Jack Spirelli here. There's an emergency in Austin. Call me back, or check in with Ewan for details. Marin should be updating him now." Jack ended the call. Harrington might be curious enough as to why the IPPC library's head of security was involved that he'd move following up on Jack's phone call to the top of his lengthy to-do list.

Or it was already at the top of his list and enough of an emergency that even Harrington was ruffled. Shit. Jack grabbed the crab and booked it back to Marin's truck. He slowed as a terrible sense of foreboding washed over him. He'd never in his life felt prescient, but he knew with complete certainty that something horrible was about to happen.

"Jack!" Marin called from the truck. "We need to go—now. Move it."

Indecision held him locked in place. A heavy weight settled over him. Pulled him down. He was suddenly so incredibly tired.

"Jack." Marin appeared from nowhere and tugged on his arm, urging him to the truck. "Come on. Let's go. What you feel, it's not real."

He didn't care. Whether it was real or imagined, it *felt* real. He was so tired. And his skin hurt when he moved.

"Ow."

A moment of clarity followed a sharp pinch to his arm.

"Yeah," Marin said. "Sorry. Move your feet, or I'm picking you up."

"Don't." The feel of her hand on his shoulder, firmly urging him forward, felt foreign. The contact unpleasant on his hypersensitive skin. His joints ached with each step he struggled to take.

Marin opened the passenger door and shoved him into the seat.

He opened his eyes, unsure how long they'd been closed.

Landscape passed by, the colors bleeding together. Buildings, trees, and sky all blurred. Greys, greens, blues. That wasn't right. Blue. He focused on the blue. The sky. Joy. So sharp it stung. His eyes burned with the beauty of the sky.

"Jack, talk to me. What's going on?"

Jack opened his mouth, moved his lips. But his tongue was thick in his too-small mouth, and no words came. He could feel the cool air on his wet cheeks.

"I'm driving as fast as I can. Just hang on."

More time passed, but the images that fled by his window were too much. The colors too bright, the emotions too full.

Better not to see or hear.

Better not to be.

JACK STRETCHED HIS NECK. He felt like he'd just gone on a bender and forgotten to chug his regular bottle of water and three ibuprofen before he went to bed.

"Hey." Marin waved a hand in front of his face.

"What the hell? Quit it." He shoved her hand away. "Why are we in your car?" He looked out the window, but he didn't recognize the gas station where they were parked. "Where are we?"

"Waco."

Over an hour from Austin. More than an hour had passed since he'd been cognizant of his surroundings.

"Jeez. My entire body hurts. Did you beat the

crap out of me when I wasn't looking?" Jack opened the car door. "I've got to stretch my legs."

Marin hopped out and followed him. "What do you remember?"

Jack rubbed at his eyes. They had a gritty, dry feel that was familiar. "Please tell me I didn't sit in the car and cry myself to sleep."

"Yeah, not exactly."

Jack stopped and turned to face her. "I was kidding. What do you mean, 'not exactly'?" But before she could answer, he remembered seeing the sky and the lightning strike of emotion that had followed. "Wait—old, crazy dragon. My house. Then weird shit started to happen."

"I'm not sure how, but this dragon's essence seems to have telepathic abilities."

Jack looked around the parking lot. No passersby looked like they were eavesdropping. "So he used telepathy to make me cry? And feel like I'd been beaten by a baseball bat?"

"That's not how telepathy works. Not usually." Marin dipped her head closer. "We use it to mind-speak, primarily with each other and sometimes with people."

"Oh, I won't forget you yelling in my head. But that's not what this was. No even remotely."

Marin cocked her head. "You remember?"

"No, at least, not exactly. It's like an old memory. Or a dream. You know the scenes and feelings were vivid when they originally happened, even though you can't pull up a good, solid image. A memory of clarity but no actual clear pictures."

"I wasn't sure I could outrun him." Marin looked at a point just over his shoulder. "So I tried extending the veil I'd created to protect myself to include you."

"Seriously? You're trying out shit you don't know how to do on me—again."

"Would you rather we still be driving north? Because I'm not sure we could outrun him. He doesn't have a physical form."

"If that's true, why is he not playing his weird mind games on me now?" Jack surveyed the parking lot again. His scalp crawled as he realized that the entity could be within feet of him, invisible to human eyes.

"He's not here; he's retreated. I'm guessing to the charity shop."

"So your veil worked."

"Yeah," Marin said. "And is still working."

Jack locked his fingers behind his neck. "Are you telling me I'm tethered to you until we sort this guy out?"

"You're welcome. It wasn't any inconvenience at all to exorcise the demon mucking about in your head." Marin took an audible breath. In a much calmer voice, she said, "Look, I know this is my fault. I'm sorry."

"Yeah. Having someone screw around inside my brain, well, it hasn't improved my mood. But thanks for the mental delousing. Truly." Jack did his very best to look sincere. "What's the distance on this veil that's protecting me?"

Marin shrugged.

Like he thought, he was tethered to Marin for the foreseeable future.

"Are we safe to head back if you keep the veil up?"

"Yes." Marin frowned. "Don't look at me that way. I'm sure. The tricky part was extending it to include you. But now that's been done, it's all good."

Jack knew there was something she wasn't telling him. But as he climbed back into the truck, he decided he was too damn tired to worry about it. His last thought as he leaned his head back was that maybe her father had provided some useful information.

3

J ack awoke with a jerk, the feeling of wind against his skin fading completely as his eyes opened. A sense of exhilaration slipped away as the world around him came into focus.

He was still in the truck with Marin, but he recognized Austin in the muted light of dusk. He scrubbed his face with his hands. "What's the plan?"

Marin didn't immediately answer. And as she continued to drive, Jack recognized the route they were taking.

"The Junk Shop?"

"We're headed to the charity shop. I'd drop you off, but that leaves you unprotected, and there's no telling if he'll try to attack you again."

Jack shifted uncomfortably in his seat. Had he been attacked? Jeez. That thing had scrambled his brains. It had gotten inside his head. It had more than attacked Jack—it had penetrated the deepest parts of his mind.

"Wait. We're going to the charity shop, where that thing lives?"

Marin nodded, her eyes still on the road ahead.

"Please tell me you have a plan."

She tipped her head to the side. "Yes."

"A not-shitty plan?"

Silence followed Jack's question.

Essence of dragon. Not a physical presence. It couldn't hurt him. Just like the dark couldn't hurt him, and there were no monsters under his bed. He puffed out an annoyed breath. Unfortunately, drawing a conclusion with limited facts didn't make it true. Now or when he was a kid.

"We need a name for this thing," Jack said. "'Unnamed nasty thing in the charity shop attic' just makes him seem creepier. And it's too long."

Without hesitation, Marin said, "Joshua."

"Joshua? Any particular reason?"

Marin glanced at him, a smile tugging at the corner of her lips. "Does Joshua strike terror in the hearts of his enemies?"

Jack choked back a laugh. "Sold."

"I'm going to open a small dimensional door in the attic. Not like at the airport. Just a small opening, as if I was ward-hopping."

"And then?"

Marin uncurled her clenched fingers from the steering wheel. "Then I leave it open. And we hope that Joshua came here in error. Or at least that he wants to return to his body as much as we want him to leave."

"You think he can't work magic in the state he's in."

"I have no idea." Her forehead wrinkled as her eyes narrowed. "Even Dad and Lachlan don't know. There's no experience within our clan of a dragon who has sustained separation from his physical body as long as Joshua has. And that's assuming it's just been since the airport incident. For all we know, it's been much longer. A dragon's essence, his anchor, isn't intended to function independently for long." Marin frowned. "The separation is uncomfortable, and I can't imagine that discomfort lessens with time."

"You think his body is sitting in that way station place?" Jack tamped down a surge of panicky claustrophobia. That closed-in, suffocating feeling was followed by a pang of sympathy for Joshua. His skin prickled, chilled by the mere thought of that place. "Doesn't it hurt you to go there?"

"You mean my hidey-hole? No. I wouldn't want to vacation there, but it's not unpleasant in any way."

Jack looked out the window. Almost dark, almost there. "It was cold. And I had no sense of time. I couldn't tell if a second or an hour had passed."

"It's not like that for me. It's just a place." Marin gave him a probing look, but she kept her thoughts to herself.

"If Joshua can use telepathy—even in a bastardized form you don't recognize—shouldn't he be able to open his own door?"

Marin tapped her thumb on the steering wheel. "If that's the case, this won't work. But telepathy isn't magic; I think it's more of a mental skill. Let's hope he has no magical abilities."

And on that less-than-optimistic note, they arrived at the charity shop.

Jack flinched at the sense of foreboding opening the car door seemed to trigger. Were those his own feelings? Or one of Joshua's mind tricks? He hovered near the truck, door still open. He couldn't walk in there without knowing if his mind was his own.

"Your veil is intact?" Jack asked.

"It is. Can you feel him?"

Jack considered the question. Did he sense an individual behind the dark cloud that pushed against him? "I don't have any sense of intent or personality. What I know for sure is that I'm afraid."

"The creepy feeling that some people get from dragons, take that and magnify it. Then you get what most people experience around a really old dragon. So if you have a strong urge to pee yourself or run away, that's not mind control, telepathy, or anything other than being in the presence of an incredibly old dragon." Marin raised her eyebrows. "The good news: that black-cloud-looming feeling means he's here."

Fear he could handle. Possession of his mind... no. But Marin had him covered with her protective veil, so whatever happened he would remain himself. "Let's do this." A couple walked by and entered the shop. "Ah, did you check the business hours?"

"Easier to get in if they're open. For you, anyway."

Since Marin actually cared about civilian casualties, he was working on the assumption that she had a plan when he followed her into the store.

A CURVED hip pressed into Jack's groin.

"Be still," he whispered into Marin's ear.

"Not much room *to* move. And it's hot."

"You're not helping. And what did you expect— it's a freaking closet." The pall that Joshua's presence cast wasn't helping Jack's mood. And from the bits of conversation they'd overhead as the store employees closed up, that pall had probably been felt by at least two former store employees. One had been institutionalized for a sudden psychotic break only two days prior. The other had become violent and attacked a customer.

Marin went completely still. "I think they're gone." She waited another minute, and then opened the door. "Looks like everyone's gone."

Jack shoved her out of the closet and followed on her heels. "Why don't people avoid this place? Can't they feel it?" He rolled his shoulders and neck, trying to loosen the stiffness a half-hour of restricted movement had caused. *He* hadn't wiggled his ass every few seconds.

"Hm. You'd be surprised. A lot of humans don't sense anything. And some who do recognize an uncomfortable feeling discount it until it fades into the background." She eyed him like a lab specimen. "Humans are weird."

"Well, those are both better options than beating the crap out of a guy for not having correct change. Prolonged exposure must have triggered those two employees' problems. I really don't understand why they don't walk away if they do feel something." Jack shook his head. "Any ideas on attic access?"

They headed to the stairs labeled "employees only."

"No. But I'm guessing there's a pull-down ladder from the ceiling someplace." Once she'd reached the top of the stairs, Marin pointed to the right. "You check over there, and I'll catch the other side."

"Theoretically, if Joshua can still do magic with only his anchor in this dimension, what exactly could he do?" Jack said over his shoulder as he headed down the hallway.

Marin's voice followed Jack into the room he was checking. "The regular stuff: sense magic, throw fire, and he's probably got some superpowers related to his age. Ha—got it!"

Red and blue lights flashed as a cruiser sped down the road. Jack hurried into the room where Marin had found the attic access. She'd already pulled the ladder down from the ceiling.

"Don't suppose you have a contingency plan if someone calls the police?" Jack asked.

"Do *you*?" Marin quirked an eyebrow at him. When he didn't reply, she started up the ladder.

Jack hesitated. There was a reason children feared the monster under their bed and the darkness. It was a visceral response to predators and the unknown—and it seemed like common sense to him.

Marin reached the top.

Jack stood with one foot on the bottom rung. Climb the stairs or not. Face the beast or run. But it wasn't a choice; not really. Jack started to climb the stairs.

When he reached the top and climbed into the dusty and unused space—there was nothing. The black cloud of malevolence he'd expected to find wasn't there. The same sense of foreboding persisted, but that was all.

"Is he even here?"

"Oh, yes." A look of concentration passed across Marin's face. "The door's open. Now we wait."

"Okay, but I don't—" Jack fell to his knees. Searing pain enveloped him.

The protective veil peeled away from his body, leaving what felt like a weeping wound. He braced himself against the floor.

If a soul could rip, it must feel like this. But then...

Howling rage, despair, betrayal.

Jack could do nothing but feel, bombarded by waves of emotions. He curled into a ball, trying—failing—to protect himself.

He tried to separate out the two pieces winding together. Him, another. Jack, Joshua. Two, not one. He was himself and no one else.

Himself.

One.

Pain turned hollow. His body was numb. And then world was a silent wash of grey.

JACK SHIFTED his head and groaned. Cool fingers stroked his temple.

"Jack?" Marin's voice. But small and uncertain, so unlike her.

"Ugh. Shit." Jack tried to sit up and failed. "Holy hell, my head hurts."

Marin half giggled, half sobbed. Completely unlike her.

Jack craned his neck to look at her and winced when the throbbing exploded into pounding. "You weren't possessed?"

"No. Just scared shitless. Can you get up?" The cadence of her voice was all wrong. Thready, panicked.

"Hm." He struggled to a sitting position, and from there, Marin lifted him to his feet. When the room stopped spinning and his vision cleared, Jack understood. "He's still here."

The pinched look on Marin's face tightened even more.

She gave him a supporting arm to the ladder, then said, "I'll go first. Let me get halfway down and then follow. I won't let you fall."

Leaving sounded like an excellent plan. As Jack carefully placed one foot after the other, he focused on one thought: one more step. By the time his feet hit the ground, he thought he was going to puke from the pain in his head. That one thought changed to: walk. Then his focus shifted to not puking. And that was how he made it to the car. One thought, one goal, and always moving forward.

Sitting in the buttery-soft leather seats of Marin's truck, Jack was seconds away from passing out. One thought, one goal. Stay awake. One thought, one goal. He had a message. "Help me."

"I know, buddy. I'm working on it," Marin said.

Jack could feel the acceleration of the car. "Help me."

4

J ack woke up in someone's bed. Not his. It happened sometimes, sure, but he hadn't been on a date the night before. And he felt like shit. If he'd crashed at some woman's house, he shouldn't feel quite this bad. He rubbed his eyes and frowned. "Help me."

"Hey." Marin poked her head into the room. "You're awake?"

"Hm. Yeah. We're at your house?"

The door flew open and Lachlan, the McClellan clan's supreme leader, walked in. Jack had only met the man briefly once before, but he was a memorable guy. He was surprised; he'd expected Marin's father, Ewan.

"Help—you don't look like you need any help. Get your ass out of bed and come down to breakfast." The giant of a man turned and left once he'd made his pronouncement.

"Welcome to Chez Campbell. I'd apologize, but really, if I started, I'd never be able to stop. Weirdly, human women find him very attractive. He got in late last night. He chartered a flight, what with all of the dragon drama brewing." Marin managed a weak smile. "You're okay?"

"Yeah. Sore, but otherwise fine. I passed out?"

"More like fell into an exhausted sleep. You mumbled a few times that you needed help, then you conked out. I woke you up a few times and you seemed coherent, so Lachlan and I decided to let you sleep it off."

"I don't remember waking up. Or how I got in bed." Jack scanned the room for some sign of clothes. "Any chance you've got my clothes stashed somewhere?"

"In the bathroom with some fresh towels. I threw everything in the wash last night."

She was turning to go when Jack remembered. "Hey—'help me.' That wasn't me. That was a message from Joshua." Jack rubbed his temple. "I think it was a message."

Marin stilled. More than a simple cessation of movement, there was an intensity to the stillness that had Jack on edge. He felt like the stalked sparrow as a housecat readied to pounce. She pivoted toward him and the moment passed. "You're certain he spoke to you?"

"No."

Marin held up a hand to stop him from explaining. "Get dressed and come down for some breakfast. You can update us both at the same time."

About twenty minutes later, Jack was feeling much refreshed after a shower and a shave. He followed the smells of cooking food down the stairs and into the kitchen.

"Tell us about this message the ancient left with you." Lachlan passed Jack a plate of sausage and bacon once he was seated.

"Morning, Lachlan," Jack replied. Jack had racked his brain while he'd showered, and he couldn't ever remember words being spoken. "He never actually said the words—but I had this really strong sense of a message: help me. Which makes no sense, I know."

Marin blinked and Lachlan raised his eyebrows.

"I mean, he'd just say 'help me' if that was what he meant, right?" Jack looked between the two dragons.

"In which language would you expect an ancient to speak when addressing a modern man?" Lachlan's expression betrayed no censure.

"Latin?" Jack asked. "Or Gaelic? Aren't you guys all originally from Scotland?"

Lachlan chuckled. "All dragons are not originally from Scotland, but I appreciate the sentiment."

"Are you trying to tell me he was speaking to me in some weird dragon way?"

Two heads nodded.

"And that's problematic for a few reasons." Lachlan wiped his mouth with a napkin and leaned back in his chair with hands clasped over his stomach. "An ancient has requested aid. It would be immoral, and irresponsible, to ignore his request."

Jack chewed and swallowed his scrambled eggs. Light, fluffy, fabulous eggs. "Even if the request is unreasonable? What does that even mean: help me?"

"As dragons age," Marin said, "they lose touch with the now. Time moves differently—"

"What she's saying is that old dragons are usually insane. She's just trying to be respectful, given my advanced years." There was a twinkle in Lachlan's eye as he spoke. Fear of aging and insanity seemed to have no hold over the man sitting in front of Jack.

"If Joshua has the ability to imprint speech on you, especially a request for help, he's not crazy." Marin lifted the coffee pot, a silent question.

Jack shook his head.

"If this ancient is as old as Marin believes," Lachlan said, "if he's from the time before, and he's sane enough to retain the concept of communication with humans...that has immense significance for our people."

"We need to figure out how to speak with him, help him with his problem, and make sure he doesn't get hurt in the process." As Jack summarized what seemed like impossible and conflicting goals, something else occurred to him. "And Joshua is seriously angry."

"That's my fault," Marin said. "When I opened the dimensional door, I invited him to leave. Lachlan thinks that whatever Joshua wants, it's here in this world. So he got angry when we asked him to leave."

"If you use your nonphysical essence to anchor your physical bodies to this world..." Jack stopped when he saw Lachlan give Marin a censorious look.

"Go on," Lachlan urged.

"Well," Jack continued, "how did Joshua's essence end up here without a body? And where is his body?"

"We don't know. But those are questions we'd very much like answered." Lachlan gave Jack a probing look.

Jack stopped chewing. Mouth full of sausage, he said, "What?"

"Lachlan thinks that there's something about you that attracts Joshua, besides your proximity to me." The subtle emphasis on Lachlan's name made Marin's dissent clear. She wasn't on board with whatever he was proposing.

"Even if it is proximity and psychic vulnerability, the ancient has made contact twice now with Jack, and Jack's no worse off. They have a connection." Lachlan crossed his arms across his chest. His massive chest.

"You want *me* to ask those questions. You do realize I become—quite literally—mentally unhinged every time Joshua touches my mind."

"But with my help, you won't," Lachlan replied.

Marin pushed away from the table. "What Lachlan means is that he'll help you connect with Joshua in a safe way that allows you to communicate with him."

"Why don't one of you speak with him directly?" That made so much more sense. And Jack was very attached to his sanity. He wasn't keen to lose it conversing with an ancient, moody dragon. One whose motives were highly suspect.

"I told Lachlan how Joshua ripped through the veil I'd wrapped around you. He's certain he could just as easily have shredded the protection I'd created for myself—implying he wanted to specifically communicate with you."

And that was what happened when you missed half of the strategy talks—you got the shit job. If only Jack had known what was happening as he slept.

That massive, pulsing ball of anger and regret

and loneliness wanted to have a sit-down with him. "Why me?" Jack asked.

"I have no idea. But the opportunity to speak with an ancient was previously unimaginable. I'll try to make a connection, but if I fail it's imperative someone speak with him." Lachlan must have sensed weakness, because he pushed his advantage. "If we don't discover what the ancient needs from us, he won't leave."

Jack looked at the remainder of his eggs, now cold, and placed his cutlery across the plate. He knew Joshua was in terrible pain. He knew that with more certainty than he knew his own feelings.

Something inside him said it was the right thing to do. He'd like to smack that something upside the head. Here was another obnoxious thought: could he live with himself if he didn't do it?

Finally, Jack said, "You'll owe me a favor."

Lachlan grinned. "I certainly will."

After some discussion, they decided that waiting until the evening wasn't wise. Especially since Joshua had already been successfully lured away from the shop, however unintentionally.

Jack proposed The Junk Shop. Using either of their homes was out of the question. And a public space meant uncontrollable variables.

"We have to swing by first. Do some prep at the shop," Jack said.

Marin did a poor job of suppressing a smile. "Jack has an Arkan Sonney living at the shop."

"Interesting. I've only met a few. They don't usually choose to inhabit dragon establishments." Lachlan cocked his head thoughtfully. "Maybe I'll get a chance to meet him."

About an hour later, when Jack unlocked the shop door, Bob was waiting patiently just a few feet away. Had he intuited that Jack needed to speak with him? That was just too much for Jack to consider in this particular moment. The idea of telepathy was difficult enough to handle, but if precognition was also on the table then his brain might implode.

"Hi, Bob."

Before Jack could explain that he was evicting him temporarily, Bob scampered away. Jack trailed behind him all the way to the office. As he entered his office, he heard the front door bells and turned around to make sure it was only Marin and Lachlan, delayed by the increasingly limited parking in the area.

"In the office," he hollered over his shoulder. By the time his attention returned to Bob, there were two of them.

Bob blinked liquid brown eyes at him.

"Are you trying to act innocent, Bob?"

If Bob had eyelashes, he'd be batting them, Jack was certain. As it was, he just gazed soulfully at Jack.

"This is your buddy from the charity shop?"

Bob dipped his head.

"That's cool that you invited him, it's just that we're about to have the nasty visitor from the charity shop come over here." Jack couldn't believe he was having this conversation.

Marin walked up behind him. "Uh oh."

"Yeah." Turning from Marin back to his guests, Jack asked, "Would you guys like to stay at my house? Just for a little while. It should be okay to come back here soon." Addressing Bob's friend, Jack added, "We're working hard to get Joshua—the dragon in your attic—to move out."

"I'll be damned," Lachlan murmured as he approached. "Nelson is certain that's not the dragon's name. He must be able to communicate with him." Turning his attention to the two Arkan Sonney, Lachlan bowed and said, "Apologies. Lachlan McClellan at your service."

Bob's friend was looking a little nervy, and Jack could hardly blame him. He'd been living in the shadow of an ancient dragon for at least several days, maybe longer. No surprise two showing up in close quarters concerned him. But when Lachlan introduced himself, both Arkan Sonney bowed.

"Ah, Nelson?" Bob's friend dipped his head. "Nice to meet you, Nelson. Will my house do for a little while?" Jack asked again.

Two heads bobbed in unison.

"Do you need a lift?" Jack winced. Did they teleport? Use public transit? Have some other mode of transport unique to Arkan Sonney?

"They've declined your generous offer," Marin said.

Before Jack could pose any more awkward questions, they were gone. "Don't suppose you have a clue how they do that? Or how they're getting to my house?"

Marin shook her head.

"I'm not sure how they even know where I live."

Lachlan snorted. "Even if we did chase them off, for a brief time, you had two Arkan Sonney in your shop. It should be raining gold in here. And such compelling creatures. I do wish they had more of a fondness for dragons."

"Bob's excellent company. Tidy, doesn't talk much, and makes the place feel lived-in."

Marin snorted. "You thought he was a rat up until yesterday."

"Not true. I thought he was something rodent-like that wasn't a rat." Jack rubbed his neck. "I guess there's no reason to delay now."

"No. It's time." Lachlan quirked an eyebrow. "Who's driving?"

Marin held up her keys. "Just on the off chance something goes awry, and Jack passes out again. Let's do this."

As Jack walked the block and a half to Marin's car, he decided he really should have negotiated a better fee. An undefined dragon favor and a flat fee and a bonus if no one died. He'd really dropped the ball this time.

Shit. He didn't want Joshua screwing with his head again. Too soon they arrived at Marin's car.

The drive seemed even shorter this time, but it was long enough for Jack feel fear and doubt. Mayeb some regret. Definitely disappointment that he hadn't negotiated a better fee.

When Marin turned onto the charity shop street, Jack could feel echoes of Joshua's emotions. He thought they were echoes. Or Joshua was there in his mind already. The line between memory and reality wavered. Jack rolled his shoulders. He could do this. "Should we have practiced—"

"Backstopping your psychic defenses and enhancing your telepathic abilities," Lachlan said. "I don't see why. I'm doing the heavy lifting, and I don't need the practice."

"Of course you don't." Jack massaged his temple with his thumb. Lachlan was giving him a headache. Remembering how badly his head hurt the last two times he'd encountered Joshua made it ache even more. He'd almost prefer a solid whack on the head. "Don't suppose anyone knows what kind of long-term damage this stuff is doing to my brain."

Neither Marin nor Lachlan replied.

Marin slowed down as they passed the charity shop and said, "Last time, it took a few miles before I noticed Jack was affected. Granted, I was a little distracted. The idea of an old dragon, some guilt over the doorway, concern about Dad kicking my butt. I had a few things on my mind."

"Does it feel like the sky is about to fall? Or is that a human reaction?" Jack asked, more to distract himself from the intense feelings of foreboding than actual curiosity.

Marin caught his gaze in the rearview mirror. "Completely human, Chicken Little."

Lachlan seemed to consider the question, and he didn't answer for several seconds. "To me it's a deep knowledge. A well that has no bottom."

A chill crawled up Jack's spine. That, too. He felt it now.

"He knows we're here. There's no doubt." Lachlan leaned back in the passenger seat and closed his eyes.

There was no wall around him. No force field. Nothing that Jack could in any way perceive. But he knew it was there, because this time was different.

This time, Jack was a visitor, not the conduit for Joshua's emotions. He was on a train that traveled through a barren landscape. But there was no train, just the sensation of gently rolling, of forward progress. And there was no landscape. Just the desolation of a life lived too long, alone.

Jack was floating. No body tied him to the earth.

He wanted to ask where his body was—but the words weren't there.

Something pulled him, reeling him back to the ground. Lachlan.

Jack knew there were questions to ask. But he couldn't remember them.

He was back on the train, but the world around him moved with urgency now. Wind whipped his hair. Cold chilled his limbs. Silence pounded into his eardrums, and he felt liquid trickle from his ears. Again, he was pulled away.

The landscape changed again. The washed-out tones and grey became a thick, sucking, pulling black. A black so deep it consumed what it touched. Jack snatched his hands away, and Lachlan's tether held tight.

The rolling motion stopped, the sensation of the train, of solid space, fell away. And then Jack fell. And he kept falling, falling, falling...

5

Jack's eyes flew open. His heart raced. Overwhelming relief pulsed through him. He'd been spared. The landing he knew would shatter him into a million pieces never came.

The first thing he registered when his heart rate slowed and his eyes would focus was one of the more disturbing sights he'd witnessed recently. Marin had her arm wrapped around Lachlan's shoulders as tears flowed freely down his face. Moved, upset, angered, Jack wasn't certain. But he was intensely uncomfortable witnessing such a private moment.

Jack turned away and brushed the damp streaks from his own face. That was when he noticed they were parked outside The Junk Shop. No telling how long they'd been sitting in Marin's truck. Jack was just fine with that. They could sit in the truck all night, the neighbors be damned.

When Lachlan eventually spoke, he voice was composed. "Joshua—he was amused by your name for him—Joshua was trapped in the in-between a very long time ago. His entire self, physical body and essence. Without an anchor in a physical plane, he was stranded in the in-between. I don't know how; that wasn't clear."

"But only his essence, his anchor, traveled to our world," Jack said. "So where is his body?"

"Dead a long time now." Lachlan closed his eyes for a moment. "It takes a long time for a dragon to starve. And in that environment, maybe longer. But I'm certain he starved. I shielded you from his hunger."

Jack flashed to that moment of weightlessness, when Lachlan had brought him back down into his own body.

"That train ride was Joshua's life." Jack shook his head. "I'm not sure why I didn't see it. Maybe I was too wrapped up in the events and the feelings to process it all."

"With me as a psychic bridge, Joshua was able to convey a story. You provided the structure, Jack, and I benefitted by watching it all."

It had played in his mind as a journey, so what Lachlan said made sense.

"If he has no body, is he a ghost?" Jack asked. But

as soon as he asked the question, he knew that wasn't right.

"No, not a ghost. His body died, but trapped in the in-between, the entirety of him wasn't able to die. When his body failed, he was left only as essence. Unable to end his life, trapped in a wasteland, he simply continued." Lachlan face tightened. "He's not insane. More sane than any one of us. But desperate for peace. I don't understand how he was spared. He had no passage of time with which to ground himself, no companionship, no tactile experiences. But he escaped the fate of every dragon who chose to stay in this world, every dragon bred to this world."

As Lachlan spoke, Jack started to get a sense of exactly what an ancient was to Lachlan and his people. Not a god, but maybe so far beyond one's own experience, so important to society, that he came close. A king? An emperor? Or maybe a wise man or shaman.

Lachlan sighed. "He didn't mean to harm you or to frighten you."

"I know that now," Jack replied quietly. "And I certainly understand his anger at being asked to return to what he would consider a prison."

"By a group of infants, no less," Lachlan said.

"You do know what he wants, don't you?" Jack hated to ask, because he already knew the answer.

Lachlan nodded.

And Jack's heart ached for the man.

Marin looked between the two men. "What? Is it that terrible?"

Jack responded, saving Lachlan from speaking the words. "He wants to die. He wants us to help him find a way to end his life."

"Oh, Joshua." Marin drew a deep breath. "But how?"

LACHLAN SAID he needed some time to review the information and to think about their options. He wanted to reconvene in the morning to come up with a plan of action. Jack wasn't sure how he could be of any more help, but he'd do what he could. Having been exposed to the dragon's deepest, most intimate thoughts and feelings, Jack couldn't help but feel a profound connection with the ancient being.

The next morning, Jack, Marin, and Lachlan met at Jack's house for breakfast. Marin brought breakfast tacos, and Lachlan brought an insane idea.

"Reborn?" Jack asked. "What does that even mean?"

Lachlan's tacos were still wrapped in foil on his plate. "You can't destroy a dragon's essence. Joshua hoped, in coming here, we would know how. But he couldn't have predicted how young the dragons are in this world."

"So if you can't destroy essence, you think it's okay to recycle it? Isn't essence a dragon's soul?"

Marin shook her head. "No. Essence isn't soul; it's essence. A snapshot of the dragon."

Lachlan leaned his forearms on the edge of the kitchen table. "Consider essence as a smaller, nonphysical reflection of the whole. Pairing Joshua's bodiless essence with a new body lacking essence should remake that reflection in the image of the new owner. It's an end for Joshua, but the energy of his essence would go on in its new form. Again, destroying that energy is beyond our knowledge, so this is the only solution for Joshua."

Jack had a bad feeling about this conversation.

After chewing over Lachlan's explanation, Jack asked, "And where does one shop for dragon bodies without their own essence?"

"One doesn't." Lachlan shifted his weight further forward. "Except for Joshua, I've never heard of one existing without the other. Temporary separation, but that's it. A dragon won't work, because all dragons will have their own essence."

"No." Jack shook his head and kept shaking it. "No way."

Lachlan quirked an eyebrow. "I haven't asked."

"You will. And the answer is no."

"I'm not asking," Lachlan said. "Joshua is."

Marin turned a narrow gaze on Lachlan. "When did that happen?"

"Last night. The rebirth of his essence through joining with another person was the only solution I could find for him. But I wasn't certain he'd agree, so I had to speak with him." A self-deprecating smile emerged on Lachlan's face. "It took significant effort before Joshua would consider communicating with me. He has a strong connection with you, Jack—for whatever reason."

"He agreed." Jack couldn't believe what they were asking.

"He asked me to present the case to you. Only because he sees it as his own death with no harm to you. The energy of his essence will continue, but it will be imprinted by you," Lachlan said. "Think of it like a sort of reincarnation, but with energy rather than soul."

"You don't know for sure that Joshua's imprint on his essence would be erased, do you? And even if it is, what would dragon essence do to a human? It has to have some effect on humans."

"Actually, Jack, it has been done. There's evidence in our mythology." Marin shot Lachlan a sidelong glance. "From long ago in our history, when the relationship between humans and dragons was very different."

"Joshua and I discussed the mechanics. It's not only possible, he's seen it done. A very long time ago —but he has firsthand experience."

"Are you telling me it's safe?" He directed the question to Marin, because he trusted her infinitely more than Lachlan in this scenario. Jack could only imagine the lengths Lachlan might go to appease or even preserve a sane ancient. But Marin...he knew Marin. They may not be close, but he knew her. If she thought it would kill him, she might let him do it—but she'd say it was dangerous.

"Lachlan? Why don't you share the mechanics?" Marin gave the old dragon a falsely sweet smile.

"It's simple, in theory. Your body and his essence can join in the in-between. Either I or Marin open a door and carry you through. You merge with Joshua's essence, and he's finally at peace. Anything of him—his memories, his feelings, his experiences—are washed away. The sum of your being—memories, experiences, feelings—will be imprinted upon the essence energy. Then we bring you back."

Jack narrowed his eyes. "You're leaving something out."

"Yes, he is." Marin's voice was tinged with anger. "We can carry you through, but I don't believe it's possible to hold on to you while you merge with Joshua. Am I right?"

Lachlan's lips thinned, and he nodded his head.

Jack's brain was doing backflips trying to sort out how the process worked. "And you're telling me that somehow, I could take on that energy and it wouldn't change me? I find that hard to believe."

"You would change the essence, because it's merely a reflection of the sum of the body and mind. That energy was not intended to exist apart from a physical body." Lachlan sighed. "To remove the metaphysical aspect, think of essence as an organ. It serves a function, but it's not intended to exist as a being on its own."

"But what will it do to me?" Jack asked again.

Surprisingly, it was Marin who answered. "It might give you a longer life. Maybe make you more resistant to disease. Prop you up a little—but it can't give you something that's not already there. It's energy, not magic, and its function is to act as a nonphysical receptacle."

"What if something goes wrong with the reset button and Joshua isn't washed away?" Jack shook his head and held up his hands. "You know what— don't answer that. I don't care. I don't know why I'm even asking these questions. This idea is insane. I could disappear into...into the freaking *in-between*. I could be stuck, just like Joshua was."

"Very unlikely. I'll be there, and I won't lose you." Lachlan inched back, making an obvious effort to give Jack more space. "Please, consider it. You're the only option. Someone with magic wouldn't work. Something about the energy of a dragon's essence and the kernel of magic inside humans isn't compatible. And while Joshua is willing—he's only agreed to attempt the process with you."

And that made Jack angry. He'd been inside Joshua's head, and Joshua had been inside his. Jack couldn't imagine an eternity of what Joshua had lived. It was unthinkable. But the solution was a no-win situation for Jack: a small chance that he'd end up lost in that same, terrible place that had trapped Joshua in exchange for a good chance the ancient would be able to rest at last. Jack gained nothing. Save the world, do the right thing, be selfless. His pulse thundered. What about him?

"Find someone else." Jack stood up and left the kitchen. His guests could find their own way out.

Jack went to his room and dropped down on his bed. Screw them and their ancients and their problems.

He didn't particularly want to examine why the question made his blood boil. It was a question, and he could simply say no. He punched his pillow. It wasn't that simple. If he hadn't *been* Joshua, if only for a few snatches of time, it would be so much easier.

"Screw them." Jack rolled over on his side, planning to try catch-up on a few more hours of sleep. He was so tired, yet as he lay there, sleep eluded him. He felt smothered by the weight of the ancient dragon's despair.

The heaviness pressed down on his lungs, until he felt like he couldn't breathe. The ache of a loneliness so dark and deep, he felt he'd never see, touch, or hear another made his heart hurt.

"Damn you, Joshua." But Jack knew it was his memory and his conscience this time—not the dragon's telepathy—that wrapped around him and squeezed until he wanted to scream.

BLEARY-EYED, Jack rolled out of bed a few hours later. He picked up his phone and tapped speed dial for Marin. "We do it now. Meet me at The Junk Shop."

"Wha—"

Jack hung up on her. He couldn't live with the guilt. Knowing what he knew, feeling what he'd felt —he couldn't live with the guilt of not helping Joshua. And that son of a bitch had looked inside his head and counted on it.

He sat down at the small desk in his room and handwrote a letter. It took him three tries, but he got it about right in the end. He sealed it in an envelope, and addressed it simply to "Kenna." He dropped it on his desk, there for anyone to find—if it came to that.

He drove too fast on the way to the shop. And when he arrived, he slammed the door of his car shut. He was pissed and he was damn well allowed to be.

Marin and Lachlan were waiting in the shop for him. As was Joshua.

"Why—" Lachlan began.

"None of your damn business." Jack tossed his car keys on the counter, and they landed with a loud rattle. "I'll be exactly the same when we're done." He directed the statement to Marin, because he still didn't trust Lachlan's motivations.

"You don't have that kernel of magic that some humans have—and this won't change that lack. You'll be the same: no magic, no fire," Marin answered calmly. She looked worried.

That made two of them.

"No strange cravings. Nothing like that. And it'll just be me coming back." Is wasn't really a question; Jack simply wanted to make sure he didn't come out of this thing and scare the crap out of himself.

"No strange cravings, and just you come back." Marin's gaze flickered back and forth between Jack and Lachlan. "Lachlan needs to bring you through."

"You can create the door?"

After getting a quick nod from Lachlan, Marin said, "Yes. I'll open the door."

"All right. Anything else I need to know to make sure this thing works?" Jack asked.

"Your physical self has to merge with Joshua's essence. At first, that energy will still be Joshua; only after you've combined will the essence rewrite itself in your image. You have to let that happen." Lachlan examined him. "You have to be ready to make that choice, or it won't work."

"I'm ready." As the words left his mouth, Jack hoped that he was.

Jack felt the moment Lachlan and he crossed the barrier into the in-between. None of the numbing cold he remembered, but the absolute stillness of the place and the warped sense of time was the same. Where had the wind come from that he'd seen through Joshua's eyes? A metaphor, perhaps.

Jack lifted his hand. He couldn't see it, but he could feel that he'd moved it. It was an odd sensation, but very different from his last experience in this place.

Marin is still young. She wasn't able to protect your physical body as well as I am.

Jack flinched at the voice in his head. Not too loud, but invasive in a way that Marin's mind speech hadn't been.

He felt Joshua, and then he felt the cold. Lachlan had let him go.

Jack was surrounded, engulfed, swallowed by Joshua. He pushed at Jack's very being. This wasn't a reset. He was being consumed. Panic flared as Jack saw himself disappearing into nothing, replaced by the great well of emotion that was Joshua. How could something, someone, so old and so vast simply cease to be? No, this wouldn't work.

Jack struggled. His body didn't function in this space, but he had will. Jack shoved back at the ancient presence with all of his will—and met no resistance.

Calm. Still. Cold. Alone.

His panic ebbed. In the stillness, Jack realized his error. For this to work, the two would have to coexist, completely share consciousness, in order for the reset to happen. Twined thoughts—but only for a moment. Could he? Cold and fear pushed, and his brain raced. One terrifying, powerless moment exchanged for an end to an ancient being's suffering. And a lifetime of guilt and regret if he refused to even attempt the trade.

Jack sent a message to Joshua and hoped it carried through the ether. He couldn't form words, and he didn't know what else to do.

The thick numbness he'd felt in place of his body faded, and he felt himself begin to float. Not an unpleasant feeling.

But it only lasted an instant. Once again, Joshua surrounded him, anchoring him in space. And this time when Jack felt that he was being swallowed whole, he counted backward from ten and tried his damnedest to believe that they truly were one— temporarily. Ten, nine...

LACHLAN'S FLASHING green dragon eyes looked down at Jack. "You said you were ready to make the choice."

Jack's teeth chattered. Holy shit, he was cold. And weak and sore. Like he had the flu. Someone had laid him out flat on the ground. "I lied." The words brought forth a racking cough.

Marin appeared with a blanket from his office. She threw it over him. "You're a complete ass and an idiot."

The worry and concern in her voice surprised him. He wasn't sure why—he'd worry about her, too, if she was stupid enough to teeter on the brink of oblivion and thumb her nose at it.

"I'm okay?" Since his teeth chattered with the words, it seemed a stupid question.

"You'll be fine," Lachlan said. "Eventually."

Curling onto his side, Jack hugged the blanket close. "Joshua?"

The tense lines of Lachlan's face eased. "At peace."

Jack nodded. He couldn't feel Joshua's presence, so he guessed Lachlan was right. "Can I have a hot coffee?"

Marin laughed. "Yeah. It's brewing now."

EPILOGUE

A few days later, Jack sat in his office contemplating the Jack and Joshua merger. He felt the same. No sudden urges to light up the furniture in a ball of fiery dragon flames. No shining green eyes. No sense of the magic that he knew was around him. In fact, no whiff of magical ability at all. Just as Lachlan and Marin had said.

Jack was giving some thought to whether his unchanged state was something to celebrate or mourn, but mostly he was just avoiding doing The Junk Shop's accounting for the week. As he contemplated the pros and cons—of having magic, of having his books up to date, of life in general—Bob trotted into the office.

That was new.

"Hey, Bob." He kept the greeting casual, because he didn't want to chase the little dude away.

Bob paused briefly but then continued along his path. He ended up next to one of the client chairs, then jumped with more agility than Jack would have suspected into the chair.

"I hope you're here to tell me your buddy's happy. Can't lie: the last few days have been rough. I'm not sure I'm up for another case so soon."

Bob curled up into a ball and closed his eyes.

Napping in the office must mean that Bob didn't have another case for him and was happy enough with the outcome of Nelson's.

He went back to crunching numbers on his computer. As he was typing, he thought he might have heard a faint whisper: "Happy..."

Keep reading for Episode 5: The Geolocating Book!

EPISODE 5

THE GEOLOCATING BOOK

ABOUT THE GEOLOCATING BOOK

The Inter-Pack Policing Cooperative has hired Spirelli Paranormal Investigations. Not so unusual, except that it's Marin's father, the Chief of Security, who's doing the hiring this time.

Personal lives collide with professional as Jack and Marin track down a magical book that IPPC covets... and that might just be more dangerous than anyone realizes.

1

Jack had been giving some thought to Spirelli Paranormal Investigations: where it had started and where it was going. What his long-term plans for the business were and how he'd ensure both the business's and his survival beyond the next case that came through the door.

"I'd actually like to see tomorrow, Bob. Several tomorrows, preferably with the business intact."

His Arkan Sonney bud looked up at the sound of his name. He didn't move from his curled-up position in the client chair on the other side of Jack's desk. He just lifted his head and blinked sleepy, puppy-dog-brown eyes at Jack. The little fuzzy guy was great company—and Jack had thought so even before he'd discovered the impact Bob had on his business.

Who would have thought that having a small, corkscrew-tailed critter living secretly in his shop would have such a startling effect? The Junk Shop had become a successful enterprise overnight due to Bob's presence. Jack remained mystified by the method, but at least now he knew to thank Bob when customers purchased odd objects in the shop he was certain he'd never acquired. Where had these mysterious items originated? Also an unanswered question. But Jack wasn't about to grill his fuzzy little benefactor.

"Sorry, buddy. Just thinking out loud. Go back to sleep."

Bob squeezed his eyes shut, let out a tiny sneeze, and settled in to nap again.

Jack scratched the day's growth of beard on his chin. He wasn't sure why, but Bob had started to hang out, nap, and visibly wander around the store a week or two after the resolution of his buddy Nelson's case. Whatever the reason, he was great company. Bob was like a warm blanket on a cold day —but for the soul.

Jack grunted then leaned back in his chair. He was going nuts. Or he needed more sleep.

He scrubbed his face with both hands. So far, he'd only come up with one solution.

The ring on his finger tightened, followed by the tinkling of the front door bells and a flash of green sparkles in his peripheral vision. Marin.

He rubbed his eyes, dry from lack of sleep, and when he opened them, Bob was gone. For whatever reason, Bob's recent sociability only extended to Jack. His furry buddy usually disappeared when anyone else was in the shop—even Marin.

Jack didn't have long to consider the Bob conundrum.

Marin came into the office and dropped into the chair vacated by Bob. "You look like shit."

"Good morning."

"Bender? Wild night with a new lady?" Marin crossed her arms. "But that's not it, because you've looked like this every morning for more than a week now. Your ladies don't last that long. And you're coming into the shop early every morning."

"Inventory." Jack tapped a clipboard on top of his desk.

"Sure, except you don't do inventory. Ever. I do it. Just like I do the dusting, and empty the trash, and refill the supplies." She uncrossed her arms and leaned back in her chair. "What *exactly* is it that you do again?"

"Come on, not today." Jack rested his forearms on his desk. "I have a proposition for you."

She tilted her head, her curiosity clearly piqued.

He opened his mouth, but the words didn't come out. Now or never—because asking wouldn't get any easier. He tried again. "I'm tired of running into every situation we encounter ill-prepared, ill-informed, and half-cocked."

Her eyes narrowed, but she didn't say anything. Finally, she said, "I can't argue. There does seem to be a tendency to fly by the seat of your pants on most of our cases. I'm not complaining; you brought it up."

She wasn't going to make it easier, but she hadn't started in with the snark. While Jack was pretty damn sure the timing wasn't perfect—when would it ever be? And if it helped him get some damn sleep... He steeled himself and said, "What do you think about a partnership?"

Marin's mouth opened. She blinked furiously. But no words emerged. Her brow furrowed and she snapped her mouth shut. Then her phone rang with her dad's programmed ringtone—"Carry On Wayward Son"—and whatever she'd planned to say was lost.

"Hey, Dad." Marin shifted her body away from Jack as she spoke. Marin listened for a few seconds and then shot Jack a look out of the corner of her eye. "No problem. Jack's with me." She tapped the screen and then placed her phone on Jack's desk.

Jack sat up in his chair and leaned toward the phone. "Ewan."

"Jack. I understand you've been busy lately."

Jack wasn't sure, but he might have heard some

amusement in Ewan's voice. He glanced at Marin, but her gaze was firmly affixed to the phone.

"Is there something SPI can do for you?" Jack asked.

"I've got a case for you. Actually, I'm acting on behalf of the IPPC library. IPPC would be your client, but you'll report to me. Interested?"

Jack still hadn't gotten a good read on Marin's reaction to the call, but work was work. "Definitely interested. You know we'll need the details."

"Naturally, if you decline the case, the details remain between us."

Marin stiffened then deliberately crossed her arms.

Jack flicked a paperclip at her. In a neutral tone, he said, "Yes, that is how it normally works."

"IPPC has recently taken an interest in acquiring magical texts," Ewan said. "We've got feelers out for book leads, in both the magical and mundane communities."

Jack caught Marin's eye and she shrugged. Jack leaned forward and said, "Sounds interesting. You have a local lead?"

"Houston," Ewan said, "But we don't have an asset there that I trust for this particular case."

Marin perked up. "Sal—I've forgotten his last name. The computer programmer guy that's worked for the firm before. Isn't he still in Houston?"

"He is, but he won't work. The book, ostensibly a

compendium of home remedies, has significant monetary value." Ewan paused, and Jack and Marin shared a speculative look as they waited for him to explain. "In addition to its intrinsic value—there aren't many undiscovered magical books, as you know—we also suspect the content is unique. It's possible there's information on geo-location."

"Whoa." Marin shifted closer to the phone. "Yeah, that's a little outside Sal's pay grade. What evidence do you have?"

Geo-locating wasn't *that* big a deal—was it?

"The IPPC librarians have traced ownership back to a particularly successful geologist that worked in the oil industry several decades ago," Ewan said. "Then it disappeared and reappeared ten years ago in the hands of a farmer living and thriving in a drought-ridden area of Central Texas."

"How did it come to your attention in the first place? Something must have tipped you off to try to trace the ownership." Marin must have seen Jack's confusion, because she lowered her voice and said, "There are no geo-locater texts."

"It's a very exciting find," Ewan said. "The knowledge base for geo-locaters is small, and we don't have any books with geo-locating information, other than some third-hand accounts. As to how IPPC learned about the book: it showed up in an online auction. The bidding pattern triggered our tracking software, primarily due to an overeager bid for what should be a relatively low-value book. Once our librarian reviewed the provenance and pulled backgrounds on the former owners, she concluded there was a high probability of a magical influence."

"I still don't get it," Jack said. "If you have questions about geo-locating, you have contacts you can ask. Clifford, the guy in the castle in Wales, for one. Apparently, he's got some kind of live chat, a direct line of communication between him and IPPC."

"That's right," Ewan agreed. "After your efforts retrieving him earlier in the summer, that was the agreed-upon solution."

Jack raised his eyebrows. His *efforts* had been storming a paranoid genius's fortified castle. "So how's the book any more valuable than Clifford the geo-locator whiz?"

"That's the issue here: the geologist and the farmer *weren't* geo-locators."

"But they were magic-users," Marin said.

Ewan's reply came across the line in one tense, harsh syllable. "No."

"Wow." Jack fell back in his chair.

"Shit," Marin said.

Silence followed.

Jack was pretty damn sure that non-magical people couldn't acquire magic. Through his recent experience with the ancient dragon Joshua—Jack didn't dwell on his complicated feelings about *that*— he'd discovered that humans had a kernel of magic or they didn't. Ewan was implying a direct contradiction with the rules of the magical world as Jack understood them.

"If mundane people are cruising around the world geo-locating, something is seriously awry, right? We *are* talking about the book imbuing its owner with some level of magical talent."

"We don't know that." But Ewan sounded grim even as he denied the possibility. "There are alternative explanations: collusion with a magic-user, a magical item—"

Marin snorted. "That would be one big battery if it's a magical item. It's one thing to use magic to encode information on a book, because a record keeper also uses magic to retrieve that information. But a book that has enough juice to allow decades—"

"Or more," Jack said.

Marin just frowned and continued. "Or more than decades of mundanes to use the book as some divining rod—not simple magic—then that is a seriously powerful magical item."

"I've never heard of such a thing, so we're talking nuclear equivalent. Or the users are figuring out how to recharge it. Potentially revolutionary." As Ewan spoke, several beeps sounded in the background. "I need to go. Here's the job. We need the book retrieved. Immediately. It's available on the open market. We need you to travel to Houston, make a very generous offer in person, but the offer needs to be contingent upon leaving with the book."

"Wait—if the book is up for auction, what exactly is IPPC's plan?" Jack could feel the beginnings of a dull ache in his temple, because he already knew the answer.

"IPPC is prepared to bid competitively." Ewan's words lacked inflection.

Yep—definitely an ache. Jack said, "Not helpful."

"Right," Marin said. "If the seller isn't already aware of the book's unique properties based on the earlier high bid, he'll be curious as hell when we outbid it."

Ewan sighed. "We're not paying you as couriers; sort it out. We'll cover your usual rates and expenses, and there's a bonus paid out once the book is safely under IPPC's control."

Jack sat up straighter. He needed a new roof. "What's the bonus?"

"Harrington will forgive your outstanding debt."

Jack's lips twitched. He owed Harrington a free job—one he'd planned to sic Marin on. "And?"

"A cash bonus." Ewan named a figure that would cover the cost of at least two roofs.

Maybe Jack would have a look at those solar panels he'd been dying to install for so long. But he was never one to quit while he was only a half step ahead. "And?"

Ewan made a snorting noise that sounded a lot

like Marin. "All right. *I'll* owe you a favor, no questions asked."

Jack exchanged a glance with Marin. There was a tiny wrinkle right between her eyebrows that only showed up when she was annoyed and trying to hide it. Jeez, how did he even know that? He shook his head. Didn't matter; no way he'd pass. "Yeah, it's a deal."

"I'm sending the file and the bidding information now," Ewan said. "Call if you have any questions, but I've got a project that's blowing up right now—so if you don't catch me, try Harrington."

As soon as Marin tapped end on her phone, Jack said, "Talk."

Marin raised an eyebrow.

"Why didn't you want the case?" Jack propped his feet up on his desk.

"We had a... It doesn't matter. It's just family stuff; nothing to do with the case." Marin studied the corner of Jack's desk intently. "I mean, it's just weird to talk shop with him, but nothing specific about this case."

"Isn't that usually when you call him? About work, when we're in a jam or need information?"

Marin shrugged.

"Jeez, Marin. You're worse than me and my family."

She perked up. "You have family?"

"Everyone has family." He thought about the

question, about the partnership offer, about how long he'd known her. More politely, he said, "Yes, I have family. I have a sister here locally. Anything else I need to know? About whatever is going on with you and your dad?"

She shook her head, then pulled out her cell from her pocket and checked the time.

Prying into Marin's family crap beyond what was necessary for the job did not appeal, so... "Right. Let's call this auction house or bookstore—" Jack checked his phone for the file Ewan had promised. "The Book Store in west Houston. Let's call them and set up a viewing. We're taking your car?"

"Uh, yes. Is your Cherokee even back from the shop?"

He ignored the question and dug out a can of crab. He didn't know when he'd be back, and he didn't want Bob to go hungry. Although when he was out of town, cans simply disappeared from his cupboard. Could an Arkan Sonney use a can opener? More accurately, did an Arkan Sonney *need* a can opener?

Jack shook his head, too distracted by the upcoming case to dwell on the mysteries of magic hedgehogs.

Jack glanced at Marin when she jerked awake in the passenger seat.

She rubbed her eyes then said, "Thanks for driving. I haven't been sleeping all that well."

Jack debated commenting on the fact that dragons needed less sleep than mere mortals like himself and asking exactly how crappy her sleep had to be to need a nap.

Con: possible lengthy personal conversation.

Pro: avoiding some terrible outcome because he buried his head and ignored a possible problem.

"I'm fine, Jack."

He couldn't miss the annoyance in her voice. "What?"

"I can see the wheels turning. You can be annoyingly transparent."

"I didn't want to pry." He shifted in his seat, trying not to squirm. "Should I pry?"

He caught her head shake out of the corner of his eye and swallowed a sigh of relief.

Several minutes passed before she said, "It's not like *you've* been at your best recently."

"Hm." He wasn't going to argue, but he also wasn't about to admit he wasn't sure what was causing his restless nights.

Joshua? Hopefully not, because merging his physical self with some ancient dragon's essence wasn't supposed to actually change anything. Except maybe stealing his peace of mind. Maybe knowing that a big, bad, ancient, scaly bastard's life juice flowed through him...disturbed him. That would wreck any guy's sleep.

Marin wasn't talking, so he had plenty of time to consider the state of his mental health—but why would he want to do that? Would that make him sleep better every night? And he needed a strategy for retrieving the book. Chance the auction? Entice with a high but not too-high immediate purchase? Scope the place out for a possible burglary, followed, of course, by a substantial and anonymous contribution to the store? He rubbed his neck. Neither idea appealed, and prison sucked. IPPC's influence had limits, and Jack didn't want to end up in prison over misjudging them.

They traveled in silence over an hour. When they

hit Columbus, Jack pulled off the highway for gas. Marin had kept her eyes closed since they'd last spoken, but hadn't slept. As the truck slowed down to turn into the station, she opened her eyes.

He rolled to a stop at the pump. "Figured we'd get some gas. You can drive the rest of the way, and that gives me a chance to read over the file."

"Or I could just brief you," Marin said.

Jack opened the driver's door and hopped out.

Leaning across the front seat, Marin pitched her voice to carry and said through the open door, "Or I could just drive. But you're a control freak." When he stepped back to the open door to respond, she met him with him her creepy dragon grin—the one that was all teeth—and added, "Partner."

"I'm not a control freak, and at this rate, you're not going to be my partner." He let annoyance creep into his voice, but swallowed a smile as he turned back to the pump. She'd been thinking about his offer.

Jack finished at the pump and climbed into the passenger seat. Marin had pulled out his laptop and left it on the seat before she'd switched to the driver's side. "Anything I should I keep an eye out for?" Jack asked as he flipped open his laptop. He pulled up the file Ewan had forwarded.

Marin had spent several minutes reviewing it, and given how fast she read, she'd probably gone through the entire document at least three times.

Zipping out of the lot fast enough to give him whiplash, she made a noncommittal noise. "Not much there beyond what he told us on the phone. A little more history on the players, but that's it."

Long before they arrived at the small store in the west Houston suburbs—located in a strip mall, of all places—he'd read the file twice. Just as Marin had said, he hadn't found much useful information.

He had discovered the reserve listing price: only a few hundred dollars. From what little he knew of old and rare books, the physical, mundane book sounded old and not actually rare. After checking online, Jack discovered the latest high bid: seventy-five thousand dollars. The dealer had to have some inkling that there was a hidden value to the book. But, wild guess, the guy had no clue some long-ago spell caster had stuffed a bunch of magical information inside the book. That, or used some other means to supercharge the magical mojo of the book.

Jack almost felt bad for the poor mundane schmoe. Jack had been that clueless guy—what seemed like a lifetime ago—but he still remembered how all of the pieces simply hadn't fit together the way they should.

Marin slowed as they cruised through the strip mall parking lot.

Jack checked the numbers on the store doors then pointed ahead and to the right. "Flip around to the backside of the strip mall. Hey, when we do the physical examination of the book, you can confirm the presence of magic, right?"

Marin shot him a narrow-eyed look. And her eyes might have looked a little greener than normal.

"What? I know it takes a record keeper to read any encoded magical text, and you can't do that. I'm just checking."

Her eyes lacking any obvious glow—maybe he'd imagined that?—she said, "I should be able to get a vibe, including whether there's more going on than simply magically recorded data."

Magical books still wigged him out. Any book could store the same information as a laptop—probably more—because the book was simply an anchor for the spells that held the information.

"I still don't get why record keepers don't pick a sturdier medium. Books seem like a fragile choice for information important enough to hide with magic."

She snorted. "That's because you don't think like a spell caster."

What had his long-time friend Kenna said? Her best friend was a record keeper. "Something to do with the function of the anchor making it easier for the record keeper to attach the spelled words to the item."

"That's it. When casting a spell, using relevant physical contexts or anchors to ground the magic can be tremendously helpful. You use magic items like any other tool, Jack. And I think you look at magic like it's a tangible thing. Your ring is an alarm system, and your glasses are basically magical binoculars. But they're not just tools. Magic is...it's pure imagination made tangible."

"Okay, so why not a typewriter? Or a stone tablet? Way sturdier, same context."

She gave him an annoyed look, then pulled into a spot in front of the store.

It had a simple sign that read "Books," but no one would mistake this tiny, shabby bookstore, tucked away on the backside of a strip mall, for a purveyor of bestsellers and genre fiction. Marin pulled into a parking space two spots away from a minivan. The only other car on this side of the strip mall was a beat-up old Civic parked in the furthest spot from the shop's door.

Jack eyed the store with some misgiving. "Any guesses on which car is the storeowner's?"

Pulling the keys out of the ignition, Marin said, "I'll refrain from forming an opinion until we see the man's stock. He could be housing some gems in there."

Jack climbed out of the truck. "Best security ever —everyone in the area thinks the place is a dump so they don't bother to break in."

"Or perhaps...not." Marin had stopped in front of the glass-fronted door and was peering intently inside. "Do you have your gun?"

"Yeah—but I'm not shooting an uber-geek civilian." The words flew out of his mouth on autopilot, but his body responded to the threat she'd identified. As he drew his backup .380, he stepped away from the door. "Plan?"

"Keep the two guys who are tearing the place apart from leaving with our book. You good with that?"

"Sure thing."

"You got the unarmed civilian to the right?" She motioned to the right front corner of the store. When he nodded, she gave him her toothy dragon grin. "I'll take the disrespectful shits throwing books around." She motioned to eleven o'clock.

Jack nodded.

Marin started a countdown from three.

3

"One." Marin pulled the shop door open.

Jack slipped in and dipped right.

A gasp revealed the exact location of a very large man cowering low in the corner.

Jack ducked down beside him—just as a shot echoed through the room.

Shaking his head as his ears rang, Jack leaned close to the man and said, "Braithwaite?"

The guy looked at Jack like he'd gone mad.

A thin line of flame streamed through the still-open door. An agonized scream followed.

"I hope you're Braithwaite, and those guys are actually robbing you, because my partner just torched one of them."

"Yes, yes, yes, yes, yes, yes."

Jack had to put his hand on the guy's arm to get him to stop repeating the word. "I'm your twelve-thirty appointment." He flashed the terrified man a grin. "We're a little early."

The shop owner breathed out a barely audible "Thank God."

Jack could see a thin strip, a slice of the shop between the register he'd hunkered down behind and the scattered bookshelves. He flipped his gaze from that narrow view to the door, then back again. Waiting.

He really had too much shit going on in his life. Someone was *shooting* at him, and he barely felt a rush. That was messed up.

Marin appeared in the doorway before he could get too philosophical.

Her movements were smooth and economical as she moved to join them. "Looks like they've moved to a back room."

"Mr. Braithwaite?" Jack touched the man's arm again. "You have a back room?"

Braithwaite fell from his crouch to sit on the floor, as if the air had suddenly left him. He nodded furiously.

Jack guessed at the reason for the sudden release of tension. "There's another exit, isn't there?"

Another nod from Braithwaite was followed by a massive crash from the back of the store.

"Shit." Marin ran to the back.

"You stored the auction book in the back room?"

Jack touched the man's arm when he didn't respond. "Mr. Braithwaite, the book?"

"Yes, yes. The back room."

Several seconds passed, then the front door opened. Jack raised his gun—not that he doubted Marin's ability to kick two guys' asses and walk away.

He lowered his gun as Marin walked in.

"They're long gone." She lifted her phone. "I got a shot of their license plate, but I doubt it'll help. I texted it to my dad—the license, and some *other* info on the book. Figured we'd use his contacts to pull the registration and a police report if it was stolen."

Jack nodded. He turned to consider the pale countenance of the shop owner.

They could hardly leave Braithwaite here to report an uncontrolled story to the police.

"Mr. Braithwaite." Jack offered him a hand up. "Let's talk expenses. We'd very much like to cover the costs of this incident...in exchange for a few small considerations."

4

When Jack left the shop, he clutched a receipt for a compendium of home remedies in his hand. While possession would have been infinitely better, IPPC now held *legal* claim to the book.

Mr. Braithwaite had been rather surprised by the generous offer for a book that he had said was "a very nicely preserved example, but otherwise unremarkable."

Mr. Braithwaite happened to be one of the few honest men left in the world, a fact that became painfully obvious when they'd begun negotiations for the book and his cooperation. He claimed the excellent condition of the book and a resurgence of interest in natural remedies had slightly elevated the value, but he stressed that the value could never rise to the level Jack was offering to pay.

"Let's hope Mr. Braithwaite's memory remains suitably vague after his vacation in Belize, and that Harrington doesn't have a heart attack when he gets the tab." Marin pulled the truck keys from her pocket. After she hopped in the driver's seat, she said, "And what was with the whole laser thing?"

"What else would you call a thin blue flame?" Jack shrugged. "I was in the moment. High-tech seemed a better choice than magic. And speaking of pinpoint laser flames, your control of fire in human form has improved, or the neighbors got an eyeful of scaly lizard lady."

She turned to him with a bland expression then backed the car out of the space.

No. She'd have to be insane to flash her elephant-sized self in a strip mall parking lot. He examined her face...and she looked too innocent.

"You're shitting me. How do we explain that away? Cutting-edge laser tech is bad enough. What, PCP exposure? Uh, filming a commercial...with hidden cameras?"

"How about a rip in time allowing dinosaurs into our world." Marin readjusted her rearview mirror slightly. "Besides, it's only a problem if there's a witness."

Jack snorted. "And you ate them before you came inside, so no worries?"

"Don't be an ass. Would you rather have been shot?"

"Not really."

She waved a hand vaguely in the direction of the parking lot behind them. "And look around; there isn't a soul. I've no idea how Elliot Braithwaite was making a living with that place. Especially in this area. It's been hit hard recently."

"The recently unemployed and underemployed are not our Mr. Braithwaite's bread and butter. If you had more respect for vintage comics, you'd probably have spotted them in the shop." Jack had caught sight of a handful in the backroom when they'd verified the book's theft. He gave her almost pristine car a hard look. "Come to think of it, you have a distinct lack of respect for all things vintage. But vintage comics might bring in some cash for him."

"Dragons live in the now. I've told you that. And sometimes it's easier surrounded by new things." Glancing out of the corner of her eye, she said, "And your Jeep isn't vintage. It's a piece of shit you need to replace."

Now she was just trying to piss him off. He opened up his laptop—then remembered her comment about the book. "What other information did you get on the book?"

"Oh, shit, that's right. Death magic. The shop, the back room especially. The book is obviously the source. Even the parking lot reeked after our shooters made off with the book."

"Death magic, as in dead people juicing up the

book and powering its magic?" When she tipped her head once in affirmation, he asked, "How in the hell did you spot that before we even went in the back room?"

"If death magic were a smell, it was stinking up the entire store."

"That's a lot of death."

She glanced at him and raised her eyebrows. "That's a powerful book."

Jack couldn't help but dwell on exactly how powerful. The little experience he had with death magic had given him a healthy respect for the sheer magnitude of magical power it generated. One death had powered a containment ward for more than a hundred years—that was serious shit.

He forced himself to turn his attention to his laptop. He wanted another look at the book's provenance, as well as the research done by the in-house IPPC librarian, and freaking out like a kid who'd just watched his first horror flick wouldn't help.

By the time he'd settled into his research, several minutes had passed and he realized he had no clue where they were headed. "Where are we going?"

"Are you going to tell me what *you're* doing?"

Maybe the partnership offer had been premature. Then again, she had just dragon-lasered a bad guy. That was pretty badass. And probably partner-worthy.

"Hey, how'd your flame victim manage to get away?" Jack asked.

"Ah. I aimed to disable—figured we wanted to question them. But his buddy just dragged him along. That was enough experimentation with non-lethal force for this decade."

Once he had the relevant docs open, he pulled up his old research buddy Christine's contact information. Married and with some unknown number of kids running around, she'd done very little freelance research for him lately. But this was an emergency. He tapped call.

"Hey, Chris. How's my favorite research assistant?" He spent five minutes updating her on the request and skirting questions about the case. The client was another matter; he asked her to copy Ewan on the results. When he ended the call, he realized they were pulling up to a cheap hotel they'd passed on the way into town.

"More private than a restaurant, and we can order pizza when we get hungry." Marin pulled into the covered temporary parking area for registering guests. "You're paying for the pizza *and* the hotel."

"What, like I wouldn't? Chris says give her a few hours and she should have a list of suspicious deaths and disappearances near the last owner's home town. It's a little place about an hour southeast of Austin."

Marin got out of the car and waited for him to

join her. As he rounded the front of the truck, she said, "You remember that back during the 2011 drought, he bought out a number of struggling family-owned farms? Not in and of itself terrible, but he managed to profit immensely by installing or upgrading irrigation systems and implementing more modern farming practices."

Jack paused. "But where'd the water come from?"

"Right. Thinking about all of those bankrupt farmers...it makes me curious to know how he died."

"Wishing a horrible and lingering illness on someone might make you a bad person." Jack opened the lobby door for her.

She shrugged. "Not if he deserved it."

Out of perverse curiosity, Jack popped off a text to Chris asking her how Albright had died. That information hadn't been included in the file.

And if the successful Mr. Albright had murdered a bunch of locals to power his water-divining book, then, yeah, the guy might have deserved a horrible and lingering illness.

And that was why they'd make decent partners: they agreed on the important shit.

Jack was in the middle of eating a piece of almost-hot pizza when Christine returned his call. He still hadn't heard from Ewan, but Marin hadn't seemed surprised when he mentioned it earlier.

Jack answered and tapped speaker. "Hey, Chris. I've got Marin with me."

"Color me shocked. How have you not flame-broiled him yet, Marin? And, Jack, I say that with love in my heart."

Marin grabbed another slice and dropped down on the bed. "He's an angel. A cheap, sentimental, slightly sleazy angel."

Chris laughed. "You guys are spending way too much time together."

Jack couldn't help noticing his longtime buddy

didn't bother to deny a word of Marin's criticism. Cheap, sleazy... "Since when am I sentimental?"

Marin swallowed a bite of pizza. "The Jeep."

Almost at the same time, Chris said, "Your car."

"Enough about Jack and his many failings." The laughter had died from Chris's voice. She was suddenly all business. "Open the zip file I sent you. There's a photo compilation inside."

"Got it." Jack clicked the file labeled "montage," then blew up the image. "Holy shit."

Marin flipped his computer around, greasy fingers and all, so she could see the screen. She shoved the last bite of her pizza into her mouth and belatedly looked around for something to wipe her fingers on.

Jack handed her a handful of paper napkins.

Marin snatched the napkins but then her attention immediately pivoted to the screen. "These look like crime scene photos. Is that legit?"

"Jack and I have a don't ask, don't tell agreement. So—no comment. You see the pattern?"

"How could anyone miss it?" One photo after another of slashed victims jumped off the screen at Jack. "How could the FBI miss it?"

"Excellent question," Chris said. "Creative wording, failing to report—but I don't have a good answer. The kids are about to get home—have to run. I'll keep poking around and will check in with additional information."

"Thanks, Chris." Jack ended the call and then set his phone on the nightstand, well away from any pizza grease.

"I'd like to know what local law enforcement have to say." Marin barely kept bits of food from flying as she spoke around the pizza in her mouth. "Similar knife wounds that would have all caused massive blood loss."

Jack winced. "I'd ask if you were raised by wolves, but the ones I've met have better table manners than you."

Marin swallowed, wiped her mouth, and then chucked the wadded-up napkins onto the nightstand. "Brachial, carotid, and femoral arteries cut—all injuries that would have caused massive blood loss. And the injuries appear to have been made with some sort of blade—a clear pattern. How could the locals not have seen it?"

She lifted a finger toward the screen.

"Hey, not the screen."

Yanking her hand back, she scowled at him. "Something's off. These should have been recognized as possibly the work of one person."

"First, there were seven murders in ten years. Second, look at the locations." Jack pulled up a county map on his computer. Pointing to the area just southeast of Austin, he circled the relevant area with his fingertip. "They're spread over four, maybe five, counties."

"Even so, seven murders in such a low population density area... Something's hinky. And where's the news coverage? Serial killer on the loose in Central Texas—that kind of thing. Someone's hushed these up." Marin rolled off the bed and disappeared into the bathroom.

Jack could hear the water in the sink running. He pitched his voice to be heard above the water. "If they didn't want the murders discovered, why a cover-up? I'd make sure no one found the bodies."

She came back drying her hands on a small towel. "We both know I'd just incinerate them. Did you get the files as well, or just the pictures?"

"We've got the files. Give me a sec, and I'll forward them." When he was done, he said, "Code red files."

"Is code red the one where I get fired if the info leaks, or the one where I have to clean your car?" She glanced at the little blue telephone box replica in her hand, and then frowned at him.

He gave her a blank stare. "The one where I leave old French fries to petrify under the driver's seat of your car. But I'll also consider firing you."

"I will be very careful."

The two of them spent some time familiarizing themselves with the files. But it was only an hour or so later that Chris sent them an update with Mr. Stanley Albright's cause of death—and then they changed the focus. Albright's death had been ruled a suicide. The sixty-five-year-old farmer turned businessman had slashed his wrists vertically. No history of previous attempts was documented in his medical files. In fact, there was no record of depression at all.

For the next several hours, they dug through the files looking for some connection between the victims, something beyond Albright to tie them together. Albright may or may not have orchestrated what were looking more and more like sacrificial murders—but it looked like he wasn't the linchpin. The man could hardly be the linchpin if he was also a victim.

Jack's phone chirped as a new text message came in. He blinked and rubbed his burning eyes. Too much reading and not enough blinking. He opened the message: *Church of the Book. And tell Chris she'd like working for us.*

He replied: *I don't work with clients who steal my contractors.* As an afterthought, he added: *Thanks*

"Hey, your dad just texted me. Have you seen anything about a Church of the Book?"

"No, but...hold on." Marin pulled her laptop closer and started clicking and tapping. "Here. It looks like a woman was questioned closely because of a previous assault against her husband. She was discounted based upon a confirmed alibi—provided by her church."

"Well, they would give her an alibi if one of them slit her husband's throat, wouldn't they?"

"Just because they use the word 'book' in the name, it doesn't mean anything. That could easily be a reference to the Bible." Marin tapped a few keys and then said, "Ouch. Her husband's injury was to the femoral artery. Sliced in the groin—now that sounds like something an angry wife might either do or have done to her husband."

"And a fantastic way to torture a guy. Don't move, buddy, or we might miss." Jack resisted the urge to cover his junk.

"Sure. The guy was worried about his dick right before he was brutally murdered." She didn't look up, just kept scrolling through the file. "I don't see any reference to the name of the church in here. That's odd, right?"

"Uh, yeah. Hey, I found a website." Jack flipped the screen around for her. "Like all good nonprofits, they've ensured there's an easy way to donate online. Three physical locations..." Jack switched back to the county map. "Yeah, all three church locations are well within that five-county region I showed you before. And there's only one pastor for all three branches. Road trip?"

"Sounds like a plan." She snapped her laptop shut. "You're driving. I read faster, and I want one more look through those files for any hint of a church or a religious group. But try not to drive like a little old lady."

"Where's all the blood?" Jack had been driving about an hour now, and it had been bugging him for several miles.

"What?" Marin pulled her attention away from her laptop. "What blood?"

"Exactly—what blood? The crime scene photos show no blood from wounds that would have bled profusely. So where is it? And going with your local law enforcement involvement theory, the missing blood from each scene should also have tied the murders together."

Marin turned off the music. "Since only about half of the victims appear to have been moved, according to the case files, and there's no sign the scenes have been tidied when the victims weren't moved, the murderer or murderers must have collected the blood. My vote's for the blood being integral to the sacrifice."

"So how does that work?"

"How should I know?"

"No super-secret dragon knowledge about blood sacrifices? Or what about Ewan? Is he ever going to get back to us on the death magic aspect?"

"When he has something, he'll let us know."

Jack's phone chirped with a text alert. "Can you get that?"

Marin entered his passcode—a code he'd never given her—and tapped the screen. "Chris is sending a background for each of the victims and a summary of some interesting financial data on the church. Give me a sec, and I'll pull it up on my laptop. On the hotspot I only use for work. That I pay for myself."

Jack mentally added cell and hotspot reimbursement to the offer he had prepared.

A few minutes later, Marin whistled. "The Church of the Book is loaded."

"Albright must have propped them up. A small church in an area with a dwindling population that's been decimated by drought—how else does a tiny church have full coffers?"

"Wrong. I've got a list here of donors that boggles the mind. Albright, the sheriff, a deputy—no, two deputies—a county judge, and a few connected politicians who aren't local to the area. And those are just the high rollers."

Jack felt a pulsing throb in his temple. "The nasty stench of that cover-up you suspected is growing stronger. How do you think Harrington would feel about a cross-county cover-up if all this goes sideways?"

"Pissy."

Jack swallowed a laugh. *Pissy* wasn't a word that came to mind when he thought of Harrington.

"Given our track record, we might just see."

"Yeah, about that—maybe let's minimize the damage?"

"I'm wounded. I always do my best."

Marin declined to respond and turned the music back up.

So things occasionally blew up. And he got shot at pretty regularly. And there was that time he was possessed. Jack figured a cleanup call to Harrington almost definitely loomed in his future.

JACK TURNED off the main drag to one of the few side streets located in downtown Lorietta. "Hard to get lost."

"Forget that. With a population of around five thousand, it's hard to imagine so may big-fish donors in the area, especially given the recent economic climate." Marin pointed. "Up there on the right. You see it?"

"Uh..." He didn't see it, unless the Church of the Book was masquerading as an old metal building. It looked more like a warehouse than a church. Then he saw the sign with clear block letters reading "Church of the Book." The sign was old and faded, and, much like the building, gave an impression of limited funds and a long history.

"Not spending their cash on rent."

"No." Jack pulled into the gravel lot and parked in the shade under a massive live oak. No other cars were in the lot. Unless church employees parked elsewhere—assuming the church was even big enough to have any—the building appeared unoccupied.

As he approached the metal building, he realized why the place had such a familiar feel. It looked like any other small-town community center in any other underpopulated Central Texas town. "If the appearance is anything to go by, I doubt the building's occupied except for services."

As they reached the door, Marin pointed to the small placard with the church's hours listed. Two services on Sunday and an evening service on Wednesdays. They might be out of luck to meet the minister or staff, since it was a Tuesday.

"Three services for a small church that gives the

appearance of being underfunded and serves a town of five thousand?" Jack asked.

"Don't forget the other two locations. The same pastor serves all three churches." She turned to try the door then glanced back at Jack when it swung open. "Maybe someone's cleaning?"

Jack paused at the threshold, then whispered, "We're thinking about moving to the area."

"Sure, honeybunch."

Jack nodded, and Marin opened the door wide.

The temperature difference as he crossed the threshold made him pause. Old metal buildings were notorious for having poor insulation and being a bitch to keep comfortable, and yet the interior of the building was cool and dry. And on a day with no services, and not one car in the church's lot.

He paused at the entrance, allowing his eyes to adjust to the dimmer light. By the time he could see well enough to differentiate large shapes, a man had spotted them and was approaching. Maybe letting the dragon with preternaturally keen eyesight go first wouldn't hurt.

"Hello. Welcome to the Church of the Book. How can I help you?" A man in pressed khakis and a polo shirt stood smiling at them. His medium brown hair was close-cropped and his smile automatic.

Jack extended his hand. "I'm Jack and this is my girlfriend Mary. We're looking at moving in the next few months. You know, get out of the city, away from the high property taxes and the traffic. We saw the sign and figured if anyone was in..."

As Jack spoke, the man shook his hand firmly and then turned to Marin. She smiled in greeting, but didn't offer her hand.

"Yes, of course. I'm Pastor Rick, and I'm happy to help if I can. What questions do you have?"

"I guess...what's it like to live here?" Jack took a casual step closer to Marin, putting her at girlfriend rather than colleague distance.

"It's quieter than Austin, certainly. We've got a mix of farmers and ranchers. Can I ask what you do?"

"Oh, sure. I'm a writer. Living in the country, writing on the porch..." Jack shrugged. "It's always been a dream of mine."

"And I do medical transcription, so I can really work anywhere." Marin had pitched her voice higher, and she sounded so unlike herself that Jack had to stop himself from doing a double take.

"Well, you won't want to be too far out of town so your internet service is more reliable. I know of a few houses that might fit the bill. Are you looking to buy or rent?"

"It really depends on what's available." Jack looked around the room, at the neatly lined up chairs and the altar. "Do you get a good turnout for services?"

"We do. I'm fortunate that Lorietta's residents are

a devout group."

Jack paused, waiting for an invitation to join the service scheduled for the following day. When none was issued, he said, "So are you from here originally?"

"No, Dallas, but I've lived here for several years."

"Basically a local, right?" Jack gave him a genial smile. "Do you live here in town? Or out in the country?"

"A little out of town."

Marin leaned closer to Jack and bumped against him affectionately. "That's what I think we should do, but Jack would rather be directly in town."

"Well, if you don't have any other questions..." Pastor Rick looked in the direction of the door.

"Right, we need to get going." Jack turned to the door, then paused and said, "One last question: if you were looking to move out of Austin, would you settle in Lorietta?"

"Absolutely."

"Thank you, Pastor Rick. We appreciate your time." Jack reached out and shook the man's hand again.

"Good luck to you both."

Jack and Marin exited the church in silence, and only when they'd both settled into the Range Rover did Marin comment. "That was weird as hell."

"Damn right it was. Sure—move to our town, but don't come to our church services. No invitation to

Wednesday's service, no tour, and no questions about our own religious beliefs. It's been a while since I've been in a church, but that should be standard. He's a man of God; you'd think he'd express some interest in our beliefs after we walked into his church."

"Yeah. And I agree, if something shady is happening in Lorietta or with the church, you'd think he'd have warned us off the town. Turn right." Marin pointed at the exit. "We can see if our pastor might be parked in the street."

"And I want to circle through the main square then get a room at that sketchy motel we passed on the way into town."

"Don't suppose I have a choice."

"Not really. What, don't tell me you have plans?"

"Apparently I have plans for a midnight break-in," Marin said. "No wards that I could detect, but they could very well be arming them when no one is there."

Jack scrubbed his jaw. "We haven't encountered anyone with magic yet. I'm betting no wards. Old-fashioned security, maybe, but no magic. This entire case has a very mundane feel."

"Except for the stench of death magic all over the bookshop, I'd agree. I don't really understand how these people got mixed up with death magic. Any hint of death magic unleashes the wrath of the entire magical community."

Jack coughed back a laugh. "We're in Central Texas—what magical community? The Lycan? They have their own problems, and this wouldn't appear on their radar. The Coven of Light? Hell, they'd join in."

"No, not the Coven. I mean, yes, they would join in—I think we know how enamored of death magic they are—but there's no indication of their involvement. And what's with the players? A judge, cops, a council member, the large geographic spread...it's all so improbable without some larger context."

"If the church is involved—and my money's on them being ass-deep—then that's the nexus. And what do all of the contributors have in common?"

"Wealth, power, influence." Marin buckled her seatbelt. "Cop up ahead. Pretend like you know how to drive and where you're going."

Jack drove exactly the speed limit as he passed the small police station with a single cruiser parked out front. Could the entire town be involved? If the minister of the Church of the Book was a key player, then what were the broader implications?

The sensation of being watched, like a bug under a magnifying glass, made him glance around the empty streets. Suddenly, this typical Central Texas small town felt like the setting of a horror flick—eerily empty and suspiciously run-down.

A few minutes later, when they were about halfway to the motel, Marin said, "Don't make a fuss, but I think we're being followed. The car behind has made the last three turns with us."

That might explain the uneasy sensation he'd been feeling since they'd left Lorietta. Unfortunately, there was a long stretch of road ahead with no turnoffs. He kept traveling, the same speed and without obviously checking his rearview mirror, until they reached the motel. He verified the dark blue sedan was still behind him, and then kept driving past the motel. "How far to the interstate from here?"

Marin pulled her phone out and fiddled with her navigation. "About three miles."

Jack had only gone another mile when the old blue sedan sped up and passed them. He took his foot off the gas, and watched as the car sped past.

"I hate to sound overcautious, but maybe skip the motel?" Marin scanned the area.

The Range Rover was hardly inconspicuous, and even less so in a dive motel parking lot. "We'll camp out at the shop. Between your place, my place, and The Junk Shop, it's the shortest drive to the church."

"You're sure that's still a good plan? If they were following us—"

"Right, I get it. Pastor Rick sent them. Let's say you're right? Getting out of Lorietta isn't a bad idea. And we'll just return...cautiously."

He pulled out in the road, ignoring Marin's mumbled reply. "Cautiously my ass."

7

J ack set his alarm for eleven that evening, just in case he fell asleep and Marin didn't keep a close eye on the time. Hitting the church somewhere between midnight and one seemed like a good idea. No neighborhood dogs abutting the church property, poor street lighting, no neighborhood watch signs, and a tiny police presence all combined to make their break-in job easier.

Marin poked her head into the room. "I'm going to sort through those last few boxes of inventory before we have to leave again."

"The junk I picked up after that big garage sale in the 'burbs shut down? I thought you finished that stuff already."

Marin gave him a narrow-eyed look but didn't respond before she left.

Oh, yeah. He'd mentioned helping with stocking

and pricing when he'd unloaded them a few days ago. And then forgot. Since Marin was still an employee—for now—she could suck it up.

He cleared some paperwork, some miscellaneous junk, and an old blanket off his couch. When he lifted the blanket, he found Bob curled up snugly under it. Bob cracked one eye open then the other.

"Mind to share, buddy?"

The little guy stood up and yawned, stretched, and then moved to the end of the sofa.

Jack still found it unnerving that Bob looked so much like a corkscrew-tailed Labrador puppy, and yet he understood more of the events around him than many people Jack knew. "And why do they call you guys lucky hedgehogs? You and your buddy Nelson don't look anything like hedgehogs."

Jack thought he saw a hint of a smile on Bob's canine-like snout. Unfortunately, without Marin, he couldn't communicate with Bob. Except for that one time, but that had been a one-off, and had happened right after he and Joshua had done their energy-essence merging thing.

Jack slipped his shoes off. "Watch the feet, little guy."

Bob scooted further toward the corner of the couch and closed his eyes.

He was such an agreeable guy. If Jack could find a roommate for the house that was half as helpful... He stretched out and fell asleep.

A nudge against his side. A nibble on his fingers. Wakeupwakeupwakeup. *A tickle at the back of his neck. Watched. Watching. Someone watched.*

Teeth scraped sharply against his knuckles.

"Ow." Jack jerked upright as Bob disappeared. "What the—"

Hands jerked his shoulders, his ankles. He tumbled to the floor.

His right hip throbbed.

His gun. He reached for his ankle holster...too slow. Pain exploded in his shoulders.

Arms twisted high above his head, he looked but couldn't see Marin.

Another jerk. This time his ankles. The muscles in his legs strained.

His head thumped against the concrete floor.

He needed to get up; he couldn't. Large hands pulled, yanking—across carpet, concrete. Concrete abraded his jaw, his cheek, the back of his head.

The pressure on his joints released. His numb hands and useless legs dropped to the floor.

A ripping sound—duct tape—and his ankles were bound. He struggled—tried to struggle—but a man slammed his head against the floor.

He tried to roll, push away—anything. Wrists taped, feet taped—he couldn't move.

Every fiber said fight... his body wouldn't move.

Acrid, choking. Smoke.

Marin...

Stinging eyes. More smoke.

Where was Marin?

One man at his feet, another at his shoulders. Joints strained, he swayed in the air, floated.

Jack swallowed back bile. The smoke. What was with the smoke?

A last glimpse of the store—one corner charred. No flames. Only smoke.

Where was Marin?

His shoulders fell; blood rushed to his head. His vision narrowed...

THE FLOOR VIBRATED. Jack's eyes watered when the floor lurched. The sudden, sharp pain in his head brought him back to the present. He was in a car, in a trunk. The same damn blue sedan that had followed he and Marin earlier, if he had to guess.

No telling how long he'd been out. He lifted his taped hands to his head. Some of the blood was dry —so a while.

Marin.

Shit. What had happened to her?

Hell, he didn't have time to worry about her. He had to save his own ass. He rolled to face the taillights. Too late he remembered his bruised hip, and a grunt of pain escaped. He lay still, waiting for some sign his attackers had heard him. But the car continued on at the same speed.

He tried again, this time steeling himself for the wave of pain. Cold sweat coated his body as his head thumped painfully in time with his pulse. He would not puke in the trunk of a car. No. Just—no.

When he'd caught his breath, he felt for the release latch. With any luck, the assholes who grabbed him hadn't thought to disable it. With each twisting effort, his head thudded. The constant reminder that he was concussed wasn't doing much for his patience. He fumbled a third time but couldn't find a release.

Shit. It was that old damned sedan—no emergency release.

And breaking out the taillights would only alert his captors that he'd awakened without improving his chances of popping open the trunk.

He rubbed his ankle against the bottom of the trunk. And they'd taken his gun. Not surprising, but it pissed him off anyway.

He inched his body away from the rear of the trunk to give himself some maneuvering room, then lifted his hands to his mouth. With enough time, he could get the tape off and at least come out of the trunk fighting. Just because they wanted him alive now, didn't mean they intended to keep him that way.

He'd worried about a quarter-inch tear in the

tape around his hands when the car decelerated. It felt like they were exiting a highway or interstate. Jack focused all of his energy on the duct tape. If they arrived before he freed his hands and feet, he'd be helpless. He ignored the tiny voice in the back of his head that said they'd be armed, and, bound or not, he was screwed. But that little voice wasn't any damn help. None at all.

Half an inch. Just a little more time—

The car slowed and turned, the crunch of gravel under the tires giving away their location: the Church of the Book parking lot. Jack would bet cash on it.

The car rolled to a stop.

8

Jack calmed his breathing, pushed away the pain, and readied himself for a final effort.

One car door opened and slammed shut, then the other. The sound of crunching gravel neared, stopped...and then moved further away.

Gradually the sound of footsteps disappeared.

Jack strained to hear any sign that someone was outside the car, but he couldn't block out the pounding of his own pulse in his ears.

He turned back to his restraints. He needed to focus on one thing. One thing at a time, and he might stay conscious and have some chance.

He gnawed on duct tape till the ache in his jaw started to compete with his pounding head. Finally the last strands gave way.

At well over six feet, Jack took up most of the

space in the trunk. Reaching his feet proved more difficult than he'd guessed. With some careful shifting and rolling, he tucked his knees up close enough to his chest that he could touch the tape on his ankles.

It took more than a dozen tries, but he finally found the edge of the tape with his cramped, numb fingers. Unwinding it in the tight confines of the trunk also proved a challenge, and by the time he'd finished, he'd exhausted himself. Without some serious painkillers or a healer, he wasn't about to put up any kind of fight when that lid popped open.

Jack

Jack's head jerked up when he heard Marin's voice. He narrowly missed pounding his head for the second—or was it third?—time that night. "Shit, Marin. Where the hell are you?"

Above the church parking lot.

"No." It might be the middle of the night and Marin might have the best camo-skin known to dragonkind, but the church was still in the middle of a populated town. And dragon Marin was the size of an elephant. "You have lost your mind."

Probably. Long story short—I'm stuck as a dragon. A few seconds of silence followed. *Hug the floor of the trunk.*

"Why?" But Jack didn't wait for an answer; he flattened himself as best he could.

The temperature in the trunk increased. As the

air grew heavy with the heat, Jack kept as still as he could. He had no clue what the hell she was doing. And even with precise control and all of the advantages of magical fire, he couldn't be sure touching the wrong part of the car wouldn't fry him.

The screech of tearing metal made his head explode in pain. As his head thudded, he envisioned massive claws tearing into metal inches from his back.

You can open your eyes now.

He could hear the smirk in her voice.

"Don't even. You try being the sardine in a tin can opened with sharp pliers." Jack lurched over the jagged edges of metal where Marin had ripped the trunk from the car.

She stretched her long, silvery neck out, giving him something that wouldn't rip his hands apart to lean on.

"You couldn't break in and just pop the damn trunk?"

All dragon, all the time. Pay attention, Jack. And hurry. They'll have heard the noise.

"You think?" Jack's hands slid down the cool, flexing scales of her neck as she turned to watch the church door. "You have an exit plan?"

We need to retrieve the book—and a knife.

"Now?" Jack did a quick inventory: concussion, bruising, muscle strain, but no broken bones. If his brain wasn't bleeding, he was probably good to go... slowly. And with no gun. "Wait—what knife?"

The church doors opened.

Marin's neck arched and her jaws opened wide. A thin stream of flame scorched the opened door.

Whoever was making their way out retreated back into the building.

"You're going to explain this terrible plan at some point, right?"

Tomorrow.

"Cute. Those guys could be escaping out the back. There's an exit on the opposite side of the building."

I melted the lock and sealed the windows.

Jack stood up taller and stretched his shoulders. "All right, seriously, what's the plan?"

Burn a hole in the building, enter, incapacitate a few guards...find a gun for you.

Marin turned her attention from the church door to him, her neck snaking around for a glimpse back to the church.

I'm stuck in dragon form...for a while.

"When we're not about to die, how about you explain that." Jack rolled his head from one side to the other. The pounding in his head was scrambling his brains, but he didn't really have time for an Aleve run.

Huge reptilian eyes stared down at him.

We need to get a move on. I have to get home before the sky lightens.

"Right." Since he'd been telling his body to move for several seconds and it wasn't complying, Jack figured he wasn't actually up to a fight. But then his second wind must have kicked in, because his legs started to work again and he headed to the door.

Marin moved her massive bulk with an eerie ease, keeping pace with him.

No windows on this side of the building, and he hadn't heard breaking glass. But there was no telling what the pastor and his congregation had gotten up to while he and Marin had been outside not communicating. "Any clue how many people are inside?"

Six.

Marin moved in front of Jack as they got close to the front door. She may have baby scales that were soft by dragon standards, but she was still less vulnerable to gunfire than he was. He kept his hand on the silvery scales of her back left haunch as they approached.

Don't get close enough for hand to hand. That knife will kill you on contact.

And Jack had his answer to several questions. A knife that would kill him—and seriously mess up a dragon. Probably how he'd been nabbed to begin with—he'd been grabbed after Marin had been incapacitated by this mysterious knife. "What's it look like?"

The scales under his hand vibrated and he walked through a small puff of steamy air. Was she laughing?

It looks like a knife.

Without warning, Marin rocked back on her muscular haunches and shot a wide burst of blue flame at the building.

Jack peered around her and watched as a hole appeared in the side of the building—and then the flames simply disappeared. Someday he'd stop expecting magical fire to behave like normal fire.

It took a moment for his eyes to adjust after the quick flash. The scales under his hand moved, and Marin was several feet in front of him by the time he could see. All of her bulk, and yet she moved with unexpected speed. Jack jogged behind her. At least the adrenaline had finally kicked in, and his head didn't explode with each step.

The hole they entered was easily twice Marin's width. She'd approached at an angle to minimize their exposure, and a split second before stepping through, she shot a burst of steam through the entrance.

As a scream shattered the air, Jack realized he hadn't even known that Marin could blast steam. He needed a dragon résumé. He would add that as a stipulation of their partnership agreement.

Heading right.

Shots rang out and Marin snaked around the corner to the right, a pale shape in the darkness.

Jack said a silent prayer that his memory of the interior was accurate, and then dove to the left.

His hip protested as he landed on the bruised area.

And there was the table he'd recalled—four feet away.

He huffed out a pained breath. Nothing but some folding chairs and open air between the angry assholes with guns and him. Add in a little moonlight, and here he was: a lovely target.

He scanned the area. Parboiled dead guy at three o'clock.

"A little cover?" He whispered the request, but he knew exactly how exceptional Marin's hearing was.

Three, two, one...

On one, Jack dove for the corpse.

The room lit up with the brilliance of a small star, and he grabbed the corpse's gun.

Half lunging, half crawling, he made it to the table. And after a few half-blind tries, he got the heavy, seventies-era piece on its side. Much sturdier than he'd remembered.

The bright flash had imprinted on his retina, and he closed his eyes, waiting for it to fade.

Too long, he hunkered down behind the thick wood table, blind. Finally, he checked the Glock 17 he'd retrieved to ensure it hadn't been damaged by its high-heat steam bath.

Seventeen rounds. The guy hadn't even fired his weapon.

Glancing to his right, he found Marin's pale form curled up in the corner. Her eyes were watchful, so she was simply making herself a smaller target.

The silence had stretched too long.

The pastor's flock had escaped through an unknown third exit, or they were hidden in a back room.

"Are we clear?"

Probably. Four left.

Steam-fried guy—and maybe a toasted second man when she'd let loose the mini-nova.

Jack searched for the second dead body but came up empty. "You good?"

Good enough.

He could hug the left wall of the building or head up the center between two blocks of folding chairs to the altar. He could only see one set of doors in the back right corner of the building.

"One door?"

Yes.

"When I hit the altar, move forward."

Jack flipped that imaginary coin that lived inside his head and headed to the wall. As he passed two windows, he checked for activity outside. Nothing.

It had easily been three, maybe four, minutes

since Marin tore off a chunk of metal from the sedan. At some point the police had to show—or the neighbors. Someone. They were making a hell of a lot of noise.

He followed the wall past the corner, but there were no windows on this side of the building. Probably because the room on the other side ran the length of the building.

As he hit the altar, Marin started along the far wall. Chairs crashed as she moved. Bull in a china shop, dragon in a church—what did he expect? She could be slippery as an eel, but that didn't change her size.

He held up a hand for her to stop. He didn't want to announce their entrance. Another chair fell, and he looked closer.

In the dim light, he could barely make out the darker smudges that streaked her side. Shit. In a whisper, he asked, "Were you shot?"

Silence.

Shit. Definitely more than once. Maybe he wouldn't have to worry about that partnership deal, since they'd both be dead momentarily. "Can you just burn the whole damn building down?"

Not if we want the book.

Jack considered the fee, the bonus, the favor—

We want the book.

Her response at least confirmed she wasn't in *imminent* danger of death.

"Right. Cover me." Jack lowered his borrowed gun and ran. What should have been a sprint turned into more of a jog. His legs simply wouldn't pump as fast as he needed. And yet, no gunfire.

As he moved the chairs silently out of the way, he asked, "What the hell are they doing in there?"

Nothing good.

"Screw this. Blow that shit up. Wait—" Jack considered the door. "Maybe to the left."

And for the second time, Marin's fire punched a hole through a wall without noticeably damaging anything else. Like she'd crisped the outer layer of an onion, leaving the interior raw.

The hole was a little bigger, and it took longer for the flames to vanish into nothing; then again, she had been shot.

"You're a complete freak of nature."

Your envy is unbecoming.

When the last flame died, he checked right then left—and found not a single pious shooter in the room.

9

"What the hell?" Jack felt Marin's hot breath blow down the neck of his shirt. He moved further into the room, giving Marin space to enter. "Clear. You wanna have a look? Check for wards?"

Stinks like death.

Marin tucked her wings in tight against her body to fit through the hole she'd made. And as she scanned the room for signs of magic, Jack checked her wounds. Three neat holes, and none of them had stopped bleeding. A thin trickle of red seeped from each wound when she moved. Her scales hadn't done jack to protect her.

"Recent death magic—as in, the book's here now?"

Yes.

She made a chuffing noise that warmed the air.

"Yeah? Laugh all you want, but you look like shit and you're not healing like you should."

Her long neck snaked around, and her reptilian eyes burned with a subtle green glow.

"Your eyes are glowing. You might fix that—or I can just paint an iridescent X on your forehead."

Her lids lowered, and when she opened her eyes the glow was gone.

There's a basement.

"In Texas? Maybe it's another exit."

Jack felt more than heard a low rumble.

"Okay, there's a basement."

He followed her gaze to a point a few feet away along the interior wall. He wouldn't have spotted it in the darkness, but knowing where to look made all the difference. "You have enough juice to blow through that?"

This time, the low, vibrating rumble made his stomach churn. Head injuries and dragon growls did not mix well. Someone was a cranky dragon.

Jack's stomach cramped and his head pulsed anew with pain. A darkness choked at the back of his throat, stealing his breath.

Death magic.

"No shit," he coughed out.

Holding his side, he pointed at the trapdoor in the floor—but Marin's jaws were already wide. Orange flame burned through the door.

Jack blinked through the haze. Stinging smoke hung in the air, and tears rolled down his face.

The cramping in his stomach had stopped—so maybe they'd interrupted whatever the hell was happening down in that basement.

He wiped his face with the hem of his T-shirt. Only then did he see that she'd blasted several feet beyond the door.

And he'd been inhaling bits of dead-guy ash.

That left three death-magic zealots doing who the hell knew what in that basement.

He looked at the narrow opening and then at Marin. "Be back shortly. If that shit starts up again, torch the entire building."

Marin huffed out a bit of steam. Then she sank down carefully on her haunches in front of the basement.

Be careful, you ass.

Jack lifted his gun in a salute and started down the stairs.

The steps under his feet were charred, but they felt solid and held his weight.

He trod softly—but what was the point? They knew he was coming. Then he felt it again: that terrible sense of dread.

He swallowed and sped up his descent.

The bottom of the steps opened up to the right, so he hugged the left wall, hoping he'd be able to quickly sweep the entire room.

Three more steps…

One man with a gun—shooting.

Jack fell to the ground and fired. Again. And again. The gunman fell noiselessly to the ground.

The world around him played out in silence. Two men standing over an open book.

One with a bloodied knife. Drops of dirty red dripped onto the page.

One with a moving mouth. Jack heard nothing.

Jack shook his head; the ringing persisted. He tried to lift his gun—but couldn't.

The room was small. His body hurt. He couldn't think. He couldn't move.

The man with the knife lunged.

The knife. *Don't touch the knife. Don't let the knife bite.*

Too late.

The knife grazed his arm.

Metal teeth ripped into him, chewed him. His left arm hung, useless.

Jack fired wildly, accurately? He fired again and then again.

His ears rang and then his attacker fell. The knife slipped from the man's hand.

Jack propped himself against the wall.

His eyes searched—found—the last man. The minister.

Who had the book.

Who wanted the knife.

"I don't think so, asshole." Jack couldn't lift his arm, couldn't aim the gun—so he waited.

Pastor Rick needed that knife. He scrambled across the small room.

And Jack waited.

Rick swooped down in a fevered frenzy, reached for the knife.

And Jack shot him. Right between his crazy, cult-leader eyes.

And then he passed out.

10

Jack. Jack. Jack.

Five more minutes. Just five.

Jack. Wake up.

Five. Minutes.

JACK

"What the holy hell?" Jack jerked and clutched his head. The instant his hands touched his head, he puked.

Each retching motion acted as a sledgehammer on his skull.

He was concussed. And Marin was yelling in his head.

Very quietly, very carefully, he said, "Have you lost your mind?"

Do you even know where you are?

Sure he did. He stopped and looked around.

Shit. "In the basement. Of course."

Status?

"Four dead guys—three shot, and you toasted one."

The book?

"Check. And the knife. Oh, hell. That guy slashed my arm. How bad is that?"

Silence followed.

While Marin tried to sort out how to tell him the bad news, he used the wall as leverage and inched himself into a standing position.

He moved his neck. His shoulders. His right shoulder burned.

One gunshot wound to the shoulder. Not bleeding, unless he rolled his shoulders.

His left shoulder had moved, but his arm hung limp. His T-shirt revealed a scratch—nothing more —on his forearm.

One magical injury to his left arm.

Bruised hip.

And a sore-all-over feeling running through his entire body.

Can you walk?

"Time to find out." He leaned away from the wall and his legs wobbled but supported his weight. "Quite possibly. We in a hurry?"

No flashing lights. Yet.

And that alone was disturbing. Good thing he wasn't actually looking to move out of Austin and to the supposed sleepy town of Lorietta. He suspected he'd just offed much, if not all, of their police force.

He headed for the knife. "Retrieving the knife."

NO

Jack stumbled and fell back against the wall. "Stop that shit. Don't freaking yell in my head."

Don't touch the knife.

"You want me to leave the biting knife that makes an entire limb numb with a scratch. Is that wise?" Jack blinked. "Wait—what the hell is going on with my arm? That's fixable, right?"

Sure.

"Shit. You have no clue."

Nope. It's definitely a good sign that you're still alive.

"Good to know." He was too old for this shit.

Jack pushed off from the wall and stumbled to the table where the book was still open. "Can I touch the damn book?"

I think so.

"You're just full of information tonight." Jack gritted his teeth then reached for the book. And it hurt about as much as he'd expected. Getting shot sucked. Book in hand, he turned back to the stairs.

Surprisingly, it didn't take him nearly as long to get up the stairs as he'd expected. He only had to stop and puke once, and he didn't drop the book. Score one for him.

He leaned on Marin as they walked side by side through the main room. She stopped when they got to the second gaping hole, the one that led outside. He walked ahead and stopped on the other side, swaying. When she'd joined him, he asked, "Where's the body of the second guy you offed?"

You stepped on him earlier, behind the altar.

"You ashed a guy, and I missed it?"

Marin flashed a mouthful of dragon teeth. Then she turned and, in a blinding moment of blue fiery destruction, burned the church to the ground.

He choked on a laugh. The impossibility of it—the ashy remains he'd stepped on unknowingly, the decimated place of cultish worship—it was just too much. He knew it would hurt, tried to stop it, but out the laughter came. And his head pounded, and his shoulder bled, and his body ached. "Let's go home."

That was when it occurred to him how screwed they were. It was still dark, but Marin wasn't fit to fly. He couldn't drive, and even if he could—what car would that be? And where the hell were the cops? The cranky neighbors? The firing squad, the witch burners? Anyone? They'd lit up an entire building, and not a soul appeared curious or concerned.

"We just wiped out the entire Lorietta police force, didn't we?"

Most likely.

"And the neighbors?"

Terrified and hiding? Do we care?

"Yeah, who gives a shit. Unless they're a part of the magic-knife, bloodthirsty book cult—then maybe it's a problem." He tried not to slur his words, tried to walk straight—but he was doing a piss-poor job of both. "Don't suppose you know of a healer in the area? Scratch that. Don't suppose you know of a way to get to a healer in the area?"

After a few moments of contemplation, they both turned to the old blue sedan with the torn-off trunk.

"Aren't you wishing you'd popped that trunk now?"

Marin chuffed out a warm breath.

Her sense of humor was coming back; maybe she was starting to heal.

"We gonna do this?"

Hell yes.

"Those wings will work like a rudder...in a pinch...if I start to pass out...right?"

Why not?

So with Marin perched precariously atop the sedan and camouflaging herself as best she could and Jack driving one-armed, they pulled out of the Church the Book's parking lot in their stolen, shredded car.

Jack glanced once in the rearview mirror. All he could see was charred rubble. The sight was more satisfying than a local brew with a medium-rare steak.

EPILOGUE

Jack felt someone shaking his arm. He opened his eyes to a blurry image of Marin in the driver's seat of a strange car. "Five more minutes, Mom."

"Cute. You're home."

He rubbed his eyes then looked out the window to find them parked in his driveway. "Wait—wasn't I driving? Weren't you a dragon?" He jerked upright in the passenger seat. "And we were in a sedan. How'd we get in this car?"

"Good Lord. The healer said you'd have some holes in your memory—but this is ridiculous." She sighed. "You made it—mostly—to that healer north of town."

"Whoa. No way. That's, like, a two-hour drive."

"Yeah." Marin blinked too-innocent eyes at him. "Let's just be glad you don't remember all of that."

"What the hell did you do to me?"

"Nothing the healer didn't fix up, good as new. So stop bitching. We're here, right?" Marin tipped her head in the direction of Jack's house.

"Okay, outside of whatever you did to torture me into consciousness long enough to drive two hours, what else happened? Clearly he sorted you out." Jack prodded the back of his head. He'd acquired a pretty nasty bump earlier in the night. That much he definitely remembered. He couldn't find any evidence of it now.

"He sorted both of us out—even though neither of us understood how you were still breathing. That knife, the one I very specifically told you to be careful of? It's designed to drain your energy when it cuts you."

"Okay—but it's not like my neck or my groin was slashed wide open. The victims we discovered had lost a lot of blood. So I wasn't ever really in any danger, right?"

"Sure. Tell my dad and Harrington that. They're both in transit, on their way to pick up that completely innocuous knife." Marin shot him an annoyed look. "You're a lucky bastard."

Maybe he was. Maybe he had some kind of mysterious edge. Maybe the knife hadn't cut deep enough. Maybe they were all wrong about how powerful the thing was or how it worked.

"Where's the book?"

Marin reached behind his seat and pulled out a plastic grocery bag. She raised an eyebrow. "Think you can manage to hang onto it for a few hours? Dad's swinging by to collect it after he and Harrington secure the knife."

"I'll manage." Jack grabbed the bag. "Uh, before we part ways—can you tell me what it does?"

"I flipped through it; I didn't study it. And I can't read it.

"Right, only a spell caster can do that. But...?"

"But—underneath the stench of death magic—it definitely has a geo-locater vibe. If I had to guess, I'd say it's likely the magical map of everything. Underground water supplies, rare minerals...hell, it might have led those goons that stabbed me and kidnapped you to The Junk Shop."

"Ah. Your freeze frame in dragon form. I wondered how that had happened." Jack winced. "Are we going to be reading about dinosaur sightings for the next month?"

"The human ability to deny the existence of magic—even in the face of scaly, winged proof—is infinite."

Jack hopped out of the car. He was surprisingly limber considering the damage he'd undergone such a short time ago. Healers were a wonderful thing. "So, no dinosaurs?"

She flashed a smile at him—a genuine one.

"Don't be foolish, Jack. You know I always eat the witnesses."

After she'd driven away in a car he suddenly realized he didn't recognize, he remembered they hadn't discussed the partnership offer.

Tomorrow.

Maybe next month.

He headed up the steps of his porch.

He'd get around to it.

Keep reading for Episode 6: The Heartbeat in the House!

EPISODE 6

THE HEARTBEAT IN THE HOUSE

ABOUT THE HEARTBEAT IN THE HOUSE

Eminent domain seizure of a magical property? No good can come of it.

Marin's dad returns to help on this potentially explosive case. With any luck, this is Marin's chance to resolve the familial tension that's bubbled since she joined Jack's firm.

But, as pressing as Marin's family drama might be, Jack's attention is riveted on the ticking time bomb he's been told will level the city of Austin.

1

———

Jack scrolled down the spreadsheet on his laptop. Even with the fifteen percent loss of stock The Junk Shop had recently suffered, it looked like they were in the black. He leaned back in his chair and looked for his furry buddy Bob. Only a bit of Bob's magical luck could make up for a fire inside the shop. Not that he could blame Marin; she had been trying to save him from kidnap, torture, and possibly the sacrifice of his soul to a magical book. What was a little dragon-fire damage when compared to the sacrifice of his soul to an evil book?

But he could hardly give his insurance company those particular details, so he'd taken the hit. And still the shop was in the black.

Bob had curled up atop of one of the sweatshirts he'd thrown on the old leather sofa in his office.

"Thanks, Bob."

Bob picked his head up from his front paws and tilted his head.

"Looks like the shop bills are getting paid this month."

Bob didn't acknowledge Jack's thanks; he just went back to sleep.

Marin had mentioned Arkan Sonney were shy about the help they gave. Really, they seemed shy about a lot of things. Jack had never seen Bob eat or exercise. He hadn't seen the guy do much but sleep. He might look a little like a mix between a corkscrew-tailed lab puppy and a hedgehog, but he certainly didn't act like either.

"Crab?"

Bob perked up.

As soon as Jack stood, Bob hopped off the sofa.

Jack retrieved one of his stashed cans of crabmeat, opened it up, and dumped it in a small bowl he kept in the office just for Bob. He set it on the ground and walked out to the main shop floor, closing the office door behind him. The bowl would be pristine when he came back, but he'd never once seen Bob eat. Jack wasn't worried Bob would vacate the premises if peppered with too many questions—their relationship had evolved beyond that. But he didn't want to offend the polite little creature. Bob was great company—and not bad for The Junk Shop's bottom line.

Marin looked up from behind the counter where she was ringing up a customer. "Here he is now. Jack, Mr. Kaisermann wanted to meet you."

Odd. Bob didn't usually stick around when customers came into the store. Maybe he was really hungry today.

"I'm Jack Spirelli." Jack extended his hand as he approached the older gentleman.

The man offered him a frail hand, but his grip was firm. "Spirelli Paranormal Investigations?"

Jack nodded. "Yes. How can I can help you?"

"It's possible I might need you to..." Kaisermann paused, and his gaze drifted away for a second, but then his expression cleared. "...*exterminate* a building."

Exterminate... Pest control? Unlikely. Blow it up? Jack knew his morals could occasionally be skewed in a direction that didn't directly align with the law, but blowing up a building? "Maybe you'd like to join me and my, ah, Marin in my office?"

Marin was technically just his assistant—but that seemed an inappropriate label given their ongoing partnership negotiations.

"Yes, of course." Kaisermann didn't seem to notice Jack's hesitation—or was too polite to show interest.

As Kaisermann made his way through the twists and turns of the display tables to the back of the store, Jack realized that the man's frail appearance belied his grace and agility.

When Jack opened the door, there was no sign of Bob—or of his sweatshirt. Jack indicated one of two client chairs.

Marin sat on the sofa, and Jack took a seat behind his desk.

Picking up a pen, Jack said, "Now tell me about this building."

Kaisermann rattled off an address on one of the major highways in town. "The government has asserted its right of eminent domain and has been pursuing condemnation of the property. They've offered a fair price, and truth be told, I'd be glad to relinquish the responsibility of the property."

Jack waited while the Kaisermann considered his words.

Kaisermann pulled on his right earlobe. "Well, the building—it's a house, really—was left to me by my father. And his father left it to him, and so on."

"The house has sentimental value?" Marin asked.

"Oh, nothing like that. It's more a familial duty than anything else." Kaisermann's bushy grey eyebrows did a little dance as his brow furrowed and smoothed. "The house is...special."

"Haunted?" Jack asked. He had some experience with ghosts. Generally, he wasn't a fan, though he knew there were better and worse ghosts. But the thought of having to exterminate a ghost gave him indigestion.

"Ah. I hadn't considered that. Ghosts, ah, they're real, are they?"

"We offer clients an evaluation of their property. We can check and let you know what we find, but in my experience it's unlikely that your property is haunted." Jack wasn't about to confirm or deny the existence of ghosts. Spirelli Paranormal Investigations existed in the mundane world as a skeptical believer in the paranormal, more concerned with debunking paranormal fraud than proving it.

"Yes, well, maybe that would be wise, just to be sure. But that's not why I'm here. No, it's the house itself." Kaisermann shook his head. "It's mad; not really believable, but... Well, just in case... I couldn't in good conscience just let them tear it down."

"What's mad, Mr. Kaisermann?" Marin asked. "We can't help you if we don't understand the nature of the problem."

"The house is...magic." Kaisermann sighed. "That's what my father was told, what he told me."

"And by magic—what do you mean exactly?"

"I'm not entirely sure. My grandfather called it a refuge. And he warned we shouldn't ever let anything happen to the house—but he didn't say why." Kaisermann pulled at his earlobe again. "There's a trust, for the house's upkeep. And you have to understand, my family isn't particularly well off, but that trust is a good chunk of change."

"So whoever set up the trust thought maintaining the house was very important."

Kaisermann nodded. "My grandfather, I believe —though I've no idea where he got the money. And while I'm not in any particular need of those funds, my father didn't have much growing up. They didn't have that kind of cash to spare."

Jack considered the facts. Where there was money, there was usually a fix. "If you have the funds, why not move the house to another location, magic and all? I'm not entirely sure what you expect us to exterminate."

"I'm not certain I *can* move it. Not with the"— Kaisermann spread his hands wide—"well, the other, intangible aspects still attached. I don't know much about the house. My father died when I was young, so he either didn't have time to tell me or he didn't know himself. But—"

"You're leery to move it not knowing what makes the house so special." Marin leaned forward. Banishing any trace of her creepy dragon vibe, she gave Kaisermann a calm, reassuring smile. "It's wise to be cautious, certainly, but if you're not certain why your father called it magical then that's the place to start. Depending on what—if anything—is there, it might not be possible to remove it."

Kaisermann nodded. "I did have a structural

engineer take a look, and he couldn't see any reason we couldn't do it. So if you can prove there's nothing special about it, then that would mean I can move forward. Or if there is a something, someone—a metaphysical or paranormal presence—then I'd like reassurance that it's safe to move. Or a way to get it out of the house."

Jack pulled a contract out of his right-hand desk drawer. After filling in a few blanks, he passed the document to Kaisermann. "If you'll fill in the address of the property, initial the space next to the fee in the second paragraph, and then sign and date on the last page, we can schedule the inspection of the property. As Marin said, that's the place to start. Note that the fee listed includes only the inspection of the property. If we discover anything, we'll discuss your options and the accompanying fees."

"Yes, that's fine." Kaisermann scanned the document and then quickly filled in the appropriate spaces. Handing the document back, he said, "When can you see the house?"

Jack pulled up his calendar on his laptop. "This afternoon? Three o'clock." With any luck, he and Marin would be out of there in thirty minutes and would beat most of the afternoon traffic.

"I appreciate your promptness." Kaisermann stood up and pulled a key from his pocket. "I hope you're comfortable going on your own?" When Jack nodded and accepted the key, Kaisermann extended his hand first to Marin and then to Jack. "I've been very uncomfortable with moving forward. This will put my mind at ease." But his tone didn't entirely match the confidence of his words.

After the front door shop bell had rung, confirming Kaisermann's exit, Jack leaned back in his chair and propped his feet on the desk. "What do you think? Someone died in the house, and there's a family legend of ghosts?"

"Or the place is just old and spooky. It doesn't take much for a legend to develop." Marin tilted her head. "Although to set aside significant funds for the maintenance of the place...that does raise the bar somewhat."

"Well, whatever the reason for the family legend, I'm betting fifty bucks we're out of there in less than twenty minutes."

"Watch it, Jack. You of all people should know better than to tempt the fates." Marin flashed him a toothy smile. "Oh, and I'll take that bet."

2

"Holy shit." Jack took his magic specs off, scrubbed at them with the hem of his T-shirt, then put them back on.

Unfortunately, scrubbing the glass clean didn't change the brilliant vision in front of him.

"Yeah. I'll take that fifty bucks now." Marin's gaze remained riveted on their client's house.

Jack could only imagine what it looked like through her dragon eyes. "Is it even safe to go inside?"

"Huh, let's see."

Jack touched her forearm as she started to walk forward. "As my soon-to-be partner and the supposedly more informed and levelheaded of the two of us —are you sure that's a good idea?"

"I can't tell what kind of magic it is, but Mr.

Kaisermann said the house is a refuge. Does that sound dangerous to you?"

"A refuge for ghosts, demons, dragons, witches, or who knows what else. So, yeah, maybe dangerous." Jack turned back to the house. He could barely look at it straight on. The walls of the house seemed permeated with magic, as if the stone façade itself were constructed of magic.

"What demons have you ever run into? Ghosts aren't always an issue. Dragons, no problem. And if there are Coven of Light witches hanging out plotting the end of the world inside, the magic would taste different." Marin cocked her head. "I think. Besides, when are you cautious about anything but driving?"

"I'm not a cautious driver; you're a maniac." The response came automatically. Jack wasn't really paying attention to her, because he couldn't take his eyes off the house.

The glasses slipped from his nose.

He blinked and found that Marin held them between her fingers.

She inspected them, and then said, "Mundanes using magic gadgets don't have the same skill and understanding as a magic-user."

"I got it." He retrieved his magic-imbued spectacles, but scrutinized the house without them: probably 1920s, pier and beam, a local stone façade that didn't look original. The house also had some other upgrades. The windows looked energy efficient and the roof was new, but the owners had refrained from adding any square footage to the house. The entire structure couldn't be more than a thousand square feet.

"No stink of death magic; nothing that looks like witch magic." Marin raised an eyebrow. "What did you see?"

For the last several months, Jack had been trying to learn to interpret the type of magic he viewed through his magic specs, but progress had been slow. Apparently, the level of difficulty in recognizing the type of magic was much greater than its mere presence. "A shit ton of magic."

"Well, that's what I see. Hard to say what, because there's just so much of it. But, like I said, nothing that's obviously death magic or witch magic, if that comforts your newly cautious soul."

"Let's go. I'll follow in your footsteps—without the glasses—so don't get me blown up or trapped."

Marin didn't respond, just pulled out the key Kaisermann had provided and made a beeline for the front door.

She unlocked and opened it, but then hesitated on the threshold. She leaned closer then away. Took a small step forward and then backed away. "It's thick—sticky, almost."

"You have got to be kidding. Like that spurned lover's ghost trap we got stuck in?"

"No." Marin stuck her arm through the door. "No. Completely different." She pulled her hand out and turned to give him a pissy look. "I'd hardly call that poor woman, left by her husband to rot in some old house in the middle of nowhere, a *spurned lover*."

"Fair enough. How about the trap laid by the crazy lady in the woods—that better?"

Marin turned her attention back to the doorway without commenting.

Probably because he was right. She'd been crazy. Possibly because her scumbag husband had given her syphilis—but that didn't make her less crazy. Or less dangerous. He shook his head; he should not feel bad.

Shit.

He would feel like an idiot, apologizing for calling the old bat exactly what she'd been. Dick or idiot—great choices. He swallowed. "Sorry," Jack mumbled.

"You should be," Marin said, then pushed her hand through the doorway again. "It's a few inches thick. Hang on a minute while I double-check that I can get back out."

Jack shook his head as she walked through the front door. Maybe the two of them together as partners wouldn't work out as he'd planned. She was supposed to be the voice of reason. Marin might be young by dragon standards—early twenties in human years, according to her driver's license—but that was still well over a hundred calendar years. Experience should equal wisdom, right? And there was also the whole two-heads-are-better-than-one philosophy. He'd clearly placed too much weight on the strategic advantages collaboration would bring to their cases.

Then again—they weren't actually collaborating.

She walked back out, giving him her toothy grin. "I get to win fifty bucks *and* raise your blood pressure —not bad for a single day's effort."

As soon as he'd made that bet, he'd known it was a bad idea. "So? What's the verdict?"

"The amount of magic involved here is astounding. There's no hindrance to entering or exiting, but I can't tell exactly what the magic is doing. It's all over, in and around the house, but doesn't serve any obvious function. You wanna give it a try?"

Jack rubbed his neck and followed her into the house.

He slowed as he crossed the threshold, waiting for something. Some sense of magic, or the resistance Marin had mentioned. But he felt absolutely nothing. No resistance, and certainly nothing he'd describe as sticky.

The interior of the house surprised him. Kaisermann's family had not only updated the house, they'd kept it furnished. The front door opened directly into a comfortable, well-maintained living room. The furniture looked mid-century modern, the rug imported, and Jack didn't spot a cobweb or dust bunny anywhere.

"Not what I expected either." Marin sat down in a green velvet armchair. "I'd say cozy. And he's had the maids in regularly."

Jack nodded. "And the magic?"

"I've still got no sense of the type, but my best guess is spell caster."

"Yeah. Makes sense. The magic is tied to the house itself, and binding magic to objects falls within the purview of spell casters. Is there any other type of magic-user that could do this?"

"With the coven, I never like to guess. 'Pursuit of knowledge at all costs' is a motto that lends itself to a broad array of magics, so even if it doesn't look like elemental magic it could still be witch related."

"Okay—but best guess?"

"Best guess: no, I still don't think it's witch magic."

Jack lifted his specs. "Think they're safe to try?"

"If the shiny lights mesmerize you, I'll take them off."

"Thanks." Sometimes, he really wanted to kick her ass. But he'd only fail miserably. He slipped the horn-rimmed glasses on. "Uh, I got nothing."

"What?" Marin took the glasses from him. "Ah, I

think you've run your battery out. When was the last time you had a spell caster charge them?"

Jack shrugged. He knew exactly when, but telling her he'd done it last week wouldn't change the fact that they were toast. He retrieved the glasses and tucked them into one of the pockets of his cargo pants. "Speaking of batteries..."

Marin stood up. "Right. Let's do a walk-through and maybe I'll get a hint of what's powering this thing."

"I don't suppose there's any chance of a magical wellspring in the Austin area?"

Marin poked her head into the kitchen. "A massive magical power source in the middle of Texas that no one's noticed? Eh." She beckoned over her shoulder for him to follow her into the kitchen. "The Inter-Pack Policing Cooperative missed the one in Prague, but that was some time ago. They've got screening in place now that they know what to look for."

Jack walked into the small 1950s kitchen. "So if there's screening, how does IPPC not know about this house? The magic practically blinded me."

Marin opened and shut several cabinets. "Hm. Excellent question." After she scoped out the interior of the oven, she stopped and turned to him. "I didn't see it—didn't even feel it—until we were pulling into the driveway."

"How is that possible?"

Marin scanned the small room, focusing most of her attention on the exterior walls. "I'm not sure."

An uneasy feeling crawled up Jack's neck. "Come on. Let's check the two bedrooms and bath. Lingering doesn't strike me as wise."

Marin once again preceded him as they walked through the living room into a small hallway. Three doors opened off the hallway. Both bedrooms yielded nothing unusual, though one was furnished more as a sitting room. All of the furnishings were mid-century, in good repair, comfortable, and clean.

Jack stood just outside the doorway of the bathroom as Marin stepped through.

"Oh, I want one of these." Marin traced her finger along the yellow tile.

"A green and yellow 1950s bathroom? Doesn't that conflict with your whole dragon philosophy of living in the now?"

"And here I am thinking you don't listen. I can like vintage yellow tile and green sinks without having flashbacks to the fifties. Besides, I'm young; it's less of an issue."

A good thing, too. Jack didn't have any desire to see firsthand what a dragon looked and acted like when it had lost touch with reality. Almost definitely catastrophically bad for all observers.

"So—anything more specific?"

Marin shook her head. "I'm getting a massive collection of magical energy. I hate to say it, but—"

"We need an expert." Jack tried not to groan. He thought he *had* an expert. But Marin was an adolescent in the land of dragons, much as it baffled the mind to think of any creature over the age of a hundred as a kid.

"Yeah. Let's get out of here, and I'll give my dad a buzz."

"So you guys...uh, you know, you're—"

"Yeah, we're on speaking terms. I keep telling you: I don't have a problem with my dad."

Jack bit back his response. Clearly something weird was going on with her family—but who was he to say? He had his own family shit.

They retraced their steps back out of the house: down the hall, through the living room, and out the front door. He couldn't help it; he held his breath as they exited the house.

Once outside, Jack did a quick check. All his parts were present, and Marin looked okay. "You're good?"

"Hm." She stared at the house. "Give me a second."

Jack stood in the drive as she disappeared around the back of the house. They probably should have checked the rear door when they'd been in the kitchen. Almost immediately, she circled back around to join him in the driveway.

"What's up?" Jack asked.

"I'm just wondering—where does the magic

stop?"

"Where the walls stop?" Jack pulled out his glasses again, and put them on before he remembered they were out of juice. "Shit." The bright light of the house startled him, and he yanked them off.

"What? I thought those were toast."

"Not toast. Definitely not toast." He handed her the specs. "Check it out."

"Come on." Marin yanked a tuft of monkey grass out of the lawn lining the driveway and then headed to the house.

"You have a theory?"

She paused on the threshold. "Possibly. Let's see if I can burn a little grass."

"Ah, that doesn't mean what you think it does." But then Jack realized her point. "Well, hell, that would be seriously freaky if you couldn't. I mean— that would be weird and very, very bad, right?" But Jack was talking to Marin's rear and her curly red ponytail. He hustled into the house after her; no way was he missing this.

She'd already moved into the kitchen when he came through the front door.

Jack joined her just as she was placing the clump of grass into the kitchen sink. He should at least appreciate that she didn't test her theory out on any of the difficult-to-replace furniture.

He watched her. Watched the grass. Back and

forth like a tennis match—but nothing happened. "I assume you're trying."

"And failing." She reached out her hand. "Your specs?"

Jack handed them to her.

After she closed her hand around them, she shook her head. "Not even a little spark."

"I don't understand. You can see the magic in here, right?"

"And feel and see it—just like before. But your specs have no magic. And my fire...it's..." She tilted her head and handed back his glasses. "I guess you could say suppressed? I don't feel as if I'm under any kind of attack. It's there; it's smoldering—I simply can't access it. Maybe blocked is a better description."

"Mr. Kaisermann called this place a refuge. A refuge from magic?"

"Possibly. But how does a man with no magic get hooked up with a spelled building that blocks magic? And how does no one know about this place?"

"And who used it and for what?" Jack felt a tingling of unease. "This house could be a powerful weapon against the Coven of Light."

Marin sighed. "Yeah. Which makes it a target. We need to find out what research our client has done; who he's reached out to; what bears he's poked."

Jack motioned to the door and, when she

nodded, headed outside. "Speaking of our client, any thoughts about whether we can move this place?"

Marin closed the door behind her. "I have some suspicions about the walls. I'm wondering if the magic extends to the foundation, perhaps beyond. I'm betting yes."

"So we measure how deep—somehow—and make sure the earth underneath is moved with the house." Jack rubbed his neck. "Yeah, that sounded way less possible out loud than in my head."

"Exactly. How do we measure it? How do we leave those magical tentacles below the surface undisturbed—if they exist? And if we do disturb them—what happens?"

"Wild guess that we don't want to know what would happen if the structure that all of that magic was tied to was destroyed."

Marin huffed out an unamused laugh. "Whatever happens, this building can't be demolished. Period. Pretty sure that's bad. Crazy bad. Shit-your-pants bad."

"Yeah—I got it. And I'm not looking forward to telling Mr. Kaisermann we don't have a clue what's contaminated or infested or possessed his house. So calling Ewan sooner rather than later would be a great idea."

"Will do." Marin pulled her phone out. "Wanna take bets on how bad this is?"

"I'm going with worse than the time we blew up

the crazy—ah—the really sad and misunderstood ghost."

Marin raised an eyebrow. "Way worse. Worse than the bloodsucking, soul-swallowing knife."

"Technically, that was a bloodsucking, soul-*collecting* knife and a soul-swallowing *book*."

Marin rolled her eyes and tapped the number for her dad.

3

Because of the street noise, Marin had called Ewan from the Range Rover. It was still parked in the driveway of the refuge, and the house lurked off to the left, looking much less innocuous than when they'd first parked.

Marin paused after explaining what they'd seen, and she and Jack both waited for his response.

"Sounds like a massive, magical bomb, waiting to blow up." Ewan Campbell, a.k.a. Marin's dad and the chief security officer for the IPPC library, sounded deadly serious. "I'm making arrangements to fly down. I should be there in eight hours—don't blow up Austin before I get there."

Jack pinched the bridge of his nose. Ewan wasn't a drama queen by any stretch of the imagination.

"Wait, don't hang up." Marin's fingers tightened around her cell. "I'm sure some assistant is making your travel arrangements as we speak, so you have a little time. Explain. Or you can leave us in the dark until you arrive—which greatly increases the risk that Jack will put his sticky mundane fingers where they don't belong."

Jack flashed her his best blandly innocent look. Since she glared back, he might have missed the mark.

"Ripping apart that building would be like setting off a small nuclear explosion in the middle of Austin. Think of the structure as the cohesive bond holding the magic together. Remove the building and you melt the glue. No glue, and all of the accumulated magic permeating the site is loosed on the city."

Jack winced. Worse than the ghost trap; worse than the bloodthirsty knife. Exponentially worse. "What about exorcising it?"

"Exorcising what exactly? Do you know why all that magic has accumulated? The Clan is familiar with the concept of a refuge, certainly—but what makes it work? How it comes into being? Not at all." Ewan sounded impatient.

Or maybe the guy was stressed. Jack didn't know how long the dragon clan had been around, but minimally, it was hundreds of years. If they didn't have the particulars on this house, then it truly was alien. And rare.

Maybe it was rare for a reason.

"If destroying the house is so dangerous, how can this refuge even exist in Texas? We're disaster central. Hurricanes, tornados, thunderstorms, hail, flooding, even the odd earthquake." Jack looked again through the windshield at the old stone house. "And yet Austin still stands."

"Wouldn't be an issue. It's highly unlikely the house could be damaged by natural phenomena. A refuge should weather anything Mother Nature generates."

Marin glared at the phone. "Nature is fine, but a wrecking ball and a bulldozer will precipitate World War III?"

"Hyperbole is hardly appropriate here. The reality is sufficiently dire." Ewan sounded about as peeved as Marin looked.

"So..." Jack faltered. Mediation didn't top his résumé, but the conversation was devolving. "Uh—maybe we should talk about this whole refuge thing. Ewan, do you have any information on what a refuge does? Other than block magical energy."

"Just as the name implies, it's a haven from magical attack. I haven't heard rumors of one in years, though. There's usually a person—a mundane—attached in some way to the house. Probably the titleholder of the property. Have you run into anyone that might fit the bill?"

"That would be our client, Kaisermann." Marin had skipped over the case details earlier and focused on the house itself. "Don't suppose you know why a mundane has the care of a magical house?"

"Experience says it'll be a mundane—no idea what the connection is."

Jack cleared his throat. "Ah, we had a few concerns about the Coven of Light—any way for us to know if this place is on their radar?"

"I don't think it is…" Ewan's voice trailed away. "I have to leave. Don't mess with the house. Destroy the structure, and—"

"Boom, we get it." Jack scrubbed his face. "Besides not blowing shit up, anything we can do to start sorting this out while you're in transit?"

"Yeah, one thing. Ask your Arkan Sonney friend if he'd be willing to have a look at the house. I'd be interested to see if he has any insight."

"Bob?" Jack shared a confused look with Marin. "Sure thing—but why Bob?"

"Just as dragon magic works differently from human magic, so does the magic of a creature like an Arkan Sonney. He may have a different and useful perspective. And I hear he's quite fond of you, Jack."

Ewan seemed surprised. Hardly a compliment. Not that Jack would have commented, but Ewan had already hung up.

"Bob—that's weird, right? *Can* I ask him to check out the house?"

Marin tucked her cell in her pocket and pulled out her keys. "I know his kind are shy, and they don't like to be acknowledged—but that ship has long sailed. You guys hang out in your office like antisocial teenagers, bonding over... What exactly do you do in there?"

"We don't *do* anything. He hangs out; I hang out. We just kinda hang out in the same room."

"Right. What was I thinking that you might actually be doing something?" Marin started the car. "Either way, Dad's right: you guys are tight. And don't forget, you helped out his buddy Nelson."

"That's ballsy." Jack fastened his seatbelt. "Fixing your screw-up hardly qualifies as helping Nelson. You're the one who accidentally left the inter-dimensional door open too long and—"

"Too wide." Marin backed out of the drive and onto the highway feeder with a careless abandon that made Jack cringe.

"What?" He discreetly pried his fingers away from the oh-shit handle.

"The inter-dimensional door was too big; it wasn't open too long. Big difference. I was ignorant, not careless."

He'd swear her nose twitched when she said "ignorant."

"Whatever makes you sleep better at night," Jack said. "Either way, the big, bad, creepy dragon got stuck in Nelson's attic, and that was all you."

Marin snorted. She flicked the radio on, then

thought again and lowered the volume. "Talk to him. Ask him for his help."

Jack tensed as Marin floored it onto the access ramp with only one hand on the steering wheel. "How do I do that? I'm not telepathic. He only communicates with other little Arkan Sonney—and dragons."

"You haven't figured out how to talk to each other? How long have you..." She laughed. "Never mind. I'll translate."

Jack didn't see what the big deal was. They hung out. They shared space. Two dudes in one room did not a conversation make—especially if one was the size of an overgrown hedgehog and had no vocal cords.

There was that one time, no, two times? He'd heard a tiny whisper in the back of his brain...but that could just as easily have been his overactive imagination. Couldn't it?

When Jack and Marin arrived at the shop, Bob was waiting. Not in the office, but in the main part of the store. Jack locked the door behind Marin without a lot of fuss, hoping they wouldn't startle him into disappearing. Bob hadn't shown himself in Marin's presence since the ancient dragon fiasco. He and his Arkan Sonney friend Nelson had asked for help with pest control, reporting "something nasty in Nelson's attic." That something nasty turned out to be an ancient dragon's essence, and its proximity to humans proved less than agreeable to their sanity.

Jack tried not to linger overlong on the mental health risks of prolonged exposure to ancient dragon essence, given the fact that he now housed that same essence in his own body—reformatted to reflect his human self, but even so...

Come on, Jack. Focus on the issues of today, not the mistakes of the past. Why had Bob suddenly lost his shyness?

"Hey, Bob. Any chance you can see the future?"

Bob's nose twitched.

Jack glanced at Marin, but she shook her head. Bob wasn't giving that one up.

"Do you mind joining Marin and I in the office?"

Bob pivoted around and, with a jaunty little wiggle of his corkscrew tail, trotted away.

When Marin and Jack joined Bob in the office, they found him not on the sofa or the client chair— his usual spots—but perched on the corner of Jack's desk. Jack estimated the height of the desk at about two and a half to three feet. Certainly higher than he'd ever seen the generally sleepy and somewhat lazy Bob jump. His small, plump body didn't look capable of the jump. Then again, Bob appeared and disappeared apparently at will, found modest treasures for the shop, and was tidier than any creature —human or otherwise—Jack had encountered.

Bob's magic worked in ways that scrambled any logic Jack tried to apply to it. He wasn't sure why he kept trying.

But they were here about the house, and Bob was looking on with keen interest, not at all like his usual sleepy self.

Twenty questions seemed like the best solution, so Jack asked, "Do you know about the house?"

Bob nodded.

Marin stood quietly to the side. Jack didn't think she could chase Bob off if she tried at this point. He looked downright excited.

"You know about the magic in the house?" Another nod, so Jack asked, "And how the city wants to tear it down?"

Bob nodded more vigorously.

"And that we need to move it before the city can demolish it?"

Marin broke her silence with a smothered giggle. Marin never giggled.

"What's up?"

"Bob says, and I quote, 'Big boom.'" She grinned at Jack.

Jack groaned. "Yeah, we know. We're trying to avoid that."

Head tilted, Bob blinked big, puppy-dog brown eyes at Jack.

Jack's store mascot was psychic. Or maybe intuitive. Or he had an underground network of gossipy Arkan Sonney friends who fed him with a constant supply of up-to-date intel.

"Do you have a Friday night poker group or something?" Jack asked.

"Uh, he thinks you have a screw loose." Marin shrugged when Jack glared at her. "I'm translating loosely. Bob will meet us there, but he has something he needs to do first. He offers his apologies for the delay."

"When's good?" Jack glanced at the clock. It was only just five.

"Midnight," Marin translated. "Any reason we're meeting at midnight?" she asked Bob.

But when Jack turned to Bob, the desk was empty. Their furry friend had vanished.

"Well, shit." Jack rubbed his eyes. "Did he at least give you any reason for the seven-hour delay?"

"Things to do, basically. He's a creature of few words. But I've been thinking we need more information on Kaisermann's family—and I know where we can get started."

Jack didn't like the cagey look in Marin's eye.

"Can we eat first?" he asked.

"Our source will be happier if she's fed, so we can eat there."

JACK LOVED INDIAN FOOD, especially curry. And this particular restaurant was one of his favorites. But it was a chain—busy, loud, and with a lot of shared seating. In other words, not a place he'd normally expect to meet and speak openly with a source. These days, everything he did had magical overtones. It was true that the world of mundanes lived in constant denial—but he hated to smack people in the face with the reality of magic when he could avoid it.

He set the stand with his order number attached on the table. The corner spot Marin had chosen ensured they'd only have curious eyes and ears on one side. He took a seat facing the restaurant's only entrance doors. "So who exactly are we meeting?"

"Penelope Smythe is...a *special* sort of friend."

Again with the caginess. This lady must be shady. "Special, as in your girlfriend? Or special, as in talented?"

"Talented. And not that it's any of your business, but we're not quite that friendly." Marin wrinkled her nose. "Fair warning: Pen doesn't particularly like people."

"No problem. Antisocial means less chitchat."

"No—she's social enough, just not keen on humans." Marin leaned a little closer and lowered her voice. "Kelpie."

Jack hadn't run into one of those before. "Some kind of sea creature?"

"Oh, no—and don't even think about mentioning the sea. She's a freshwater beast, not salt."

"And never the two shall meet?" Jack shook his head. "If you guys are friends, then dragons must pass muster. What's the deal with humans?"

"First, we're more friendly than friends. Dragons

are like puppies to her. You guys, on the other hand, are more like gnats."

"That's more than a little unflattering. You're sure we shouldn't have waited to order?" Jack didn't mind avoiding the cost of an additional meal—but it seemed odd, especially given the fact that he ranked among the lower orders by kelpie standards.

"With what you're paying her, she'll be happy to pick up her own tab. She's charging us by the hour, and you will smile and pay when you get the bill."

"Naturally, I'll pay for any services we use." But he'd smile about it when hell froze over.

An older woman, hair neatly swept up into a tidy bun, entered the restaurant alone. Just as Jack had decided she was their dinner appointment, a younger man came in and hurried to catch up with her. A couple with small children—no way, not at a business meeting. A teenager with a nose piercing and weirdly colored hair—too young. A man in his twenties alone—wrong sex.

Then Marin stood up and waved.

The cotton-candy-haired girl waved back with a bright smile. Maybe not cotton candy—maybe more sea foam. Hell, like he even knew what sea foam meant. It was green, but not the color you got from being in the pool too much. As she approached the table, Jack could see a small metal dragon hugging the outer shell of her left ear.

"Hi, Pen. How are you?" Marin hugged the girl.

Marin with her bright red curls and unusual height and Pen with her not-chlorine-green hair, piercings, and short stature didn't even warrant a second glance from grandma, family with kids, or single guy. Oh, and he'd missed the tattoos. Also a green-blue color; he couldn't tell what they depicted because her billowing shirt would gape just long enough for him to catch glimpses of color along her collarbone but no specific pattern.

Of course they could talk about magic here. None of the patrons would care or even notice. Man, he loved Austin.

Pen held out her hand. Jack stood and shook it. She had a surprisingly businesslike handshake. Not something he expected from a five-foot-nothing teenager.

Then he stepped back and looked, truly looked, at her. Diminutive height, flawless skin, and the overall look she cultivated made her appear young —but those lavender eyes were anything but. He experienced the same chilling creepiness he'd felt the first time he'd encountered a dragon. What she presented to the world was not the reality of herself. "Good to meet you." He forced the words out.

He hated the feeling, but he was experiencing a moment of gnat-likeness.

"Hm. You're different from the rest." She placed a finger on her chin and tilted her head. Even her mannerisms had an affected cuteness.

"Just human." Marin spoke dismissively, as if *what* he was—or wasn't—had no part in their conversation today.

A catlike smile spread across Pen's face. "All right then; that's a mystery for another time." She reached inside the large purse that was slung across her shoulder and pulled out a card. She handed it to Jack with another feline smile. "I'll just go order. Be right back."

Jack sat and then looked down at the card in his hand. Beautiful blues and greens edged out with delicate gold scrollwork. "Fine antiques and collectibles? How is that relevant to our case?"

Marin seated herself across from him. "She has an extensive knowledge of the history of Austin. People may be insignificant in and of themselves— but they create beautiful things. And those pretty pieces are much more valuable with their human history intact."

"You mean provenance, right?"

"Yes. But an object's history of ownership can also have significance beyond the provenance. A cute story sells well, a tragic one even better. But a *true* tragic tale can have real power." Marin gave Jack a warning glance, but a hint of amusement tinged her voice. "Pen tells a mean story. Be careful."

Jack glanced over his shoulder and saw Pen was still at the counter ordering. "How old is she?"

"Very." Marin stared back at him blandly.

Jack eyed the card and then Marin. Dragons as puppies. It was an interesting image.

"Quit looking at me like that." Marin snatched the card from his hand.

Pen returned with a large glass of soda, a basket of naan, and her order number. As soon as she sat down, she tore into the naan. Literally.

Jack couldn't take his eyes off her teeth. They looked white and even—like any other teen who'd spent a few years in braces. But then—a flash, a tiny moment where two images met, one superimposed over the other. Even, white, human teeth faded. Crowded, sharp, sharklike teeth flashed atop the false image of orthodontic perfection. Again, a chill crawled up his back.

And since when did horses have pointy shark teeth? Either he needed to do a little research on kelpies—or legend got the whole horse thing wrong.

Marin kicked him under the table.

He glanced away. When he looked back, the bread was gone.

"So, Pen, what have you found on Mr. Kaisermann?" Marin asked.

Pen patted daintily at the corners of her mouth with her paper napkin. "His family has been in Austin for three generations. Before that, the Kaisermann family diverges into a German branch and a Polish branch. I'm rather partial to the Polish side of the family—there were a few jewelers in that branch." Her eyes glittered with an unearthly light. "But I suspect you're more interested in the family tree with connections to a refuge?"

Jack exchanged a quick glance with Marin—but he couldn't read anything in her face.

"No, no. Little Marin didn't spill the beans. But really, a refuge, in Austin? She didn't have to."

"So you know about our problem?" Despite Marin's caution, Jack couldn't help but hope that they might have found an ally. Allies were good when dealing with unexploded magical bombs.

Pen flashed him a darling grin, devoid of any sharp edges or fangs. "I couldn't care less. That's *your* problem."

Jack tried to wrap his head around that. How would the city of Austin exploding in a cloud of magical dust *not* also affect Pen? Including her home, her business, maybe her life.

"Oh, don't think so hard. You might bust a blood vessel in your tiny little human brain. Humans come and go. Cities rise and fall. It's the natural order of human civilization. And I do love a good scavenge." She smiled sweetly, revealing a dimple. "But I wish you the best of luck. Citywide destruction would be...mildly inconvenient."

Before she could elaborate—if she ever intended to—the waitress arrived with his and Marin's food.

"Please eat," Pen said. "Mine will be along shortly."

Marin started in on her tikka masala, so Jack took his cue from her. And he did love a good palak paneer.

Pen leaned forward and inhaled. "Lovely. So, the Kaisermann family's German roots. There was once a refuge in the Black Forest—oh, years ago."

"And by years, you mean what exactly?" Marin asked.

Pen waved a dainty hand in the hair. Jack noticed for the first time that her nails were painted a shade of light blue-green very similar to her hair. "More than a decade, less than a millennium."

Marin sighed. "Pen, sometimes, your sense of time is less than useful."

Tiny little frown lines appeared on Pen's forehead. "It's all in my notes. Silly girl, sometimes the story is bigger than the details. Pay attention."

"Apologies." Marin's lips were tight, but the corners pulled up at the edges.

Jack guessed laughing at the ancient, sharp-toothed creature might be perceived as a slight.

"Where was I? Yes, the Black Forest. There was a house, deep in the woods, a place to hide from the ill-intentioned magical beings of the day. Humans feared the dark, and places deep in the woods, in those days."

"They still do," Jack interjected.

Pen raised a fine, pale green eyebrow. "True." She sounded surprised. But then she gestured dismissively. "That human fear of all things unknown became the refuge's protection. A word here and there about witches and children and cannibalism"—she snapped her fingers—"and the refuge was safe from human intervention."

The waitress interrupted them with the delivery of two meals—both ordered by Pen.

Now aware that sharp teeth lay hidden beneath an illusion, curiosity pulled at him. He knew her predator's teeth would rip apart flesh as easily as the bread he'd seen her shred. Jack made himself look away.

Eventually, Marin asked, "What's the connection between the house in the Black Forest and the refuge here in Austin?"

Jack looked up and found that Pen's noodle dish had disappeared.

"Between the houses? Oh, nothing at all." Pen began eating the remaining curry with no particular haste. But then she paused, wiped her mouth, and her eyes narrowed. "That house deep in the forest came to an unfortunate end. Overtaken by a coven. Tainted." The hint of a snarl emerged—the impression given but no sound heard. But the anger—fury, even—disappeared as quickly as it had manifested.

Jack fought the urge to stand up and leave— quickly. Then his brain turned back on and he remembered that the coven he knew—the Coven of Light—was no friend to him or his allies. The enemy of his enemy and all that? Maybe. But Pen seemed closer in definition to foe than friend. And then he caught sight of her plate.

Even eating with beautiful table manners and cutting all of the meat into tiny, bite-sized pieces, half of Pen's curry was gone.

Marin kicked him under the table again. He'd be black and blue before the end of this meeting.

"So, it's the caretaker family that the Black Forest refuge and ours share?" Marin asked.

"In one, my little dragon." Pen smiled with an almost maternal affection.

Pen really did have a soft spot for dragons. The pastel hair and frail appearance had faded into the background, overshadowed by sharp, hard edges. The more Jack shared Penelope's company, the more he saw of what he believed was her true self.

"But the family has no magic. How could they create a magical place with so much power?" Jack asked.

"No human is capable of creating a refuge." Pen stared at him. Her pale lavender eyes grew huge in her face, giving her an alien appearance.

The hairs on the back of Jack's neck stood at attention.

She blinked, and her face softened, looking again like a normal human teenager.

Jack exhaled. He hadn't realized he'd been

holding his breath until those freakishly bright purple eyes had blinked. "So how are they created?"

"A house becomes host to the magic when a refuge is needed." Penelope patted her mouth and stacked her second empty plate atop the first.

"Needed by whom?"

"By whomever needs it." Pen's nose wrinkled. "Such simple creatures with such limited, linear thinking."

As the simple, linear-thinking creature in this equation, he figured pushing for answers wouldn't get him much more. Jack looked to Marin for a cue, but she simply lifted a shoulder.

Pen made the decision when she stood up to leave.

"Thank you, Pen." Marin leaned in and kissed the air near Pen's left cheek.

Pen hugged her. "Report and invoice are in the mail."

And then she left, leaving behind a faint scent of...spring?

Jack sniffed the air: the sweet smell of blooming flowers, the fresh smell of crushed grass—but underneath, a hint of fishy decay.

Jack watched the door close behind her then turned to Marin. He shook his head. "Just bizarre. And what's with mailing the report?"

"She means email. Trust me; she's very technologically savvy. And, yes, a bit bizarre—by your standards."

"So, you going to tell me why we're not paying her for information on refuges? It's obvious she knows something."

"Two different types of information. If she has it, we can't afford it. And no telling what she knows. Disinterest in humanity coupled with a fascination for the artifacts of human life, well, it makes for an odd hodgepodge of information."

Jack looked at the door where Pen had exited and felt that creep along his spine again. As he followed Marin out of the restaurant, he couldn't help but wonder: how many more ancient, powerful, and not particularly friendly beings lurked around the next blind corner?

5

Several hours passed before Pen's report arrived in Marin's inbox. As Jack and Marin had waited, they'd done a little research of their own. Neither of them turned up anything online about magical refuges, and none of the sources they'd trusted enough to ask seemed to know much about them. Ewan probably had some nuggets he hadn't shared—but he hadn't yet arrived from Prague.

Jack had sent a follow-up email to the client. Nothing too specific, just that he had an expert coming to take a look at the house. Marin had looked like she might keel over when she heard him explaining there'd be no charge since they'd booked the expert without the client's prior approval.

It pissed him off. He wasn't a cheat, just perpetually two inches shy of broke. And charging the client for Bob's services when Bob didn't charge Jack—that was just shitty. He wouldn't abuse the client's or Bob's trust that way. Keeping the client in the dark about IPPC...that was entirely different, and Jack had no moral qualms on that front.

When they'd updated Ewan on the plan to meet Bob at the house around midnight, he'd claimed he could make the meeting. Seemed tight to Jack, but as of a few minutes ago Ewan had confirmed by text he planned to be there.

It was right at eleven thirty, so Jack printed out an old-school paper copy of Pen's report—no laptop for this trip—and then he and Marin left for the refuge in her Range Rover.

About five minutes into the drive, Jack flipped to the last page. "Pen may have questionable eating habits, but she certainly came through. It looks like the Kaisermann family has been affiliated with more than just one refuge."

"She said as much at our lunch meeting."

Jack braced himself against the door as Marin took a turn too fast. The pages crumpled in his fingers. He had to unclench his teeth to reply. "Yeah, but she's listed three here."

"And if she's listed three, there are probably more. She wouldn't reveal an undiscovered and still operational refuge. Not for the price we're paying. Possibly not for any price."

"Speaking of, aren't we owed an invoice?"

Marin stomped on the gas and switched lanes. "Once I'm sure Austin's around to stay—then you'll get the invoice. No point in raising your blood pressure if we're all going to die."

"So practical and yet so pessimistic." Jack tried not to imagine a sum, failed, and decided he could wait for the real number. "What do you think of the family connection? Three refuges—four if you add ours—two countries, and one family."

Marin glanced in her blind spot then crossed two lanes of traffic. "Too many coincidences become a pattern."

"Agreed. What I don't understand is how Kaisermann could be as unaware as he appears. How do you have a family background tied to a mystical house and not know it? No family myths, no guesses as to why the house has to be maintained. Just a sense of duty to keep up the property. That's strange."

"You keep forgetting that you have a skewed viewpoint. You have this... It's like a talent. You see the magic that exists around you."

"Yeah—with the help of my magic-seeing spectacles."

Marin snorted. "That's not what I mean. You may not literally see the sparkle and shine of magic without help—but you see its impact on the world around you. You have an awareness that most humans not only lack, but that they actively work to

KATE BARAY

avoid." She glanced at him from the corner of her eye. "It must be genetic."

"Or maybe I have ninja-like observation skills. Give a guy some credit," Jack said. "Although I really don't understand how someone misses a dragon sitting on top of a moving car."

Mari's lips pressed tighter together. "Circumstances dictated that particular solution; I never said it was a good idea, just the only option." She shrugged. "Most humans possess a constitutional inability to accept magic when the evidence is right in front of them. You're different—and I don't think it's your PI training." She arched an eyebrow. "Or your ninja abilities."

Whatever Marin said, he'd been a decent PI back before magic had jacked around with his and his friends' lives—so he definitely had mad ninja skills.

"Okay, so say our client can't see magic even though it's right in front of him. He has a strong sense of duty either to the house directly or to his family—is that due to some magical influence? Or he's just a conscientious guy?"

"We should have a little chat with Mr. Kaisermann after our midnight rendezvous with Bob." Marin exited the highway and this time cut across three lanes of traffic.

"Yeah." Once he was sure impact with another car wasn't imminent, Jack pulled out his phone. He sent a quick email then stuffed it back in his pants pocket. "I've requested an appointment at ten tomorrow morning. We need to provide him with a more extensive update anyway—and by then, I'll know what IPPC decides is legit to pass along."

"Sounds like a plan." Marin pulled into the driveway a few minutes before their midnight appointment. After she parked, she gave the house a hard look. "Did you notice the other detail Pen included about those three houses?"

Jack eyed the simple, well-maintained, and in most ways very ordinary house. "Yeah. They all had a history. If the Hansel and Gretel story she told us over lunch was any indication, the stories were provided as cover to protect the homes from mundane interference."

"Yeah. I wonder why our little gem doesn't have some terrifying story attached to it." Marin shut the engine off.

"Are you kidding? Attach some story to the house and you draw attention. We live in the age of reality TV and sensationalism. We've moved from being terrified of the dark to being both terrified and fascinated. Absolutely ordinary *is* the cover story."

"You're not wrong."

"You remember the other thing your friend mentioned over lunch, that humans didn't create it?"

"I've been thinking about that." Marin shifted in the driver's seat, getting more comfortable. "Pen has a different view of the world and a bizarre sense of humor. Maybe she truly meant the *houses* aren't connected. The actual structures."

"Shit, that's right. She said something about the house being host to the magic. I would have asked, but she made it clear she wouldn't answer any more questions. Host is an odd choice of word; it implies a guest. So what type of guest is this house hosting? What type of magic?"

Even in the poor light, Jack could see that Marin looked annoyed. "Or whose? She might have chosen her words carefully, no connection between the houses, but—"

"There could be a connection between the magic inside this and the three other houses." Jack suddenly felt very small. "I have this weird image of all this magic roiling around under the surface. You know, like those illustrated pictures of magma they had in our earth sciences book as a kid?"

Marin snorted. "Because we both had earth science as kids. Sorry—I know what you mean."

"Well, the magic had to come from somewhere. *Someone* had to make that house happen."

It wasn't as if there was this burbling, powerful mass of mindless magic roiling under his feet. He sure as hell hoped not.

"Hey—you okay?"

Jack shrugged off the uncomfortable feeling of insignificance. "Yeah. Of course. Let's say the house is possessed by some benevolent entity that protects its occupants—nuts as that sounds—but then how does the house get hooked up with the humans who act as caretakers?" Jack pulled out a second file, one that contained a background on Kaisermann. "What if Kaisermann is holding out on us? Maybe he knows more than he's saying."

Marin's lips twisted. "Really? Is that the impression you got?"

"No." Jack flipped open the client's file again. "Widowed, no children, no criminal background, excellent credit, lifetime Austin resident, retired at sixty, volunteers at the food bank. He's the perfect responsible, dependable person."

"No one's perfect. We're missing something, because everyone has flaws and secrets."

"Whatever it is, it's not jumping off the page at me." Jack rubbed the back of his neck. "I can have Chris do a more thorough background on him—but she's already been pretty damn thorough."

"Skip it. Let's wait to see what Kaisermann has to say tomorrow morning then go from there."

Another set of headlights shone up the drive and a second car joined them.

"Three minutes to midnight," Jack said. "Ewan must have managed to snag the IPPC jet. But agreed; we'll have a nice chat with Kaisermann tomorrow."

Marin opened her car door but abruptly stopped and didn't get out. "You have got to be kidding me."

Jack walked around the front of the Range Rover,

and then saw there were two people in the other car. At first, he thought Ewan had a driver. Then he saw Ewan was driving and a woman was in the passenger seat.

She stepped out of the rental car.

Not just a woman. Heike, Ewan's girlfriend.

As Jack approached, Heike pushed her short blonde bob back out of her face. Even in the dark, he couldn't miss the rock on her left hand. Not Ewan's girlfriend—Ewan's fiancée...or wife?

6

—————

Jack closed the short distance between himself and Heike. They'd met before, months ago, before Jack worked with IPPC. He'd been helping out his friend Kenna, and Heike had been a part of the solution.

A genuine smile spread across his face. "What an unexpected surprise."

Heike smiled and reached out her hand. "I heard you could use a spell caster."

The faint German accent she'd had the last time they'd met had almost vanished. Probably from speaking a lot of English...with her maybe husband. Jack shook her hand, and then turned to Ewan.

The men briefly shook hands.

Jack wasn't sure where he stood with Ewan after hiring his daughter. He didn't look like he wanted to roast Jack slowly or turn him into bits of ash, so that was a decent start.

Jack turned to find Marin still sitting in the driver's seat with the door open. If he had to drag her butt out of the car... He wasn't sure what he'd do, but he'd make her pay for it. God, he hated family drama.

She jumped out of the car as if she'd read his mind, then shut the door with a little too much force.

"Heike, it's nice to see you. I didn't know you were coming." Marin gave Heike a quick hug, and she looked happy enough to see her. "Dad."

The curt nod in her father's direction told a different story.

Jack pulled out his phone to check the time. "Midnight on the nose. I'd rather not keep Bob waiting..."

"Of course." Heike headed toward the porch, and everyone else fell in behind her.

Still as no-nonsense as ever, Heike was, however, much softer around the edges than Jack remembered. Probably because she was happier—and safe. He knew a little of her history, and he wondered if Marin did as well. Maybe he'd ask when they weren't in the middle of a city-leveling crisis...or not.

When the group reached the door, Ewan opened it and went in before Jack thought to stop him.

Hopefully Bob hadn't arrived yet—or would stick around when a stranger opened the door.

Jack was close on Ewan's heels, but he didn't immediately see Bob. He scanned the room, looking for some sign of him—and there he was: perched atop the mantel. If Jack didn't know better, he'd swear the little dude could teleport.

"Hey, Bob. How's it going?"

Bob sat, rocked back on his haunches, much like a dog, and watched as four people filled the small living room.

"Thanks for doing this." Jack remembered a little belatedly that Bob liked the formalities, so he hurried to correct the omission. "Bob, I'd like you to meet Ewan Campbell, Marin's father, and Heike Schlegel. And you know Marin."

As soon as he'd started the introductions, Bob had stood up. He performed a careful little bow with each introduction.

"It's a great pleasure to meet you." Ewan returned Bob's bow with one of his own. "Bob?"

A split second later, Ewan lips tugged upward in the hint of a smile.

Jack assumed Bob had replied to the curious note in Ewan's voice. Because Ewan, like Marin, would be able to communicate directly with Bob. Maybe Marin was right and Jack needed some formal method of communication with his friend.

Heike dipped into an approximation of a curtsy.

"Hi, Bob. Thank you for meeting us." Marin had closed the door quietly behind her, and now she stood next to Heike.

Ewan approached the mantel where Bob was perched.

"Oh, he's a little shy of strangers," Jack said.

And while Bob did back up, it looked like he was simply trying to keep Ewan within his line of sight.

"I'm just having a look at the mantel. Bob says the mantel is the heart of the house. No surprise there; that's an old concept." Turning to Marin, Ewan said, "What do you think—original to the house?"

Marin did a visual inspection. "I think so." Looking at Bob, she asked, "Do you mind?"

When Bob rocked back on his haunches into a sit again, she approached to examine it more closely. "Yes. I'm pretty sure. What are you thinking?"

Ewan considered the mantel, and then his gaze swung wide to encompass the room. "I think this is a spell caster problem, and it had a spell caster solution. We can't move the house, but what about the heart—the mantel—of the house? A little rejiggering of the magic..."

"Oh, you want me to—" Heike looked a bit pale —but maybe it was the lighting. "Oh, I don't think that's possible. At least, I don't know how I'd move quite so much magic."

Marin squeezed her eyes shut.

"You guys wanna clue in the non-magical guy?" Jack looked around the room. Only Bob seemed pleased.

Marin opened her eyes. "If the mantel is the heart of the house—in other words, an object symbolic of the whole—attach *all* of the magic to the mantel and move the mantel. Theoretically, no big magical boom."

Bob squeaked. At least, Jack thought the noise originated from him. He didn't even know Bob could make noises, but given how excitedly he was hopping up and down on the edge of the mantel and that the noise came from his general vicinity...it looked like Bob could squeak.

"Okay, Bob seems pretty sure that's an excellent plan." Jack glanced back at his furry buddy. "Right?"

Bob had stopped hopping, but he nodded several times.

"The only problem, Jack, is that someone has to shove all that volatile magic into that tiny little object." Marin looked less than thrilled by the prospect.

"That's me." Heike lifted her hand. "I'm the only spell caster around. That *is* why I'm here. Attaching magic to objects is a spell caster talent."

Ewan made a grumbling, annoyed noise. "You're here as a consultant. As a consultant, do you think a spell caster made this house?"

Heike didn't hesitate. "No. No way in hell."

"Exactly. Manipulating magic that has an unknown source—that's hardly in the realm of spell casting." Ewan clasped her hand and threaded his fingers through hers. "That's a bad idea."

"It's your idea. And if you think Lizzie or Harry have time to fly out to Texas—well, think again. And I'm equally qualified."

"Not to be a naysayer," Marin said, "because I'm on board whatever your decision, but you're only equally qualified because *no one* is qualified to do this. No one's done something like this before, have they?"

Everyone looked at Ewan. He was the oldest person in the room. Barring Bob—but who knew Bob's age?

"There's a lot of magic here." Ewan ran his hand through his hair. "I've never heard of a refuge being moved, and this mass of pure magic being manipulated—no, no idea."

"A little nudge to test the waters should be safe enough." Heike took a tiny step away from Ewan, and said, "We talked about this."

Ewan shifted away from Jack and Marin, more squarely facing Heike. "Now is not the time."

"Now is exactly the time." Heike crossed her arms. "This is what working in the field looks like."

Jack had a sinking feeling he was experiencing a marital disagreement. An ongoing marital disagreement.

Jack tipped his head in the direction of the hallway. "We'll just go check the rest of the house while you guys—"

But neither Ewan nor Heike was listening. They'd lowered their voices, but the intensity had escalated.

"Let's go." Marin beat a hasty retreat down the hall.

"Hey—are they married now?" Jack asked when he caught up to Marin in the bedroom.

"Good Lord—we left poor Bob in there." She dropped down on the edge of the bed.

"I think Bob can take care of himself. Hey, speak of the devil."

Bob was curled up on one of the decorative pillows at the head of the bed.

"You can seriously move when you're motivated." Jack smiled. He wasn't surprised that Bob had made a hasty exit. He seemed a low-drama kind of guy. "What do you think? Is Heike going to blow us all up if she fiddles with the house's magic?"

Bob looked at him, and then—he shrugged.

"Did you see that?"

Marin turned around. "What?"

"Uh. Nothing. Maybe this isn't a great idea. We have—what? Another two, maybe three days before the final appeal is resolved and the court determines damages? We can hold off for a better plan."

"If there's a better plan, Dad will come up with it.

Did you see how wigged he was? And they're...
they're *mostly* married."

"What the hell is mostly married?"

"They're human-married."

"What—there's a dragon-married? What the hell
is that?" Jack lifted his hands. "Never mind. I don't
want to know. So long as we get this shit sorted out
with the house—"

"We will."

"Right, I mean without triggering some
catastrophic event that kills all the little gnatlike
humans."

Marin laughed harshly. "The dragons don't fare
well in that scenario either. Pen's sense of perspective
is heavily warped. Accept it and move on." Her gaze
shifted over his shoulder. "We can head back now."

"You with us, Bob?"

But Bob had once again disappeared.

"Crap. Marin, we lost Bob."

Marin paused in the hallway. "He's not especially
social—not with anyone but you—so no surprise
there."

Jack followed Marin back into the living room,
but reluctantly. He thought Bob's retreat was more
likely a desire to preserve his small, furry hide than
an expression of social anxiety.

This time, whatever went awry, it wouldn't be his
fault. Small comfort to his corpse.

7

Heike stood near the mantel, once again examining it closely.

"We reached an agreement." But Ewan didn't sound like he'd actually agreed to whatever Heike was about to do.

"Wanna share the plan?" Marin stopped just inside the living room, leaving only enough space for Jack to walk past.

Jack glanced from Ewan, who wasn't pleased, to Heike, who appeared puzzled, to Marin, who looked like she wanted to leave as much as he did. "Maybe I should get the Rover warmed up for a quick getaway."

Heike was too preoccupied to respond, but Ewan and Marin overtly ignored him.

Jack took a breath and prayed to whatever gods

might be listening—the dragon gods, if they had them.

Finally, Heike looked up. "It's fine. I'll just poke a little. I'll try to herd the magic into the mantel...after I disconnect it from somewhere else in the house."

Jack raised his hand. "Not to bash a perfectly good plan—but isn't that exactly what we're trying to avoid with the demolition? Disconnecting the magic from the house?"

"This is on a much smaller scale." Marin bumped him gently with her elbow. "Remember our first case? At the end, and we did that group hug thing?"

What the hell was that supposed to mean? The end of their first case had been a massive explosion... Ah. Marin had "disappeared" him momentarily into the place she hid out when she ward-hopped. "Yeah. Sounds good. I'm all about group hugs." Only when they transported him away from big magical blasts, but no need to bust Heike's confidence by saying it.

At least they had a backup plan. Although it sounded like Marin was leaving her dad and Heike to fend for themselves—which was odd.

"Okay. It's basically a ward, right?" But Heike's question was rhetorical. Her upbeat tone implied this was her version of a pep talk. "All I have to do is unravel the magic from the physical anchor—just like I would any ward."

He knew from past experience that Heike had serious spell-casting skills. She'd been hired by a ruthless egomaniac back in the day, before she started working for IPPC. And that guy had been particular about his employees—only the best for evil mastermind bad guys.

But this was *a lot* of magic.

And Bob had disappeared.

And Ewan seemed worried.

Jack stepped a little closer to Marin. If he remembered right, they had to be touching to zap into Marin's hidey-hole.

"Press your thumbs." Heike blinked and looked away from the mantel, then corrected herself. "Sorry, cross your fingers. Whichever."

She ran her hand across the mantel until it met with the outer wall of the house. Fingers splayed against the wall, she closed her eyes and stood very still.

Jack held his breath...but nothing happened.

He forced himself to take a breath, because— what was he? Twelve?

Heike's eyes popped open and she lifted her hand away from the wall. "I can do this. It's not quite like spell caster magic, but it's similar. Give me just a second."

Ewan wore a pained look. The guy clearly adored his wife. He knew what Jack knew: Heike was a badass spell caster. But that didn't seem to lessen his concern. Love did that; it made all the stakes higher.

"Let me try this again." Heike ran her hand along the wall, tracing a line visible only to her. She stopped and closed her eyes.

A crack split the air. The room trembled. It vibrated, sparked, and then grew dark.

Jack fell to the ground. He looked for some sign —of what? A shooter in the dim light? The telltale flash of lightning signaling a storm? A crack in the middle of the floor leading to hell?

Light returned to the room and Jack could see the comfortably stuffed sofa, the pleasant wallpaper, the decorative pillows. It all looked so terribly normal.

He'd drawn his gun without thought, and he held it loosely now, feeling like an ass. Or that twelve-year-old he'd felt like earlier. Right up until he saw Marin.

She crouched low next to him, completely still —transfixed.

He said her name quietly, but she didn't respond.

He touched her shoulder.

She didn't move. And she looked scared.

Jack scanned the rest of the room, and he found Ewan and Heike similarly immobilized.

And then a ripple, like a muscle twitching, passed through the room.

Marin grabbed his arm and pulled herself up. "It's alive."

"What?" Jack glanced over his shoulder, looking to see if Ewan and Heike had similarly recovered.

They had. Their heads were bent close as they exchanged urgent words.

"When Pen talked about the house hosting magic, she meant the house is host to some magical being."

"Well, shit." Jack looked at the gun in his hand and then holstered it. Hell of a lot of good a gun would do.

8

"Heike felt a pulse." Ewan's voice sounded harsh in the sudden quiet of the living room.

"Yes. A pulse. An artery runs along there." Heike pointed to the right of the mantel, where she'd touched the wall earlier. "It felt like a point of attachment. Wards are simply magic connected to physical objects, yes? I thought this line of magic was a place where the magic connected to the physical structure of the house."

"But it was more like an artery sending magic out into the structure." Ewan's gaze focused on the mantel, and Jack thought he saw a hint of green in the depths of the dragon's eyes.

A crawling sensation made the hairs stand up on the back of Jack's neck. This cozy little nest of a house got weirder by the minute. A living house, a trembling house, a house with magic literally pulsing through its body... Jack couldn't reconcile that with the home that he saw around him. "We need to leave. Unless there's a good reason we're having this conversation inside the belly of the beast."

He didn't wait for them to answer; Jack walked out the front door. Once in the front yard, the tightness in his chest and the crawling sensation running along his skin stopped.

And his brain started to work again.

Bob hadn't seemed certain what they were doing was safe. But he also hadn't warned them that they were about to do something terrible.

Marin, Heike, and Ewan were close on his heels.

Addressing his question to the two people who had the ability to communicate directly with Bob, Jack asked Ewan and Marin, "Did either of you get any hint from Bob that the house might bite back if poked? More importantly, that the thing is actually alive?"

"Arkan Sonney are known for their brevity, and he did say the mantel was the heart of the house." Marin sounded a little more flippant than the situation called for. But as easily as he could spot her pale face in the dark, he couldn't pick out enough detail to read her expression.

"So what you're saying is that hindsight is twenty-twenty, but we didn't get a clear warning."

Jack tried to keep the irritation out of his voice, but it was a half-ass effort. He was tired.

"If I'd received a clear warning from Bob," Ewan said, "we wouldn't have proceeded. But speaking with an Arkan Sonney is muddled. There's room for interpretation."

"And error," Marin said.

Heike sighed. "I should have realized. But all of that energy masked the biorhythms. When I touched on the artery, I should have seen—"

"No offense, but I don't think you're the only one who's feeling like an ass. We all feel like grade-A idiots for missing the obvious." Jack rubbed his neck. "I keep looking at it thinking it's going to look back with big glowing eyes. What are the chances it understands language?"

"Slim," Ewan said. "We'll have to find some other way to communicate with it. Bob saw more than us, as I'd hoped, but I doubt there was any substantial communication between him and the creature inhabiting the house."

Marin and Jack locked eyes. They said in unison, "Kaisermann."

"Your client, yes. He might be the key, but fair warning," Ewan said, "IPPC didn't find anything noteworthy in his background. If he has a magical talent, it's well hidden."

"Probably even from himself. The man couldn't be more average." Marin pulled the Range Rover keys from her pocket. "We have an appointment with him tomorrow—or today, rather—at ten. Unless we're worried about leaving the house unsupervised...?"

"No." Ewan opened the passenger door for Heike. "We've got a confirmed late check-in with our hotel, so we're set for tonight. Let's reconvene after we've all had some sleep, after your meeting."

Marin's step faltered. She quickly recovered and opened the driver's door. "I'll give you guys a ring afterward."

On the way home, Jack expected some acknowledgment of how Marin's family dynamic had played into the events. Or an explanation of her stepmother's presence. Or something about why her dad was ditching their client meeting tomorrow.

Nothing.

As Marin pulled in front of the shop, where Jack's car was still parked, he finally asked, "You wanna tell me anything?"

She stared straight ahead. "You wanna give me that partnership agreement?"

Jack pulled out his phone and tapped the screen a few times. "Done."

That pulled her out of her funk. She turned to him with a frown. "Are you messing with me?"

"No. Check your email. Fifteen percent ownership, non-negotiable. We can revisit in a year or two."

If they were both still alive and kicking.

She turned back to stare down the street. "I left to give them some room—no big deal, right? Maybe even kind of nice of me."

She seemed to be looking for affirmation, so Jack threw up his hands. "Yeah, sure. Newlyweds and all that. I mean, I've never been married, but—why not."

"Well, he flips. Acts like I'm incapable of doing even the most basic of things: find a place to live, get a job, and don't get me started on the cooking." She sent a glare his way that he was glad not to have earned. "Cooking. I mean, how hard can it be? Like I'm going to starve."

"You eat a lot." It was an unsolicited comment, and he had no clue why he said it. Just tired, probably.

Her narrowed eyes lit with a green fire. "I'm a dragon. I don't eat a lot for a dragon. And who are you to talk?"

"What are you saying?" Jack glanced down at his midsection. "I run."

"And the bigger issue is, dragons don't do well outside the clan. So I hear, though I can't say I see any evidence of that. I'm doing fine. Maybe it was a little rough at first, but I'm good, right?"

He nodded. Jack had forgotten, but she'd said before that the clan stuck together. "I don't get what the issue is now, though. Whatever he's said in the past, Ewan seems cool with your choices now. I mean, he hired us for a job." Jack would keel over in shock if his sister—or, God forbid, his mother—hired him for a gig. "That's damned supportive."

Marin just shook her head like he'd lost all his sense. "Says you. He's totally checking up on me."

"You need some perspective. He hired us for that book-retrieval job—directly. He could have had Harrington call. That's what usually happens." Jack held up a hand. "No, hold on a minute. Then he left us to it. He let the no-talent human and his daughter retrieve a valuable book. That's trust."

She scrunched up her nose. "But he came this time."

"Are you kidding me? We asked for help." Jack couldn't help but lose his patience—this was ridiculous. She sounded like a teenager. Or what he imagined teenagers sounded like. "You're normally so reasonable. Take a step back and look at this without all of your weird family baggage. I think he's trying. Hell, I wish my family was half as supportive."

Marin crossed her arms. "You really think so?"

"Good Lord. I just said it. Yes, I think so. He's not even coming to our client meeting, and I don't think that's so he can have a little alone time with your stepmom." Jack bit back a groan. He couldn't believe he was giving this advice, but: "Ask him."

"What?"

This was downright painful. "Ask him how he

feels about you living in Austin, working for me... hell, ask him how he feels about you making your own meals." Jack gave her an exasperated look. "Who the hell usually makes your meals?"

"Oh, we have a chef." But she wasn't really paying much attention to him. She seemed to be chewing over his advice.

What the hell had the world come to if he was the guy providing family counseling?

9

The next morning, Marin arrived at the shop a few minutes after Jack. She didn't mention their conversation from the night before, and neither did Jack. But maybe she'd sort her family shit out now. If she did, maybe Jack wouldn't hold his breath every time he ran into the guy.

Kaisermann showed up fifteen minutes early for his ten o'clock appointment.

After he came through the front door, Marin locked it behind him and flipped the sign to closed.

He followed Jack and Marin back into the office. "You have news, don't you?" Kaisermann looked from Marin to Jack. "Something's there, isn't it?"

Jack walked behind the desk and indicated the client chair. After Kaisermann seated himself, Jack said, "Yes. There's something there."

"I knew it." Kaisermann collapsed back into the chair. "Forget what my father said. I felt it in my bones. It's a ghost?"

Marin perched on the edge of the sofa, her hands clasped in her lap. "No—not exactly a ghost. But something has definitely taken over the house."

Jack realized belatedly that he and Marin should have come up with some kind of reveal strategy. "Magic is real, and your house is alive" seemed somewhat abrupt.

"Well, whatever it is, can we exorcise it?" Kaisermann's color wasn't looking so good.

"Can I get you a drink, sir?" Jack thought back to the background on Kaisermann. He didn't think the old guy had any medical conditions they needed to worry about, but...

"Mr. Kaisermann, we think you might be able to help us resolve the issue with your house." Marin lifted her hand when he started to sputter a denial. "We're aware that you're not involved with the magical aspect of the house. But it seems your family has some connection to whatever is living in the house."

Jack watched as Kasiermann's face turned from pale to ruddy. He rolled his chair over to the mini-fridge and retrieved a bottle of water.

Jack handed Kaisermann the water bottle. "We know this is surprising, but the stakes are high. The house can't be moved while the...ah, the guest is in residence. My expert tried to communicate with the entity, but with no real success."

Sort of true. Jack hadn't been able to grill Bob any further, because he'd been absent since last night. And as far as he knew, Bob didn't have an actual conversation with the house—although it would be nice to know for sure. Any insight into the psyche of the pulsating magic mass would be just fine by him.

Kaisermann had drunk several mouthfuls of water and his color was returning. "And you think I can communicate with it when your expert couldn't? I don't see how."

"It's the family connection," Marin said. "We did a little research on your family, and there's a connection going back years between your family and houses much like this one."

"You traced my family history? I don't know about that—well...you said the house can't be moved with this creature in it. What happens if I simply allow the city to demolish the house?"

Jack and Marin shared a glance. Time for the ugly truth.

"It's possible—probable, actually—that there would be an explosion."

Kaisermann laughed. "A magical explosion. You're kidding me." His eyebrows beetled together. "What exactly are you charging me to prevent this magical explosion?"

Marin gave Jack a subtle shake of the head, then said, "We understand your skepticism. Your evaluation fee will be sufficient. Given the nature of the problem and the far-reaching effects destroying the house would have, a private organization has stepped forward to absorb any costs."

"That seems very irregular." Suddenly Kaisermann lowered his head and covered his eyes with his hand. When he looked up, he gave Jack a weak smile. "Ridiculous. We're talking about magic. It's not like I can get a second opinion. And I know, in my bones I know, there's something not right about that house."

Marin wrinkled her nose. In a quiet voice, she said, "If it makes you feel any better, there's solid evidence to suggest your house is a refuge of sorts. That the inhabitant might have a fundamentally benevolent purpose. It probably played a part in keeping someone safe from a truly terrible magical event."

A rather generous interpretation of the minimal facts thus far gathered—but Jack wasn't shy of a little spin, and he nodded agreeably.

"Well, if the thing is so benevolent, it would be neighborly of it not to blast the neighbors before they have a chance to clear out." Kaisermann pulled a handkerchief from his pocket and blew his nose.

Jack debated correcting Kaisermann's perception

of the size of the blast—but what was the point? It wouldn't go that far.

After all of the pallor and stress and sneezing, Jack wasn't sure Kaisermann was up to a confrontation with his living house.

Kaisermann's features hardened. "So how do I talk to this creature?"

Or maybe that was the real question.

10

After deftly avoiding the "how" question that Kaisermann had posed, Jack and Marin made arrangements to meet him at the house at two o'clock that afternoon.

That gave Kaisermann time to prepare himself to enter the house—something he was clearly reluctant to do. And it gave Jack and Marin a few hours to dig around for a viable method of communication between a human and a house. Jack wasn't holding his breath.

After Kaisermann left, he and Marin had bounced around a few ideas. Thus far no brilliant revelations had been made.

"Do you think Penelope might give you some idea?" Jack rolled his chair back and propped his feet on his desk.

"We have a very specific kind of friendship—one that does not include me picking her brain." Marin stretched out on the couch with her hands behind her head. "I doubt she'd know anyway. That's not the type of information that interests her. The story behind a vase or a mirror—or a house—sure. Besides, she's not currently available. She's off on one of her treks—she calls them scavenges—and can't be reached."

"Just a thought. Any other ancient, freakishly knowledgeable resources we haven't tapped?" As Jack spoke, an image of Joshua flashed through his mind. Which was profoundly disturbing. He didn't know what Joshua looked like, because he'd never seen the dragon's physical form. He couldn't because Joshua's physical form had long ago decayed into dust. And yet he saw a massive black dragon...and he *knew* it was Joshua. In his innermost self, he simply knew.

"Jack?"

Jack jerked himself back to the here and the now. A chill went down his spine. He was always here and now. He was no dragon, lost in the past.

"Jack!"

"What the hell?"

"You need to get some more sleep or something. You're off your game." Marin was still lounging on the sofa, but her cell was in her hand.

"I'm fine. What were you saying?"

"Just that Dad checked in with the IPPC librarian and they were working on it, but he's not hopeful."

Jack shifted his feet off the desk and picked up a pen. "Let's consider the possibilities." He tapped the pen on the blotter on his desk, then started to scrawl a few random thoughts.

"It helps if you say them out loud."

Jack looked up from his short list. "Yeah, not sure about that. I've got Vulcan mind meld, pictures via telepathy, and genetic language."

"*Star Trek*?" She might not have rolled her eyes, but he could hear the judgment in her tone.

"Are you kidding me? *Star Trek* is the answer more times than you'd think." Jack considered his list. "Granted, probably not this time...but frequently."

"And genetic language?"

"So, consider that there is a genetic component to the relationship between the Kaisermann family and the house. Why that family? Why one family?"

"Genetic language," Marin said. "If there's a genetic component and the Kaisermann family have some ability that isn't readily recognizable by the rest of the magic community..."

"And that ability lets them communicate on a different level, beyond language."

Marin raised an eyebrow. "That's usually called telepathy, and dragons have that ability. If the house needs a telepathic connection to communicate, it could easily have reached out to Dad or me."

"But what if you're tuned in to the wrong frequency? The house is talking, but you're not hearing."

Marin sat up. "Oh. I never really thought about it, but Bob doesn't exactly come across crystal clear. Maybe we have overlapping but not entirely compatible telepathic communication. But if Kaisermann has some latent ability, wouldn't the house be reaching out to him?"

"Who's to say it hasn't? You saw his reaction when we said something had taken over the house. And he keeps saying that he feels in his bones that something is odd about the house."

"Well, that's the first question when we meet up. 'Mr. Kaisermann, have you had secret dealings with the entity that inhabits your house?'"

Jack grunted. "I think I can manage a little more subtlety, thanks."

"Sure." Marin's wide-eyed, unblinking stare said otherwise. "We should also talk contingency plan. If Kaisermann can't reach out to the house, or he can't convince it to retreat to the mantel and let us transport it somewhere safely away from civilization, then what?"

"Any chance you and Ewan could disappear the house, magical blob and all, into the in-between place? You took me there to escape a blast—would the opposite work?"

"My gut says that is a very, very bad idea—but I'll ask Dad."

Jack gave the various outcomes some consideration. "It's possible we simply walk away from this meeting in a stalemate."

"A stalemate at this point is a loss. We're running out of time."

Jack massaged the point where his shoulder and neck met. It seemed the pinched feeling kept getting worse each day. "Communicate with the alien being inhabiting the house, hope Kaisermann can not only speak its language but well enough to explain the situation, and pray it doesn't hold the city of Austin hostage. Is it too late to take a vacation?"

11

J ack drove to their appointment with Kaisermann. He wanted steady nerves when they arrived, and Marin's driving put him on edge.

Twenty peaceful minutes later, he pulled into the driveway. He shut the engine off then took a moment to examine the house.

"It looks so harmless." Marin sat in the passenger seat, also staring at the house.

"Hell, for all we know, it is harmless. The place is supposed to be a refuge."

"I've been wondering about that. A refuge for whom and from what?" Marin asked. "In every conflict, there are at least two sides. What's the conflict and who chooses which side receives refuge?"

"Does it matter?" Jack asked. They were too far

into this mess. It wasn't like they could stop and evaluate the morality of dismantling a strategically important outpost...or a possible haven for an enemy...or an ally. The thought of an Austin post-magical apocalypse made his eye twitch and his neck hurt. "And maybe the house doesn't take sides. If its magical signal jammer works indiscriminately, then there are no sides."

"Switzerland, huh?"

"Let's hope."

Marin sighed. "It seems such a waste. As rare as these houses are, and the practical applications—"

"Which include being co-opted by the Coven of Light. Better it's moved far away from a mainstream, well-populated area."

Kaisermann drove up in an older silver Prius and parked next to the Range Rover.

"About that." Marin opened her door. "We need the alternate house location from Kaisermann. And we should discuss whether IPPC should assume responsibility for the house."

Jack suspected Kaisermann wouldn't let go of his responsibilities so easily, however uneasily they sat with him. Jack exited the car and turned to greet Kaisermann.

He stood in front on his car, watching the house. "Still gives me the creeps, even after all these years. I can't remember the last time I actually went inside the place."

"About that..." Jack ignored Marin's half-smile. "You say the house gives you a strange feeling. Is there anything specific you can point to?"

Kaisermann shifted uncomfortably. "I'm not sure what you mean."

"Mr. Kaisermann, if there's anything, anything at all, that relates to the house that you haven't told us, now is the time." Marin gave him her best, most engaging smile.

When she kept the glowing eyes and teeth under control, she was a very attractive woman. And Kaisermann must have agreed, because he relaxed under the shine of her smile.

He gave Marin a rueful look. "Nightmares. Not for years, but all of a sudden they've cropped up again."

"And how are these nightmares tied to the house?" Marin asked.

"Sometimes I'm inside the house, sometimes outside standing in the driveway looking at the house." He paused and glanced at the house. "Like now."

Suddenly Kaisermann stopped, distracted as Ewan and Heike pulled into the driveway.

"These are your experts? The ones with the organization that's paying for this...this extermination?" Kaisermann seemed relieved to be interrupted—which made Jack all the more curious as to the nature of these dreams.

"Yes, that's right." As the couple exited the car, Jack said, "This is Ewan Campbell and his wife Heike."

Heike and Ewan shook hands with Kaisermann but deferred to Jack for explanations. Jack figured less was more, and simply said they'd be helping. "Mr. Kaisermann was just telling us about some odd dreams centering around the house that he's had over the years. Mr. Kaisermann?"

Kaisermann shuffled a step back from the group, then another. Jack didn't think the man was acting consciously. Kaisermann started with some hesitation, but then the words flowed. Perhaps he was relieved to finally share the odd visions he'd lived with for so long.

"Wherever I start, I end up in the living room. The lights pulse on and off and there's a thrumming vibration coming from the walls. I can almost hear— but not quite—something off in the distance. I feel like I should be able to hear...but I try and I can't. Then I have this terrible feeling that I should be doing something. I'm so frustrated. And there's this anger. And then it's dark and I'm lost." Kaisermann blinked several times. "That's it." He looked around at the faces of the four people who encircled him. "What does it mean?"

"Marin and I might have a theory." Which Ewan and Heike would be hearing for the first time, since Jack hadn't updated them. "We're hoping the house is trying to communicate—just isn't on the right wavelength. Or station."

"I don't want to talk to it—whatever it is." Kaisermann backed another few steps away from the group.

Enough with the carrot; time for the stick. Jack cleared his throat. "Mr. Kaisermann, we're expecting a large—no, a very large—explosion should this house be moved with its visitor still in residence. We don't have much of a backup plan at this point," Jack caught the slight tip of Ewan's head—they did have a backup plan?—but ignored it for now. "So in order to prevent a potentially catastrophic event, we need you to at least try to have a conversation with the house."

Kaisermann stood, stunned, in the driveway. Finally he said, "Aren't you people supposed to be professionals? Why do you need me?"

Jack took a breath, about to spout some amazingly persuasive garbage—or not—but was interrupted when Marin touched his shoulder.

So he waited as Kaisermann stood in the driveway of the possessed house, eyes darting between the house, the paranormal professionals who couldn't help him, and the street. Jack could guess exactly what the guy was thinking: face his nightmare, let the pros take care of the mess, or run.

At least that gave them a thirty percent chance. Math didn't actually work that way—but that thirty percent lie let him stand here in the driveway and wait—rather than pressuring a guy who was already under too much strain.

Finally, Kaisermann said, "Yes." His feet remained firmly planted—but at least he'd said the word.

12

It was Marin who got Kaisermann into the house. After politely waiting for what seemed like several minutes, Marin looped her arm in his and simply walked up the drive.

She didn't pause at the porch steps, and, since Ewan had the foresight to beat them to the door, it was open when she and Kaisermann arrived.

By that time, Kaisermann had acquired a much more purposeful step, and he surprised them all by passing the threshold ahead of Marin.

Once he was standing in the living room, Kaisermann said in a small voice, "It's much more cheerful than the dreams." He suddenly seemed old in a way he hadn't before.

Jack hadn't caught the nightmare quality of the man's dreams as he'd relayed them. His recounting sounded slightly odd, but nothing about what Kaisermann had described seemed sinister.

But Kaisermann's pallor and demeanor expressed exactly how frightening he'd found the dreams. Even now, as he commented on the cheeriness of the room, the man seemed to shrink in on himself.

Heike walked from the front door, across the room, to the mantel.

Kaisermann tracked her movements until a few feet shy of the fireplace and then his gaze skittered away.

"Mr. Kaisermann?" Heike said using the German pronunciation. "Sir?"

But Kaisermann seemed not to hear. He kept his head averted from the fireplace, as if he couldn't stand to look at it.

Ewan moved into his line of sight. "Do you hear something?"

"No. No, nothing. I don't hear anything at all." With each pronouncement, Kaisermann's voice rose in volume and he shook his head with increasing agitation.

Ewan approached the man and calmly but firmly placed a hand on his back. "You're not crazy. Whatever it is, we believe you."

Kaisermann calmed down a little and then made eye contact with Ewan. "You can hear it too?"

"No, but I believe that you do. But I might be able to…" Ewan grasped the man's shoulder with a firm, reassuring grip. "If you help me."

Jack poked Marin in the ribs and then whispered into her ear, "Vulcan mind meld—*Star Trek* is always the answer."

"Not remotely the same thing. Telepathy is easier if you're touching," Marin replied in a hushed voice, and then shushed him.

Kaisermann's eyes widened. "Okay. What do I do?"

"Accept that it's trying to speak to you." When Kaisermann nodded, Ewan said, "And that it doesn't want to hurt you."

Kaisermann looked confused. "I'm not sure. I think she's angry."

Jack would bet cash that Ewan had gambled. And maybe he'd guessed wrong, but the gamble was a good one: the guy and house were talking.

In an even, calming voice, Ewan asked, "Do you know why she's angry?"

Kaisermann's eyebrows beetled and a tear rolled down his cheek. "Not angry, lonely."

Jack had been watching Kaisermann and Ewan so intently that he'd missed Heike. But her movements flashed in the corner of his eye and he turned to find her at the mantel, running her hands along the wall, much as she had before.

Quietly, she said, "The magic is surging."

Jack nodded. Whatever happened, they'd certainly awoken the thing by bringing Kaisermann here.

"Mr. Kaisermann!" Ewan shook the man's shoulder.

Kaisermann's distant gaze sharpened. "Yes. I'm here."

"Can you tell her about the house? That we need to move it?" Ewan asked, his hand still on Kaisermann's shoulder, but passive now.

Marin inched closer to Heike, moving slowly so as not to startle Kaisermann. She tipped her head at Ewan.

Was this the backup plan?

Just in case, stay close to Dad. He'll get you out.

Marin's dragon voice echoed in Jack's head. Great. That was the escape plan—not the backup plan. So long, Austin. It was nice knowing you.

"She doesn't understand." Kaisermann's voice was small, swallowed by the dense air.

Jack shivered. The change had occurred so slowly that he'd missed it till now. The house was cooler and the air thicker.

"Tell her that we want to move her and the house, but we need her to be smaller." Jack looked at Ewan. Could be hear what was happening in Kaisermann's head?

Ewan said, "She needs to pull her magic back,

into the heart, the hearth. And then we can safely move her."

The air became almost un-breathable. Jack's lungs hurt with each pull of breath.

The floor rippled, like the shivering skin of a beast.

Lights flickered on and off—but it didn't come from the fixtures. The very walls luminesced. Pinkish light, then red.

Jack felt like he was inside a reptilian womb. The pulsing beat of a heart, the air thick and moist, a chill to the air.

A massive shudder and then the house was silent. No thrum of a heart pulsing magic echoed in his ears. And the air was once again only pleasantly cool.

He shifted his weight, and his joints cracked. How long had he been frozen still in that one spot?

He caught sight of Kaisermann, stooped and tired. Ewan led him to the sofa and the man collapsed in it.

He looked distressed. More distressed than he should, given that there wasn't a bunch of magic pulsing all around them. Then Jack had a strange pull of guilt. "It's not dead?" It was a freaking house...or magic blob in a house. Why did he care? But the thought bothered him.

"No...I don't think so." Kaisermann's head shot

up, as if he'd just realized what he was hearing and saying. "Surely not?"

Ewan sat down next to him on the sofa. "What do you think?"

"She's not here." Kaisermann's tone was cautious.

"There's no detectable magic." Heike moved away from the mantel and sat next to Ewan on the sofa. "Not in the hearth, either."

Kaisermann considered her words. "I think she's gone. Not dead. I think she understood and she left."

"Any idea why this house? Why Austin?" Jack paced across the small room, loosening stiff joints.

"Someone needed refuge." Kaisermann turned to Ewan. "Do you think it's safe to move the house now?"

"But who needed refuge?" Jack asked.

Kaisermann shrugged. "She didn't say." And he didn't seem the least curious about the answer.

Ewan shot Jack a warning look then answered Kaisermann's question. "Yes, you can make plans to move it."

"But what was she?" Jack asked.

"I don't know." Exhausted and looking every bit his age, Kaisermann wobbled as he stood. Once his feet were firmly under him, he asked, "Can I go home now?"

Marin appeared at his elbow, once again looping her arm through his, but this time it was to steady not his nerves, but his body. They disappeared through the front door together.

Once the door had closed behind them, Jack turned to Ewan. "What's the deal?"

"He can't answer any of your questions. The connection he had with that creature wasn't exactly telepathic. More of an instinctual thing. It felt like a psychic umbilical cord between mother and child."

That explained the icky inside-a-womb feeling Jack had. "If that's true, it's no wonder Mom was peeved at being cut off. Kaisermann's dad passed unexpectedly. I wonder if there was some piece of information he would have passed along to keep the connection alive between the—whatever that thing was—and the family."

"Possibly. One thing I can tell you: she was old. I wouldn't be surprised if she was the same being that inhabited the Black Forest house hundreds of years ago."

"Yeah, I got that as well," Heike said. "Really big, lots of magic, and old. That's about all I got, though. Oh, and the magic surges pulsing through the walls."

Marin walked back in. "I think he's good. By the time we got to the car, he seemed to be more himself. He just wanted to go home and, I think, forget about all of this." She flashed Jack a smile. "Good thing he doesn't owe us anything, because my guess is it would be hell to get him to acknowledge this night ever happened, let alone cough up any cash."

Heike stood up. "Are we ready to put this house behind us?"

Three responses, all emphatically affirmative.

13

After a very brief discussion in the driveway of the formerly possessed house, Marin, Heike, Ewan, and Jack had all decided to grab a bite to eat at a local Mexican place that Marin and Jack frequented.

The meal had been fabulous and the booze had flowed. Something about a battle fought that hadn't been a battle at all had everyone keyed up, and the bar tab proved it.

Since the dragons were almost impossible to get drunk, Marin and Ewan had promised to drive, leaving Jack and Heike to drink themselves under the table.

It was well after dark when they all made their way outside, leaving a very satisfied waiter behind.

Jack was about to wish Ewan and Heike safe travels home, when Marin said, "Hey, Dad. Do you have a second?" She grabbed Jack by the arm as he started to slip away. "Jack here had the brilliant idea that I should ask you about something that's been bothering me."

Jack tried to tug his arm free, but Marin held tight. "I'll just wait in the car."

Marin didn't reply, and she didn't let go.

"Sure. Are we talking in the parking lot?" He seemed a little confused.

They'd been eating chips, queso, and guacamole for hours, and now she ambushed the guy when they were a feet away from their cars. Jack could understand his confusion.

It took a little headache-inducing thought, but Jack finally got it—and she was brilliant. Having a hasty escape nearby when having a "family" discussion could never hurt...but did she have to drag him into it?

Marin had finally let go of his arm, so he made his way to the Range Rover—one very cautious step at a time. He snuck a glance to see if she'd noticed his escape—and blinked.

What the hell had he missed? Everyone was hugging and looking happy and teary-eyed. Well, Heike looked teary-eyed; the dragons just had smug, toothy, dragon grins. Either way—it looked like reconciliation was in the air. Not that he had a lot of first-hand experience with his own family.

Maybe he was a little drunker than he'd thought,

because he thought he might be feeling the first flutterings of jealousy. Yeah—he had to be wasted to think he wanted that kind of acceptance from his uptight, middle-class, suburban, neighbor-one-upping, judgmental family.

He squinted, wobbled, caught himself with one hand on the hood of the Range Rover, and hollered, "Can we go home now?"

EPILOGUE

Things had been pretty quiet. Bob had returned from a three-day walkabout. Whether he'd been visiting friends or simply seen the wisdom of a hasty exit from the Austin area, Jack didn't know. And he wasn't likely to find out anytime soon, since he still hadn't cracked the communication barrier. He needed to get on that.

But not today. Marin was in the shop, and Bob was correspondingly absent.

"Hey, what happened to Kaisermann?" Jack asked from behind his desk. "You said you were going to follow up with him."

"Yeah." Marin looked up from a dusty pile of newspapers, magazines, and old books, all stacked on the small table that served as their unofficial stock-processing area. "Where did you get this stuff?

He slouched in his chair and fiddled with some loose papers. If he looked busy, maybe he could skip processing what had to be a mildew-fest of newspapers. "No clue. Someone might have dropped it off. Kaisermann?"

"Right. He's decided to embrace his retirement fully. He's moving to Belize. Which is where I'm moving if you don't start sorting some of the useless stock you bring in."

Jack ignored the gibe. "Belize? Why does that sound so familiar?"

"The bookseller? The one we bribed to keep his mouth shut about the nasty, soul-stealing book? He took the cash and had a party in Belize for about a month."

"Ah. Good thing you keep up with the little details." Jack rolled his chair over to the mini-fridge and pulled out two beers. He lifted one in the air. He'd been off booze for a few days after that whole drunken scene with Marin's parents. But he'd fully recovered from his hangover, and all the dust motes floating around were making him thirsty.

"Sure." Marin took the offered beer. "And the book guy did make it back into the country. He's still selling books out of that shabby little shop."

"I know. I'm just giving you shit. Chris blind-copies me on all the assignments you give her. And we didn't bribe him to keep his mouth shut about the book. It was the fire damage you caused trying to catch the book thieves."

"Yeah. That was a good cover story. Some garbage about cutting-edge tech. Didn't you tell him it was a laser that zapped his store?"

Jack shrugged. "Lasers are cool. What guy doesn't want to believe in lasers? Especially nerdy bookseller guys."

"Who also sells comics," Marin said. "Oh, and Chris doesn't blind-copy you on *everything.*"

Jack blinked. Was Marin doing research on him? Chris wouldn't—

"Gotcha."

He let it pass. Because he'd just realized that there seemed to be convergence happening. Kaisermann picking up and moving so suddenly. Their bookseller who had just happened upon a nasty, soul-stealing book and a bizarre cult of money-grubbing murderers. And Belize. "You don't think there's something brewing in Belize, do you?"

Marin downed a quarter of her beer in a one long pull. "I hear Belize is a nice place to visit."

Shit.

Jack and Marin's next adventure, Entombed, *is available now! Keep reading for an excerpt.*

EXCERPT: ENTOMBED

PROLOGUE

Belize

Hunger. A twisting, gnawing ache of emptiness. For flesh, for blood, for marrow. Thought slithered away, lost in the pulse, the pain, of want... need...hunger.

Time passed.

A spark lit inside the creature; its instinct to live flared. The creature narrowed the pain, focused it. Its world became a small, dark place, filled with a greedy lust to consume. The hunger overwhelmed it, chasing away not just thought but also instinct.

Waking, sleeping, no, up, no, down, always hungry, its world still small and dark.

Time passed.

The spark flared again. Instinct pushed the creature forward, pushed it to explore its small world. It began to wallow in the dark. It felt dirt against its body. It felt the scrape of rocks against its skin. The stink of its own blood filled the space. Unlike the hunger that dulled, this pain sharpened its senses.

And the blood brought insects. And the insects were food.

A pitiful, meager food—not filling its belly, but giving it some sustenance. It was enough.

Slowly, it began to move beyond instinct. It began to think. To strategize. To consider escape from the pit that confined it.

It whispered into the dark, calling forth larger creatures to consume. It grew stronger. It called louder.

And then it found a human mind.

Connected with it. Read it. Learned the human's language. And in the learning, it remembered itself...himself.

He was awake. No longer dormant, no longer dulled by hunger and pain. Awake and ready to be free of his prison.

CHAPTER ONE

Jack read the email one more time before shutting his laptop. An intriguing offer: free international travel, a hefty fee for the southerly jaunt to Belize, and an even heftier sum for a brief consult. No strings, no commitments. All he had to do was listen to the prospective client pitch a case. If the job wasn't a fit for Spirelli Paranormal Investigations, he could walk away with a tidy little windfall. And if he did take the case, well, the payout would probably set him up for a year of property taxes and some repairs to the house.

It was a good deal. Probably too good. He could hardly overlook the fact that his prospective client hadn't revealed his—or her—identity. But the cash...

He checked the time, then left his office in the back of The Junk Shop for the retail area. He wanted to catch Marin before she headed out for the night.

She was flipping the shop sign to closed, so he had about five seconds before she was out the door. To do whatever it was she did in her free time. He didn't know—didn't want to know—so long as she showed up to work at The Junk Shop and was available for cases. Their recent partnership agreement had already twined their lives closer together than was ideal.

He walked into the retail area as she was digging her car keys out of the bag slung over her shoulder.

"You ever been to Belize?" he asked as he walked between the display tables.

She paused, keys clenched in her hand. "Why? I thought we'd decided to give Belize a miss. No payday, remember?"

That was when Belize had been the focal point of a series of interesting events. Now it was a new HVAC system and a tree trim, not to mention his property taxes, if they took the case. His house had become a demanding mistress lately.

"And if there was cash involved?"

She flicked a few stray strands of bright red hair away from her face. "Is it enough to justify the cost of leaving the country and getting entangled in some kind of supernatural jurisdictional quagmire?"

He'd considered contacting Harrington. For about two seconds. As the head of the Inter-Pack Policing Cooperative, a European agency intent on becoming a global policing organization for all things supernatural, paranormal, or magically enhanced, Harrington wasn't always concerned with the best interests of the little guy. Since Jack was very much the little guy, he only brought Harrington and IPPC in when it was absolutely necessary.

And Harrington could be a moralistic ass. Especially galling, because IPPC and even Harrington himself didn't always stick as close to the ethical high ground as they might.

Screw it. The anonymous client paid better than IPPC. So much better that Jack was willing to annoy both Harrington and his new *junior* partner by taking the meeting...unless Marin knew something he didn't. She had exceptional connections. Being a dragon—both long-lived and a part of the magic-using community—would do that.

Weighing his options had kept him occupied longer than he'd realized, because the sound of

Marin clearing her throat interrupted his thoughts. When he met her gaze, she looked annoyed.

"Have you spoken to Harrington?" When he still didn't answer, her eyes narrowed. "Eventually he's going to get tired of being our own personal 9-1-1 service."

Probably true. But that street ran both ways. Spirelli Paranormal Investigations was a solid resource that IPPC had relied on more than once. "No, I haven't specifically mentioned this case. I don't run all my cases by him. Do you?"

When she didn't respond, he said, "Harrington has excellent spies. He probably already knows about this offer, as well the migration of two former clients to Belize."

"My point exactly; both of those cases involved IPPC. You still don't think they need to be brought in on this one?"

Jack shook his head. "If they're interested, they'll have their own investigation. They might even have an explanation for some of the unusual news coming out of the area."

"Maybe. I'm not sure migratory birds altering course to avoid Corozal Town, and the rodent population in a tiny town outside Corozal suddenly dwindling, would be flagged as suspicious by IPPC."

"You noticed, and Harrington has an entire staff tasked with monitoring news for weird phenomenon. I'm sure he knows. Hell, your dad is probably halfway through his investigation."

"My dad's on sabbatical."

"I'm sorry—what?" Jack had the very strong impression that the head of the IPPC's magical library never took vacation.

"Sabbatical. Three months." Marin's eyes flashed the creepy glowing green of an annoyed dragon. "Don't ask. I don't know why or even where he is."

"Well, that answers the IPPC question. They're already understaffed. They don't need to get involved in this particular case when they're down their chief of security."

Marin crossed her arms. "All right, how much are we talking?"

Not everything was about money. Okay, most things were—but that was hardly his fault.

"A lot. And that's to show up. More if we take the case."

"And the client?"

"That's tricky." He'd forwarded the email to Chris, his go-to tech gal, but she was on her fourth kid—or was it the fifth?—and sometimes she was busy with life. He pulled his phone out of his pocket and flipped to his email—where he found that she'd already responded. Maybe he'd imagined five—probably only two or three. "Chris says no-go on identifying the client from the email."

Marin's arms dropped to her sides. "That's curious." After only the barest of hesitations, she said, "Fine. If you're in, I'm in. What? Don't look so shocked. You think I like sweeping up, emptying the trash, and de-funking your and Bob's bizarre finds?"

"Bob's the man. Don't knock his special finds. He's keeping The Junk Shop in the black." Thinking about the shy little fuzzy critter made Jack want to smile. Bob was like that; he was a smile waiting to happen. "You know what? I think you like tidying the place. You do way more cleaning than you have to. It's a *junk* shop. People don't expect pristine."

It was an old argument. She thought their upscale clientele required a higher standard than he was willing to maintain, and now that she was a partner, she expected him to do more to maintain the place.

Not gonna happen.

Marin pursed her lips. "Getting out of the shop occasionally is a good thing. And it's been two, three weeks since we've come close to being blown up. I haven't even gotten a papercut. My body's in shock from all the risk-free living."

"Cute."

"And it's about time for the shop to shut down for a week or so. I'd hate to train our clients to expect regular hours."

Jack shook his head. "And yet the shop needs to be tidy."

"Being unpredictable fits our brand. Dirt does

not." She pointed a finger at him. "We take the case, but you're dealing with any fallout from IPPC. Like I said, my trump card is on some mysterious sabbatical. When do we leave?"

"I haven't said yes, so—"

"But you will." She walked through the door.

Jack flicked the screen of his phone and pulled up his email again. He tapped a brief message to their new anonymous client: *We're in.*

To read Marin and Jack's next adventure, grab your copy of Entombed!

ALSO BY KATE BARAY

ABOUT THE AUTHOR

When Kate's not tapping away at her keyboard or in deep contemplation of her next fanciful writing project, she's sweeping up hairy dust bunnies and watching British mysteries.

Kate is from Austin, Texas (where many of her stories take place) but has recently migrated north to Boise, Idaho, where soup season (her favorite time of year) lasts more than two weeks.

She's worked as an attorney, a dog trainer, and in various other positions, but writer is the hands-down winner. She's thankful readers keep reading, so she can keep writing!She hopes you enjoy reading her stories as much as she loves writing them!

CPSIA information can be obtained
at www.ICGtesting.com
Printed in the USA
BVHW091051160921
616889BV00017B/1192